The Munich girl

A Novel of
the Legacies that Outlast War

Phyllis Ed

WHOLE SKY BOOKS
EXETER, NEW HAMPSHIRE

Ring, Phyllis Edgerly, author.

The Munich girl : a novel of the legacies that

outlast war / Phylllis Edgerly Ring.

pages cm

ISBN 978-0-9965469-8-0

1. World War, 1939-1945--Fiction. 2. Man-woman

relationships--Fiction. 3. Kindertransports (Rescue

operations)--Fiction. 4. World War, 1939-1945--

Underground movements--Fiction. 5. Historical fiction.

6. War fiction. 7. Romance fiction.   I. Title.

PS3618.I5396M86 2015   813'.6

QBI15-600213

Book cover and interior design by Marina D. Kirsch.
www.marinakirschdesign.com

Poems of Erich Mühsam originally published in *Der Krater* (1909),
and their English translation courtesy of Gary Bachlund. http://bachlund.org

Special thanks to Ed Fusco for assistance with Eva Braun photos.

WHOLE SKY BOOKS
EXETER, NEW HAMPSHIRE

Dedicated to the memory of two exemplary martyrs.
You served the cause of love and justice with
moral courage until the very last breath.

Erich Mühsam
6 April 1878-10 July 1934

Those who comfortably acquiesce
and say 'we cannot change things'
shamefully desecrate human dignity
and all the gifts of their own hearts and brain.

Fr. Alfred Delp, S.J.
15 September 1907-2 February 1945

Only together with God is man human!

PART I

THE FORK IN THE PATH

Die Gabel im Pfad

CHAPTER 1

August 21, 1995
Boston to Munich

Panic ignited a fuse in Anna when the 747's hatch door sealed shut.

Breathe, her therapist always urged when these attacks had ambushed before.

Look around, count things. Pull yourself back into your surroundings.

The flames darted around her, dissolving behind her eyelids in a copper haze as she squeezed them shut.

Then, as quickly as it had begun, the roaring in her ears subsided and the flames faded. She heard only the clink of seat belts, a murmur of voices—everyday sounds of a cabin full of passengers in the moments before a plane climbs into the sky.

When she had teased Hannes about the way he coached her through these flashbacks like a husband at a delivery, his reply was tinged with sadness. "You *are* giving birth, Anna. To the life you deserve to have back."

How would she have made it through these last months without this man she'd barely met, who felt like someone she'd always known? He had begged her to fly first-class, even bought the ticket, but she'd insisted on traveling in coach, just like last time.

On the plane that never left the ground.

Despite his protests, she was flying without him because no matter how he wanted to help, she still had to face these attacks alone, plunged into the remembered terror of lying helpless, unable to make herself heard above the screams.

The handkerchief was now a damp, rumpled ball in her fist. Her other hand had a death grip on the armrest.

"Everything all right?" a flight attendant asked.

Anna's gasping breaths were making her chest ache. She drew a longer, ragged one. The woman gave her hand a squeeze.

Behind them, a crew member delivered instructions to men happy to stretch out in the emergency row. Anna had asked for a seat in front of it because it was possible to climb over a seat to get there if doing so through the aisle became impossible—or deadly. Of course, the exit row wasn't always the best option. Those rigid door handles—

"Got that?" The voice snapped Anna's attention back into her surroundings.

"Direct passengers this way and say, 'Leg, body, leg. Sit, and jump,'" one man parroted back to the crew member. The words echoed inside Anna like a mantra, a chorus she'd heard over and over while lying in searing pain.

"One of you opens the door, goes out first, and gets down on the ground to help. The other stays here and tells passengers: 'One leg out, pull your body through, other leg follows. Then sit on the wing and jump.'"

"And get the hell away!" The man's laugh was raucous.

"Better?" the attendant beside Anna asked.

She shivered. "Yes, thank you. It's silly—I've flown so much."

"But not since May, Mrs. Dahlberg. I know." Her features melted into sympathy.

Then she was gone as the pilot announced departure and the crew readied for the first of air travel's two most dangerous events. It surprised Anna how much calmer she felt. This latest attack had brought more images than any of the previous ones, suppressed horror from that burning plane, just months ago, at this same airport. But now, aware of her surroundings, she knew that what she saw around her was what was really happening.

The plane finished taxiing and lurched to a halt before the acceleration that would launch it skyward. *This* was the moment, she remembered: the abrupt stop and unexpected pitch forward before everything had gone so terribly wrong.

Anna raised the handkerchief to her nose. On the back of each seat, a compact screen showed the cockpit's view of the runway stretching out of sight.

I've done it, she marveled. After the inferno she'd witnessed—and survived—she had boarded a plane again; ridden out the fear, as her therapist had assured her she would.

All because of a mysterious friendship she was still trying to understand. Anna smoothed the handkerchief in her lap. The embroidered monogram formed a Kleeblatt, the word her German mother, Peggy, always used for four-leaf clover. Her mother had hidden this in her bureau and never shared it, nor explained why she had it.

Anna now knew whose monogram this was: someone who'd become as famous as she aspired to, though for none of the same reasons. A woman who had loved a man the whole world despised, and chosen to die with him. And Anna's mother had loved her.

Staring at her neighbor's screen, Anna watched its view of take-off as though mounted on the nose of the plane. Only weeks before, she'd never have been able to imagine this, yet here she finally was, on her way to Munich.

More surprising, as the runway sped beneath the plane in a blur of silver on the screen, was that her source of comfort was a careworn handkerchief that had once belonged to Adolf Hitler's mistress, Eva Braun.

———

Anna had found it six months earlier when an argument with her husband rolled in like a thunderstorm. Lowell had arranged an appointment she didn't want, on the drizzly Tuesday that would have been her mother's 83rd birthday. Or, as the last day of the month, the date on which Peggy celebrated in years with no February 29.

Before Anna could pour her first coffee, a terse conversation suddenly stirred the morning peace like a rising squall.

"Today?" she blinked, barely awake. "You want me to come down to *The Fighting Chance* office today?"

"Uh, huh." Lowell didn't look up from sorting the stacks of paper with which he'd covered Peggy's table in the breakfast nook. The Bavarian benches on three sides held similar piles and he'd claimed the chair at the end for his briefcase.

"Appointment's at 10." His voice was deep with its morning timbre. Sunlight through the window highlighted flashes of white that threaded his dark hair. "My day's booked. I'll have to meet you there."

Sometimes, Anna decided, *you feel as curt as those bloody Nazis you spend so much time researching.* The kitchen's chunky cuckoo clock showed quarter to nine. She had planned to go back to bed after he left for the university, explore papers of her mother's she'd unearthed in this house they came home to each day like a purgatory.

After Peggy died, Lowell insisted that her house wasn't ready to list, especially in a New Hampshire winter. They'd moved into Peggy's Cape here in Marsden and listed their own house, two towns away. Lowell's father had also died months earlier and though Anna planned to resume her own writing projects now that she'd left her job at the university press, she spent her days sifting through others' possessions instead.

Peggy's rooms were frustratingly full because every other home she'd known had been yanked, if not bombed, from under her. Nothing could convince her to leave it, especially after Anna's father had died. When Peggy left his hospice room for brief seconds, he had rasped at Anna, "She'll need someone strong, now."

How can you still know her so little? Anna had wondered. She was coming to realize that he'd known what her mother had allowed him to believe, about both of them.

Anna missed Peggy's strength as she faced the "firsts," the anguished anniversaries that follow a death like reopened wounds: first Thanksgiving, first Christmas. And now, Peggy's birthday.

Her hand shook as she groped down a cup from the cabinet. She kept reaching for things from her own home, finding instead these objects from childhood—tossed from one time frame to another, never landing long enough to feel present in either one.

Lowell managed the changes by strategizing like a general. As he unveiled his latest battle plan last night, his smile had nearly reached the pale eyes he increasingly needed to shield from light, and Anna realized how much she missed his hopefulness, and his willingness to include her in it.

"I don't understand why this has to happen today," she began.

He peered over his glasses. "How many ways do we have to go over this, Anna?"

"But you just brought up this idea last night." *When you finally held me, touched me. After months of ... nothing, in the midst of all this sadness.*

He'd introduced the "decision" in bed after surprising her with caresses that temporarily thawed a frozen place between them. These had been merely tactical, she realized now, Lowell's conjugal politicking, like lunch with his department head to gain support for a grant. It had been so long since they'd touched each other she had forgotten, willed herself to forget, that even in this, Lowell served his own agenda.

After some sips of coffee, she asked, "Why does this all have to happen so fast?"

The crack of his pen on the table made her flinch when he whirled to face her, and he saw it, she knew. She trained her gaze on where the cuff of his white shirt retracted up his wrist, the gouge he'd made on the surface of her mother's table.

"Because life's moving fast, Anna! We damn well better get our heads above it."

She stood frozen, the sound of her heart pounding in her ears. Why did he have to act this way? Didn't he know by now that she was on *his* side?

He tilted his head back and continued in the deliberate tone he probably used when addressing inattentive students, "You need to go meet the new editor so he can assign you something quickly." His eyes narrowed. "I'll get rid of those other incompetents, and you'll be the staff writer. Rather than write for peanuts, you'll get a real paycheck for it, now."

But you never asked. Simply announced this is what you've decided. For my *life.*

"You'll find a way to fit in your projects." His tone rendered these pedestrian—like errands, laundry. "But this is *real* life." He gestured to the papers spread across the table. "With bills? Plus two goddamn mortgages, thanks to your mother's bad timing, not to mention her bad planning."

Anna recoiled as though slapped. The lump swelling in her throat was going to choke her, or unleash tears she couldn't bear to let him see.

Things went reasonably well when Lowell felt in charge and things went his way. His approach vacillated between thrust and parry, threaten and bully, or soothe and seduce. Anna knew she relied on the last as proof he really did care. But now that seductive cosseting only came when he was looking to consolidate his own gains.

In bed, through his initiation of what had long ceased to be what she'd call making love—and Anna had given up trying to initiate it herself—his decisions became "theirs." In their childless marriage, perhaps this was the only procreation possible.

His tone was appeasing, now. "I wanted a sabbatical, time to launch my book. Instead, I've had to teach. We both have to make sacrifices. If we keep Dad's magazine and cut costs, we'll have extra income while we settle your mother's estate."

His Army-veteran father had started a military-history magazine and nurtured it to considerable success. "We can pay this new editor half what that other jackass wanted, and I won't have to take his crap anymore. I don't know why Dad did but I guess the ties of battlefield comrades run deep." He gathered his papers and packed them in his briefcase. "If you write some articles, I publish book excerpts, and this new guy writes as well as his clips show he can, we can unload those dilettantes Dad kept on."

Anna knew he was eager to give the magazine a World-Wars focus. "Perfect timing, especially for bringing out my book," he said. "The 50th anniversary of VE Day is May 8 but there isn't a *single* story assigned about it. We need to hit the ground running."

No prior consultation, I'm handed a new job, and it begins today, of all days.

The Second World War was the one thing that still stirred Lowell's enthusiasm. He'd inherited his drive to "figure out" Hitler from his father, who'd fought in Europe and been passionate about military history. Lowell's tenure as history professor might be their source of income but it was his Third Reich research he cared about most.

Now, his mammoth manuscript was going to be published by the university's press. The sight of all his books about Nazis still gave Anna the creeps. Why try to understand someone like Hitler? Yet she admired what her husband had uncovered about National Socialism's sinister world, and the madman who reigned over its ruinous years.

The magazine *would* make a good platform for bringing out Lowell's book. Writing about the war might not be her first choice, but she'd find some interesting angle. This was part of Peggy's history, after all, and she'd been in Germany in the midst of everything that happened there. *It's not as if I'll be doing this forever.*

She pinned back her unruly dark curls in a wide barrette and decided to wear one of Peggy's Hermés scarves in honor of the day.

When she crossed the hall to her mother's bedroom, Anna encountered the same electric hush waiting every time she entered now. She opened the bureau's top drawer and released the *Je Reviens* fragrance that permeated everything Peggy wore, incubating between wearings in the chrysalis of this drawer.

Resting on top was a scarf Anna had never seen, a design of leaves in ochre, sage, and scarlet. It always puzzled her that frugal Peggy had such expensive scarves. She pulled it out and saw that beneath it was an old brown-paper envelope and a folded square of white cotton. A handkerchief.

She didn't remember her mother having one of these, either. "Frightfully unsanitary, especially now we've got these lovely tissues." Anna could still hear the lilt in her mother's English. Most Americans only heard her German accent, no matter what language she spoke, but Anna always detected the subtle British in Peggy's English.

The very last time she'd called, she asked Anna, "Can you come over? I've had a visitor—it's about your father. I need to talk with you."

It had been an impossibly hectic time—busy for Lowell, which always meant busy for Anna—so she put her off. The following day, Anna found Peggy unconscious on her living-room floor and never had the chance to talk with her again.

As she'd waited for the EMTs, scenes from her mother's television flashed and flickered in the dark room. Anna first thought it was an old black-and-white movie with the sound turned down. Then she realized these were home movies, though she didn't recognize anyone. Relatives from Germany, perhaps. The scenery looked like the Alps.

One scene in vivid color showed three women in traditional German dirndls gathering purple iris in a field. The sequence was filmed from the ground, as if the photographer had hidden among the plants to document the cheerful outing. Overhead, a bright spring sky took up half the scene with its billowing clouds.

Anna had sat mesmerized, as though watching for something—or someone—she knew. Perhaps her absorption had simply been her retreat from the unbearable situation. In that silence, Peggy seemed very close, yet nowhere near the waxen-faced body on the floor. The films had felt like a portal to another world, one to which her mother had somehow already travelled.

Later, when she thought about her mother's phone call, Anna wondered whether Peggy's visitor had been Rod, her father, bearing some otherworldly message. Her mother had been "sensitive" all her life, subject to psychic experiences, though she never wanted to talk about it—even seemed a little afraid of it. If Anna's deceased father was her "visitor" that day, had he been some angel of death sent to fetch her?

It was one of the few times Peggy had ever asked for much of anything. If Anna let herself dwell on it now, the weight would pull her under so far she'd never resurface.

She lifted the handkerchief from the drawer to have a closer look. Yellowed with age, it was embroidered in one corner with tiny satin stitches that formed four small circles that resembled a cloverleaf. She folded back the envelope's flap just far enough to see that it held newspaper and magazine clippings. *More* things to sort through. The clock at Peggy's bedside showed there wasn't time now.

Anna was already late when she drove away from the house, dragging her feet as she often did now. Going out into the day had become … difficult.

Lowell might run late, since this development with *The Fighting Chance* had come up so fast, and she certainly didn't want to arrive early to sit with a complete stranger in a meeting neither of them had arranged.

As she crept through the college town's slow-moving traffic, she remembered that the magazine had moved since her last visit. She turned the car around, resigned to arriving even later. The building was in the older part of Marsden near the river. She parked quickly and raced up two flights of stairs to a suite of offices at the top.

Kathy, the receptionist she'd met just once, flashed a smile from where she sat at an uncluttered glass-topped desk. "Found us!"

"So glad that sign was out front. I'm already late."

"No problem at all," Kathy started to rise from her chair. "The conference room's down the hall on the right."

"Don't get up," Anna headed her off with a wave. "I'll find it."

She hurried into a hallway that curved to the right, with all of its doors on the left. The farther she walked, the darker it grew. Like a tunnel.

Fitting. I'm already in the dark about all of this.

She paused, listening for the sound of voices but the quiet in the shadowy dark was the exact opposite of what she'd expect in a place usually so busy.

"Hello?" The voice, deep, reverberating, male, startled her when it sounded from somewhere ahead in the shadows as she jerked around quickly. "Anna?" it spoke again.

As she strained to see down the curving hallway two observations collided in her mind: the voice wasn't Lowell's, and, even so, the speaker had said her name properly. Unless she introduced herself, people never pronounced the name Peggy had given her with a German "a" at the beginning. Instead, it was the "ANN-a" of American English.

"I'm sorry to be late," she called back. "I forgot the office had moved."

The approaching figure was backlit from somewhere down the hall. The man's head was bowed slightly and though she couldn't see his face, she could tell, even in the dim light, that he was a few inches taller than Lowell's five-foot-nine.

"I'm sorry you've had to find your way in the dark. The electricians were here yesterday and we don't have these lights working yet." He reached to shake her hand. "Thank you for meeting with me on such short notice. I'm Johannes Ritter."

The hand he closed around hers felt warm after the raw February cold. His voice, though nearly without accent, delivered his name with fluid German precision: Yo-HA-ness, and rolled the "r" at the beginning of Ritter.

"But call me Hannes," he added quickly. "Is it all right if I call you Anna?"

"Of course. How often do you hear *your* name pronounced correctly?" she wondered aloud.

He hesitated, as if he hadn't understood, then laughed softly. "Well, you probably know how it is. I get 'Hans' or 'Hanes'—someone once even called me 'Harness' no matter how often I corrected him. Let me take your coat and I'll show you the way."

Anna felt his fingertips touch lightly on her shoulders. She stuffed her gloves into the pockets of her dark wool jacket and shrugged out of it.

He draped it over his arm as he fell into step beside her. "I'm looking forward to working with you, Anna. I apologize for the mess. We're still unpacking."

As he led the way, she thought, *How nice, to hear the sound of my name. My own name.* Too bad they couldn't prolong this agreeable exchange before she met with Lowell's inevitable displeasure. Why was she already worrying about whether he would embarrass her in front of a man she'd barely met?

The light ahead of them grew brighter and Hannes's silhouette turned back toward her. "There really *is* light at the end of this tunnel."

The curving corridor terminated abruptly in an archway beyond which the room was—circular. Its walls were painted a pale saffron and a skylight flooded the space with light, including the round table at the center.

"So *this* is why the wall is curved."

"Interesting, isn't it?" Hannes was hanging her coat on a rack just inside the door. "The natural light is so nice, I often work in here." He moved to where she stood gazing around the room. "A good place to put heads together democratically, wouldn't you say? No front or back—or sides, for that matter."

And no Lowell.

Anna was stunned. "M-my husband isn't here yet?"

Hannes turned to look at her. "Why, no. He and I spoke yesterday and he phoned this morning. Was he supposed to be here?"

Once again, she felt blindsided.

If Lowell's absence was a shock, what came next nearly took her breath away as she faced Hannes, who gazed back with concern, as though some error in the situation might be his own. In this room the color of daylight, she saw that he had a striking, nearly stereotypical Teutonic appearance—golden-brown hair, eyes the vibrant blue of a cloudless June sky, and a face almost an exaggerated parody of handsome: like sculpture or hand-cut glass. Gemstones. Things with planes and angles and facets.

He was asking her something. She really needed to focus.

He repeated the question: "May I get you some coffee or tea?"

When she'd been too distracted to answer, he continued to look at her in that concerned way, as though he'd somehow been remiss. "Is everything all right?"

"Yes—coffee would be great. Excuse my confusion. With all the changes lately, sometimes ... I lose track."

His smile was kind as he nodded. "Yes, I think I know what you mean."

The lump rising in her throat made her feel desperate to shift his gaze away.

"What do you like in your coffee?" he asked.

"Cream, or milk. Please."

"Make yourself comfortable," he invited, then seemed to leap from the room.

Probably can't wait to get away. I must have been gaping like a fish.

She really did need to get out more. She moved to the table and set her purse and leather satchel on a chair, then drew another one closer to where folders and a yellow legal pad lay on the table. She was unpacking her pens and notebook when he returned carrying two mugs. He set them down, took a seat beside her, and asked, "What would be most comfortable for you, today?"

Looking at the earnest beauty of his face, Anna had absolutely no idea what he was asking. The word "dazzle" made perfect sense in a situation like this. She'd looked it up recently and the list of synonyms had spelled out this phenomenon quite precisely: *temporarily deprive of sight, confuse, overwhelm.*

"I'm sorry?"

"I was wondering what your time is like today." His voice gave way just a bit on his last words. He blinked rapidly several times as he reached for his coffee. Perhaps he was feeling as odd, and a little nervous, as she. "I don't want to impose on it."

"Oh, no. It's fine," she said. "I planned on being here as long it takes to figure things out, maybe send me home with an assignment or two."

He nodded. "That sounds good."

Anna took a breath. "I must say, this is about the last thing I ever imagined doing, writing for this kind of magazine."

A smile tugged at the corners of his mouth. "Me, too."

"Really?" Her tone showed her surprise.

"Ja." When he raised his eyes to meet hers, Anna realized he'd used German. "I was part of adjunct faculty at the university. That's how I met Lowell. But the budget cuts ended that, so this opportunity is timely."

"Have you done this kind of work before?" Then she added, "I mean, you've already been interviewed and hired. I don't mean to—"

"It's no problem at all that you ask. I worked as editor for a few German publications, one an English-language magazine. I've also written and published for my teaching work. History, and German. And English."

"So you've lived in Germany?"

"I *am* German. I grew up in Munich."

"How did you come to speak English so well? If I'm not rude for asking."

"My stepfather was from Philadelphia; my mother is German. They met in Germany after the war. I learned to speak English—*American* English—almost before I spoke German. I understand you also speak German?"

Anna hesitated. "Nur ein bisschen—*Only a little.*" She added quickly, "Fast immer mit meiner Mutter—*Almost always with my mother,*" as if to discourage the possibility.

A wave of sadness rose as she realized she might never speak it again, despite the fact she sometimes felt self-conscious about it. Though never with Peggy.

Anna looked away as her vision blurred. *Please, please. Not here.*

Hannes's tone was encouraging, even playful. "How fortunate, that you shared this 'mother' tongue."

She smiled at his wordplay.

"It must have made her very happy," he said.

Anna knew it in an instant, then. His tone and expression—the eyes that showed gentleness she found both reassuring and familiar—these all conveyed it unmistakably. This man was genuinely modest, unaffected.

"I'll miss speaking German with her." She touched the scarf. "Sometimes, I wear her things, to feel close to her."

"That was hers?"

Anna nodded. "She always had a new one for her real birthday, February 29th. I know her whole collection but I'd never seen this one." How had she rambled into telling him all this? She really was spending too much time hiding at home.

"Perhaps she was saving it for you?" He looked shy, hesitated a moment, then said, "Since my stepfather died, whenever I am missing him, I often find something that belonged to him. It can feel like … a gift he has been keeping for me."

Anna stared at him for several seconds. "That's *exactly* how it feels."

"Well, it looks very nice." He shifted in his chair. "If you don't mind, I thought we might begin by talking about the 50th anniversary of the end of the war in Europe. Since that issue must be out before May, we only have a few weeks, but I think we can manage it. The fact it is a special issue gives us more options. It also provides a way to change the magazine's focus, as Lowell wants to do."

The sound of her husband's name felt like an intrusion. How providential they had this chance to talk together before he inevitably took over.

"We already have a lot of good material we can use." Hannes's tie, pale blue silk dotted with a darker design, fell forward as he stretched to retrieve a notepad and slide it in front of them. He turned toward her and reached across the top of the page with the mechanical pencil in his left hand.

Beneath handwritten notes was a bulleted list. Anna's gaze followed where the pencil led as Hannes explained, "Lowell has lots of excellent material, with excerpts from his book about the end of the war." He pointed to the words "Fall of Berlin"… "The Reich's final days." His hand dropped to the phrase, "Bunker Days." "And the Allies' advance through Germany." He circled the word "liberation."

"We can also use articles of mine related to the British and the Russians." He leaned back in his chair. "Much of what we need may already be written."

Anna experienced a curious mixture of relief and disappointment. "Maybe you don't need my help, not right away."

"Oh, no, no!" Shaking his head, he said, "I have some ideas that could round things out very nicely, even attract readers the magazine doesn't usually reach." He glanced at her, then down at his notes. "But I hope you won't think I'm suggesting them simply because … you are a woman."

Anna watched him easily now, observing with actual enjoyment the openness of his speech and expression. "Well, I *am* one, after all. I'd love to hear your ideas. But might we have a little more coffee, too?"

"Oh … yes. Excuse me— "

"No, let me," she intercepted him as he moved to rise from his chair. "And pardon my being so direct." She met his eyes and felt the charged spark of their electric blue. "If I'm going to be part of things here, I need to know my way around."

"Indeed. Let me give you a tour, then we can get some more coffee and discuss what I have in mind."

Anna followed as he led the way out of the room's sunny circle. The magazine's former editor, her father-in-law's Army buddy—even Lowell himself—would have had Kathy running and jumping for the coffee no matter how busy she already was. Things really were going to be new and different around here.

CHAPTER 2

A phone message from Lowell was waiting at home:

Things were a circus, so I couldn't get away. Won't make it home for dinner, either, but I'll see you tonight.

Anna moved to the dining table and unpacked the books Hannes had sent home with her. Now that there was no need to figure out dinner, she could sit with the portrait that hung here and think about her assignments.

"Women news correspondents made big discoveries in Germany at the end of the war," Hannes had said about the first of his article ideas. "They would never even have those jobs, if not for the war, ja? What do you think about sharing this history through *their* voices? My aunt, Charlotte Wald, was one. She would be happy to talk with you."

From conversations Anna had heard Lowell have with colleagues, she knew that Lee Miller had used Hitler's tub to take her first bath in weeks in his abandoned Munich apartment at the end of the war. Another woman journalist was among the first to photograph atrocities at Buchenwald concentration camp near Weimar.

But it was Hannes's second idea that filled her thoughts now as she studied the portrait on the wall in front of her. Anna had seen this image of a young woman looking back at the viewer over her shoulder during every meal she and her parents had eaten at this table. She'd always known whose face this was, though never known anything about her. Now, Hannes wanted her to write about this woman.

"Hitler's mistress?" she'd asked doubtfully when he introduced the possibility.

"His *wife*, actually, but only for a day or so. One of the best-kept secrets of the Third Reich—a real surprise at the end of the war, not only for the Allies, but the Germans. Even some of those who knew her had no idea."

He had reached into a box and handed her two books. "These are the more reliable biographies. The better one is German. Just let me know if you need any help."

"I can probably manage." She really would need to get going, though—hit the ground running, just as Lowell had said. She was still a bit surprised by the subject of this assignment: "Who was Eva Braun?"

Who, indeed? Anna stared at the face in the portrait. The eyes were crystal clear, their gaze inescapable. There was a silky quality in the hair that fell to bare shoulders, an eagerness in the expression, if a slight petulance across the mouth. Yet the proportion in this drawing was off, as though the artist hadn't gotten the angles of the head and shoulder quite right.

"I don't know how much you'll be able to find about her but anything is bound to be more than most readers have seen," Hannes told her. "Much of what was circulated after the war, and since, has been inaccurate. Like urban legend."

Then he'd paused. "But would this really interest you?"

"Well, it's not what I was expecting. You don't think readers will be ... put off?"

"Are you put off?"

"It's just—the association with Hitler." Anna shrugged, "I guess if Lowell can spend years immersed in everything about him, it only seems appropriate I learn something about the woman in his life."

Then she'd mentioned the portrait.

Hannes spun back around from where he'd been packing folders away in his briefcase. "You mean photograph?"

"No, it's a portrait. A drawing, in something like charcoal, but reddish-brown."

He'd listened closely as she explained how this had been a fixture in her family's home, one that eventually blended into its surroundings as fixtures often do.

"It was found after we took Berchtesgaden," Rod always announced to any guest at the table, whether or not they'd asked about the portrait. Berchtesgaden, the town near Hitler's Alpine retreat, hadn't been "taken," but had extended immediate, unconditional surrender when the Bürgermeister walked out to meet American troops on the outskirts of town.

"My father commanded a unit that arrived in Munich at the end of the war. He acquired the portrait there," Anna explained. "It was never clear just how."

Hannes's gaze had fastened on her as she described this piece of family history.

Once, after glasses of her favorite Riesling brought a flush to her cheeks, Peggy had mused, "Perhaps they forgot where they left it, or never got round to picking it up." Anna had imagined it forgotten at some Munich framer's after the war, stashed under dozens of canvases in the bombed-out shell of a building.

"Maybe Eva didn't care for it," Peggy said once. "Thought it a poor likeness."

Anna remembered how inexplicably flustered this remark made Rod, who displayed the portrait like a trophy, as though he had captured Eva Braun herself.

Yet through all the years it hung in their home, Anna's mother had seemed curiously detached, almost indifferent, about this booty that so obsessed her husband.

"I think we should hang it in our bedroom," he'd once taunted with a sly smile.

"Suit yourself," Peggy had replied with one of her elegant shrugs.

But he had chosen the more prominent setting of the dining room, where Anna had spent hundreds of meals with this face; where he could tell his story over and over. "Of course it's her," he'd bluster if anyone questioned its authenticity. "Says 'Fraülein Eva Braun' right on the framer's label in back." His pronunciation of "Frow-line" must have made Peggy cringe.

During all the years that this face had been such a presence, when Anna recalled the tyrant this woman had loved, she often thought Eva looked more like Hitler's daughter than his girlfriend. Lover. Her own father's bullying possessiveness about the portrait had made her feel protective of it in a way she couldn't understand or explain.

"Might I have a look, sometime?" Hannes had asked. "Perhaps this could help illustrate the article."

"Sure. Let me get started on all this homework you've given me." Anna rolled her eyes with a smile. "Then we'll have you come to dinner so you can meet 'Eva.'"

When she called Charlotte Wald in California that night, her pen raced over her notepad as she struggled to keep up with the voice made gravelly by years of cigarettes.

Charlotte leapt from topic to topic. Anna didn't even have to ask many questions before recollections poured forth. While Charlotte insisted she was undergoing cancer treatment and mustn't talk long, she kept launching into memories of wartime Germany.

"No one asks, talks, about those days anymore." She sounded sad. "Sometimes, you'd think they never happened, when they were such a cataclysm at the time." After a pause she said, "I'm glad Hannes encouraged that you call. How is he?"

"Oh, I've just met him," Anna told her. "I'm grateful he agreed to take the job."

Within the first ten minutes, she had what she'd called for, a detailed glimpse of a female war correspondent's life. Charlotte had accompanied U.S. troops and been among the first to enter Hitler's Berlin bunker in May of 1945 after fire ravaged it, and water collected and stagnated inside it. With excerpts from her war coverage and that of other women journalists, this article would be dispatched quickly, as Hannes had predicted.

Then Anna mentioned her second assignment and was shocked to discover how much Charlotte seemed eager to recall about Eva Braun—and about *Peggy*.

"We only met a few times, when we were both working in Berlin, but I liked your mother so much. She saw the looming dangers when others were lulled by the impressions the Nazis tried to make. She had that mix of backgrounds, too—German *and* British—which made things complicated for her as time went on in Germany."

There was so much Anna didn't know about her mother's life, especially the war years. Peggy had sometimes talked about them in sharp, sudden detail, undoubtedly as memories had surfaced. More often, she hadn't talked about them at all.

"She *knew* Eva Braun, didn't she?" Charlotte asked, as though she'd suddenly remembered this.

Anna nearly gasped. "My m-mother?" She couldn't have heard the other woman right. "Why, no. At least, I never heard that she did."

Every cell of her body seemed to be alive with listening, now.

"Well, I may be confused. There's so much water gone under the bridge. But one of the foreign correspondents once told me she'd seen a woman she thought was your mother talking with one of Hitler's secretaries. That's what any of us who ever saw Eva Braun before the war took her for, you see. But that was who she meant."

Anna wanted to hear more, but felt desperate to steer the conversation toward anything she could learn about Hitler's mistress. Charlotte's voice was faltering and the interview might have to end soon. "You had seen Eva? Before the war?"

"Oh, yes," said Charlotte. "She was right there in front of us, hidden in plain sight. But she was the exact opposite of what we'd have expected."

"How do you mean?"

"Well," Charlotte said, "her clothes should have tipped us off that she was his mistress. None of Hitler's secretaries or the frumpy Nazi wives had such flair, nor such an extensive wardrobe, though always in very good taste."

"You mistook her for one of his secretaries?"

"If anyone noticed her at all. She was quite pretty, but also incredibly everyday. *Ordinary.* We were accustomed to seeing Hitler with flamboyant actresses on his arm, though he swore his only bride was Germany. If we'd understood what sort of person he really was, his choice of Eva Braun would have made perfect sense.

"You see, in his personal life, he was incredibly bourgeois, wanted someone he could come home to. Those beautiful women he was always photographed with were just for show. They weren't up to the role he had in mind for a partner.

"But Eva Braun was, and knew how to play it very effectively, a consummate actress, really. As so many women have been." Charlotte broke off in a hoarse chuckle.

Astonished by this outpouring, Anna realized Hannes had likely known what a good source his aunt would be for both subjects. She'd arrived at Hitler's Berlin bunker the same day the Russians had displayed a surprising discovery they'd made in its rat's maze of claustrophobic rooms: photo albums with Eva Braun's initials on the covers.

"There we were, sitting in those ruined buildings looking at her pictures of family and picnics, and scenes of Hitler's house in Berchtesgaden with Ribbentrop and other Nazi bigwigs eating cake." Charlotte's tone was amazed. "And scores of photos of Eva, when she wasn't playing photographer.

"'Who on earth *is* this woman?' we wondered. Many of us had covered the news in Germany before the war and couldn't believe our eyes as we looked at those photos.

"Witnesses who'd been in Hitler's bunker described how, young as she was, Eva had been a calming, dignified presence. Everyone had been spiraling out of control, dying for it to be over, but the Führer kept going on crazily.

"She didn't even *have* to be there," Charlotte pointed out. "He'd urged her to get to safety in Berchtesgaden. Makes you wonder why she stayed. Perhaps her being there finally helped bring it to an end. If she went with him, he might finally go quietly.

"The journalists got it all wrong afterward," Charlotte added. "That's what happened in the big rush to criminalize everything remotely associated with National Socialism—or Germans. Your mother probably experienced how, after the war, simply being in Germany rendered you suspect, no matter how much you'd suffered or how opposite your own politics or views had been from the Nazis."

Anna felt a shiver run up her spine. Her mother never once talked about this. When the subject of being in Germany during the war, and being

German, had come up, she'd either diverted to a new one or praised the Americans and other Allies.

"After the war, Eva Braun made a likely pariah for people's ire, as they maligned her with every defamatory stereotype you can dredge up about a woman," Charlotte said. "And mostly, it was men doing it, showing how 'informed' they were, when they really hadn't a clue. Even Nerin Gun, her biographer, admitted he'd missed the chance to spot who she was early on. She was labeled shallow, grasping, insignificant—certainly, that last was part of why her role remained hidden, even for people who knew her.

"But those presumptions are nearly the precise opposite of fact," Charlotte sighed. "That's the mistake we made, basing our calls on our own experience and assumptions.

"Then scoundrels like that actor, Luis Trenker, published absolute trash about her. Plagiarized trash, at that, from someone else's diary. And yet people swallowed it like gospel. Well, you know. They still do."

Finally, she said, "It's nearly midnight your time. Have I really talked that long?"

"I'm thankful you have," Anna said. "Especially before I've started my research."

"Be sure to read between the lines. And do take into account that she was a woman, and German. And the times she lived in."

"It was an extraordinary time for women like you, wasn't it?' Anna asked.

"Well, yes and no. When we came home, we were expected to go back to life as we'd known it, as our mothers had known it. But none of us could. Most of the women correspondents couldn't make a marriage last. We'd tasted too much of life on our own terms and you didn't find men who could manage with that. Well, I did, but he was Jewish, and German, ironically. He was lucky to get out. And I'm lucky to have him.

"Feel free to call any time. And please give my best to Hannes when you see him," she said, then rang off.

Exhausted, and wildly curious, Anna wondered how she'd ever sleep. When Lowell finally came home, she was in bed absorbed in the pages of Nerin Gun's biography of Eva Braun.

"You're all set?" he asked. "You and Hannes worked things out?"

Anna began to describe her meeting with him, and the call with Charlotte Wald, but he cut her off, in search only of confirmation that his plans were going forward.

"He assigned a piece about Eva Braun I think is going to be especially interesting," she tried again.

"Save it for the page, Anna. You know it'll lose its edge, if you talk about it. Just get going."

In a way, it was a relief not to feel as though she had to report to him. Perhaps he was going to hand this over to Hannes and give her breathing room in it all.

Switching off the bedside lamp, she settled in for sleep. She'd left her mother's Hermés scarf on the bureau and a hint of that Worth scent it carried reached her as she lay in the dark.

Leap year or not, Peggy, your birthday's been quite a day.

A month later, Anna spread her notes out on the dining table, astonished to see how much she'd already learned about Eva Braun's life.

The table was clad in one of Peggy's many embroidered cloths, white damask with clusters of yellow and purple pansies along the border. She'd wanted to set a pretty table as she brought out her mother's Dresden porcelain. She had also used Peggy's recipe for a Viennese Tafelspitz meat dish after she learned how much Hannes liked it, and how homesick he seemed for Germany.

"You went to all this trouble?" His expression had grown soft, his eyes bright.

"It's not your mother's. But hopefully it's close to *my* mother's."

"Consider yourself an honored guest," Lowell told him. "It's one of her best."

The men discussed the magazine's anniversary issue, for which Anna had already finished her article about women correspondents. It had taken several tries to arrange this visit as Lowell was out of the house earlier each day and home later each night. Even tonight, once they'd finished the dessert of Peggy's buttery-rich poppy seed cake, he had pled needs at his office and hurried off.

Anna had finished Nerin Gun's biography about Eva Braun and started reading the one in German. In it she'd discovered a photo of Eva almost identical to the image in the portrait. It had been taken in 1929, the year the 17-year-old met the 40-year-old Hitler where she worked in a Munich photo shop. Given the timing, this photo that the portrait seemed to mirror might be the first one Eva had given her famous lover.

"The photo's so lively, while the portrait feels static," Anna told Hannes. "I've always thought the proportion in it seemed off, and the photo shows that's definitely true. Maybe some friend at art school made this disappointing attempt."

Also, while the face in the photo showed artless innocence, the woman in the portrait had a far more knowing look in her eyes, and across her mouth.

"More coffee?" Anna asked as she paused.

Hannes extended his cup for her to fill, then smiled as he set it back in the saucer. "Did your mother teach you how to make this, too? Nice and strong?"

"Not too strong?"

"It's perfect. And very hard to find in America."

"Hope it won't keep either of us awake."

He rose from his chair and moved toward the portrait, leaning in closer to study it. "Would it be all right if we take it down to get a better look?"

At her assent, he lifted it off the wall and carried it to where she sat, then turned it over. The framer's label on the back showed a Munich address: No. 7 Promenade Platz.

"Do you know where that is?" Anna asked.

"The business is gone, with the damage from the war. But I know the place, ja."

She smiled. For all his pitch-perfect pronunciation, whenever Hannes aimed for English's informal "yeah" it always came out German – "Ja." His English Achilles heel.

"I believe it is a bank, now. Right across from the Hotel Bayerischer Hof."

"Oh! I know where that is," Anna said. "My mother took me there for tea, once—a room with a huge stained-glass dome overhead."

"That sounds like it."

"It was obviously part of happy memories, though she was sad about all of the destruction," said Anna. "It's hard when places you know have changed so much."

"Curiously, that lounge was about the only part of the hotel to survive the war." Hannes looked up from where he'd been studying the uneven typescript on the framer's label, which showed the words "Frl. Eva Braun" and the date: 22-8-1936.

He turned the portrait right-side-up and set it in the space Anna had cleared for it on the table. "Ah, yes," he said. "The year is right here, too."

"Where?"

He pointed to the portrait's lower right corner, his finger hovering just above the glass. "Written over the signature line."

Anna looked closely and finally saw the numbers 1-9-3-6 scrawled across the base of where the artist's signature appeared like a small tattoo on Eva's shoulder blade.

"No wonder the signature always seemed so indistinct." The numbers were scribbled in an odd, angular way Anna had always thought part of the signature.

That year, 1936, had been a turning point in Eva Braun's life. At twenty-four, she'd already survived two suicide attempts since meeting Hitler. Anna had discovered that quite a few of the women who'd gotten involved with him had attempted suicide.

The year had been the triumphant one in which Eva was finally established as Hitler's mistress with a house of her own in Munich. It was also when he had finished renovating his Berghof retreat in the mountains near Berchtesgaden and established Eva as mistress of the house with extensive quarters next to his own.

As Anna described these things for Hannes, she wondered, "Could this have been a housewarming gift when she moved into the Berghof, or the house he bought for her?"

"Possibly." Hannes smiled. "You really are doing your research, becoming quite a detective. Did you notice the initials?"

"What initials?"

"Right behind the date."

Anna leaned nearer to look. "Well, yes, that does look like an 'A' to the left of the '1.' I think I've noticed that before."

He was watching her, as though waiting for something. "And the second one?"

She glanced up. "*Is there a second one?*"

He reached to trace its outline above the glass.

Anna's gaze followed his hand, noting the firm outlines of the veins on the back, the long fingers, tapered at the tips. "Right here. Two vertical lines set close together, to the right of that first letter. Although the first number in the date partly covers it, there could be a cross bar between them."

"An ... 'H'?" Anna wondered, then turned to face him open-mouthed.

A and H—the initials all over her notes about Eva Braun, not only to save time but because writing the name of this man and having it around brought such aversion.

"My—*God!*" she exclaimed finally.

"Do you see it?" he asked.

She nodded, shocked. Unless a viewer knew something about Hitler's voluminous artwork, as Anna had come to in recent weeks, and understood the significance of that year in Eva's life, it would never occur to them that he had drawn this.

"Oh, someone probably copied this from that photograph it looks like. Put his initials on it," Anna said dismissively. "People created all kinds of fakes after the war—sold them on the black market. Did whatever they had to to feed their children, right? My mother used to talk about how awful it was. How she couldn't wait to get out."

There was a pause before he answered, a long enough one that Anna turned to see whether he'd heard her.

His eyes were fixed on the portrait. A knot of muscle showed in his jaw and something about him felt drawn back, the slightest bit. Finally, voice low, he said, "It was ... difficult, that's true. People did things they might otherwise not have done."

His tone and phrasing had grown stilted, as though finding the English was suddenly challenging. Anna had noticed this in his speech before, perhaps when words came to him in German, first. She had to remember that English wasn't the language in which he would think all the time.

Then she realized it might be his family's experience she'd referred to so casually, that of millions of women—families—in the war's aftermath, living in rubble with hunger and fear, perhaps not even a full roof overhead if they had anything more than a cellar to live in. She was opening her mouth to apologize when he spoke.

"But think about it, Anna." His voice seemed stronger, less hesitant now as he reached for the portrait. "What's the year on the label?"

"1936."

"And it's clearly original, as the frame appears to be."

"But someone else could have drawn it, even then," she said.

Hannes replaced the portrait on its hook then turned to face her.

"But what have you just been telling me? Part of her agreement with Hitler was that she had to stay invisible. Almost no one knew what part she had in his life. Even when she died, few people did. In 1936, only his servants and her family were aware of the relationship. What would be the point of faking anything back then?"

Anna stared at him as he talked.

"Perhaps some other artist she knew had those initials. But given the odds of that, and the significance of the year for her, and the relationship, what seems more likely?"

Then he added, "One reason the Vienna academy rejected him was that his portraits were judged so inferior. You said yourself the proportion here is off."

Although she knew little about how it had come into her father's possession, Anna imagined the portrait had been filched from the small Munich villa Hitler had given Eva, what she'd called her "little Braun house." That, Anna's research was revealing, was where many items associated with Hitler's mistress had been looted.

"This is how *he* saw her," she recognized suddenly. Anna could see now that the image resembled photos of Geli Raubal, the niece with whom Hitler had a tempestuous relationship. One of the women he'd known whose suicide attempt had been successful.

Hannes watched her quietly.

"Do you really think this was done by … him?" she asked.

"A lot of things point to the possibility."

"My God! If it's true, then my father displayed this all those years when he absolutely despised Hitler!"

"If he acquired it as war booty, there was probably little explanation about where it came from," Hannes said. "My guess would be either her Munich house or Hitler's apartment there. If this *was* his gift to her, it had personal meaning for them both."

Anna studied the image of Eva Braun's face. "I always knew this was linked with her life. But never *this* kind of connection."

Seated back at the table, Hannes was watching her, chin resting in his hand. "I think it's time for me to thank you for this evening of lovely hospitality and excuse myself so you can get to work." He smiled. "I have the feeling it won't be the coffee keeping you awake tonight."

CHAPTER 3

After Hannes left, Anna settled in bed with the German biography of Eva Braun. Despite her excitement, she dozed off and never heard Lowell come home. Parsing out the biography's German was hard work, especially after such a full day.

The next morning, a pot of coffee beside her, she was back at the dining table with her notes, reflecting on the portrait's possible history.

She heard Lowell's rapid movements and loud sounds in the kitchen. Moments later he appeared. "You're still working on that?" His tone was slighting.

"I think I'm in the homestretch," Anna said cheerfully. Whatever would he say when she told him who the portrait's artist might be? She looked up to see him staring at her and felt a familiar sinking sensation from her throat to her heart.

"I'm down to my last shirt, Anna. This damn thing's taking over your life."

She let a few seconds go by, then asked, trying to keep her tone light, "Am I the only one in this house who knows how to operate a washing machine?"

She saw the anger in his eyes. "Who the hell's keeping house? If you want to work from home, keeping up that home is part of the bargain. My job's bringing home the money, remember? To do that, I need clean shirts."

Anna set down her pen as she looked up at him, determined to keep her tone reasonable. "Lowell, there are just two weeks before this deadline. I have it because of plans *you* made."

"Yeah, but you're overcomplicating things, the way you always do. Everything that can be said about that woman has *been* said. Round it up, boil it down."

Anna asked levelly, "Is that how you conduct your research?"

"What the hell's there to research? You're wasting too much effort on one story."

"No, Lowell," Anna felt her heart pounding. "I've already filed one article, remember? This is the second, on a very tight deadline. Unlike yours, which were already written. Of course, we both know what a timely opportunity that is, when your book's about to come out."

Something old—and practiced—had added this last, some part of her that always took responsibility for trying to shift things away from the kind of unpleasantness this conversation was eroding into. She could have left it there.

But something else suddenly refused to give him another inch. "Right now," she enunciated the words emphatically, as *he* often did, "I'd like to get this finished." She could feel the fury at the edge of her voice, straining to get in.

"Then the housework, which, unlike deadlines, will actually *wait*, will be right there when I'm done. I can have myself a regular marathon with it. Do nothing but housework for *weeks*." Her voice rose on this final word.

Go ahead, get angry. Part of her was almost eager that he would.

But after a long pause, he shook his head, that patronizing tactic he was bound to reach for. "You're making too much of this. Frankly, I was disappointed when I heard it's what Ritter assigned you."

When Anna didn't reply, Lowell said, "She was a *nobody*, Anna. In the scheme of things, she just doesn't matter."

"To you, you mean? Or to 'historians'?" Anna spoke the word derisively. "Yes. That's a point you and others have made plain enough.

"But believe it or not," her voice grew quieter now, "she matters to *some* people. We look at her life. Then maybe we look at our own, and begin to see things."

Lowell all but snorted, "What? More ways men have wronged women?"

"No, Lowell. We see the truth. About what it is we don't do, when we could make different choices. And we begin to see what it is we do instead."

He put his hands up then turned away. "You're in over your head, and some feminist bullshit is probably the reason. It's time to fish or cut bait, Anna."

"Fish or do laundry, you mean."

His back was to her as he left the room. He returned, shrugging on his jacket. "Look, I don't have time to waste on this. I've got things to do at school, and now," his tone was caustic, "I guess I'll have to stop off at the cleaners on the way."

Anna knew he'd paused for effect and didn't look up.

"I was just trying to talk some sense about this but I've obviously wasted my time." After a moment, he added, "You should understand, though, that nothing is certain. The issue may not even have room for this."

Just the sort of bomb he'd drop.

"I simply plan to keep my end of the commitment," Anna leaned back in her chair and looked up at him. "Have you thought about what this could do, if approached the right way? It could attract women readers—the ones statistics say actually buy magazines. Or are they as unimportant as Eva Braun was?"

She pushed her chair back and stood up. If anyone was going to walk out on this unpleasant exchange, she was about to claim that privilege, this time.

He'll find some way to get back at you, a voice warned as she moved toward the stairs. *Well, it can't stop me, if I don't let it,* a stronger one decided.

Shortly after she stormed upstairs and slammed the bedroom door, she heard in her mind the lead for her article. She'd drafted almost the whole story but this had stayed just out of reach. Anna reached for the pad and pen on her bedside table to write it down:

They called her "stupid cow" though she was smart enough to capture the man she loved when everyone—he, most of all—said he'd never marry.

Considered insignificant by those around Hitler, she was one of the Third Reich's best-kept secrets and filmed the private lives of many notorious Nazis.

Eva Braun paid a big price for the name "Hitler" and it was hers only for a day, and now no one ever calls her Eva Hitler. Her life with the Führer mirrors Germany's: he first seduced, then neglected and abandoned them. Finally, he led them into the jaws of destruction.

The article knit together easily after that. When Lowell stayed out late again, she sat at her computer until midnight, when she knew she was done. After these compressed weeks of learning so much about someone's life, it all came full circle at last.

While she worked, Eva Braun's face looked back at her from the photocopied photos Anna had spread on the floor around her chair. It was a circular timeline that stretched from the year the teenage Eva had met Hitler in Heinrich Hoffmann's Munich photo shop to the spring day the 33-year-old elected to die with him in a Berlin bunker as Germany was on the brink of defeat.

The years between had brought long spans of endless waiting for his return, his calls. In the sixteen years of their relationship, when you added up the actual days Eva had spent in Hitler's company, it wasn't even as much as a year.

Anna wrote of Eva the "ordinary Munich girl" no one took seriously who, at the end, was the only person Hitler trusted, the only one who could interrupt, speak directly and honestly to him. The one who had made him feel he could come home to a private life like any other man.

Eva who, Anna was surprised to learn, was credited at the war-crimes trials in Nuremberg with an action shortly before her death, an interception of one of the Führer's last written orders, that had saved the lives of 35,000 Allied prisoners of war.

Then there was Eva behind the camera, the avid documenter whose insignificance allowed her to draw close to Hitler and his inner circle. Thus, she'd created the legacy that outlived her, the hundreds of photos and hours of film footage that millions still watched, trying to understand just what had happened, and why it had.

And finally, there was Eva the paradox. Slavishly devoted to Hitler, she never joined the Nazi party, had Jewish friends, and a churchgoing Catholic's conscience. A well-brought-up girl from a respectable, even conservative, Munich family, she had chosen the utterly disreputable life of a mistress. This, in her time, had sentenced her to a furtive, secretive existence. She'd had access to more wealth and comfort than most people could imagine during the war years, yet she'd confided to trusted friends that she was little more than a bird kept in a gilded cage.

After giving the manuscript one final read the following afternoon, Anna looked at the portrait and realized, *I'm a little sad to be finished, after all this time I've spent in your life*. Hannes had given her until April 15, a deadline she knew was close to his own larger one, and she had beaten it by almost two weeks.

And she knew just how she hoped to celebrate. Since he'd enjoyed that meal the other night, she would invite him for tonight, or arrange a time over the weekend. If Lowell chose to stay busy and remote, then she'd have Hannes's company to herself.

Following a week of rain, the tulips had bloomed bright in the beds around Peggy's house. Anna had wanted to shake off the weight of winter and dress for the new season, evoke the same lightness and vitality she could feel stirring inside her. After weeks of wearing nothing but sweaters and jeans, she had chosen a 1940s dress she'd bought at a vintage shop last year but never worn. Its silk print was a palette of lush spring colors in a flowing shirtwaist with a V-neck and three-quarter sleeves.

Her coffee-colored eyes watched from the mirror as she drew her long, wavy hair away from her face and clipped it behind her head, then added gold hoop earrings. She slipped on suede pumps the same violet as that in the dress's floral print and felt … pretty. And excited to deliver her manuscript. And just last month, she'd hardly been able to push herself out the door.

When she arrived at *The Fighting Chance*, Kathy wasn't at her desk. Anna lingered over it, listening for the sound of voices. She thought of heading for Hannes's office, or the conference room, but didn't want to seem intrusive.

The phone rang. She could answer it, at least—even use it to let Hannes know she was here.

Anna tossed her folder on the desk and hurried around it. Her eyes scanned for the list of the office extensions, which was right beside the phone. She picked up the receiver and said, "Good afternoon, this is *The Fighting Chance.*"

"Oh, hallo?" The female caller paused. "May I—speak, please, to—Herr *Ritter?*"

She emphasized the name, rolled its r's perfectly, then added emphatically, as though there might be some possible confusion, "*Hannes* Ritter?"

"Yes, of course. Please—hold. Ein Moment, bitte," Anna said reflexively.

She quickly transferred the call to his extension, the buttons for which her fingers had already started to hover over anxiously. Then she replaced the receiver in its cradle as rapidly as if she'd been holding a red-hot potato straight from the fires of hell.

What if he wasn't in his office and the call rang back here? *What if he's in the conference room? Perhaps that's where Kathy is. Maybe they're in a meeting.*

What if she'd transferred a call he'd—

Anna's heart leapt when she heard Hannes announce his name as he picked up the call. Turning to look, she realized that the sound was coming from his office a few doors away across the hall. She could see that its door was ajar.

"Wh-who is this, please?" he was asking in German. "It is a little hard to hear."

Oh, God—she'd never even asked who the caller was. She'd felt caught off guard, dispatched the call instinctively—

"*Du bist es? Wirklich?*" Hannes was asking now, using German's familiar "you," the one reserved for family, and other intimate relationships. Anna heard the delight in his tone as he exclaimed, "Is it really you?" and continued in a stream of excited German—eager, *affectionate,* "I was beginning to think I wouldn't hear from you."

Anna felt a searing flash in her chest. She was an eavesdropper. She should … leave. Close a door. Do *something.*

But she stood rooted, afraid, even, to move. Her heart seemed to pound through the soles of her feet. She felt herself straining to hear, not wanting to.

"Of course I can meet you," he was saying.

Anna swallowed, hard. Felt … adrift.

"You mean I'm really going to see you, *tonight?*" His voice was growing more alive with happiness.

Anna was awash in sickening waves; felt obtuse. As mortified as if she'd been caught by a video camera doing something embarrassing. How idiotic, to have imagined all of that about tonight. When here, clearly, he had a whole other life, one she'd certainly never know anything about. Or be part of.

"I can leave soon—perhaps in an hour. When will you be finished?" His voice was animated, its tone so warm. "I know, sweetheart. They never give you enough notice, or enough time. Where are you staying?"

Gasping in a breath, Anna looked around for scrap paper. Kathy kept an orderly stash in a red plastic tray next to the printer. So organized and neat, Kathy was.

Anna couldn't think. What should she write? Simple, short. Just a few words:

> Hannes,
> Here is the story. Any questions, just call. Have a good weekend,
> Anna

She scribbled the words hard and fast with the pen she'd picked up and been holding since she'd answered the phone. She would leave this clipped to her manuscript here on Kathy's desk. She could always call later to say she'd left it.

Then, the sound of Hannes's laughter rippled down the hall, first one bright burst, then a second, longer one.

Anna felt a stab of emotion near her throat.

His beautiful laugh. Always sincere. Never used to try and mask discomfort or nervousness, to seem congenial or make a good impression. Anna had discovered that Hannes only laughed when it seemed to surprise even him, as though carried off unexpectedly by its eruption from somewhere inside him.

Get out, an inner voice ordered. *He mustn't see you. You'll never be able—*

"Very good, I'll see you then," Hannes's voice was lower, softer. "Ich freue mich, auch—*I look forward to it, too.*"

Anna didn't hear the rest because she bolted out the glass doors of the office suite's entrance straight into Kathy.

"Oh, hi, Hon! Were you looking for me? The copy machine's down so I went to use the one in the chiropractor's place. They're always so nice. I swear, we can't keep a machine of ours running. I keep telling Hannes we've got gremlins—hey, are you OK?" She suddenly stopped and looked at Anna.

Anna could feel the quaking that was bound to show in her voice. "Fine. Thanks, Kathy. I'm running behind and I have to go. I just dropped off my story. It's on your desk." She felt as though she wouldn't even be able to speak Hannes's name without giving her feelings—such embarrassing, unexpected feelings—away.

"Well, *congratulations!*" Kathy reached to pat her arm.

"Sorry to be in such a rush." Anna added a weak smile, then turned to hurry down the carpeted stairs.

Kathy was standing with her back to the office's glass doors, through which Anna had already seen Hannes stride out to her desk.

She raced down the stairs and out to the car as rapidly as she could without actually running, her heels clacking crazily on the asphalt of the parking lot. She gunned Peggy's noisy diesel Jetta sedan to life and was nosing it toward the exit when she caught sight of Hannes out of the corner of her right eye. He had emerged from the building's front entrance and, hand still on the door handle, was looking around. Then he seemed to spot the car, where Anna had stopped as she waited to pull out into traffic.

She steeled herself not to turn or look his way. Then she realized she'd either have to make a left turn across the line of traffic coming from both directions, or drive past him if she turned right. Either way, the traffic wasn't allowing her to go anywhere.

From the periphery, she saw Hannes moving toward the car.

Suddenly, a man driving an old green Toyota waved her out. Hannes was jogging toward her now as she turned out onto the street. She reached to throw an appreciative wave to the angel who'd provided this escape, averting her face from where Hannes had drawn nearly parallel with her car near the lot's exit.

Anna fixed her eyes straight ahead as she sped away, now the traffic was finally moving. She held her breath the distance of a block until a sob caught in her throat. Tears heaved up in a hot gush.

It was so rude—disingenuous—to act as if she hadn't seen him. But she couldn't have faced him, couldn't bear to look at his face, so full of his recent joy. How could she begrudge him that, especially when he was so kind?

Because her heart wanted his response on the phone to be for *her*, for all she'd imagined being able to share with him.

If only I'd never come here today. An inner voice added: *If only you hadn't indulged in that pathetic fantasy like a schoolgirl. You're turning fifty. What were you—*

Anna wrenched away from the goading blades of these thoughts. It was true. She had somehow lost perspective, risked embarrassing them both. Maybe this was how women suddenly made bizarre mid-life choices.

Her thoughts were beginning to quiet when the memory of that female voice asking for Hannes resurfaced like a tennis serve lobbed back at her face.

"I *couldn't* have talked to him," she heard herself cry as fresh tears coursed over the ones that had already begun to dry on her face. Her head felt as though it were held in a vise. Her throat was raw, and a dull ache throbbed behind her eyes.

I'd have dissolved into this mess at the sight of him.

As if all of her ridiculous, pitiable—now utterly dashed—hopes would have been plain in her face. Like the last girl left when everyone else has been picked for the dance.

Still shaking when she reached home, Anna hardly remembered the drive there. Spring bulbs were blooming in Peggy's flowerbeds, along with the forsythia that always grew so wildly out of control. Anna remembered her father cutting it back to stumps she hadn't believed would ever grow again. Yet here it was, and so it had, year after year.

The house was a dark reprieve for her aching eyes as she stepped out of the sunlight. She caught sight of her ravaged face in the hall mirror as she slid out of the suede pumps now grown heavy on her feet.

When she set her things on the dining table, she discovered that Lowell had left a note. She couldn't remember the last time he'd done this. The notepad-sized sheet was resting on top of a slender paperback at her place at the table.

Anna lifted the note to peer at the photograph on the book's cover, which showed an American soldier displaying a mocking Nazi salute, and the title: *Collectors' Guide to "Liberated" Adolf Hitler Memorabilia.*

Then she read the note:

> *I know I came off like a hard ass. End-of-term, getting things ready for the book's release. I was probably a shit, and I'm sorry.*

Anna stared at this final word. Lowell encouraged moving on, putting things behind them. But he never apologized. Looked for ways to avoid it, she knew. And here it was. In print. She read on:

> *Thanks for all you've done to help with the magazine. I found this book in my office and thought you might be interested. There's a small section about items that belonged to EB. I won't make it home for dinner tonight, but how about a nice meal out somewhere this weekend? L.*

His words flowed over her comfortingly. There was a time when he'd seemed to delight in finding ways to surprise her, leave things like this for her to discover. She'd found it sweetly, even vulnerably romantic. The Lowell most people didn't know. The one he shared with her.

Anna glanced at the book's cover again and saw that it pictured the "Kleeblatt," Eva Braun's four-leaf-clover monogram, in one corner, although this one was drawn to look more like a butterfly, as her monogram sometimes was. She flipped through the pages, pausing to look at photos that catalogued Hitler's looted possessions, including china and silver services found in his homes in Munich and Berchtesgaden after the war.

She'd save this for later—heat a bowl of the Asian soup she'd made last night and take this upstairs to read in a nice hot soak.

The telephone's answering machine flashed a "2" as she passed by the table in the front hall. Anna paused, then reached to press the retrieval button. The first message reminded about Lowell's upcoming dentist appointment.

The second made her heart skip when she heard the sound of her name:

> *"Anna! Where were you racing off to?"*

Hannes's voice, gently scolding, sounded more German than English.

"I wish I'd had a chance to thank you properly. I was already two pages into your story when Kathy came in to say you'd left. The piece is wonderful. You've told us so much, and raised important questions."

There was a pause of several seconds before he concluded:

"I'll be away this weekend. I hope we can talk when I'm back next week. Vielen Dank—Tschüss – thanks very much—bye."

Anna rested her forehead against the wood of the adjoining doorframe as the words died away. She felt an impulsive urge to save the message, or play it back.

Before there was a chance to do either, she pressed a button firmly to delete it, clear her head of that moony nonsense. Hopefully her article met the magazine's needs and they could continue in a pleasant, professional relationship.

Her heart jumped at the sound of the phone.

She felt drained, ready to collapse. Certainly not like talking. And what if—

Anna snatched up the receiver decisively.

"I'm glad you're home." It was Lowell.

"Thanks for your note," she said.

"You found the book?"

"I did. It looks very interesting."

There were a few seconds of silence, then he asked, his tone teasing with challenge: "Are you ready for some big news? *Two* pieces of it?"

A note. And now this. Lowell hardly ever called about anything anymore.

"Sure ... " she replied uncertainly.

"Which do you want first? The good news? Or the other good news?"

"Oh, Lowell. *You* decide. Just don't keep me in any more suspense—"

"We have an offer on the house, on *our* house," he shot in.

"My *God!*" Her tone rose along with her enthusiasm.

"A good offer. One I think we can go with and close on soon. Their financing looks solid and they want to move fast."

"I can't believe it!"

"We can sign papers by the end of next week, the agent says. They've just got one quick inspection they want done, then everything should be all set.

"And the other news," he continued, "is that I got another call today with an invitation to speak next month about my book, and the War. In Germany."

"Lowell!" Anna exclaimed. "So much wonderful news in one day!"

"It's quite a jackpot." Then his tone grew more serious. "But we'll have to move fast with the house, Anna. I wanted to give you a heads-up. I know you're trying to work on your assignment—"

"Oh, I've finished it. Dropped it off today." What providential timing after all.

"Well, that's great. We can plan on getting over to the house this weekend and begin clearing it out."

"And let's not forget that dinner you mentioned."

"Absolutely," he said.

"I'm so glad you called, Lowell. It's good to hear this news today. Congratulations."

"I'm going to give Hannes a call. He's the one who helped me make the connection with the university in Munich. He may have some ideas about how to prepare. Between that, and the house, there'll be a lot to do in these next weeks."

"Maybe I should go over to the house tonight?" she wondered.

"Nah. It can wait till the weekend. Give yourself a night off." His tone was indulgent. "I should be home around midnight."

A little later, Anna eased into a bath fragrant with lavender salts. Relaxing back, she sipped steaming miso broth, wielding chopsticks to capture the soup's long noodles and bright vegetables.

What a day for Lowell. How glad she was that she'd been here for his call. He had worked so hard, for so long, struggling to mask his disappointment when the recognition he longed for didn't come. You could measure the degree of his disillusionment by the impatience and displeasure he showed with whatever posed an obstacle to his plans.

At times like those, though he'd appear detached and indifferent, Anna knew how his thwarted ambitions smarted. He'd grow more suspicious, and critical, intolerant of anything illogical—or, that most deplorable of possibilities, "hysterical." Like those "antics" of his mother's that had stolen the time and attention subsequently denied her young son. Lowell had nothing but contempt for such "weakness," Anna knew. Above all, never sacrifice your credibility by losing control.

In the beginning, he had charmed her like a playmate before he'd begun devolving into what so often felt more like a disapproving parent. They met during her junior year at Smith, when the irresistible edge of his sexiness was fueled by his intelligence, a mixture both competent and creative. Where so many of the men had seemed like boys, immersed in superficial things, Lowell had exuded awareness, depth. Talented—on a full scholarship at nearby Amherst College—he had chosen her, after she'd wondered—worried—whether anyone would. Anyone worth being chosen by.

What had attracted him to her? Had she enough perspective to know? She imagined he found her open and willing, knew he could be himself with her—as much as he was prepared to show, anyway. She also allowed him the control he seemed to need. It was sometimes almost a relief, when it wasn't confining. When it was, she had learned how to wait for it to pass.

She'd learned how stay out of the path of his drives in every way but one: the children they'd never had. With each successive disappointment, each pregnancy that never brought a live birth, Anna watched something fade in Lowell.

In time, he'd been home less and less, blaming his extended work hours on the demands of his job. She knew he let work consume his life because he never stopped waiting for the acknowledgement he felt was overdue. Perhaps today's news, and the publication of his book, would begin to fulfill him.

She set her empty soup bowl on the floor beside the tub and reached for the catalog from Lowell. The section about Eva Braun showed a half-dozen photos of wardrobe items like an evening dress Anna knew had fetched five figures at an international auction. Other pages showed jewelry, silverware, and table linens.

Most carried Eva's trademark Kleeblatt monogram, engraved on silver or hand-stitched on fabric. In one photo, a handkerchief showed the monogram as a quartet of small, conjoined circles embroidered in one corner.

Water sloshed over the side of the tub as Anna bolted up, remembering the texture of stitches under her thumb. *It couldn't be,* part of her insisted as she reached for a towel. This was probably ridiculous—but she had to go see.

She had forgotten all about the discoveries in Peggy's bureau, had liked the scarf so much she'd never returned it to the drawer. Hurrying to her mother's room, she pulled the drawer open to find the square of cloth and the envelope. *Surely, there was no way—*

She set them on the bed, then switched on the bedside lamp and reached for Lowell's book to find the photograph. Beads of water dripped off her limbs onto the hardwood floor. She drew a quick inhalation of astonishment. This handkerchief's clumsily hand-stitched design appeared identical to that of the one in the photograph.

It *had* to be some odd coincidence. Peggy had loved four-leaf clovers, anything associated with luck. But Anna had never seen anything like this in her things before.

She unfolded it and saw that the square of plain white cotton had a simple banded hem on four sides. In one corner, embroidered in tiny white stitches were four converging loops all roughly the same size that formed the letters "EB." The vertical line of the "B" extended down between them, like the stem of a cloverleaf.

Settling cross-legged on Peggy's pale blue coverlet, Anna reached for the envelope. Its brown-paper surface was soft and worn with age. She slid the contents out carefully and saw that it was a bundle of newspaper and magazine clippings about a half-inch thick. Most had been torn from *Life* magazine and its competitor, *Look,* those coffee-table companions of childhood she'd pored over each week the day they arrived, looking for photos of animals, or movie stars.

The earliest of the clippings were newspaper articles without photos, or ones that only pictured Hitler. They announced his death, and that of the woman many had been surprised to discover had not only died with him in Berlin, but been his wife at the time.

Finally, in early June of 1945, the single *Life* magazine cover Peggy had saved bragged that the issue included the first available photo of "Hitler's woman." The brief text, filled with inaccuracies, was essentially a long caption under a photo-portrait of Eva Braun in a narrow-waisted dress, a photo that probably dated from 1943 or '44.

Articles from later issues, some as late as 1947, told more of Eva's story, usually with lots of errors. These were accompanied by photos of her at different ages, and of her sister, sometimes misidentified as Eva. In several instances, Eva's name had been crossed out in the caption and her sister Gretl's written above it in blue ink.

At the bottom of the pile was a sheet of small black-and-white headshot photos of Peggy, no doubt photographer's proofs sent in this envelope addressed to her. The date in its postmark was October 1932. Her mother would have been twenty.

She looked happy and relaxed, and very pretty. Anna recognized one shot in which she gazed at the viewer directly with a warm smile as the photo that had sat on Rod's bureau as long as Anna could remember. Peggy always said it was her favorite.

By the time she'd read all of the clippings, her mother's coverlet wrapped around her shoulders, Anna felt the same combination of familiarity and unanswered mystery that she had when she'd done the research for her article.

What in the world were these doing here? Her mother would never keep something like this unless it had significance. Instantly, Anna remembered Charlotte Wald's words, that night of her phone interview: "She *knew* Eva Braun, didn't she?"

CHAPTER 4

Anna first feels the chill of cool, wet grass under her bare feet. Ahead of her, a building's façade gleams white in shadowy fog. The sun rising behind her illuminates and draws it out of the gloom into the first light of day.

High above a valley, embedded in the mountainside, the building's pale expanse shows a portico of arches and masonry columns studded with stones. Similar stones underfoot lead across a patio to a corner formed by two wings of the house. The entrance is just beyond, up two broad shallow steps.

The breeze and her breathing feel comingled. The door is open a few inches, wooden surface warm beneath her hand, like the sun on the crown of her head.

The entry hall's vaulted ceiling is supported by squat columns that remind her of oversized chess pieces. All is dim, unlike the dawning light outside, as if the fog has sought refuge here. The only light comes from the crack at the base of a door.

In an instant, Anna stands in the room beyond it, near the marble mantel of a great hearth. Fire blazes with roaring force. A small group is gathered around it, dwarfed by the room's high, coffered ceiling and elephantine furniture. Their attention is on Lowell, who speaks uninterrupted, like a lecturing professor.

Anna listens for his pause, steps forward to speak, but makes no sound. Lowell continues as though he hasn't seen or heard her. The others don't notice her, either.

Lowell's voice fades. The flames' flashing light writhes toward her in spasmodic bursts of orange and gold. Their roar escalates to a screech.

Anna spins around to find the vast space deserted. Where fire cast shadows on the walls, there is scorching, exposed lathing, plaster crumbled on the floor.

Her foot bumps into—a body, lying prone, head twisted to the right, face hidden. Sunlight streams through a window nearly as big as the wall itself. Anna sees the angle of a wrist, the curve of fingers, gazes down tenderly at Lowell's elegant hands.

Then she wrenches back in horrified recognition. These hands won't move again. This posture of death is like a tree felled from its heights.

The battered walls blur into ones Anna doesn't recognize as she pulls up and back, higher and higher, throat straining with the hammering of her heart.

Beside her, breathing sounds shifted from a soft rumble to a tiny whistle.

Lowell's snores, right there. Home. Safe.

Morning light was just beginning to appear through the bedroom window. All that Anna had seen in her dream was receding into vague mist. Thank *God*.

Only that image of Lowell lingered. She blinked it away.

He was usually awake first, these days, and she was often fast asleep before he got home. She had so much to share with him. But he was never here to talk to.

She hadn't had a dream she remembered in such a long time—nothing like this. Maybe she'd dreamt of him because of his invitation from Germany.

But what was that house? And the dream's horrible climax, a scene that made her heart clench each time her mind went back to it.

Perhaps it was a warning. She needed to pay attention to her life, to their life, after how absent she'd felt in these last mournful months. That silliness about Hannes seemed truly embarrassing now. Yesterday had been a day of extremes, in all of her feelings.

She decided to get up in this early light, the quiet house, and start organizing her thoughts. She and Lowell had lots of changes ahead of them over these next days.

***

August 21, 1995
En route to Munich

The plane's droning engines drew Anna's attention back to her surroundings. The cabin was filling with savory aromas as the flight attendants distributed dinner trays, and the pilot announced their flight's progress in both English and German.

Outside in the dark, Anna saw undulating tendrils the color of pale jade— the Northern Lights—dancing in the sky somewhere over Newfoundland. During the flight, she'd been too absorbed in memories to reach for the reading material in her carry-on.

Her dream back in April had been a harbinger of so much to come. During the years she'd looked for acceptance in Lowell's academic world, she often discounted her dreams, suppressed what they might offer.

But from the day she discovered that her mother's life had some connection with Eva Braun's, Anna's dreams had shown a presence and power she couldn't ignore.

The dream also brought a kind of punctuation mark on her life with Lowell. At the time, she couldn't have imagined what would follow, any more than she could have imagined flying to Munich without him like this. But nothing that had transpired in the months since her mother's death felt anything like the life that had preceded it.

When she joined Lowell to finalize the closing on the house they vacated after Peggy's death, it was the first time in years they'd spent so much time together. Anna was eager to tell him about the handkerchief and the magazine clippings about Eva.

Perhaps the dream had presaged how this would go, how her inner hunger to connect would, once again, meet the wall of his impassive indifference.

"Your mother always had a fascination for odd things," he said when Anna showed him the articles. "And she was German, after all. Those revelations must have seemed huge in that post-war chaos. Magazines were a luxury. Your father probably got them for her. They were still in Germany then, right?"

Anna nodded.

"Maybe *he* was the one who collected those," Lowell suggested. "You know how obsessed he was with that portrait he brought back. Your mother hated Hitler, and everything about the Nazis. Why would she be interested in his mistress?"

"But what about the handkerchief?" Anna insisted, even as she began to feel like a child trying to debate the professor. In just a few analytical assessments, Lowell had deconstructed her ideas; deflated her excitement.

"What about it?"

"It looks just like one in that book you gave me, has the same monogram."

"What does? Some embroidery?" He took it from her, scanned the surface, then shook his head as he handed it back. "A clover's a pretty common decoration. Germans are always going on about luck."

"But it's exactly what Eva Braun's monogram looks like. And Charlotte Wald, the war correspondent, *asked* me whether my mother knew Eva Braun, She said she thought people had seen my mother with her."

"How long ago is that, and how old is she? Who knows if she's even talking about your mother? Trouble with you is, you hear what you want to hear."

Something flared in Anna, ready to protest, then dropped back, as if a soft hand restrained her. There was some truth in what he said, and it stung, though it was what she should have expected. She had planned to tell him what she'd learned about the portrait of Eva but knew then that she wouldn't bother. Trying to explain further would only leave her tongue-tied, the way it always did in the face of his insistent logic.

Lowell had *decided*, wasn't even listening now, if he ever had been. Since his father's death, and Peggy's, it was as though something in Lowell, some last vestige of possibility, had moved out. They had plenty to do that day. It was time to focus on that.

Besides, an inner suggestion reminded, *you can talk to Hannes. He will listen.*

A few days later, Anna ducked out of spring rain into the foyer of the magazine's office building. Music echoed down the stairwell as she climbed higher, along with a soft thrum of rain on the roof. When she opened the glass door to the office suite, tones of a stringed instrument leapt toward her as though suddenly amplified.

"Come by. Anytime," Hannes had said when she phoned. What in those words made her feel more welcome here than she did in her own home?

As though cued by the question, the music shifted to a cadence that impelled her forward, like advancing waves, then struck an old ache near her heart. She paused to lean against the wall that curled around the conference room like a nautilus shell. Sound was palpable through it, as she recognized the music.

Her mother had played this second movement of Beethoven's Seventh Symphony, but only when alone. Anna sometimes came home from school to hear it pouring from the living room's small stereo. When Peggy heard her close the back door, the music stopped abruptly and within seconds, her mother would appear with an air of having been waiting for her all along, though her eyes always looked red, and sad.

Once, when she was about eight, Anna asked Peggy to play the music. Her mother had made a face, as though teasing, but her voice had been grave. "Nein, Liebling. It makes me cry." Anna never asked again. Doing so would have felt like hurting her mother. She already knew she couldn't ask *why* it made Peggy cry.

As a teenager, she unearthed the record with this music like a sad secret, and wept as she listened. It evoked a memory of standing beside a door with her mother on the other side. The door's surface had a dark design, like a butterfly. Anna recalled tracing its shape as she waited, her heart a weight of sadness in her chest.

One night, shortly after she had asked Peggy to play the music, Anna had stood outside her bedroom door calling for her. With uncharacteristic gentleness, her father had finally come and led her away. His eyes looked sad that day, too.

At the entrance to the conference room now, Anna caught her first glimpse of Hannes where he sat near the center of the room playing a chestnut-colored cello. He wore dark jeans, a maroon button-down shirt, and an expression of rapt concentration. His face, cello, shining crown of hair, and the hands that worked the bow and strings with fluid grace were all lit from above by the skylight. Its surface was being pummeled, now, as rain poured down in a crescendo that matched the music.

Anna had just enough time to view the scene, like a snapshot, before the music ceased, as it always had with Peggy.

Hannes's blue gaze flashed up to meet hers over his music stand, like light sparking off a diamond.

A stab of apprehension struck near her solar plexus. She was that child outside the door—now suddenly thrust open, prodding her heart to pounding.

"I-I'm sorry if I interrupted."

His smile etched lines from his jaw to the corners of his eyes. "I'm just finishing." He stood, as though coming to greet her, but the bulky cello made that impossible. "Come in, please," he gestured from behind it as he turned toward a case that lay open on the floor and eased the instrument down into it. "I've been practicing what I'll play with the university quintet. I'm hoping to record it."

"A musician *and* a recording artist."

"Oh, not that kind of recording. It's for a gift."

Anna remembered the phone call she'd answered on her last visit here.

"For Mother's Day," he added. "It's one of her favorites."

After a moment, Anna said, "I think it was one of my mother's, too."

"Really?" His tone showed interest. "What I love about playing it is, it always feels," he paused, as though searching for his next words, "like finding something you have felt was missing, that has been there, all along."

He snapped shut the clasps on the instrument's case. "One of my musician friends says it makes him feel 'Gija Hoda.' That means something like 'dizzy with God.'"

Studying his face, Anna noticed an almost imperceptible imperfection in the handsome features: the left eye looked just a little smaller, as though it were retreating, less of its surface visible behind his eyelids. She didn't recall seeing this before.

"I bet this will make your mother very happy," Anna said.

"I hope so," he shrugged. "What she says she wants most is to have me back in Munich. This gives her a little of that. And playing helps me focus for the big push."

"Oh, the deadline?" Anna turned toward the conference table covered with layouts of the magazine's pages. They were due at the printer Monday. He'd obviously been working hard at the drafting table and computer nearby.

"Where's everyone else?" she asked. "You're not doing this alone?"

He grinned. "Lowell must have confidence in me. I should take it as a compliment. He has high standards."

She shook her head, unbelieving. "The others have gone? The few that were left?"

"Lowell let them go some weeks ago."

"Even Kathy?"

Hannes nodded.

"I figured he'd at least keep some of them part-time, to help with the deadline." Anna's anger at Lowell was rising. "This, of all deadlines."

"Oh, I knew this was coming—and I'm more than halfway through now, since my best writer got her work to me early." His smile was warm.

"How do you manage?"

"Too much coffee. Staying up late. Some of my habits haven't improved very much since my student days."

"Well, you'll get home earlier tonight," she declared. "I'm staying to help."

"Anna … " He looked uncertain.

"Unless you'd *prefer* to be on your own."

"I'd prefer not to impose on you."

"It's no imposition. I have the time. And I'm a pretty good proofreader. "

"Now *that* will save me a lot of time," he agreed. "Maybe you can start with the pieces I've written?"

She nodded as she moved toward the table.

"And, before you're drafted into this, let's not forget that you had something you wanted to talk with me about, ja?"

What Anna had planned to share seemed a long way from her thoughts now. "Let's deal with this, first."

After Hannes helped her get settled, the next hour passed quickly as they worked in companionable silence. "All done," she said triumphantly when she'd stacked the last of the proofread layouts at one end of the table. "Except for my stories, of course."

"I'm nearly finished, too." He was framing an ad with slender border tape. "I'll make us some coffee."

"I can do it."

"Absolutely not—you've done enough. I'll fix us a little something to eat, too. And speaking of your articles, did you see those pages?"

Before she could answer, he added, "Oh, no, I have them right here," then lifted the sheets from the drafting table and brought them over. "I'll be right back," he said and disappeared down the hall.

The magazine had never looked this good. Anna had to hand it to Lowell. Turning it over to Hannes had been a smart decision.

To illustrate her article about Eva Braun, he'd used a color photo of the portrait and grouped around it a collection of smaller photos of Eva at different ages. She was a doe-eyed toddler, a teenager costumed for Karnival, an athlete reaching high for a swan dive, and, as she was so often in life, a photographer coaxing a group together on the terrace of Hitler's mountain retreat. There was also a color photo of her standing alongside Hitler, the kind of image Anna knew was rarely seen during her lifetime, as he'd forbidden it. He needed German women to believe he was a bachelor forgoing a private life in service to the Fatherland.

When Anna uncovered the pages of her story about women war correspondents, she encountered the riveting gaze of a dark-eyed woman in a black-and-white photo. With her hair swept up in a luxuriant cloud, she emanated a striking glamour even her military khakis didn't diminish. Alongside this photo was a smaller color headshot of a woman with waves of snowy hair around a lined face with a deep California tan.

Both were Charlotte Wald, Anna realized.

Hannes returned and set a tray on the table then ducked back down the hall to retrieve a white carafe and two mugs.

"You made us a whole meal!" Anna called after him.

"Only a very pedestrian supper, German-style."

The platter held slices of rye bread, two types of cheese, ham, tomato slices, pickles, and a small pot of tawny mustard.

"You deserve a much better thank-you than this." He set a paper plate and napkin beside her.

After they'd eaten in silence for several minutes, Anna said, "My stories look wonderful. The whole issue does."

Covering his mouth, he said, "Thank you" from behind his hand.

"And Charlotte Wald is beautiful. She's your aunt?"

He finished his mouthful and said, "Yes. Well, technically, my stepfather's sister. His twin, actually."

"She was so helpful. Gave me lots of good direction. I was also very surprised to learn she'd met my mother."

His eyebrows arched upward. "Had your mother ever mentioned her?"

"Not that I remember, but something about her seems familiar. And do you know, she told me she thought she'd once seen my mother with Eva Braun? I couldn't believe I'd heard her right. She did say she might be mistaken."

Hannes's gaze was directed toward his plate.

"By the way, I've been meaning to ask—why do you go by 'Hannes'? I noticed the by-line in your stories is your full name."

He seemed to consider his answer. "The man I'm named for was 'Johannes' in our family. To avoid confusion, I'm 'Hannes'-- 'Hänschen' when I was small. I know my mother's missing me when she uses that."

"Hänschen?" Anna asked. "Like the song?"

He rolled his eyes. "Ja, ja."

"What's it called?"

"'Hänschen klein'."

"Yes!" Anna was delighted as she remembered. "My mother and I sang it all the time. ... '*Hänschen klein, ging allein, in die weite Welt hinein ... Aber Mutter weinet sehr, Hat ja nun kein Hänschen mehr. ...*'"

Hannes tipped his head back and smiled. "Your voice is very pretty."

"I *loved* that song! And it's perfect—out goes little Hänschen into the wide world and his mother's sad because he's gone. Then home he goes again and she's happy." She smiled. "Just like you. I've always liked that name."

She had a happy childhood memory of sipping lemonade with Peggy near the seashore in Maine surrounded by people with brown faces—black folks. So curious. There'd been a Hänschen that day, a shy but friendly boy she'd played with while Peggy visited. Her mother occasionally spent time with German-speaking friends this way. Rod had seemed very angry when he learned about this afterward. That, Anna realized, was probably why she hadn't asked her mother more about it.

"My mother's business keeps her so busy, I'm surprised she has the time to think about anything else," Hannes said.

"She's still working?"

"Yes, at 75, still fully in charge of her Saint Anthony's Bakery—Sankt Antonius Bäckerei," he added in German, then smiled. "Best bread in Munich. Now in three convenient locations."

"She's not ready to retire?"

"Not a chance. Mutti lives for two things: her family, and her work."

"What sort of work did your father do?"

He had finished eating and sat silent, his gaze casting about the surface of the table as though looking for something he'd misplaced.

Anna said quickly, "Please excuse me if—"

"No, no. Just … sometimes, my thoughts go to German, first."

His voice sounded strained, as though forcing the words out. A muscle twitched in his jaw, and a slight wince made his eyes blink more rapidly. These facial shifts were subtle, as though he were accustomed to trying to mask them.

She reached across the table. Its span only allowed her to touch his fingertips.

His head shot up instantly.

"I'll stop prying," she said gently.

He swallowed, then said, "I am named for my mother's first husband. Who most likely died in the war. At the front, in the East."

He raised his eyes to meet hers. "Odd way to put it, I know. During the war, and long after, they read the names and serial numbers of the dead and missing on the radio, hour after hour. And posted them at the train stations.

Many soldiers just … didn't come home. Families never knew whether they had died or not. He was one of them."

A shadow of sadness enveloped Anna. What if you hadn't been listening, when a name was read? And what if you did hear the awful news that way? But even worse must be to never hear anything at all.

"You're named in his memory?"

He nodded. "Like many stories from that time, it's complicated."

"Lots of situations in families are complicated," she said softly.

He took a breath. "The way Mutti tells it, she went to church, to pray for an answer. The women were always pressured. To be faithful. To never forget the men at the front. She felt confused, because her heart told her Johannes Ritter was dead. He'd already been reported missing."

Anna flinched inwardly at the sound of his name referring to someone in such dire circumstances.

"They were both young, barely in their twenties. She'd had a dream in which he said good-bye. She couldn't tell whether she'd dreamed it or he'd actually been there in their room. The last time he'd been home was for a few days' leave in the summer of '42, not long before Stalingrad. She says it was as though part of him was gone already; that he'd only come home to make sure she was all right. He helped her find work in a bakery. That reassured him she would at least have enough to eat.

"So, after he was reported missing, she went to the church to pray to St. Anthony, patron saint of lost causes, missing objects—and persons. The priest there, a Jesuit, always encouraged her to trust her heart. The Gestapo later arrested him for helping some of those in the resistance who plotted to kill Hitler.

"After she talked with the priest, she says she 'knew' Johannes was dead. She prayed in the church, and heard the words, 'Go and feed my lambs, now.' The bakery where she'd been working had been bombed out. But she had the opportunity—"

Hannes stopped abruptly, as if something had caught in his throat. He reached to take a sip of coffee, then continued, "To work in a children's home. She took that as a sign." The corners of his mouth tugged upward toward a smile that didn't reach his eyes.

"I think she was simply grateful for whatever she had. It certainly was never enough. Since Anthony is also the patron saint of bread, she decided after the war to pursue her trade in his name. It wasn't easy. Baker's guilds didn't allow women then."

His eyes looked glossy when they met Anna's. The narrowing of his left eye appeared even more pronounced now.

Again, she wanted to reach toward his hand, but checked the impulse. "I hope I can meet her, when we all make this trip next month."

"I'm counting on it."

Anna decided to let him steer the conversation where he wished. His next words were a shock.

"We don't know who my father is." A shrug raised his shoulders and he released them with a sigh. "Not even Mutti."

"Hannes," Anna nearly gasped. "I'm—"

"Das—this was the story for lots of women, afterward," he added quickly. "There were many fatherless children in Germany then. For many reasons. "

His tone had changed, Anna noticed. Grown taut. Detached.

"I'm fortunate my stepfather was so kind to me."

Yet you never call him your father, Anna mused. Hannes's English had also grown more accented, and he'd slipped into German, briefly.

"It was chaos, at the end. So many women on their own. They're the ones who rebuilt Germany," he said. "They were often very brave, suffered so much. And received little acknowledgement. This was the subject of my thesis. The women professors encouraged me; the men said to focus on the war. They never understood that my goal was to uncover the story of those who endured in spite of it, or never wanted it at all."

After a short silence, Anna said quietly, "I'd like very much to read it. I think that's a remarkable subject, and I imagine no one ever talks about it. As if Germans—and the women, especially—somehow had no right to own the things they'd suffered through."

His features softened as he watched her.

"Speaking of history, I've made some more discoveries, in my mother's things."

Hannes leaned forward, as though eager to know more, or perhaps eager to change the subject. "That's what you wanted to talk about?"

She felt a flutter of trepidation as she recalled the conversation she'd already attempted about this. "Now that I've talked with Lowell, I realize it may seem silly."

Hannes's features collapsed in a small scowl. "Why would anything that interests you be silly?"

She reached into her leather satchel and withdrew the well-worn envelope, then removed its contents and spread them out on the table.

Hannes shifted his chair closer and began examining the clippings, his long fingers paging through them gingerly. As she watched, Anna noticed that several of the articles included photos he had used in the layout for her article.

"Where did you say you found these?"

"In a drawer in my mother's bureau. Where she kept her scarves."

"And you'd never seen them?"

She shook her head. Why did she suddenly feel nervous, like she was waiting for a test grade? Because she could still hear Lowell's derisive words.

"Well, this is very intriguing," Hannes said.

Anna then showed him the photos of Eva Braun's belongings where she had bookmarked them in the catalog, and brought out the handkerchief for him to see.

He studied it closely as he compared it to the one pictured in the book. "The monograms look identical," he said matter-of-factly. "How did your mother get this?"

"I'd love to know." Anna glanced away at the pages he'd created for the article about Eva. "But maybe Lowell is right, that none of this means anything."

"Do you think he would be interested if these were, in fact, connected with Eva Braun, and with your mother?"

Anna looked back at him for a long moment. "I-I don't know." But in her heart, she realized that it seemed unlikely.

"If these were with your mother's belongings, it would suggest to me that she was interested in Eva, at least. And the handkerchief looks just like the one in the photograph. Doesn't that seem to imply some connection?"

Anna was about to share Lowell's trivializing responses when Hannes said, "But what I find particularly interesting is how the captions for some of these photos have a correction made in ink—Eva's name replaced with that of her sister, Gretl. Did you know that Gretl is frequently misidentified in photos as Eva?"

Anna shook her head. "No. I mean, Eva was fair, and Gretl's eyes and hair were dark. How could anyone confuse them?"

"They did," he affirmed. "Quite a lot, after Eva's death—both people who'd never seen either of them, and those who had known them both. Whoever made these corrections knew the difference. Does the handwriting look like your mother's?"

"Well, it's block-printing. But it does, yes."

He was watching her now, a smile drawing the lines like parentheses on his face again. "I wonder what kind of story this handkerchief has to tell? And why your mother kept these things?"

Anna shook her head. "I simply don't know."

"Maybe, with your good detective work, you're being invited to find out." His eyes twinkled. "Perhaps even write another book about Eva Braun. There hasn't been one in English for a long time."

"Oh, that's much too ambitious," Anna said. "But I would like to find out why my mother had these things."

Then she added, "Thank you for listening. For giving me such an encouraging response."

He looked up at her as though surprised. "Well, of course. I'm very interested. I appreciate that you share them with me."

She checked her watch. "I suppose I'd better go. I'm not abandoning you?"

"Anna!" he exclaimed. "Heute hast du mir den Himmel gebracht!"

The German caught her off-guard for several seconds.

Yes, her inner voice agreed, *you've brought me heaven today, too.*

CHAPTER 5

The pace of Anna's days sped up as Lowell generated long to-do lists and only two weeks remained before their trip to Germany. Most mornings she was at the kitchen table, pen in hand, as he delegated tasks for his book's pending publication.

"The publisher needs background for publicity. Can you review my résumé, pull out some things that would strengthen a press release?" he asked one morning.

"I'll write a release, if you like."

"That's their job," he said gruffly. "But sure. See what you can come up with."

His requests took little time, and he'd even acknowledged that the release she drafted was far better than the publisher's.

Anna dispatched his lists, then turned to what drew her more irresistibly than ever, perhaps because it made her feel closer to Peggy. As she followed the pull of this call, Hannes's companionship felt like an unanticipated inheritance, too.

Her days had resumed a rhythm like those she'd previously spent in the workplace, where she'd managed her work life in order to maximize what she could of her private one. But now, it was home life that felt like the job, and the hours immersed in research that was the life she wanted.

Hannes's observations about the articles from Peggy's drawer had spurred her to revisit them and study their photographs. She'd been doing the same with photos in the two Eva Braun biographies he'd given her and was rereading the one by Nerin Gun, watching for clues. What was she searching for? Would this preoccupation lead anywhere? *Did* those items of her mother's suggest some connection with Eva?

During the long evenings when Lowell was away, she pulled down more books from the shelves in his study, ones about the war, the Third Reich. And Hitler. While she didn't always relish the reading, she knew it was necessary, to expand her understanding.

Most works about Hitler mentioned Eva Braun in no more than a sentence or two. Sometimes there were longer references, but that was in volumes of nearly a thousand pages. Why did this companion of his remain such a cipher?

Anna's favorite photographs were those of a younger Eva, between the ages of seventeen and twenty-five. These typically showed the effervescence that had prompted Hitler's photographer, Heinrich Hoffmann, to hire her although she had no prior experience. He knew the appeal that her pretty face and lively nature would have for his male customers, the ones most ready to spend their Reichsmarks for the latest camera equipment. Maybe he'd also sensed how much Eva would please his biggest—and most important—client.

What was evident in the few photos in which Eva appeared with Hitler was how stiff she seemed. While her face showed a smile, or an expression like that of an adult coaxing a child, her stance told a different story. It was a guarded posture, arms crossed in front of or behind her, as though bound—or, perhaps, holding herself in place.

Her demeanor in these was also yielding, deferential. Most other photos radiated her vibrant spirit, or she posed with confident elegance. But in the shadow of Hitler's presence, she was unmistakably muted.

Hannes had given Anna the photos he'd included with her article. One of them spoke volumes about the paradox of Eva's tethered life in its golden cage. A professional quality portrait, it showed her with a silver fox fur clutched to her throat, her gaze unfocused and downcast in an expression Anna could only characterize as bleak. Like someone who had received bad news, or reached a place of inescapable reckoning.

From her hairstyle, Anna knew this had been taken toward the end of her life, when she'd let her hair grow nearly to her shoulders in the style she'd worn at her sister Gretl's wedding in 1944. Perhaps this was the wrap she'd worn that chilly June night high above Berchtesgaden. Maybe this had been taken then and mirrored her realization that there would likely be no wedding for her, as the Führer remained firm in his assertion that marriage was both a political and personal impossibility.

This photo reminded Anna of one she'd found of her mother sitting at the table staring into space with a similarly desolate expression. Rod must have caught her off-guard and thought she was daydreaming. But Anna could see the sadness.

The biography by Nerin Gun described a visit he had made to the National Archives in Washington, where he viewed the dozens of Eva's photo albums that the U.S. had confiscated after the war. Anna was determined to find a way to see them, too.

The week after they met the magazine's deadline, Hannes called to say that the issue was back from the printer and offered to drop off copies for her and Lowell.

"It's nearly dinnertime. Will you stay and eat?" Anna asked.

"Oh, I'm sorry to say no. I have a rehearsal."

"Ah, yes. Your concert," she remembered. "When is it?"

"Next Sunday. I can visit for a bit, though. I have some other things to show you."

A little later, he was seated in the chair at the end of Peggy's kitchen table. As Anna settled on the breakfast nook's bench to his left, he unfurled a length of paper on the table. It was a fax from the university in Munich.

"I talked with some of the faculty there, who heard about the seminars Lowell will give, and sent them a copy of your article," Hannes explained. "This is an invitation. They would like for you to present, as well."

Anna looked up from where she'd been laboring through the fax's German. "They—present what?"

"About Eva Braun." His smile was encouraging. "They really liked your article."

Anna sat silent as her mind struggled to take this in.

"You can simply introduce the topic, some of the facts you have collected. The students in these classes will have plenty of questions, believe me," he said.

"*Classes?*" Anna emphasized the plural.

"Yes, well, a few. Which can be in English, if you wish." The light in his eyes sparked. "Anna, these professors are ones with real interest in this subject, and in helping you find good source material in Germany. You can go deeper with research—they're excited you're American. They think it gives you objectivity."

He stopped, alternating between glancing at her and looking down at the table as a furrow appeared between his brows. "Perhaps I've misread your interest."

"No," said Anna. "It's just that this all keeps getting ... bigger. And I'm no academic."

His blue gaze watched her closely. He blinked slowly a few times before he said, "All you have to be is who you are. That is, if you want to do this."

"Well," she sighed. "I can't seem to stop following this trail."

"And you have already done so much good work!" His tone was enthusiastic as he leaned in close. Anna felt the warmth of his exhalation on her cheek. "You don't have to know where it's leading. Treat it like an experiment."

He eased back in his chair, as though giving her space in which to consider.

"How soon will they need an answer?"

"You can think about it for a few days, certainly. I know this is short notice. I'm sorry if I'm pressuring you."

Anna smiled. "Is this what you call pressuring? It's the most encouragement I've received about anything in a long time!" She studied the fax again.

"Is it clear?' His tone was quiet, now.

She nodded. "I'd love to try this. I just don't want to disappoint them."

"There's no chance of that. These are the women who have supported my research about women rebuilding Germany post-war. I think you'll enjoy meeting them."

Perhaps one was the voice on the other end of the phone that day at the magazine. "Don't any men teach women's studies?" Anna wondered aloud.

Hannes looked surprised, then said, "I do. Well, I have. But men need to be thoughtful about it. Women have been written *about*, for a long time.

Once there is more of their own words, and voices, maybe then men can get more involved."

Where in the world did a man like this come from? Was it his mother's influence? That of other women, of a special one in particular? A flicker of jealousy made Anna feel both defeated and ashamed.

Hannes stood up slowly as Peggy's clock cuckooed six times. "I'd better get going." Reaching into his shirt pocket, he withdrew a gold-colored object. "You have a birthday this week, I believe?"

"Why—that's right. It was yesterday" Anna said, surprised.

Lowell had had flowers delivered, the usual two arrangements he always sent when he didn't remember until the day arrived.

"Then I am sorry to be late. Happy Birthday, Anna." As he extended it toward her, she saw it was a gold-plated mechanical pencil. The striped detail on the side was nearly worn smooth, but the tiny monogram was clearly visible.

She glanced up at him, unbelieving. "Is this *hers*?"

His smile was gently teasing. "Aren't those her initials? That curly Kleeblatt she had emblazoned on everything?"

"Where did this come from?"

"From her house, in Munich. In *Bogenhausen*," he added, specifying the district where Eva Braun had lived.

"Hannes, this is incredibly kind." Anna felt lightheaded. " I'm not sure just how many more surprises I can take in one day."

His hand touched down lightly on her shoulder and she heard his soft laugh. "We'll stop with these two, for today."

He withdrew his hand, slid it into his pocket. "It only seems appropriate that a writing instrument, of all things, should come to you."

"However did you find it?"

"Some of the magazine's advertisers are militaria dealers. One was in Germany after the war and brought home a lot of her things. He also buys them from widows of soldiers who did the same. This was discovered between floorboards in her house. Someone had thrown a rug down over it, so it took a while before anyone found it."

He had put on his jacket and was moving toward the back door as Anna jumped to her feet to keep up with him. "How do I even begin to thank you?"

"*Use* it," he said emphatically, sky-colored gaze bright as his words intercepted hers. "To formalize this new journey you're embarking on." The smile lines deepened around his mouth.

"Danke," Anna blurted out finally. "*Vielen* Dank."

"And, I thank you," he returned in German with a small bow. "Now—off to practice!"

After he left, Anna moved to the dining table, now covered with books in which she'd marked references to Eva Braun. Hannes had encouraged her to present from the research she'd already done, but it didn't seem like enough.

What had struck her as she'd read the articles Peggy had saved was how, with virtually no facts at all, news sources of the day had made all kinds of assertions about Hitler's mistress. As a result, most of what had been published about her was inaccurate, often defamatory, just as Charlotte Wald had said.

But what voice had there been to speak for Eva by then?

Anna recalled Hannes's observation about women being the subjects of men's writing, from men's perspective, rather than having voice of their own. She felt determined to unearth some sense of Eva Braun's voice.

She found it in the few letters of Eva's that the biographers had included, mostly brief, congratulatory messages or thank-you notes. The one exception was the last letter penned to her best friend, Herta, from the bunker where Eva died with Hitler just days later. Dated 22 April 1945, it was among the last letters she wrote, and ranged widely between reassuring her friend with a tone reminiscent of a parent's, expressing appreciation for her with tender affection, and wild speculation about whether to believe in eleventh-hour hope, or accept that the end had truly come. One cryptic line stood out, for Anna: "You cannot imagine the things I do for him, how they affect me personally."

The biography by Nerin Gun included a handful of entries from twenty-two pages of a diary Eva had kept in 1935. These were sporadic, made over a single season, a spring that was achingly beautiful everywhere except in Eva's anguished heart. These entries may have been her only safe outlet for wrestling with the confusion and hurt that led up to her second suicide attempt, made on the day of the last entry. Her pain was palpable.

When Hitler—much like Lowell—sent flowers for her twenty-third birthday but made no call or visit, she wrote, "Now my office resembles a flower shop and smells like a cemetery chapel."

Several more lonely days of disappointment later, her hopes rallied: "*Yesterday he came quite unexpectedly, and we had a delightful evening.*"

Then, a weekend of more highs and lows:

> "*He came on Saturday, when there was the Town Ball. ... I spent a few wonderfully delightful hours with him until 12 o'clock and then with his permission I spent two hours at the ball. On Sunday he promised I could see him. ... I felt I was sitting on hot coals at Hoffmann's, expecting him to arrive at any moment. In the end we went to the railroad station. ... just in time to see the last lights of his train disappearing. ... I am racking my brains to find out why he left without saying good-bye to me.*"

A March 11 entry captured the depths of her roller-coaster ride of euphoria and despair:

> "*Why do I have to go through all this? If only I had never set eyes on him! I am utterly miserable. I shall go out and buy some more sleeping powder and go into a half-dreamlike state, and then I won't think about it so much. ... He only needs me for certain purposes. ... When he says he loves me, it only means he loves me at that particular instant. Like his promises, which he never keeps. Why does he torment me like this?*"

Nearly a month later, Hitler invited her out to dinner, along with her sister. She sat next to him for three hours without their exchanging a word. Later, he handed her an envelope with money in it, "*as he had done before ... but not so much as a greeting or a loving word.*"

29 April 1935: "*I am in great trouble, very great trouble.*" Ironically, ten years later, this date would become Eva's wedding day, in a Berlin bunker—the same day that Anna had been born. Eva's little pencil had come to her on the date of its owner's death, which occurred the day after her marriage to Hitler.

Finally, on 28 May:

> *"I have just sent him the crucial letter. Will he attach any importance to it? … If I don't get an answer before this evening, I'll take pills and gently fall asleep into another world.*

> *"I haven't had a good word from him in three months. … Maybe it is another woman. … But there are so many other women. Is there any other explanation? I can't find it. God … If only somebody would help me. … the uncertainty is more terrible than a sudden ending of it all."*

This voice in the diary was about the age of the students Anna would address in Munich. What would it be like to read these words together? Surely some would have already experienced the pain of frustrating or unrequited love, the paralyzing sense of immobilization it brought.

In this suicide attempt, as in the first, Eva had held out for weeks, then months, with almost no contact from Hitler as his political activities took him far from Bavaria, and from her. Feeling abandoned, she'd sent a last-minute message to him before taking her drastic step.

Anna began leafing through one of Lowell's more illustrated books about Hitler. As she searched for scenes from Eva's sad, confined days, one image was startlingly familiar, though she'd never seen a photo of it before.

Eva wore a traditional dirndl with a red-checked bodice over a blouse with puffed sleeves. Her earrings, gleaming in sunlight, matched a pendant around her neck set with a garnet-colored stone. What caught Anna's eye was the armful of irises she carried as she reached to gather more under a brilliant sky dotted with colossal clouds.

Recalling the scenes playing in silence on the television the night Peggy died, Anna hurried to the living room. Neither she nor Lowell did more than watch evening news here, so the videocassette was still in the player. She switched it on and felt her heart turn over as she realized whose home movies these were.

Holding down the rewind button, she found the scene she sought quickly. It was about a minute long and followed Eva and two women, all dressed in dirndls, as they picked irises in a field, the ragged profile of the Alps on the horizon. The same scene as the one in Lowell's book.

In her final hours, Peggy had been watching Eva Braun's films. But how had she come to have them? Had this been what she wanted to talk about?

As the videotape continued, Eva frolicked with her sisters and parents in a small waterfall. Scenes shifted quickly to lakeside picnics, and a segment in which Eva and friends were crossing a stream in bare feet, holding the hems of their dresses high above their knees. Subsequent scenes showed her playing with her Scottish Terriers, water-skiing, and practicing gymnastic routines on a set of parallel bars.

After so many images that showed only frozen moments, it was mesmerizing to watch Eva's lively presence in motion. She looked vivacious, graceful, happy, usually at the center of the action, yet always aware of those around her, encouraging their participation. Animals of any kind absorbed her attention completely in these outdoor scenes in which Hitler and other well-known Nazis were markedly absent.

Then a large white building emerged on screen from behind fog. Lit by early-morning light, its columns and portico, the two shallow steps leading to an arched doorway in the corner—*every*thing was the same. What Anna had seen in the murky mist that had seemed to follow her inside that night she dreamt of Lowell—and Hitler's Berghof, she realized now.

She gazed at it, fascinated, then stopped the machine and turned off the television. As quickly as recognition had come, something inside began to pull away. She could imagine Lowell's tone, his reaction: that it was all just imagination.

She had mentioned the dream to him that morning afterward, mostly to acknowledge her relief. "I'm so happy you're right here. I had a scary dream about you."

He had looked disgusted. "Do you know how foolish you sound, when you harp on that stuff?"

Anna had experienced a flush of heat somewhere near her belly that had leapt toward her throat, stretched like a band, as though the two ends were pulling in opposition to each other: Lowell's dismissive reaction insisting one thing, while she knew the other to be true, even if her mind didn't understand why, and she couldn't find words to explain it. It was as though his discounting of her experience sought not just to diminish, but *prevent* this part of her.

Resolve had dawned then, stronger than any habitual accommodation she'd previously yielded to the presumed sovereignty of his demands. She suddenly understood that there were things she needed to shield from his unwillingness for her to be different, see differently, than the way he believed she should. She'd always felt hurt, full of doubt, after such exchanges. Now, she was determined to prevent them occurring at all—to protect what Lowell might never be able to recognize or understand, but could endanger.

Anna settled back at the dining table and picked up Hannes's gift to study it more closely. What had Eva used this for? Shopping lists? Those diary entries? The thought brought a tingle that traveled up the back of her neck.

She'd go to Hannes's concert next Sunday, enjoy time with him and let the memories keep her company after he was gone. The same way Eva Braun had.

She'd known him such a short time, and he had a life of his own that would take him back to Germany soon, something Lowell had mentioned just yesterday, though Hannes hadn't. If she were honest, the shift in her feelings toward her husband had to be related to what she felt from Hannes. And for him. What she'd longed for from Lowell.

She knew she couldn't look to him for this, whether or not Hannes provided it. Yet how wonderful it felt when he did.

What seized her heart then made it feel like a stone in her chest. Was this how you became unfaithful?

CHAPTER 6

On impulse, Anna clipped a rose from one of Peggy's bushes to give to Hannes after his concert. She said nothing to Lowell about her afternoon plans, and he was already out of the house early that Sunday morning. The May day was sunny and warm so she decided to walk the mile and a half to the campus.

During the hour-long concert of Beethoven's music, Anna drank in the shifting expressions in Hannes's earnest features as though committing them to memory. When audience members crowded around the musicians afterward, she saw him exchange a kiss on both cheeks European-style with an attractive woman who gave him a large bouquet.

Anna turned away and left the hall through one of its side doors. A short while later, the sound of a car horn startled her as Hannes pulled up alongside her in a small station wagon. She knew he didn't have a car, usually walked or rode a bike to the magazine's office. He must have borrowed this to transport the cello stored in back, along with the extravagant bouquet and the black tie he'd taken off.

His expression looked happy as he rolled down the passenger-side window and leaned over. "Well, hello! Can I give you a lift?"

Anna hesitated a moment, then reached for the door handle.

"The concert was wonderful," she said as she fastened her seat belt. "I didn't want it to end."

"I thought I'd seen you. But then, I couldn't find you."

She handed him the rose and shrugged, feeling foolish. "My offering looked so puny. I guess I chickened out."

He cradled the flower in his palm, then raised it to inhale the fragrance. Anna had chosen one of the more velvety red ones whose bloom was just beginning to open.

"It's beautiful. From your garden?"

"My mother's, yes. She'd have loved that music."

He looked at her reproachfully. "I would have been very disappointed not to receive this. Almost as disappointed as I was not to find you." He set the rose across his lap carefully, glanced over his shoulder, and steered the car out onto the road. "Have you had a good week?"

"I have, thanks. Still seems kind of unreal that our trip's just days away."

She was contemplating how she'd tell him her discoveries about Eva's films, and her dream of Hitler's Berghof, when she saw Lowell. He was leaning into the driver's side window of a nondescript sub-compact, forearms resting on the top of the door, body rocking side-to-side, that way it did when he was pleased with himself.

The young face looking up at him wore a blaze of red on the lips parted over a wide smile. Strands of long, corn-colored hair curled in the breeze toward Lowell's face.

He was wearing his pale yellow Ralph Lauren shirt, the one Anna had ironed just yesterday, remembering their spat a few weeks ago. That day she'd finished writing the Eva Braun article all the way through in one sitting. She could smell the heat of the iron, imagine the pebbly texture of the Oxford cloth against her hand.

Lowell was lowering his face into the car to meet that upturned mouth. A hand with lacquered nails reached up to touch the nape of his neck.

And, in case Anna's mind tried to introduce doubt about what she'd just seen, there was Lowell's Saab parked a few yards farther down the street, facing the river. How could so much appear before her eyes in drive-by seconds? The way your life did, when you were dying.

Beside her, Hannes was silent.

The expanding obstruction in her throat was going to choke her.

Hannes drove a little farther and turned the car into a small parking lot.

"You saw?" The words leapt to Anna's mind, but didn't get past where her voice felt snagged in her throat.

How she hoped he hadn't. Could she act as though she hadn't, either?

As he parked in a shaded space, Hannes's eyes showed that curious fast-blinking wince. He shut off the engine and turned to face her, then reached and laid his hand over hers.

She wanted to feel arms around her; run as far and fast as she could, all at the same time.

"Anna," he said softly.

She pressed her right hand over her mouth, staring through the windshield as tears stung her eyes.

"My *God*," she breathed. "So ... so ... *public*."

Why did she feel so mortified, as if she were at fault? It was clamping off her breath, threatening to wrench forth the sick sensation knifing at her stomach.

"Am I the very last to know?" she said finally.

"I ... don't know."

"Did *you* know?" she wondered suddenly.

She heard him inhale then release the breath in a sigh through his nose. "I certainly did not want to."

A spark of anger made her snatch her hand away. "How long have you known? Did he talk with you about it?" Her voice, previously strangled, seemed to be spiraling out of control now.

His head shot up as he met her gaze and said firmly, "Absolutely not."

His expression a tight mask of discomfort, he said, "I don't ... look for ... these kinds of things. So, I *do* tend to be one of the last to know."

"How did you find out?" she asked quietly.

"I ... saw something. Similar to what we just saw. When I was leaving campus one night. It was dusk. At the time, I—"

"The same person?" Anna demanded. "She must be a student."

"I'm not sure."

"Were you going to *tell* me?" Anna felt spurred by hurt, and embarrassment, even as she realized how unfair this was. And how awkward it must be for him.

"I didn't know what I was going to do, Anna." His eyes darted back and forth as though seeking something. "I wanted … to be mistaken."

Light blazed in his eyes with his next words. "I'm sorry, now, that I've done anything to help him. Once I introduce him, that first day in Munich, I want nothing more to do with him."

He reached for her hand again. "But I am here for you, Anna."

She drew a breath to hold back the sob ready to burst from her throat.

"I'd go back there right now," Hannes said. "Knock him against something—*through* it," his nostrils flared as he enunciated the word, "for being such a selfish idiot." This last came out with German pronunciation: ee-dee-OHT.

Anna blinked rapidly, avoided looking at him.

"But I want this Munich trip to happen, Anna. For your sake."

"Oh, Hannes! How can I possibly make this trip? Now?"

"You make it for yourself," he asserted. "*Your* reasons. Your needs. I'll be there, and there are people I would love for you to meet," he said. "Who want to meet you."

Anna couldn't imagine what she'd do next. A part of her still couldn't believe that she'd seen what she had, there by the river. And it wasn't as though she wanted to face him about it. There was only one likely outcome if she tried—the ugliness of Lowell cornered by truth he'd somehow find a way to turn back on her.

She just wanted it to all go away. Like another death, she thought grimly. One that comes out of nowhere, as Peggy's had; leaves you wishing you could find some way to leave the life you find yourself in, too.

Her fevered thoughts raced back to the scene. All those nights Lowell hadn't even come home, let alone been late. How long had this gone on? Were there … others?

But what did it matter? Something had already begun to close down inside her. Now, it was as though a gust of wind had finally slammed it shut. There was nothing left to protect or fight for. Except, as Hannes suggested, the remnants of her own life that had nearly been buried underneath.

"I'm sorry we aren't traveling together," he said. "I could rebook my flight."

"No, no. Don't do that." As always, Lowell had wanted to save money, so they didn't have a direct flight the way Hannes did.

"I'll be there at the airport," he said.

"But your plane leaves *hours* after mine!"

"I want to be there."

She looked away as the next thought overwhelmed her, as if she'd suddenly been knocked off balance. "I don't know how I'll get through these next days."

Hannes was quiet for a few moments. Then he suggested evenly, "You have choices here, Anna. You don't have to talk with him. You can decide about that later."

"But he'll know!" she cried.

"*Know?*" The light in his eyes flashed. "Know what?"

His voice was louder, angry, as he added, "Ich denke—" then switched back to English, "I don't think he has the sensitivity to know anything about you at all!"

His chin dropped toward his chest, then, as his expression grew guarded.

Anna stared at him, unable to think of what to say.

"I apologize if that is ... blunt. Or I am the one being insensitive," he said slowly. "This must be more difficult for you than I can even imagine."

"It's not as though things have been especially good between us," Anna said quietly. "A failing marriage is seldom one-sided."

His mouth tightened in a small grimace, the way a child's might look apologetic. "But I shouldn't be so outspoken. It's really none of my affair."

He looked instantly anxious, said quickly, "Oh—I am sorry. My English—"

As the laughter overtook her, Anna had a mental image of a wave capsizing a wobbly dinghy. She let herself be dissolved in the sudden, unexpected hilarity, let its spasms drag her under; wring tears from her in a far more pleasurable release than crying could ever be. The more his words echoed in her mind—his attempt at apology, as much as what he perceived as his gaffe—the harder she laughed, each new wave swamping her in intense and unexpected freedom.

"Oh, Hannes!" she gasped at last, laying her hand against his arm. "Talk about perfect timing!"

"Or imperfect," he shrugged with a clownish smile. "I'm grateful it helps you laugh." His look made something inside her flutter as she tried to catch her breath.

It was true. She could act as if she didn't know a thing. In fact, the prospect even felt surprisingly empowering. She *wanted* this trip to Germany, she realized. And as he'd reminded, her opportunity in Munich had come through her own efforts.

"I'm sorry you had to witness this," she said finally. "I should just go home, though it feels like the last place I want to be." She stared out the passenger side window at the trees, which had finally leafed out in a full canopy of bright green.

"You know," Hannes broke the silence. "This is a time when some women might go shopping. Run up a big credit-card balance. That may not be your style. But doing something for yourself you've really wanted—"

"—would be a far easier way to get through these days," Anna realized aloud. The idea came with a sudden rush of excitement that both shocked and delighted her. And what a supreme breaking of the rules it would be— against the grain of everything that was Lowell. All she'd need to tell him was that she had some last-minute research to do.

"If I could," she said, "I'd go to Washington. Spend the next few days looking at Eva Braun's photo albums, in the National Archives."

Hannes's face came alive. "That's brilliant!"

"When I get home, I'll call the travel agent—"

"No—let me," he insisted. "I know someone who can get this arranged quickly. And at no cost to you."

"Oh, Hannes. I couldn't."

"Trust me," he said, his expression decisive. "Airline employee's perks."

Anna looked at him doubtfully.

"Would you like to go tonight?"

Now she really was shocked. "Is that even possible?"

"Actually, the hotel can be reserved at the same time, so let me do that, too."

She grabbed his forearm, trying to catch his gaze. "Only if you tell me the cost."

"Anna, I've already *told* you," his smile was broad and beautiful as he turned it toward her. "There will be no cost involved for me, or for you."

He arched an eyebrow cryptically. "There may be an invoice or two to the magazine's 'business office.'"

Anna's mouth dropped open.

"For the hotel, a few meals. Maybe a taxi or two." His expression sobered. "Only if you agree, of course. It seems legitimate enough. After all that good work you did on the article, and so quickly. Why not submit for a few expenses?"

It was Lowell who would receive these bills.

Hannes's eyes gleamed. "If it were closer, I'd drive you myself. But I have no car, and you need every bit of the time now."

Anna wished he *could* come with her. But he must have so much of his own he needed to do before their trip.

"Shall I take you home?" he asked. "I can make calls to book your travel while you pack." He glanced at his watch. "I'll have to call Germany. That's all right?"

"Of course," Anna nodded, still feeling dazed by it all.

After a short conversation in German, Hannes booked her a flight to Washington that left less than four hours later, then used the borrowed car to drive her to the airport.

Anna felt queasy anxiety about the possibility of Lowell suddenly appearing at the house. Unlikely as it seemed, given recent history, she still shrank from the thought, her shoulders stiff with tension as she rushed to gather and pack her things.

"If he comes home, I have more than enough to talk his ear off about," Hannes said, as if reading her thoughts. "And let's blame this whole idea on me, OK?"

She slumped in relief as his arm circled her shoulders encouragingly.

"Everything is going to be just fine, ja?"

Her eyes filmed over with sudden tears as she nodded.

A few hours later, she arrived at her hotel, a short distance from the National Archives. The city's humid air felt thick against her face when she stepped out of the taxi. She planned to stay three nights and fly home Wednesday, savoring every hour of reprieve from Lowell, home, and a life she couldn't seem to recognize any more. The only advisory she'd given him was a short note she'd left on the dining table.

Something still lurched inside her whenever that scene by the river resurfaced in her mind. But by tomorrow morning, she'd be turning the pages of Eva Braun's photo albums, something she'd never have imagined— and certainly not before Thursday night's flight to Munich.

Once she'd settled in the cool comfort of her room, she ordered a supper of Maryland crab cakes and salad from room service. She didn't pick up the first call when it rang through, but instead called Hannes, as he'd requested, to tell him she'd arrived.

On what was probably Lowell's third try, Anna prepared herself, like someone getting into character, then answered brightly, "Hello?"

"Jesus, Anna! Where in the name of God *are* you? What the hell's going on?"

Before she could answer, he asked, incredulous, "You didn't even talk with me?"

Her mind tossed out the first two truths it was sure of as she recalled the afternoon's unwelcome scene: "I couldn't reach you. You weren't in the office."

"You didn't even leave a damn message?" His tone was rising now.

"I left you a note, Lowell. You found it, obviously, since you knew where to reach me—"

"Only after Hannes Ritter told me how. Just what the hell is going on here?"

Anna took a deep breath. Something inside wanted to scream: *What's going on is that you're a faithless bastard!*

Instead, she replied as mildly as she could, "This opportunity came up, with a very narrow window of timing. I didn't want to miss it, so I had to act fast."

"Could you be any more irresponsible? Our trip is four days away."

"Actually, this is part of my preparation for that," she told him. "I'm pretty much all set with packing for Munich."

"Yes, well, you have a lot more time on your hands. I'm not ready, and was counting on you to make sure that I am."

Anna's voice was cool. "I wish you'd told me."

There was a long silence before he spoke again. "Is *that* what this is about? Is this some way of getting back at me?"

Anna felt a ball of heat rising inside her, one that vacillated between rage and fear. *He wants the advantage. And I have to be at fault for him to get it.*

"Lowell," she asked quietly. "Whatever would I have to get back at you for?" After a brief silence she added, "I figured you'd be so … busy, over these next days, that you'd hardly notice I was gone."

"Well, I damn well do," he snapped. "I need to talk with you about some things."

Something in his voice had changed, taken that tone it did when he was going to introduce something unpleasant. Was this how he was finally going to tell her?

Anna braced herself. *Stay agreeable. It keeps him off guard.*

The nightmare of what life with him had become was coming to an end, she reminded herself as she turned toward the room's broad windows, gazed down at the twinkling lights of the traffic seven stories below.

"There's been a change of plans. I need to make some different arrangements," Lowell said. "It looks as though I may stay on in Germany— teach for the semester."

"Really? Our trip's going to be extended?"

"Not ours. Mine."

His words fell on her ears like boulders.

"We'll need for you to come back here and pick up some slack at the magazine, hold things down at home. And there'll still be papers to sign."

Anna's head was spinning now, a dull ache beginning to form at the base of her skull. All she could think was: *Who is this "we"?*

"I-I don't understand. Have you talked with Hannes?"

"Oh, I've talked with him," his tone was steely. "Enough to see what a meddler he is; more of a liability than an asset, at this point. Did he put you up to this?"

"He helped me arrange—"

"I thought so. Just how much is this going to set us back?"

"The air fare and hotel won't cost a thing. Hannes was kind enough to see to that. Any other expense will be minimal."

"Once we're finished in Munich, I'm going to fire him," Lowell declared.

Anna felt a plunging sensation near her heart and swallowed hard. "What will happen with *The Fighting Chance*?"

"Well, if you hadn't gone off on this badly timed expedition, you'd be here to discuss it. I'm not going into it now. When will you be back?"

Anna was beginning to experience that same defeated spin she always did in these interactions. The words about Hannes had hit like painful loss, and the fiery lump was back in her throat, along with teary sadness.

She reached for anger instead, drawing herself up tall in it as she squared her shoulders, her thoughts racing: *You want to know when I'll be back? So you can bring her to the house, you treacherous son of a bitch? My mother's house?*

Bolstered by outrage, Anna suddenly perceived a surprising option, one that would confound and madden him. Her tone turned deliberately breezy. "Actually, I'm taking things day-to-day, depending on how much progress I make."

This pre-emptive strike brought a rush of adrenaline. Whatever had prompted it? Fury about the plans for Hannes? Lowell's continuing deceit and betrayal?

There was nothing left to save. She could tell him whatever she liked, leave him able only to guess at when she might reappear. It was a heady, liberating sensation.

"Then you can be back tomorrow?" he said.

The arrogance of his presumption nearly made her laugh out loud.

"Probably not that soon." To keep things unpredictable, she added: "Of course, I *may* get back sooner than I expect. I asked Hannes to drop off some things at the house."

She hadn't, though perhaps now she might. She was on a real streak, almost as though she couldn't stop herself.

"WHAT?!" Lowell roared like the cornered quarry he was becoming. "Tell him not to bother. And I need to know when the hell you're coming home!"

His voice was loud enough that Anna had to hold the phone away from her ear. She felt a twinge of remorse for the undeniable pleasure she was experiencing as she baited him. Her next response seemed to arise like an inspiration.

"Oh, don't worry," she fibbed for the third time. "I've given him a key."

She would, she decided, and wished she'd thought of it before she'd left.

"You've *what?*"

"Yes. He's been kind enough to get some information together for me. Is that a problem?" she asked, feigning concern. "Or have you already told him that you won't be keeping him on?"

"For chrissakes, of course I haven't. And I'm warning you, Anna, if you want to make this trip, you'd better not tell him either. I'm keeping him on for this connection in Munich—and because his German's better than yours. I'll tell him once we're there."

Lowell's mean-spirited reference to her skills bit like a barbed hook as it touched a nerve already raw. "Then he'll have the inconvenience of having to come back here to tie things up," she said.

"That's no problem of mine." His voice was leaden.

Anna stared at the wall in front of her, unblinking as tears began to cloud her vision. This assertion, so reflexive for Lowell, felt repugnant in a way she couldn't imagine never noticing before. It was like discovering a rotting carcass hidden somewhere in the house.

She suddenly felt almost equally unclean for having lied to him, wanting so desperately to hurt him. How could she feel such hurt and hate and sadness all at once?

After a silence he demanded, "And since when have this guy's needs mattered so much? Why the hell does he know more about your whereabouts than I do?"

The question, both the injustice of it and the underlying truth, struck like a blow.

Another realization had also dawned. She'd started to wonder just why Lowell was "keeping her on," despite his obvious preference for where to spend his time. Then she realized: *the will*. Her mother's estate, now nearing settlement. Those were the "papers" he'd referred to, assets that would be "theirs" while they were still married.

Her reply seemed to come forth of its own accord, surprising her: "Why am I concerned about Hannes? Concerned about basic human decency, you mean?"

He started to reply but she cut him off, her voice cold with inflexible anger, "I don't like the accusation in your tone, Lowell. I'm astonished you'd even ask such a nasty thing. Need I remind you which of us has been away from home so much lately?"

It was all she could do not to slam the phone down, as she recognized the possible scope of Lowell's strategizing. Was he planning to set himself up with his young lover, start a new life, in Germany? Maybe even have a *family*, an inner voice suggested.

Even angrier, now, she was also starting to feel sick. Lowell was saying something but she hadn't heard him. She was no longer listening, only letting the weight of realization sink in. She'd been so naïve, so trusting. But wasn't he supposed to be the one she could trust? She didn't know who he was anymore, if she ever had.

Inwardly, Anna pulled far away, as though the hundreds of miles she'd put between them still weren't enough distance. How she wished Hannes were there. She'd tell him, of course; call and forewarn him.

After standing up to Lowell this way, she suddenly felt so weak that she couldn't imagine doing anything but collapsing into bed. Thank God she wasn't at home, wasn't any closer to him than the proximity of this miserable call.

His words were louder against her ear now, as though trying to force themselves into her emotional retreat: "Did you hear me?" His tone was brusque with impatience. "Are you going to be able to do those things before we go?"

She drew in breath deeply, didn't answer.

"Anna? For God's sake."

"At the latest, I'll be home late Wednesday afternoon," she said. "Whenever I get back, there'll be time to pick up or pack whatever you want."

"You're going to be away until the day before we *leave*?" He was shouting now, his tone infuriated.

"I told you, I'm deciding as I go," she repeated, her tone flat. "I can't say when I'll be home. If you have errands, leave me a list."

Cold sweat was creeping up her neck as her knees shook beneath her. Anna felt spent, unable to handle one more round.

"As usual, you'll want the last word, so consider that you've had it. I have things to get ready for tomorrow. I'm going to hang up now, Lowell. Good night."

She set the phone down, managing not to slam it. Still, she pressed it into its cradle for long seconds as though the whole horrible exchange would erupt back up in her face if she didn't.

Within moments, it rang again.

Her limbs were quaking as she moved toward the window and set her forehead against the cold glass. She felt both freezing and fevered.

The phone's ring sounded insistent as she gazed out, the city's lights blurring before her eyes in the inky darkness. Finally, the last ring died away.

Her mind seized on the memory of that dream image: Lowell in the gloom of what she now knew to be the great hall in Hitler's Berghof, shadows towering up the walls. The guests had huddled around him as he held forth, just as the Führer so often had when his company was grouped before the fireplace, dwarfed by the room's massive dimensions. No matter how she'd tried to get Lowell's attention, he ignored her, as though she weren't there. The way he always had, unless he wanted something.

Then, stamped on her awareness, the dream's climax: that body, face-down. Evidence of destruction, plaster dust and rubble, scorch marks on the walls.

She'd recoiled so hard when she recognized the figure sprawled on the floor that she'd woken to where Lowell lay snoring beside her on one of those many nights she'd never heard him come home, after he'd stayed out so late.

Hannes had urged she make her own life her priority, focus on the unfolding discoveries about Peggy and where they might be leading.

The prospect of Germany was suddenly irresistible, somewhere she imagined she could do what she wanted, go where she wanted; teach again, and write. Stop giving her time away to Lowell's needs like unpaid staff, always postponing her own projects.

Her own life.

Hannes had offered his help, and his company. All this was waiting now, no matter what Lowell did or did not do.

Of course, Hannes had his own life, that woman's voice on the phone.

But whatever surprises Lowell had in store, her own might turn out to be just as big. Maybe even bigger.

CHAPTER 7

Most of Anna's first morning at the National Archives was taken up with acquiring researcher's credentials and finding her way around the enormous building. Finally she'd donned the requisite white cotton gloves and settled at a table in the resource room, much like a library's, where Eva Braun's thirty-three albums were stored.

At first, Anna had tried to view them in chronological order. But this proved impossible, because Eva and whoever helped assemble them—there were captions in several different sets of handwriting—certainly hadn't organized them that way. While some albums covered specific time periods, most appeared patched together any which way, with childhood photos alongside ones taken near the end of Eva's short life.

Anna lost all track of time in the windowless room, and forgot to stop for lunch on her second day, when the announcement came that all visitors had twenty minutes to conclude their research and leave the building by five o'clock.

Over the three days of her research, she felt most affected by photos that depicted what she thought of as Eva's "real" life, the one she lived in her Munich house, in the company of family or longtime friends. Something about her life with Hitler seemed more artificial, like a dramatic role.

As she paged through the albums, Anna felt a sharp, sudden sorrow as she studied Eva's lively images and bright expressions. Most radiated such hopeful-looking happiness, when her life was so doomed—captive in an unending limbo in which the effervescence of her vivid personality had nothing to meet and welcome it, and nothing to illumine, beyond what felt like the confines of a small, dark cave. She had gradually suppressed these qualities in herself, as if the invisibility that her role demanded had finally been absorbed completely.

In photos from gatherings in Eva's home, ones where Hitler was never present, a humble-looking chair with a caned seat and floral-print cushion assumed a personality of its own. It was used frequently for posed shots, many playful or humorous, and Eva's artist friend, Sophie Stork, had even painted a little watercolor image of it on a divider between two of the album's pages. This chair had also been featured in a photograph of Eva's living room taken by an American journalist after the war, Anna recalled.

Immersed in the albums, Anna felt the hours rush past each day. Then, in the next-to-last album, she encountered a shock. On a page of eight small black-and-white photos was a shot of someone aged about sixteen, smiling back at the camera from where she stood beside a passenger rail car in a large train station.

Anna felt as though she'd turned the page to discover her mother standing there looking back at her. Or herself. The posture, expression and smile— all were like Peggy's. But the face itself was somehow different, its features more angular, especially the nose and chin in the way Anna's own was, but Peggy's hadn't been.

Then Anna recalled that there'd been some sort of accident that had altered her mother's appearance. It wasn't ever anything she wanted to talk about, and she'd almost always been scrupulous about applying make-up before anyone had a chance to see her.

As she reached for the last of Eva's albums, Anna told herself: *I must be seeing things—or imagining them. My eyes are tired.*

On her final morning at the Archives, she raced to get through the remaining few albums before she had to leave for the airport. If only she'd known how much more time she was going to have after all.

Despite her plans, Anna arrived home from Washington just hours before she needed to be back at the airport for the Munich flight. Lowell wasn't home when she arrived by taxi late that next morning.

Waiting on the dining table was a terse note—no greeting, just the single command:

I'm mostly packed. I still need a carry-on, packed with the following:

A numbered list followed.

Thankfully, Lowell's list was short.

The eclectic pieces of her parents' luggage were corralled in the closet in the spare bedroom at the back of the house. As Anna dragged them out, she recognized a blue-canvas carry-on with a gold Lufthansa logo.

It was her mother's "ready" bag, and had to be at least thirty years old. Anna felt a spasm of sad nostalgia as she unzipped it.

Peggy had always kept one of these so that if she had to leave home on short notice, she'd have the essentials gathered in one place. In recent years, the bag had proved useful for several impromptu hospital stays.

But Anna knew the real reason for this ready-packed resource. If you'd ever had to leave a burning building in the middle of the night, race to a cellar or shelter as bombs pounded your street, you took precautions like this later. When you'd had to abandon your home in terrified seconds in order to survive, lost everything but what you were wearing or carrying with you, you never forgot. You planned for the future.

In fact, Anna had learned, the best resource during wartime was actually something you could wear on your back because you often needed your hands free for scrabbling over and around rubble.

Dispatching Lowell's demand would be even easier than she'd thought. She'd swap her own carry-on for this, since hers had more room for his things, and then she could bring the sweet comfort of this piece of Peggy's life with her.

As she began unpacking the contents onto the daybed pushed against one wall, Anna could almost predict what she'd find. As a child, she'd encountered an earlier version, a loden-green make-up case, in those days, and pored over what it contained.

There were similar items here. One set each of summer and winter clothes, always with pants instead of skirts, in later life. The requisite underwear, and stockings or socks. The most essential of toiletries: usually a bar of soap, though this had been replaced here with a travel-sized bottle of shower crème, a more multi-purpose product. Toothbrush and paste, a wooden comb, a white glass jar of moisturizing cream, and a well-used lipstick in a soft red, more coral than scarlet.

And here it was, at last—the rectangular gold Longines watch with its no-nonsense brown leather band that Peggy had so often worn. Anna had long wondered where it was. Wrapped around it was a pastel silk scarf Peggy often wore over her hair.

Beneath a tin of bobby pins were two ballpoint pens, a folder of writing paper, and a slim paperback of stories by Rosamunde Pilcher, Peggy's favorite. She'd said that rereading them was like revisiting a painting; it never yielded the same experience twice.

At the bottom of the bag was a wide, flat box of typed onion-skin paper about two inches thick. The box cover had the words, "Private. Please keep out" in Peggy's scrolly handwriting. There looked to be at least a hundred pages, perhaps more.

The first showed a title, Fellow Travellers, with contact information that included a Munich address and Peggy's maiden name, "Adler."

Anna flipped through some pages and saw that dates and places were noted in a few places, like a diary. Glancing at the first page, she read:

February 1928

What a wave of relief when my train crossed the border into Germany at Simbach. Escaping Austria was like release from prison, from that tirade of Father's."

Simbach? Where Eva Braun had attended the English sisters' convent school? Anna flipped through the fragile sheets. What *was* this? A memoir? A novel?

The phone's jangling made her jump, and by the time she reached the nearest phone in the downstairs hallway, Lowell had already started to leave a message.

"I'm here," Anna gasped as she snatched up the receiver, feedback from the answering machine screeching in her ear. "I'm getting your carry-on ready now," she said, as if to mollify him. Why did she feel as though she'd been caught out past curfew?

"Well, thank God for small miracles." His tone was sarcastic. "I was ready to make this trip on my own."

"The weather finally cancelled the flight I'd planned to take. I had to wait till this morning. Did you get my messages?" Anna noticed the winking number on the answering machine and realized he likely hadn't.

Her flight had been delayed more than five hours due to thunderstorms, then cancelled. After a night in the airport and a few hours of fractured sleep, she'd flown home this morning on a flight that left just minutes after the sun crested the horizon.

"I had so much to do, I never even made it home last night." He sounded accusatory, as though she were somehow implicated in this.

Anna's heart sank when she realized where he must have been. However would she get through these coming days? At least she hadn't had to see him. By the time she did, Hannes would join up with them at the airport.

"Why were you down there?" Lowell asked

"The National Archives," Anna replied blandly. "For research."

There was a silence, as though he were waiting for her to say more. Then she heard him sigh. "Well, I hope your head's on straight. You need to be ready to leave the house by 2. I'll be home then." He rang off without saying good-bye.

How she wished there were time to call Hannes, but there was barely enough to get everything together. She'd have to be careful at the airport, keep all possibilities for tension to a minimum. Once they were finally in Germany, there'd be a chance to tell Hannes about the hours she'd spent with Eva Braun's photo albums.

There wasn't likely to be much sleep on tonight's flight to Munich, either. It was time to get going, and she still had her own things to pack.

August 22, 1995
En route to Munich

Anna startled awake, then realized she'd dozed. It was several seconds before the sounds in the plane's cabin reminded her where she was.

The in-flight movie was flashing scenes of a high-speed car chase as her uncommunicative seatmate excused himself to get in line for the restroom.

This was the flight to Munich she had finally found the courage to make—by herself—months after the one she'd been hurrying to pack for that day in May. Glancing at her watch, she saw that the flight's progress was a little past the mid-way point, with about four hours remaining before they arrived. She reset her watch to German time, five hours ahead, where it was already August 22, the date on the portrait of Eva Braun.

Although it was past midnight back in New Hampshire, Hannes was probably tending to last-minute details before his own flight later today. Anna imagined the worried expression his dear face often wore over these last months—the one he'd showed when she moved off toward her gate to board this flight alone.

Back in May, she first became aware of his presence in the hospital room days after the burned-out shell of that other plane had been cleared from the runway. How surprising to wake and find him beside her in the stillness of what she eventually recognized as some kind of medical setting. She didn't know how much time had passed—it felt like one long, jumbled sleep of feverish illness.

At first, her body was a dense mass she couldn't seem to move. Then her leg seized with pain she couldn't associate with any cause. As she looked around, she felt herself recede from a world of dream-like images, ones that had felt familiar, like home, and appear in a space in which everything was unknown—except Hannes.

His head was lowered, where he sat reading. She gazed at him for moments that felt as long as hours. When she finally spoke his name, he was on his feet and beside her seemingly in the same instant.

"*Anna!* You're *awake!*" He drew close and she saw that his eyes were red, his features haggard. He closed his hands around hers, where it rested on top of the covers.

"She asked uncertainly, "I've been asleep?"

"Oh—*yes.*" He dabbed at his face with the back of one hand, took a shaky breath. "For quite some time."

These were *tears*, Anna realized. But *why?*

"You don't know how happy I am to see your eyes," he said.

"How … long has it been?" Suddenly, a lot of questions poured into mind. "Where am I now?"

"A couple of days," he said. "You're in the hospital. This is where they brought you after—there was an accident, on the runway. Do you remember?"

His gentle grip on her hand tightened then.

Scanning back in search of an answer was like turning a corner into a room stacked with file folders. You knew what you sought was there, but *where*? She began by tracking the first details that surfaced: "There was such thick smoke, and fire."

Her thoughts felt their way along toward what loomed like a doorway she'd been avoiding. "Where's Lowell? He got out? I *know* he did. I *saw* it," she insisted.

Hannes's forehead creased deeply. After a pause, he affirmed, "He … did."

"Where is he?"

Hannes then paused so long, alternating between looking at her and looking away, Anna knew what the answer must be. His hesitation already revealed what he probably didn't begin to know how to tell her.

She shrank back into the pillows, her grasp loosening in his hand.

"Lowell … died on the runway, near the plane," Hannes said finally.

Anna's mind, as though under someone else's control, erupted in its first sharp recollections: curling her body down low, away from the black, suffocating cloud. Trying to keep track of Lowell as she struggled to move toward an exit.

Then, being slammed back into her seat by one, then another of the figures flailing, bolting, in the blackness. Unbearable heat tearing at the side of her leg as she tried to pull away, a sudden terrible pain that felt as though it might snap her leg right off.

Darkness. Alternating with waking to screams, and stern voices intoning their rhythmic, repeated command: *this way out.*

But she couldn't get up, couldn't see. Only feel the most agonizing pain each time she opened her eyes. And the *flames*, and choking smoke.

In the scenes she witnessed afterward—and she still wasn't sure just where and how she had witnessed them—she watched Lowell through one of the small cabin windows as he hurled himself to safety down the plane's inflatable slide. Perhaps that had really happened.

She had also seen him through a window on a train as it pulled out of a station.

Drawing back from these spasms of memory, she reached under the bedclothes with new understanding toward where her right leg throbbed and occasionally stabbed with fresh pain. It was wrapped in a gauze-covered armor that felt inches deep.

"Your leg is hurt, but they say it's healing well," Hannes's tone was encouraging. "I need to let them know—"

The interruption was the sound of someone coming into the room. Then a second person was standing alongside the first, who announced, "Well! You're awake!"

As a man in a lab coat appeared in the doorway, the nurse who'd been the first to arrive told Hannes, "Now she's awake, you'll have to go."

"I'd really like to stay."

Anna felt small, like a child among adults. "You can't leave." Her words emerged in a weak trickle compared to the cry of alarm they'd started out as inside her.

All of them turned toward her, looking surprised.

Sensing that the man standing so unnervingly close held the authority, she tried to turn toward him, seek out his eyes, though it was hard to keep his face in focus.

"You have to let him stay. I *need* him to stay." She fought to shift from a childlike cry of panicked terror toward a more reasonable, we're-all-adults-here sort of tone.

Then her gaze shot back to Hannes. "You're the only person here that I *know*!" Surely the sheer logic of this would trump any regulations.

Where had her world gone? How had she gotten here? Why didn't she remember?

Hannes's features were suffused with tenderness. He tried to get closer but was barred by the sentries in surgical scrubs on either side of the bed.

Anna summoned strength again and extended her left hand toward him, wincing at the pain it ignited in her leg.

This time, he reached past the nurse to scoop up her hand in his. "Let me at least stay while you talk with Anna, so she won't feel so alone. Would that be all right?"

And so began the steady companionship he had offered in the months ever since.

Days later, Anna finally saw her injuries. Remarkably, the doctors told her, nothing had been broken. She'd sustained second-degree burns on her upper leg, and that other curious mark in the midst of them.

"In these kinds of situations, people can't see where they're going and things like this do happen," one of the kinder doctors had bothered to tell her, as though this would somehow ease her awareness about what had happened that day the plane's cabin had been engulfed in flames and smoke. When she'd been trampled by someone trying to escape and the result was this brand, this imprint of a shoe sole, left behind in her flesh.

What Anna kept to herself, like some shameful secret, was that once she saw it, she knew exactly whose mark this was, even recalled moments of awareness when someone in the smoky chaos had stepped not over, but directly on her.

She had come to think of it as Lowell's last assertion of her expendability. She wouldn't even have known whose imprint this was, were it not for that incident in the parking lot earlier that day. It wasn't as though she knew what the soles of his shoes looked like, after all. Who, other than police detectives, paid attention to things like that?

She knew the irregular contours of his worn underwear, the jagged spines of his signature, the smell of his shirts, and the alabaster hue his face took on as he slept. But until that afternoon, she'd certainly never noticed the footprint he left behind him, no matter how often he had sped on ahead impatiently.

After they parked the car that day of their flight and were walking to the airport shuttle stop, he had tread squarely on a newly blooming tulip. It was waving like a small red flag in an island between rows of parking spaces before Lowell flattened it.

Anna stopped to look.

"For Christ's sake," he snarled, "If we miss it, there isn't another for a half hour."

In his wake, beside the shattered flower, the cross-hatched pattern of his shoe sole was etched into the moist, dark soil. Anna experienced a sudden, engulfing sadness—for herself, for him. For the destruction and ending of so many things.

It had been cool for May, with a stiff breeze off the bay near the airport. She'd stooped to retrieve the flower's petals and slip them into her jacket pocket, where she had also placed Eva Braun's gold pencil. Miraculously, although they'd had to cut off some of her scorched clothes at the emergency room afterward, Anna's jacket had survived. She later found the contents of its pocket intact, including remnants of this flower, shriveled to slender wisps.

As she hurried to catch up with Lowell that day, Anna watched him dodge a car that had begun backing from a parking space without seeing him. Thankfully, she hadn't had to hear whatever it was he shouted at the driver.

Just as she hadn't had to see what happened when, having been warned in advance, Lowell had still gone his insistent way. Once he reached safety on the runway outside the burning plane in which Anna was still trapped, he hadn't seen something else: the emergency vehicle that, in its rush to save lives, had claimed one that day.

Anna was scheduled to be released from the hospital when Hannes arrived and, looking hesitant, told her, "There's someone I've wanted—"

Before he could finish, a face appeared inside the door wearing an expression of almost childlike excitement. As the woman approached the bed, Anna could see that under a mass of dark, glossy curls she appeared to be in her thirties.

Here she was, the woman in his life, even younger than Anna had imagined.

"I'd like to introduce my sister, Renate." He smiled at his companion. "However, like everyone in the family, she never uses her *real* name. So, this is Nati."

Anna stared at him for several seconds before she found words. "What a lovely surprise." She turned toward this new visitor, more confused than ever. "But, don't you live in Germany?"

Nati nodded. "I work for Lufthansa and fly into New England every so often. Hannes wanted us to meet when I last came to Boston, but there wasn't time."

She paused. "I am so very sorry. About all that has happened." Close by the bed now, she gathered Anna's fingers in a gentle squeeze.

What a kind, sweet face she had. Just like her brother.

"We need ... to talk with you, Anna." Hannes seemed impatient, even nervous. "Bring you up to date."

"To see how we can *help*," Nati intercepted, as though trying to divert him.

"But first," he persisted. "We need to tell you about Lowell's funeral."

In the cascade of abrupt changes and endings, Anna had literally slept through it, like Rip van Winkle; been spared it, she realized. All those faculty snobs she never knew how to talk to—and his sister, Connie, whom she'd always simply resorted to interviewing. Connie's life was the only thing she ever wanted to talk about, anyway.

Lowell's funeral. Already over.

With the pain medication, even when finally awake, Anna had had little awareness of how much time was passing. The hours since she'd regained consciousness felt like a cottony cocoon, a long, waking dream.

But why did she feel nothing about Lowell? Only guilty relief, as though now that she didn't have to think about him each day, she didn't want to think about him at all.

Yet, some inner voice suggested, there was remorse due. Some accountability. She was still here. And, had *wanted* him gone. And now he was. Just like the dream.

"We ... " Hannes paused, and then said, "I hope it won't seem impossibly presumptuous, what we did. It involved quite a few... lies. Or deliberately obscured truths." His features drew into a kind of frowning grimace.

Nati picked up the thread in her accented English. "Because you could not be there, we told Lowell's sister and her husband that we have connections with you. From Germany. Of course," she added with a quick laugh, "we *are* from Germany."

"We gave them the impression that we are family. Of your mother's," Hannes cut in, looking even more uneasy. "So that Nati could stay at your house, and everything would be the way you left it."

He had gazed at her for long moments, then said, "We weren't sure what was going to happen," before he turned away quickly.

"We also wanted to make sure you were represented at the funeral," Nati said.

As Anna's eyes tracked back and forth between where they stood on either side of the bed, she was suddenly plunged into a gray haze. Nati was in her line of sight when her vision finally began to clear.

"Are you all right?" Nati asked anxiously.

Anna nodded, then said, "How can I ever thank you?"

"Come home," Hannes's tone was emphatic, his expression strained, as though he were holding something in check.

"They believed you?" Anna asked. "About our being related?"

Brother and sister exchanged glances again, as though deciding which would reply.

"I guess Connie only ever saw my family a few times, after the wedding," Anna realized aloud.

"In fact," Nati said softly, "Connie's husband thought that you and I were somewhat alike." Dark-haired, with wide-set eyes so brown they were nearly black and cheekbones that shaped her face as though it were outlined, Nati did look a lot the way Anna had at the same age.

"Let me stay with you," she offered. "After you come home. I have already taken the time off, for the visit we were planning in Germany. I would like to help."

Anna gazed at her, astonished. They'd met so many of her needs. How could they feel more like family than anyone other than Peggy ever had?

This proved even more the case in the days that followed once she returned home. Though the medication still made her days indistinct, Anna felt cared for in a way that often brought Peggy to mind. As Hannes visited each evening, she enjoyed watching his interactions with Nati, who shared lots of family stories with her.

"What smells so good?" Anna wondered when she woke to the scent of fresh bread one morning.

"Oh that's the master baker." Nati looked surprised. "He's never *baked* for you? Why, that is our Hannes's meditation! Mutti is always telling him how much happier he'll be when he stops trying to change the world and settles down as a baker. She believes the bakery is a perfectly good place to change the world, you see."

Waiting on the table in Peggy's breakfast nook were six German-style Brötchen, crusty rolls that pulled apart to reveal soft, doughy centers, still warm.

"I think perhaps he has a little bit Heimweh, yes?" Nati said as she poured cups of coffee for them both. "How do you say it? Home ..."

" ... sickness," Anna finished for her as she savored her first mouthful. "These are exquisite! I don't think I've ever eaten them this fresh."

"Our mother insisted we learn to make them. But Hannes is the true baker." She rolled her eyes with a shrug. "Mine are like stones."

Anna spread a generous portion of butter on her second half. "He's out, already?"

Nati nodded. "Up early, like the elves, to make these. Then, straight to the office."

Where he was likely embroiled in more negotiation. Most activity had ceased at *The Fighting Chance*. Lowell's sister had initially claimed that ownership should "stay in the family, especially since you have no heirs." Tactful as always, Connie.

Hannes had been courteous, even gallant, during the meetings the three of them had with Anna's attorney here at the house. Anna was still too weak to go out.

"Too weak to deal with her, anyway. Let her have the damn thing. And I think she likes you, by the way," Anna told Hannes. "I'd swear you were flirting."

"Ach," he looked sheepish. "I simply want her to see me as sympathetic."

"That's a side of you I haven't seen."

He feigned hurt. "Sympathetic?"

"No," Anna said. "Calculating!"

He smiled slowly. "Only because I have *your* interests at heart."

Though he'd charmed Lowell's sister with his diplomacy, he'd had a firm objective in mind: that the two women broker a sale of the magazine to an interested buyer—the militaria dealer he'd befriended—then split the profits after all expenses were paid. At last, Connie had agreed.

"It really should all come to you, Anna," he'd said. "But I guess it's not worth dragging things out." Hannes agreed to stay on as editor for a short transition period before he returned to Munich in the fall to teach at the university.

"There's so much room here," Anna told him one day. "And you're at the house so much of the time anyway. Why don't you move in, let your apartment go?"

At his surprised expression, she added, "It only seems practical. I mean ... I hope I'm not being bold." *Or inappropriate,* her thoughts added.

"It's very generous. I would be honored to stay at Gästehaus Anna. I can pay—"

"Absolutely not," she cut him off. "Just move your things over soon, so you don't lose another month's rent."

The day he moved in, he was keeping her company while Nati ran an errand. Anna was on the sofa relaxing into the pain medication's first waves of relief when she remembered it suddenly: Peggy's bag—and the manuscript. That day she'd come home from the archives.

"Oh, no!" she cried. "The *bag!* Oh, no—*no!*"

Hannes looked up from where he sat reading, his expression alarmed.

She leapt to her feet. Then, features convulsed in pain, collapsed just as quickly when her leg gave out under her.

Hannes was across the room in an instant, wrapping his arms around her, guiding her back onto the sofa. "*Anna,*" he scolded softly, looking confused. "Was machst du? You must be careful," he cautioned, speaking in German before he remembered English.

His hands cupped her wrists as she lay back. For a moment, she could feel the beat of each of their pulses there, his and hers. The pain in her leg subsided, but her anguish only seemed to grow.

"The manuscript—it's *gone!*" A sob seemed to shake her whole body. "I should have made time, that day. Should have *looked.* But we had to get to the airport."

She was dissolving into an overwhelming sorrow that felt the way losing Peggy had, like losing her all over again.

As Hannes watched warily, his eyes showed recognition. "Ach, nein, nein, Anna—Alles OK," he said soothingly. "Einen Moment—Give me a minute. Promise you will stay quiet, here, until I come back?"

She nodded as he moved off, wondering, as she wiped away tears, why she cared so much about this when she didn't even know what it was. Why did the thought of losing those pages of Peggy's seem like a death? When the real death—Lowell's—was something she hardly seemed to think about at all?

She looked up and nearly yelped as Hannes returned and she saw the box.

"But … the bag." She shook her head. "I put it under the seat. On the plane."

How could this even be possible?

"You've been through so much already," said Hannes. "I have been waiting. For what seemed the right time."

Anna took the box, stared in amazement. "How can you have it?"

"It was right there on the sofa when Nati and I came into the house. Because I knew Lowell's family would also be coming here, I put it away."

Anna gazed at him as though from a dream. Then she remembered Lowell's call that day, the anxious rush to get ready, when she'd barely arrived home from her impromptu trip to Washington and had to head right back to the airport. She must have set the box aside when she'd come downstairs to answer the phone and forgotten it.

"I guess I had a lot on my mind," she said as the memory of that day descended: Lowell stiff, distant. Hannes asking thoughtful questions about his book, as though drawing some sort of fire away from her.

When Anna had broken in to say she was going to one of the airport shops, Hannes had glanced up at her knowingly. Lowell hadn't said anything.

Hannes had been there at the airport that day, she realized. With everything that had happened, not knowing. When the gate for her flight with Lowell had been changed suddenly, Lowell had come to find her.

"I never said good-bye to you," Anna remembered. The remorse felt as strong now as it had that day. "Oh, Hannes. I wanted to come back. But Lowell—"

Tears came at the most confounding times, now. It was all so confusing. Lowell's death brought only a desert of feeling, like a blank wall. But the thought that she might never have seen Hannes again and hadn't said good-bye was suddenly unbearable.

"Anna, it's nothing." He rose to fetch a tissue for her then returned to where he'd been kneeling beside Peggy's Toile-print sofa.

She laid her hand on his arm. "I have you to thank? That this wasn't lost?"

"I only found it right where you left it." His smile etched curving lines on either side of his face, the ones she'd missed seeing now that he seemed so serious and worried about her much of the time. "I lost track of it, for a while. For me, only one thing was irreplaceable that day." His eyes shone so brightly she could hardly bear to meet them.

Anna lifted the lid of the box and glanced down at her mother's pages. It was the same as it had been for days now, this price she paid for the medication's relief from the pain. Whenever she tried to read, the words quickly disappeared in a blur.

"I read some of it," Hannes confessed. "While you were in the hospital. Once I looked, I couldn't seem to stop. I'm sorry."

"Oh, that doesn't matter—but would you help me read it?"

He looked confused.

"It's the medication. Not just that it makes things blurry, but I feel dizzy when I try to focus."

"You want me to … read it to you?"

She nodded, feeling a little shy. "Didn't you say you'd already read it?"

"I shouldn't have, I know."

"*Hannes*," she pleaded. "I don't care about that. But there's still so much I don't understand." She shook her head helplessly. "It's like there's a trail, in front of me. First one clue, then another. Now this."

He sat silent, listening.

"I had a dream. Or vision. I don't know what to call it. Back in April. After I'd found those things of my mother's. I dreamt that Lowell was dead. In the Berghof."

"You mean—"

"Yes. *That* Berghof. And it still feels so real, it's as if it just happened."

"How do you know that's where it was?"

"I watched some of Eva's films—turns out my mother was watching them the night she died. There was a shot of the Berghof—exactly what I saw in my dream."

Perhaps she'd dreamt this because she had watched those scenes, as she'd sat in shock beside Peggy's body. Anna struggled to focus. "You probably think I'm crazy."

"Anna, you know that's not true. I just want to be sure you don't overdo things."

"I feel like I've woken up in someone else's life and all I have is questions and no answers. I don't know what this manuscript is. It may even be fiction. But if my mother did have a connection with Eva Braun, this may tell me what it was."

He nodded slowly.

"You'll help?"

"Of course. I'll do whatever I can to help you, Anna."

She handed him the box of pages.

"Right *now*?" he asked, surprised.

"If you would. I waited once, and nearly lost them. I don't think I can wait again."

And so, the sound of Hannes's voice, smooth and resonant, became inextricably linked with the tale that began unfolding from Peggy's pages.

PART II

The Path of the Fellow Travellers

Der Pfad der Mitreisenden

FELLOW TRAVELLERS

The Leap Year Angel

CHAPTER 8

February 1928

What relief when my train crossed the border into Germany at Simbach. Escaping Austria was like release from prison, from that tirade of Father's last night.

When Aunt Winnie announced he would come to Salzburg, I foolishly let myself think it was to visit during my school break. Once he'd reviewed my school report, however, he left to ski in Berchtesgaden.

I don't ski, and wasn't invited. But he took that redhead he brought along, the one whose ridiculous hair looks like mashed carrot. He really has no taste. She barely spoke to me, beyond introductions, and him, always carping about manners. Guess they're not so important for some things.

In my first year at boarding school, I'd have been wrecked when he did something like that. Now I know Salzburg's just something to check off his list, make sure the school is worth his money.

Thank heaven I have plans to spend the Fasching holiday in Munich with Mutti and Aunt Paula. Aunt Winnie begged me to wait until Father comes back. Isn't it too bad he didn't have the courtesy to tell us when that would be? That's what I wanted to say. Instead, I told her, "I have to be there tomorrow. They've made special plans."

They want to spend time with me. They plan for it.

I felt bad, lying, but I couldn't wait to get away. I knew my father's sister would never call Mutti to check on this. They haven't spoken since Mutti came back to Germany six years ago. I've grown used to traveling between people who no longer speak to each other, have decided they are enemies. Or, at least Father has. I just wish I didn't have to always do it alone.

When Father returned last night, I was upstairs in the room at Aunt Winnie's where I stay during vacations. He never offers to have me with him in England, and Mutti can't afford to visit me in Salzburg. She saved a long time for this trip for Fasching. He would never pay for it.

I'd hoped to get away before he came back. There was a big hollow in my stomach when he called me downstairs.

"You're *leaving*?" he began shouting. "You selfish, ungrateful girl. Does it mean nothing I've come all this way?"

There was sweat on his lip, just below the curving line of his mustache. The lump that filled my throat seemed to reach to my ears.

I don't know what happened next—I felt like I floated somewhere outside my body.

The redhead stood just a few feet behind him.

My words struck out, "You think I actually believe you came here to see me?"

The slap was like a wall hitting me. I thought I'd gone through a wall, but it was a sideboard I'd careened into, setting everything on top into a rattling I felt in my teeth.

I hate you, I hate you, I HATE you, my thoughts raged.

Aunt Winnie's posture stiffened, head retreating into her neck. She cast a warning glance at me, softened with a hint of imploring, before she and the redhead moved into the drawing room and closed the door.

He and I stood alone over the long minutes he beat me not with his hands, but his words. At one point, he actually had spittle at the corners of his mouth.

Then he said, "It's enough I had to lose a child, but that—"

He brought himself up short, turned on his heel, and left.

I was waiting for him to grab me, strike me. Forbid me to make the trip to Munich to see Mutti. But, instead, there was only this sentence that hung in the air.

I stayed frozen like a statue in the foyer for long minutes, as though he'd suddenly return, enraged not to find me rooted like a commanded soldier, or a dog.

When I heard the women's voices behind the door, mixed with his deeper tones, my plan came quickly. I crept upstairs, finished the packing I had left, penned a brief thank-you, and slid it under my aunt's bedroom door. Some of us still have manners.

I used the servants' stairs to reach the deserted kitchen, sandwiched some cold meat between two slices of the bread I found in the pantry, and left by the back door. The sound of the piano meant they'd be there for hours if Father had asked my aunt to play.

The station clerk said I'd missed the overnight train, but a local to Linz left in ten minutes. From there, I could make a connection to Munich, arrive even earlier than I'd planned. It meant waiting in the Linz station overnight, but at least I'd be out of Salzburg.

Now the morning sun was painting Simbach's shuttered buildings in lemony light as the train from Linz huffed to a stop. It was a big station for such a small town, probably because Simbach sits directly across from Braunau, Austria, on the River Inn and is the first or last stop in Germany, depending on which way you're going.

A girl stood alone on the platform, looking somewhat chubby in her boxy school uniform. But who ever looks good in those things? I was glad to finally be wearing regular clothes again.

Wisps of hair had wriggled free of her braids and fluttered in the blasts of steam the locomotive puffed out as it came to a halt. She looked as eager as if she'd been waiting for this train since it left Linz at dawn.

Where was the conductor? The girl hurried alongside the train, gaze scanning the carriages. Then her shoulders sagged, as though she didn't know what to do next.

I unlatched the outer door of my compartment, thrust it open, leaned out, and called, "Fräulein? Fräulein!" until she looked my way.

"Are you going toward Munich? Quick—come and join me."

She stared back, her moon-shaped face pale. Then she broke into a smile as she loped toward the carriage, tan suitcase banging at her hip.

The locomotive began panting, as though readying to depart. Surely the conductor saw someone still needed to board?

"Danke!' she exclaimed as I reached down to help heft up her suitcase, then grabbed her gloved hand and pulled her in.

"Your bag can go up there." I pointed to the overhead rack as I pulled the carriage door shut. Together, we struggled to lift up the suitcase.

"It is so heavy," she apologized. "I bring so much, I never know what I'll need."

"I do the same."

"Du hast mir den Himmel gebracht—du bist ein Engel," she declared, collapsing into the seat across from me.

"Oh, no, *you* are the angel. I was going crazy without someone to talk to."

Within seconds, there was a lurch and the train rolled forward slowly. We exchanged a look of surprise.

"Are they running late?" I asked. "I thought it usually stops for longer here."

She nodded. "Maybe because so many are traveling home for Fasching."

She pulled off her patterned woolen mitten and extended her hand. "I am happy to meet you. My name is Eva—Eva Braun."

Anna sat upright as though yanked from a reverie.

Hannes glanced up from the armchair where Peggy so often sat knitting or reading.

Before he could speak, Anna's thoughts streamed out aloud: "Simbach is where Eva Braun went to the Marianhöhe convent school. That same year. And my mother went to school near Salzburg. Her father's sister lived there. *Winifred!*" she remembered. "I met her, once, when I was little."

Hannes still made no reply, only watched her, the lines on either side of his mouth deepening.

"But it's a common name," Anna said. "This was probably some other Eva Braun."

His tone was neutral when he asked finally, "I wonder how many of them attended a convent school in Simbach that year?"

She stared at him for several seconds, then fell back against the pillows piled behind her. "But, there's no mention of the convent."

"Not yet, that's true. Only Simbach. And the school uniform she's wearing."

As her eyes widened, he added, "I've gotten so involved in reading. Are you having pain? Getting tired? Should I stop?"

"Stop? Are you *kidding*?"

She saw the concern etched in his features. She *was* tired. Felt knocked off balance. But she certainly didn't want him to stop.

"It's just ... so unexpected."

He checked his watch then thumbed through the remaining pages cradled in his lap. "Let me bring you some more tea." He rose and set the manuscript pages on the end table beside his chair.

"But—"

"I think you should take your next dose soon," he urged. "You mustn't let the pain get ahead of the medicine."

"But I want to hear the rest!" Anna protested, like a child about to be sent to bed when the party was just beginning.

"I know, I know," he said softly. "There are about 10 more pages in this section. If you take the medication, there'll be plenty of time to read them before you get drowsy. Then you will rest, ja?"

She nodded. Then parroted, "Jawohl."

He was moving toward the kitchen and paused to look back as he shook his head with a smile.

"Do you think it's really—Eva? *The* Eva?"

"Anna, remember, I've already read some of this. And I'm worried that it may be too much for you, right now."

"I'm fine," she assured. "Really, I am."

A little later, once she'd settled with her tea and taken the medication, Hannes continued reading Peggy's words.

As I reached for Eva's hand, the door to the main corridor slid open and the conductor seemed to fill it with his blue uniform.

"Where did *you* come from?" he asked my companion accusingly.

I smelled schnapps on his breath. And saw tears gleam in Eva's blue eyes.

"From Simbach, where she waited for this tardy train. It's not as though she was invisible."

His head snapped back.

"With no one there to help, she barely made it on board," I accused.

"But I saw no one at Simbach!"

"It's hard to see, when you're not on the platform yourself." Then I asked Eva, "Do you have your ticket?"

Nodding quickly, her expression like a chastened child's, she started digging in her leather shoulder bag.

The conductor was weaving in the doorway, tapping his boot impatiently. Just like most of these useless bloody uniforms, throwing their authority around. God help you if you actually need their help. They'll be too busy having a nip and a smoke out of sight, as this joker obviously had. Probably been drinking since we'd left Linz—he'd even neglected to announce some of the stops.

When Eva found her ticket and handed it over, he snatched it without a word, fumbling for the hole punch dangling from a chain on his waistcoat. Then he thrust it back without looking at her, muttering to me, "Your parents should have taught you better manners."

"My parents taught me people should do their jobs, especially when jobs are scarce. And that men who want to be taken for gentlemen should behave like one."

I took great satisfaction in saying this, though I did so in English.

Across from me, recognition sparkled in Eva's eyes.

As he stared at me, I asked in German, "How long will it be to Munich?"

"A little over an hour," he mumbled. When he lurched back, the door his bulky frame had propped open slid closed with a thump.

Eva burst into a shower of radiant giggles. "Now I *know* you are an angel."

"As I was starting to say before we were so rudely interrupted, I'm happy to meet you, Fräulein Braun. I'm Peggy Adler."

"Nein, nein—*Eva*," she insisted. "If you don't mind." She used German's familiar "du" pronoun. "I think I should be on a first-name basis with an angel, don't you?"

"Yes, let's dispense with formality," I agreed, relieved. I reached into my rucksack for my Lucky Strikes. "How about a smoke? Help us relax after that ordeal?"

Eva's eyes were like stars as she reached for one tentatively, then settled back in her seat after I lit it. Her lids fluttered shut as she took an extended drag, then exhaled with luxurious pleasure. "How wonderful. It's been a *long* time since I've had a cigarette. And I've wanted one so often."

As I inhaled deeply on my own, she said, "You speak English, and your name is English, too, yes?"

I nodded. "My real name's Margarete, but I never use it. My father is English, and I lived there until—I came away to school in Austria."

I'd been very close to saying, "Until my parents separated."

"I love what you told the conductor!"

"Oh, in English, you mean? You understood?"

"Absolutely!" she replied in heavily accented English, then lapsed back into her Bavarian German. "I thought I'd choke, trying not to laugh!"

"Are you studying English at school?"

"No. They're called English sisters, but teach us French, ironically," Eva shrugged.

"Très continental. So how do you know English?"

"Oh, not so very much. From films, mostly."

Now that she'd touched on one of my favorite subjects, the time and kilometers flew past as we talked about actors and music, jazz, dancing—and clothes. When I pulled out a movie magazine for us to look at, her chubby face came alive as she offered succinct assessments of the actresses' clothes.

"I had to hide my magazines at school. Under the mattress," she said. "My family thinks I'm going back next fall, but it's not the life for me. I haven't told them yet. The Sisters or my family."

"Sounds like we've made the same decision. I'm not going back, either." The thought of the scene that likely followed my unexpected departure last night launched a plummeting sensation in my stomach.

"Don't you want to be out there in life—really *live?*" Eva said. "These are modern times, nicht? Not our grandmother's days. There's more to life than finding some lord and master and being under his thumb. I swear I'll never live in such a prison!"

"You know," I decided to confide as I leaned forward to light us fresh cigarettes. "My mother's more independent now."

I stopped, suddenly. What was I doing? I never talked about the divorce.

Eva was looking at me kindly. "Oh, my parents had a time, too. When I was small."

"My parents divorced," I relinquished, finally. "After the war."

Might as well get it over with. I'd probably never see her again anyway.

She reached across the gap between our seats for my hand.

"My brother was killed, just before his nineteenth birthday. Right near the end of the war." My voice was suddenly growing tight.

"I am so *very* sorry." Eva moved to the seat beside mine and was offering a soft handkerchief.

"I tried." I could barely get words out now. "To tell them. I *knew*, you see."

I had seen it before it happened, that final end that was so horrible not only for Peter, but so many others lying there around him in that muddy, hellish mess. That place I didn't want to see. Didn't want to look. But it had kept coming back.

When I had tried to tell them—*beg* them—not to let him go, Father had called it morbid. Wicked. Been enraged that I would even suggest the danger that loomed.

Then, afterward, he'd looked at me as though I'd *made* that terrible thing happen to Peter, simply because I'd seen it ahead of time. And tried to warn them. Ever since, he's acted as though I have to choose between him and England, and Mutti and "those Huns who killed your brother."

"My mother came back to Germany," I said, glad to have her handkerchief as I wiped my eyes. I hadn't cried in so long. Maybe it was because I'd tried so hard not to during these last days around Father.

Long-suffering Mutti. Beautiful at eighteen, she had enchanted him, though not so thoroughly that his infidelities hadn't started as soon as she was pregnant with Peter.

"It was such a terrible time," Eva was nodding. "In our family, we felt it, too. Things were never the same. Afterward."

Her eyes looked more solemn than solicitous now.

"I don't understand why men are all so infatuated with war. When it's so horrible." Her tone was angry. "And there are so many interesting, beautiful things in the world." Her nose wrinkled in disgust. "Their stupid politics. Sometimes I think they haven't stopped playing with their childish games and toys."

After a few moments of silence, I asked, "What will you do, if you don't go back to school?"

Her expression was decisive. "I'm going to work in films. I've studied it all carefully and I know you have to work hard. Naturally, it will require sacrifices. But everything has its price, if your dream's going to come true."

She paused to stub out her cigarette in the ashtray in the arm of the seat, then flipped its metal cover shut and pressed her hands to her pudgy cheeks.

"But first, I have to get my figure back. The food at the Kloster is so *heavy*. All that dough and sugar. And it's so boring in that one-horse town that sometimes it feels like eating is the only pleasure."

Then she asked, "What will *you* do, if you don't go back to school, and Salzburg?"

"And *England*," I added. "My father's always telling me I can't have it all, that I have to choose. I guess I finally have." I shrugged. "I don't know. For now, my mother and I will be visiting in Munich with her sister, my Aunt Paula."

"Oh, my mother has a sister Paula, too—that's why it's my middle name," Eva said happily. "Will you stay on, in Munich?"

"I'd love to, but Mutti will need to get back home, near Kassel. Now that I'm not going back to Austria, I'll go with her." Which is all I've ever really wanted anyway.

"They won't try to make you go back?"

"Well, I'm not going back. It's only because my father's been paying for school that he's insisted I be in Austria, where his sister can watch me."

"They treat us like such *children*!"

"It feels like being trapped under glass," I agreed. "Like an insect in a laboratory. Always bossed around by some man's rules." *While all the women try to make him happy—or look the other way when he makes you miserable.*

But Mutti wasn't like that. While I knew she longed for me to have the education Father was willing to pay for, she wouldn't force it.

"Well, I'm no child, now—and certainly no insect!" Eva laughed, then proclaimed proudly, "I turned sixteen last week."

"Happy birthday! Which day?"

"The 6th."

"I'm sixteen, too, this month," I told her. "On the 29th."

She clapped her hands. "A real Leap Year baby! I'm one, but not on the actual day. It's very good luck, you know."

"Well," I said, "I'm going to need it."

"Oh, don't worry. Kindness like yours will always come back to you. I'll certainly never forget it."

Outside the window, villages and snowy fields had been replaced by the broad avenues of the suburbs as the train slowed through the outskirts of Munich.

"I love being back home." Eva watched the scenes flying past. "It's like I lose part of myself, when I have to go away."

"Time for one more smoke," I offered the pack. "My mother and aunt don't know I'm coming this early."

"My family doesn't, either," Eva said. "I couldn't wait to get away. Took the earliest train I could."

"We have quite a lot in common," I chuckled.

"Let's go for coffee, since we've got time," she proposed. "I'll treat you to some cake, too, to thank you, and celebrate our birthdays. And our freedom!"

"And when we stop," she added, "I'll get my Brownie out of my suitcase so I can snap a photo of you. It's not every day I meet a Leap Year angel!"

Hannes gathered the manuscript pages together and placed them in the box on the table beside him.

As she tried to take it all in, Anna gazed out the living room's bay window to where soft rain had started to bead on its surface.

"There was a photo," she remembered. "When I looked through the albums, at the National Archives. I told myself it must have been someone else, someone who looked like my mother."

"What sort of photo?"

"Old, tiny. Hard-to-see. Black-and-white. The kind a Brownie camera would take. Like so many of the early ones in Eva's albums.

"My mother's face—well, it's complicated. She was in an accident when she was about twenty and it changed her face. That's why I doubted the photograph."

Had she really heard those descriptions and exchanges Hannes's steady voice had read? It was as though she'd fallen into those scenes and forgotten that she and Hannes were here at all. Her own voice was fading, throat turning dust-dry as the medication drew its shroud around her, merging everything in a fuzzy haze.

"I'd convinced myself it couldn't be her." Anna reached for her mug and drained the last swallows of mint tea. "But it *was* taken beside a train, in a big Bahnhof that looks like what I remember of Munich." Then she recalled the photo's caption, in Eva's cramped script: "Der Engel. Eine Februar Fräulein."

And every detail associated with the Peggy in these pages fit her mother's life. The estranged parents, one British, one German, parted eventually by the divide of political boundaries, her father's infidelities, and the death of her brother, Peter, in the trenches in France in 1918.

But Eva. Eva *Braun*. Was it really possible that whatever connection her mother had with her had begun *this* early in their lives?

"You must rest now, Anna." Hannes's tone was firm as he took her mug and set it on the coffee table then reached for the afghan folded on the back of the couch.

"There will be plenty of time to talk about this later. Aber du musst ruhen, ja? Es ist sehr wichtig." He sounded so much more authoritative in German. Did he even know he'd slipped into it? Had she even heard him correctly?

"You mustn't get overtired."

"I know, I know." As her head began to nod, she felt like something was slowly pulling her out of the room.

"But it *is* Eva, *the* Eva Braun, isn't it?"

Her blurring gaze searched for his eyes. "There really *is* some connection between it all. The handkerchief. The magazine clippings. The photo I saw?"

He nodded slowly. "It would seem so."

Her lids were lowering, now, as the medication exerted its force. "Wherever will it all lead?"

Hannes spread the afghan over her, then tucked it around her shoulders before he smoothed back a few curling locks of dark hair from her forehead. "You can chase it in your dreams."

He leaned closer and said near her ear, the last words that drifted in. "And yes, it's Eva. The next chapter proves it, without a doubt."

He was smiling at her as she woke from deep, dreamless sleep two hours later.

"Perfect timing! I can make you something to eat."

"Hannes," Anna's speech was thick. "The doctor talked about my weaning off the pain medication."

He looked doubtful.

"I know it won't be easy. But I have to, eventually. I'll have something to eat, but I'd like to delay the next dose. Start increasing the time between them."

After a long pause, he said, "Only an extra hour or so, to start. And you need to eat a good meal, and agree you won't try to do anything else today, after the next dose."

"And you'll read another chapter," Anna added quickly.

He looked confused, said with a small scowl, "What kind of bargaining is this?"

"It'll keep me distracted. Oh, please—I could hardly bear to stop last time. The medication always wins. If I get off it, you won't have to do this."

It was obvious that he was reluctant.

"You said yourself the next chapter will tell me more. You know I'd stay up all night to find out what's there."

"And wind up back in the hospital," he said, shaking his head. "Nati is not going to be happy with me."

Once he'd served the lentil soup that his sister had left warming on the stove, and finished his own, Hannes retrieved the manuscript and led them back into Peggy's world.

FELLOW TRAVELLERS

The Scars Won't Show at All

CHAPTER 9

Munich
6 October 1932

I was surprised, after my appointment at Fotohaus Hoffmann, to learn that Eva was "only a shop girl." This revelation came as I was leaving the photographer's shop on Munich's Amalien Strasse and nearly collided with an obviously tipsy Heinrich Hoffmann as he lurched up the sidewalk.

Now, I understood why he hadn't been here to keep my appointment. I wouldn't have recognized him if it weren't for the photos in his studio. He was featured in several alongside the severe-looking man whose image seemed to dominate the place, the one with the odd brush of a mustache, dark forelock, and startling eyes. They were either mesmeric or foreboding as they looked at you, neither option very pleasant.

During my photo session, I'd learned that Herr Hoffmann prides himself on being the official photographer for "the Party," and especially for its rising star, the man with the strange eyes and mustache.

I was just closing the shop door behind me when Hoffmann approached, belched softly, and said, "Guten Tag. Was our Fräulein Braun able to help you today?"

"Oh, yes," I replied before thinking, "and I know I'm going to love the photos."

His expression blank, he slurred, "Wha' photos?"

"The ones she took."

His face began to turn the same beet color already showing on the tip of his nose.

"But, she's only a clerk!" Irritation flared in his voice. "I pay her to—"

Then that Munich oddity, the wind known as "der Föhn," gusted and halted him mid-sentence as he groped awkwardly for his tie. It passed just inches from my face as it arced back over his right shoulder. I seized the distraction to excuse myself and hurry toward a tram clanging its bell at the corner.

Wasn't Eva full of surprises? She must have seen the opportunity in my appointment to use a situation to her advantage. To both of ours, really. With luck, it would show Hoffmann how capable she was, especially after he'd been too busy indulging in a lunch comprised of drink, by the look of things, to honor his appointments.

I'd arrived at Hoffmann's about an hour earlier for the sitting I arranged with him by telephone yesterday. The woman behind the counter exuded such crisply courteous authority that I took her for the shop's manageress, if not its actual proprietor.

She looked confused as she asked, "The appointment was for today? For *this* time?" and began paging through a red leather appointment book. She seemed familiar, though in the confusion I couldn't place why.

"Yes, Thursday, the 6th, at 11 o'clock," I always hated having cameras pointed at me. And now, when my hair still didn't quite cover the scars that, while fading, felt like angry wounds meant for someone else, it had been all I could do to get myself here, especially since it was Rod's idea, not mine.

"I can't seem to find any appointment," she said, her tone apologetic as she closed the book. "Herr Hoffmann isn't here, you see."

Perhaps this was my chance to put off the whole damn thing. I felt as ambivalent about it as I sometimes caught myself feeling about Rod. He had left England and was overseas at Yale and asked me to do this. Now, I could honestly say I'd tried.

The woman's lips were pursed, eyes narrowed, as though she were puzzling something out. "It's no problem!" she announced suddenly. "*I* can take your photograph. Just like that day at the Bahnhof, yes?" Her eyes flashed friendly recognition. "It is good to see you again! I was confused, looking for 'Fräulein *Margarete* Adler'—but now, I remember you are Peggy, yes?"

"That's right," I smiled and gave the hand she extended a gentle squeeze. "This is a wonderful surprise." It was Eva, the Munich girl, from that day on the train. But how different her slight figure and silver-blonde hair made her appear now.

"What is it—four years ago? We were both planning our escape!" she laughed.

The confidence was back in her smile as she darted to the door. After turning the key in its lock, she adjusted the small, clock-shaped sign in the front window to indicate that the shop would reopen in an hour. Then she lifted the telephone's receiver from its cradle and set it on the counter before reaching underneath for a leather handbag and a camera case about the same size. "Come, the studio is just upstairs," she said, moving toward a set of narrow steps at the back.

I followed as she led the way up the dark tunnel of the staircase to the floor above. It was all my muddled thoughts could do to keep up—with her pace, and the spontaneous course of action she seemed to be charting.

Upstairs, Eva escorted me to a chair with a small table beside it then began adjusting several large lights on tripods around it, training them on my face. "Are you having this portrait done for a special occasion?" she asked.

"It's ... for a friend. He's away, and asked me to have one taken for him." He'd also asked me, as Father kept doing, to return to England, rather than stay in Germany. Why couldn't they understand that Mutti's being here made it feel most like home?

Eva had taken out the camera she'd brought with her and was peering through its viewfinder, trying out different angles as she aimed its lens at me. "I'll use this, rather than the studio camera," she explained. "With the help of these lights, and a few tricks, we'll get good photos—and it will feel more natural than making you freeze in front of that big monster."

I nodded gratefully.

"You seem a little tense, though. You need to relax a bit, yes?" she coaxed with a smile. "I want you to feel so comfortable you'll forget I'm here. Just like you're having coffee with a good friend. Don't worry, I've done this before."

"Oh, it's fine," I said, though I seemed to croak out the words as an unwelcome lump took over my throat. It was suddenly very difficult to have someone so fashionable and pretty staring at my face so intently, with all this insistent lighting.

"Have you had a look in the shops this week?" Eva asked. "There's a salon near the Karlstor that's offering a wonderful new facial made from pineapple and coconut."

At the mere mention of this, tears filled my eyes. I couldn't make them stop, and the lights only made it harder.

"Oh! Oh, my!" She shut off the lights and was beside me, dropping to her knees.

It took everything I had to find my voice. "It's ... the scars. I was in an accident this summer, and he hasn't seen me like this yet."

"Oh, there, you mustn't worry." Eva was patting my arm softly. "Is *that* what's troubling you?"

My efforts to hold a dam against my emotions failed. The words came out in gasps. "It's not just the scars. They had to fix ... my face. It doesn't look the *same*, now."

It was a stranger's face I didn't seem to know or recognize, but had to move about in the world from behind now. Like a mask that must be worn as some sort of punishment for the rash decision of saying yes to a man neither of my parents would have approved of. One who drove too fast, and had been drunk enough to walk away from the accident with only a broken collarbone, and no apology.

Aunt Paula kept reminding me I could have died when my face went through the car's windscreen. I'd never told anyone I felt as though part of me *had* died that night.

"I don't feel the same anymore, either," I told Eva.

There was a brief silence before she replied, "But you *are*. And still so very pretty—just a different kind of pretty. Still that same girl who was so kind that day I felt so lonely. I would know you anywhere." Her pale brows knit together in a stern little frown. "I hope this man the photos are for knows how lucky he is!"

I covered my eyes as my shoulders began to heave with tremors of tears.

"Oh, there, you just need to have a cry." She hurried over to the handbag she'd set on a shelf nearby and returned with a handkerchief embroidered with tiny flowers. Then she brought a wooden chair and set it beside me. "And let's have a smoke," she decided suddenly, leaping to her feet again to fetch her purse. "That will help you relax."

"Will Herr Hoffmann mind?" I asked, voice hoarse as my tears finally subsided.

"If he's not here, then what does it matter?" She gestured in the air with one upturned palm as she reached into her bag with the other hand. "I've got some nice new pancake makeup—I'll touch up your face a bit. You have really beautiful skin. What do they say? Like an English rose?"

She withdrew a petite, ivory-colored cigarette case, pressed it open and extended it toward me on her palm.

I was already feeling better as I leaned my cigarette into the flame from her monogrammed lighter.

Eva lit her own and closed the case with a snap, eyelids lowering as she took her first deep pull on the cigarette. "Is there anything better than the start of a smoke?" she asked, her unfocused gaze directed off toward the door. "Did you stay in Munich that day?" she asked as she pulled a tortoiseshell-colored compact out of her purse.

"No. I went back up north with my mother."

"That's right—you're the *real* Leap Year baby, with a birthday every four years. You get to be 'young' for so much longer!" She set her cigarette down in a square glass ashtray on the table and began daubing bisque-colored foundation onto a cosmetic sponge. She reached to apply it in soft pats on my chin, nose, and forehead, then blended it in with feathery strokes. "That means you've had another real birthday this year."

"I did," I said, tilting my head back as she smoothed foundation along my jaw line. "It makes me five, if you count it that way. And how was yours? A good day, I hope?"

"Oh, yes! One of my very best." She looked eager to share more. "I have an admirer, you see. Someone I've known for a few years. He gave me a lovely gift."

She held up the bracelet on her right arm for me to see, a simple gold-wire design that held a faceted stone of moss-colored tourmaline. "With earrings and a necklace to match."

When I complimented this, she eyed me meaningfully. "It's the very first jewelry he's ever given me. It's always been candy and flowers, before."

I nodded my understanding.

Eva had taken up her cigarette again and blew a thin exhalation of smoke. "A lot has changed since that day on the train, nicht? We're not schoolgirls any more, but women, with men in our lives."

"How did you meet him?" I hoped it was all right to ask.

The enthusiasm in her voice made it obvious it was. "Why, right here at Hoffmann's. Well, on Schelling Strasse, where Herr Hoffmann used to have his studio."

She paused dreamily, in recollection. "I'd barely worked there three weeks. Afterward, I didn't see him again for a while and almost forgot about him until he started showing up now and then with little gifts. But mostly just to talk and visit. After a while, he began inviting me to dinner, and the theatre."

The animation that had filled her face faded as her voice trailed off. "But now, well, he's got very important work and I don't see him as often as I'd like. He keeps saying he's a confirmed bachelor, but won't he be surprised when I bring him around?"

She punctuated this last with a long blink of assertion, lips pressed in a small, knowing smile. "You know how it is with men. We're *always* having to figure out something. Get around them, somehow. They keep us busy that way."

"Sometimes they do," I agreed.

"It's like this little chance for us to get reacquainted. If Herr Hoffmann hadn't confused his appointments, and you and I weren't willing to work around that together." Her voice dropped to a more conspiratorial tone. "We have to seize our opportunities where we find them, don't we?"

Church bells chimed the half hour as Eva pulled the ashtray nearer to extinguish her cigarette. "I'd best get started. We often close for lunch, but the customers will expect us to be open again soon."

She snapped the lights back on and reached for her camera.

Happy to relax with her this way, I stopped worrying about the photographs. The studio felt private—with none of those photos of that foreboding-looking man.

As Eva worked her camera, it seemed to be an extension of her. Her appearance was so different from that day in Simbach and during the long ride through the Bavarian countryside. Her face had been wide and round, then, her schoolgirl's hair limp, even a bit stringy, and a pale brown color as drab as a vole's.

Now, it resembled the silk inside an ear of new corn, sinuous where it framed her face in glossy waves that reached to her chin. It was the platinum hue women usually chose to suit men's taste, or experimented with when they had an adventurous nature. A far more drastic transformation than I would consider.

On Eva's small, sleek head, it was alluring, however. It beckoned like cashmere, yet also had an aura of the sacrosanct, as though it—or she—were charged with some sort of power accessible only to the gods.

Her features appeared more angular, now, as did her slender frame with its erect posture. She wore a blouse of taupe-colored silk tucked into a slim skirt of fawn herringbone tweed, a look both subdued and elegantly stylish that made her seem older than she was. It also displayed her small waist to fine advantage.

The shy duckling I'd met that cold February day, face as doughy as the cream cakes and sweet noodles she'd eaten at the convent, was now a regal, confident swan.

Although her face was thinner, it still rounded out like a small, genial moon when she relaxed into a smile. It was a canvas of quicksilver contrasts: pensive, brow-furrowed one moment, as she focused in, then all businesslike efficiency when she directed me through a series of shots. When she seemed satisfied with her efforts, her expression held warmth I'd swear I could feel on my skin. Enveloped by her tinkling laughter and warm encouragement, I decided that more women would obtain photos of ourselves we actually liked if the experience were as femininely hospitable as this.

I was about to ask whether she'd thought of doing this kind of work on her own, when she said, "We're nearly done. Your skin and hair look so nice, and the scars won't show at all. Your man will like these very much, I think."

She peeked out from behind the camera with an expressive wink. "There's no better gift you can give him than a good photo of you, especially when you have to be apart. I try to have one done at least three times a year, and always for his birthday. And it's the very first gift I gave him, right after we met. He's promised he's going to draw a portrait of me from it one day." She laughed quickly and added, "He teases it'll be worth a lot of money, because my face is going to be famous. Like a film star's."

There was a girlish quality in her voice, an almost guileless lack of sophistication I suddenly found touching. She was so earnest, so determined to help.

"These will be the last shots, so let's try for the very best," Eva said. "Think about something that makes you feel *truly* happy, then send that to me with your eyes."

Her voice and mannerisms seemed almost to shimmer, now. These were what stirred the happiness I suddenly felt, gratitude for the sweetness of companionable time like this, when I hadn't even expected it.

"Drop your head just a little—more, more—that's it! Right there. Now relax your left shoulder, just a bit."

"*Perfekt!*" Eva's voice was triumphant. "We've got it!"

"It's really her," Anna said as Hannes finished. "It really is Eva Braun."

"Yes. And now, you really have a bargain to keep."

She nodded and took the pill he'd brought for her.

Poor Eva. If you only knew how very badly the portrait would turn out. When you were such a pretty subject. Anna's thoughts trailed away as her head swam with fatigue. The scenes Hannes had read felt as immediate as if they had just surrounded her, and as distant as a long-ago dream.

Hannes's caution had been justified. Her leg was throbbing, the price she was already paying for delaying the medication. "I think I'll sleep right here, tonight," she decided. "The thought of the stairs seems daunting."

"This is just what I worried about." His tone was admonishing.

"Hannes, don't fuss. I just need time for the medication to kick in. But would you be willing to get something for me upstairs?" She described where he could find the sheet of little photos she'd discovered weeks before, and the old envelope that held it.

"Eva was right," he remarked as he came back downstairs a few minutes later. "The photos do look nice. How long have you had them?"

"They were in that envelope, in the same drawer as the news articles."

Anna studied the sheet of thumbnail-sized proofs again. "I get the feeling my mother really cared about these, as much for the circumstances in which they were taken as anything else. And the return address—"

"Fotohaus Hoffmann," Hannes affirmed quickly, handing over the envelope. "I think this rules out that these pages are fiction, don't you?" he added with a smile.

Anna heard the sounds of Nati letting herself in the back door.

"A quick hello, but nothing more," Hannes said firmly. "You need to rest. Especially now that you have so much more to think about."

The road's uphill grade is so steep, Anna's destination appears only as a roof hovering above the slope. She climbs in near-vertical ascent until wide marble stairs appear on the left. They rise precipitously toward the sky, like the sides of a pyramid.

Her breath is coming in gasps as she uses both hands and feet to scale the stairs, like climbing a ladder. She collapses at the top onto a broad expanse of flagstones that feel cold and smooth against her cheek. A gunmetal sky releases spatters of rain that darken the patio in patterns like spreading shadows.

She can see the arched doorway of the entrance, but getting back onto her feet, navigating even this last short distance, feels as out of reach as the sky. Perhaps she will die here. If death brings release from feeling she has to keep trying, it might be welcome.

In an instant, she lifts away from the flagstones and floats like a leaf to where the door lurks in shadows. The sun is shining now from above the mountain that flanks the Berghof to the south. Its light illuminates the razor-sharp roofline, and the semi-circle of the breakfast room, where it bows out from the angular building like a rounded belly.

"Is everything all right?"

The speaker asks this question in English with a German accent. She is dressed in a dirndl that makes her a voluminous silhouette where she stands just inside the entrance, whose door is now open. "Do you remember where you are?"

Anna tries to reply, but her voice makes no sound.

"Can you hear me? Anna?" The woman's voice is louder, its tone of concern more discernible. "Please—just a minute," she says, moving off out of sight.

How does she know me? Anna seizes the opportunity to slip inside unobserved. The door to the great room with the fireplace is open. She drifts into its cavernous space.

Will Lowell be here? Is this the only place she'll ever see him, now? Or, even here, will she still be invisible to him?

There is no furniture, no evidence of anything to do with human life. The massive window at the far end of the room has no glass; it has become a gaping portal through which a frigid breeze gusts in from the valley below.

At first, the sound Anna hears is like small crackles, until it becomes a roaring when she turns to find the room engulfed in flames. Heat blazes out, lashes at her.

Reflexively, she pulls away, though there's nowhere to flee. She hears a yowling, terrified scream as if it comes from somewhere other than inside her.

The flames leap out, reach around her, holding her, though there's no heat or pain. She struggles to escape, but they hold her firmly. Just like on the plane. No escape from the flames. In the dark, like the black, choking smoke.

"Anna. Kannst du mich hören?" The voice is a man's. "Can you hear me?"

"Alles ist gut, Anna," The voice is against her ear, now. "Du bist hier, mit uns. Du bist sicher. Es ist jetzt sicher.—*You are here, with us. You are safe. It is safe now.*"

───────

Anna felt soft warmth near her lashes as they fluttered open; someone's face was near her cheek. What confined her was loosening, arms relaxing their hold around her.

A small lamp glowed in the corner of the living room. Hannes's face was above her, where she lay on the sofa, and Nati's behind him, watching her with anxious eyes.

"What? Where did—" Anna felt too dazed to speak.

"You were having a dream," Hannes said quickly in German, then switched to English. "I'm sorry if I scared you. Nati came to check on you, then came to get me."

"You were moving about," Nati explained. "We didn't want you to get hurt."

Anna remembered how she'd fought to get away from the flames and looked at Nati apologetically. "I hope I didn't hurt you. Either of you."

"No, no," Nati assured.

"It was so real," said Anna. "I thought I was going to die, trying to climb the mountain. At Hitler's Berghof—just like when I was there before."

At this, Nati's eyes grew very wide.

"There was fire everywhere. I couldn't get away." Anna's voice broke as her breath caught in a sob.

Nati came around from behind Hannes and perched next to her on the edge of the sofa, then slipped a slender arm around her shoulders.

Hannes moved off and returned with tissues that he folded into Anna's hand.

Her body was trembling, tears erupting each time she tried to speak. Why, even when she could no longer see them—knew it had been a dream—did the flames feel like a terror she couldn't escape?

"It was the same as on the plane." She covered her face with her hands.

"Don't try to talk, now," Hannes urged.

A little later, after Nati had brought them tea, he told Anna, "I should have stayed with you. With all that we read today. I should have realized."

In the succeeding days, as Anna weaned herself off the medication, it was as though a veil that had masked her flashbacks suddenly lifted, exposing them like unwelcome intruders. One afternoon, she awoke from a nap to what appeared to be flames all around the sofa. Across the room, the chair where Hannes usually sat was empty. At the sight of it, Anna felt more sadness, even, than fear about the flames.

Within seconds, she wakened fully to find him at the end of the sofa, head curled into his shoulder in sleep. He didn't stir when she spread her mother's afghan over him.

He must be getting exhausted, and his Munich teaching semester was drawing closer by the week. The next day, she overheard him talking with Nati in the kitchen. They were speaking German and Anna felt hesitant to interrupt.

"I haven't. I haven't had the chance," Hannes said, keeping his voice low.

"When do you plan to?" Nati asked after a short silence.

"I don't know. She's been through so much. Every time I think I've found the way, something happens."

"You know I'm leaving Friday?"

"And now, there are these frightening dreams." Anna heard urgency in his voice.

"*Hannes*," Nati's tone was plaintive. "You have to talk with her. *Tell* her."

So, Anna realized, her intuitions had been accurate. He didn't know how to tell her that he needed to leave. She could at least make it easier for him.

He spoke again. "None of this would have happened if—"

"*Nein*, Hannes. *Bitte,*" Nati cut him off. "That's just crazy!"

"You don't understand." His voice dropped so low that Anna had to strain to hear him. "I urged her to go. I felt so sure that—" He broke off suddenly, then, after a pause, added, "I can see now what a terrible mistake that was."

"You must stop this," Nati insisted. "It certainly isn't going to help Anna. And she needs help." After a pause, she said, "I met someone, at the café near the university. She's a counselor who helps people with this kind of thing. She said she'd talk with Anna, if she's willing."

It was true then. These flashbacks, whatever they were, were weighing on *them*. On Hannes, especially—perhaps enough to make him regret ever having encouraged her to go to Germany. And now, he was feeling *guilty* about it.

Before either of them could speak again, Anna moved through the door into the kitchen. "Of course I'll talk with her," she said. "If you think it might help."

They both looked startled. Hannes's expression grew uneasy.

"Oh, *Anna*." Nati approached her.

"I didn't mean to eavesdrop. But truly, I'm ready to try anything." Anna's voice caught in her throat. "I can't keep living this way, and I don't want either of you feeling trapped here."

Hannes looked pained, as though bracing for what she'd say next. "Trapped?" he burst out finally.

"Hannes, I don't know what would've happened if you hadn't helped me. I am so grateful." Anna turned to him. "You have *nothing* to blame yourself for. How you can even think that way, when you've both been so generous? I know that you have your own lives. I know you need to talk with me."

Anna halted, in a flash of memory. This was just what Peggy had told her she needed, and then, so quickly, she'd been gone. And soon, Hannes and Nati would be.

Her head was growing light. She'd been standing all this time and suddenly felt weak. It was so difficult to imagine being here alone. Was this what her mother had felt?

Hannes stepped forward and said softly in German, "What I need is to be here."

She stared back, tried to take in words the exact opposite of what she'd expected.

He glanced at Nati, then back at Anna as he switched to English. "I wanted to tell you that I'd like to stay, to help you. Especially since Nati must return to work. And," he added, "I would still like for you to come to Germany." He looked at Nati again, as though seeking corroboration.

Anna felt struck dumb.

"I know it's probably very difficult to even imagine, right now. But in time. When you are feeling stronger. Perhaps we can even make the trip together—when the time is right," he added quickly as Nati cast him a warning look.

What had happened? Anna wondered. She'd been ready to tell him she knew he must go. Now, she felt dizzy, could barely keep her balance, or think of how to reply.

"What about your work, this fall?" she mumbled at last.

"There'll be time, Anna. Don't worry. For now, I think my place is here."

Where she would rather have him be than anywhere. Though what he meant, and what she wanted, were surely two very different things.

Then she was in his arms as he set her down gently on the sofa.

Nati was handing her a glass of water. "You looked faint." She shot a glance at Hannes. "Perhaps it was being bombarded by so many of my brother's ambitions at the same time!"

"Guilty as charged," he agreed, raising his hands.

"It might also be time for you to have something to eat," Nati suggested.

"And for me to make myself useful and go tackle Nati's shopping list," Hannes grinned. "If you'll both excuse me?"

Before Anna could reply, he was gone.

"I'm really going to miss you," she told Nati a little later. "I'm worried that Hannes feels he *must* stay."

"No, it is not like that," Nati shook her head. "You see, after your accident, he—for a time, it didn't look very good for you. And Hannes," she hesitated again, then said, "he was very worried."

Although Anna couldn't put her finger on why, it felt as though Nati had deliberately substituted these last words for different ones.

"He wants so much to see you get well, and to come to Germany. We both want that."

"The way things are now, I just don't know," Anna shrugged.

"Do not worry, about any of it," Nati said as she hugged her. "But please believe him. He really wants to stay."

On the morning that Hannes drove Nati to catch her flight out of Boston, Anna decided to continue reading her mother's manuscript.

She found the place where he had left off and was surprised to discover that while the pages looked just like all the others, typed on Peggy's ancient Silencia typewriter, it wasn't her own experience Peggy had described in this next chapter, but Eva Braun's.

FELLOW TRAVELLERS

In the Service of the Reich

CHAPTER 10

Obersalzberg, near Berchtesgaden
Late afternoon, 6 October 1932

When Eva saw the two puppies waiting on the terrace at the Führer's Haus Wachenfeld, she hoped one of them might be for her. He knew how much she longed to have a dog for company. And those silky, tumbling armfuls were so delicious to gather against her, their fur as sun-warmed as the stone flags of the terrace beneath her knees.

The trip to his retreat on the Obersalzberg high above Berchtesgaden had set out from Munich in the early afternoon. Such excursions, where others were also present, were inevitably awkward, because the Führer, cordial and gallant as he always was in company, still treated her with a curious reserve, as though he hardly knew her.

Eva couldn't decide whether this made her feel younger or older than she actually was—as though she had to play a part she wasn't rehearsed enough to portray confidently. Unsure of what would be the right thing to say, and what would not, she tended to smile diffidently when others spoke to her, then demur with a polite question, rather than say much herself.

The puppies were a pleasurable way to pass the time during which she waited for Adolf. Because always, her relationship with him was one of waiting.

They'd been lovers for nearly a year. More and more, she waited, and knew less and less, never sure when she'd see him next, or how they'd spend the time together. Others presumed she was one of his secretaries and

Eva knew that even for those women, the rhythms of his schedule—and his moods—were unpredictable.

The drive down to Berchtesgaden had passed quickly, with Eva riding in the front car with Adolf and his driver. The other men had ridden in the second long Mercedes that trailed behind them all the way from Munich. When they'd arrived at the house on the Obersalzberg hours later, four men filed out of that rear car and clustered at the top of the long drive, lighting cigarettes eagerly.

The sky was cloudless. Up so high above the valley, the sun managed to pierce the autumn chill, although a breeze still flapped their coats around their knees. The men gazed about, remarking on the majesty of the mountainside vista that, on first encounter, always struck visitors as impossibly unreal, like a movie set.

The Führer went inside immediately, traversing the path and stairs in his quick tread with its short strides. He always went in alone first to talk with the staff and ensure all was in order before he welcomed in his guests. Sometimes, Eva knew, he went from room to room to inspect them, or see that the table was set properly.

She watched him go, yearning to follow. Or, to join the men in their companionable smoke. But not with Adolf here.

Instead, she removed her Leica from its brown leather case and checked to see how many rolls of film she had grabbed in her mad dash from Hoffmann's shop. Like most of Adolf's invitations, this one had arrived with last-minute notice shortly after she'd finished Peggy's photo session, when the Führer's driver came into the shop to request Hoffmann's presence.

"Damn it all, I still have work to do before his campaign next week!" Hoffmann had protested, flustered by the command appearance. Eva knew he'd also had a considerable amount to drink during the "lunch" for which he'd abandoned Peggy's appointment. He completely surprised her when he ordered, "*You* go, since you're so eager to play photographer."

Her heart skipped a beat.

"Oh, yes," he added sternly before a hiccough interrupted his speech. "I met the customer with the portrait appointment. She said you were a regular *artiste*." Then his expression softened as he added with a wink, "Ja, go. I wager he prefers a pretty face to an old Party bore like me!"

Eva would have worked a week without pay for this opportunity, and here he was handing it to her. Thank God she'd taken time with her clothes that morning.

Hoffmann looked at her meaningfully. "I don't imagine they'll return today."

She nodded, disappearing into the coatroom where she and Hoffmann both knew she kept an overnight case for such occasions. She had mere minutes to retrieve her things before the two Mercedes roared away from the curb out front.

She was escorted into a seat in the back of the first car, which carried its important passenger up front beside the driver. Adolf turned to greet her and chat amicably as the cars made their way through the congested streets. Once the surroundings gave way to flat countryside broken by occasional spires of tall poplars, he faced forward and fell silent as the car accelerated to close the distance between city and mountains.

At Haus Wachenfeld, Eva and the others waited until one of the house staff came to summon them inside and the men hastily stubbed out their cigarettes. Now, they were all outside again, the men huddled a respectful distance behind the Führer as he ambled around the quadrangle near the terrace on the chalet's west side. Most of the men pulled up their collars against the breeze as they strained to hear him.

The quadrangle offered level surface for walking and unobstructed views of the Untersberg mountain across the valley to the north, and the towering peaks of the Watzmann toward the west. Eva found this setting impossibly chilly for the breakfasts the staff insisted on serving there, though delightful for coffee in the late-afternoon sun.

It was three years almost to the day since she'd first met Adolf. Some days, she barely remembered that girl she'd been, the one high on a ladder in Hoffmann's old studio on Schelling Strasse near closing time that October day when she met "Herr Wolf"—and he first laid eyes on her. For that is what he called himself, then. And that was how it was with his eyes, which laid hold, caressed, commanded.

Nothing in life was simple anymore since that first afternoon the tinkling bell above the shop's door announced him. Eva had caught a shutter-swift flash of a figure in a loosely belted trench, broad-brimmed hat obscuring the top half of his face. The mouth under a dark brush of mustache wore an expression of resignation.

But when he raised his eyes and the resigned look disappeared at the sight of her, she felt as though this man really *saw* her. And that what he saw pleased him, which, in turn, pleased her very much, too.

Eva hadn't seen his eyes, at first, but she felt them, on her legs. Felt them like a horse feels the hovering presence of its rider above the saddle on its back.

On the top rung of Herr Hoffmann's ladder, almost to the tin tiles of the ceiling, she was reaching high over her head for something Hoffmann had stashed there, something that had nothing to do with what she really wanted at Hoffmann's. She'd hoped for so much more when he hired her.

As she descended the ladder, counting her steps on the rungs silently to herself, she finally saw Adolf's eyes. It was a very long moment, one of those sudden contests of locked eyes where each dares the other to look away.

After that first encounter with his crystal-blue gaze, she couldn't imagine how she'd held out so long without blinking or looking away. A combination of innocence and ignorance, perhaps.

Yet that was before she knew him and learned how much he liked this game; how disappointed he was when others wouldn't engage when he threw out the challenge, but lowered their eyes submissively. That was necessary only when he was angry.

As she let the warmth flow into her smile that day, it was he who withdrew his intimidating, penetrating gaze. Swung it in another direction awkwardly, as though pretending to scan the camera lenses in one of the display cases.

Naturally, he greeted her, first, "Good day, Fräulein." But before she could answer, Hoffmann pulled his attention away.

It was during those first evenings when she was a guest at the Hoffmanns' Bogenhausen home that several things became very evident about Adolf. One was that when he spoke, he held court. All others were listeners.

He always deferred to women, however, sometimes gently teasing them, or kissing their hands, his voice warm with charm. Yet while he presented himself in a self-deprecating manner, it was still he who controlled the flow of interaction and exchange.

His teasing of men was more heavy-handed, what he might characterize as "mannish," something he settled back into like a detached, amused observer. And curiously, while robustly vocal as a public speaker, in private conversation he often spoke in such mild and unobtrusive tones as to be nearly inaudible, particularly out of doors.

Unless his topic snared his emotions, as it obviously had today while he and his companions traced their laps around Haus Wachenfeld's quadrangle. At times like that, Adolf was rendered unable to speak and walk at the same time.

First, his voice escalated into ringing tones that eventually reached thunderous, explosive force. Then, as though physically engaged with an adversary, he held forth, stopping abruptly in the midst of a methodically paced stroll, one unalterably consistent in its stride, speed, and direction—until these eruptions shattered it.

His listeners, several paces behind, like drivers suddenly halted by the vehicle in front of them, stumbled over themselves or each other in their effort to accommodate the unexpected shift. They also snapped from a posture of straining close to hear him into a slight backwards recoil, as though armoring themselves. Otherwise, they moved not an inch until he did, nor offered any reply or remark.

The Führer's vacillating rhythms required that listeners, rather than lapse into reverie as he talked, must constantly monitor his tone and adjust their response accordingly. Some were far better at it than others, so such scenes could be quite entertaining to watch.

Eva felt empathy for those whom she knew to be sincere. But for the ingratiating sycophants who lapped around him like besotted dogs, she felt only contempt. The truly sincere managed to keep their footing around the Führer, she realized, because they already had a secure footing with themselves.

Those like Esser and Hoffmann were, most often, unafraid, as she was, to speak directly and truthfully to Adi. It was possible; one just had to learn the way to go about it. It required a blend of self-assurance and dignity, together with infinite respect for the Führer's authority, something that couldn't be faked, though so many of the ambitious believed it could. They didn't realize how much their very mannerisms gave them away.

In some regards, Adolf was a most predictable person. The path he took around the quadrangle never varied, any more than did his daily routine.

But within that certainty, his moods, like a composition of music, could unfold multiple variations. Like an actor playing several parts in the same production, he valued and relied upon these changeable aspects of himself, Eva knew.

And once he started talking, particularly when his monologue reached a crescendo fueled by emotion, as it just had, it could be a long wait. She needed to keep herself busy, and her work at Hoffmann's had shown her the way. Moving with the grace of the dancer she had once aspired to be, she found a spot close enough to keep him in view yet an unnoticeable distance from the conversation. It was the perfect blind, much like a hunter's, from which to participate in the scene, while he and the others failed to notice. As she wielded her growing collection of Halberstadts and Leicas, she had filled half a dozen albums and Hoffmann had used many of her photographs in postcards and materials he prepared for the Führer's campaigns.

Her hours behind a viewfinder also afforded her the perfect opportunity to obtain valuable intelligence and information. There was advantage in being esteemed pretty but unimportant, a perception that determined the degree of discretion that others did or did not use. And many in the Führer's inner circle were astonishingly indiscreet.

As Eva's own role called for more complex kinds of discretion, she developed a sentry's vigilance regarding those around the Führer. An overheard conversation, a gesture, an expression that unmistakably said one thing while the speaker's words said another, these were all potential resources too valuable to be overlooked.

While the hours she spent alone with the Führer were relatively easy, the ones in the wider company around him brought challenges. There, her appearance, manner, and even courage weren't always enough counterweight to others' strategies to capture and hold him, as she herself longed to do.

The solution was to find the way to reach him that no one else could. With careful observation and listening, she gathered bits of information and made use of them during the hours when Adolf sought her company alone.

As the men strode the perimeter of the quadrangle like a team of surveyors, Eva moved alongside or just ahead of them, clicking shot after shot. It was difficult to catch good photos of Adolf, who grew self-conscious when alone before the camera. But when surrounded by others, he relaxed. With careful telephoto work, Eva could pluck him from their midst like a jewel from sand.

That day's efforts yielded a cache that was bound to provide what Hoffmann could use for the following week's tour before the big election of 6 November.

Eva returned to where she'd left her camera case at a table on the terrace and began to pack her equipment away. As far as those around her were concerned, her reason for being there that day had been fulfilled.

At the sound of the car in the driveway, Anna slid her mother's pages into their box and set it on the table beside what she now thought of as Hannes's chair.

"Can I make us some coffee?" he called from the kitchen a few minutes later.

"That sounds great. Thanks."

Once he was settled across from her and she'd asked about Nati and her flight, he told her, "Nati also talked with Karen. The therapist. She's willing to come here, could even come tomorrow. Do you feel ready?"

Anna said nothing for a few moments, then nodded slowly.

"Is everything all right?" he asked.

"Yes. I'm just a bit tired."

She felt him looking at her and wished he'd stop.

"You've read more of the manuscript," he said quietly.

Anna gaped at him.

His eyes were soft, his voice kind. "There's a way that you have, afterward."

"What sort of way?" Her tone was defensive.

"As if you're somewhere else."

She directed her eyes away from him, towards her lap.

"Berchtesgaden, perhaps?"

Anna nodded. "I heard you drive in. I thought you might think it was too soon."

She looked up at him, finally. "My vision's back to normal, and I'm feeling better. If you think it's a problem, you could always read to me."

Hannes shook his head. "I think this journey is one that you—you and your mother—need to make together, now." He looked at her imploringly. "Just promise that you won't push any harder than you are ready for, ja?"

"Ja," she smiled and took a sip of her coffee. "I promise."

He was watching her closely all the time now, on guard for any signs of a flashback, Anna knew.

A little later, she found the page where she'd left off, and continued reading.

Eva settled on the terrace to play with the pups again. She'd discovered they were intended as gifts for two of the Party members who'd come with them that day.

People always seemed surprised at how unhesitatingly she went to any creature, bird or dog, squirrel or cow. During childhood visits to the village in the Altmühl valley, where her sometimes strict, sometimes kindly grandfather was Herr Doktor Veterinaire, Eva had learned that, with humans, it often felt as if she had to walk on eggshells, though not even sure why. But in the transparent presence of animals, who showed very clearly how they felt, and what they needed, she always knew where she stood. They met her as they found her, a constancy she had found almost nowhere else.

That was especially true when she was sent away from the family to her grandparents' house in that shell-shocked time after Vati returned from the Great War. That was when the happy rhythm of life she'd known in a household of four females had disappeared forever.

All because Vati went to that place where the bad women were. Eva didn't see him there, and no one had told her, but she knew it right away, when she woke in the middle of a December night in Advent, one full of stars in an ink-black sky, and moonlight on the snow that heralded the nearness of Holy Night and Christmas. That was what made it so awful, the blighting of such a special time.

Though only nine at the time, Eva already knew how babies came, how they were made. She had watched too many animals under her grandfather's care not to know, and he approached that part of life with matter-of-factness that never made her squeamish.

She knew why men went to those places where those women were, even though she never talked about it. Well, maybe a little, with her friend, Herta.

What she discovered when she awoke that Advent night brought a kind of outrage, along with a stifled fear. Her leg was numb. She had a memory of a weight holding it down so she couldn't move, as though in a dream.

There were smells that night, in her bed, and on her skin, ones she knew went with those places where the men went, and the things that happened there. Fruity perfume, sickly sweet. All her life, she would despise, in an instant, anything that resembled that smell. For reasons she couldn't explain, she felt the same way about pearls, and lace on undergarments.

There had also been the rank stench of old wine, or spilled beer. And that other smell, the one she'd smelled before, though she hadn't known where it came from. And the stickiness, on the cover of her feather bed.

The memories made her angry, then sickened, then afraid. She tried to talk about it, but only once, with her older sister, Ilse, who then talked with their mother. Weeks later, Eva was the only one sent away, to her grandparents' home, when Mutti and Vati stopped living together.

Mutti said that Ilse must stay in school in Munich, and Eva's younger sister, Gretl, was too young to be away from home. So, Eva had to go away alone, to a school full of strangers where she never made a single friend. Thank goodness Oma and Opa had been there.

Then, one day, they were all a family again, in the new apartment in Munich, and no one ever talked about what had happened. The anger stayed with Eva, but could never be spoken. She thought about it during Mass, sometimes. Anger at the selfish, mindless defiling of what was sacred. Revulsion at this fate of women, and daughters. Rage at an entitlement as unjustly demanding as it was undeserved.

But with Adi, it wasn't that way. However much others railed against her arrangement with him, it was different. Vati, especially, so livid that "his" girl might be "spoiled." That *he* might be humiliated, is what he really meant.

Vati, who was so adamant about what her future should be, what was required of her. Who looked at her with those slithery looks out of the sides of his eyes, showed only disinterest when she tried and tried to please him. Called the things she loved silly, stupid. Well, she had found her own destiny, her own future, at last.

How they worried and hounded her—Vati, Mutti, Ilse—insisting that she was throwing her life away with "that man" who still had not proposed marriage.

Whatever passed between her and Adi could never be discussed with anyone. But whatever transpired between them, he always *asked* her. Never demanded, or took. He received it like a gift, and offered himself to her in the same way.

No matter how things went between them, when they were alone together, he asked, first, with a vulnerability and shyness that left no question for her heart about what the answer would be. She could rise above anything, any disappointment, when she had the chance to lie with him in her arms, and he was quieted and content as a child.

"Fräulein?"

With the two pups cuddled in her lap now, Eva looked up in the direction of the voice, though she could see only the outline of the speaker where his uniform was silhouetted by the sun behind him.

"It would make a very nice photo, the three of you," the adjutant said, then gestured toward where she had left her camera on the terrace table, whose sun umbrella was buffeted every so often by the breeze.

"*Darf ich?* – may I?" he asked.

"Certainly. Please," she said.

"They are like little bear cubs." He indicated the two furry bodies she'd gathered against her. He retrieved the camera and angled around until the bright sun, low in the sky, was on her face, making her squint as he clicked off the shots.

It would be very nice to have the photos, yet Eva knew what would come next. The young man, quite handsome, particularly in uniform, would say a few more polite things designed to continue the conversation. It would be necessary to head him off, using good manners, a pleasant tone, what the nuns had taught at the Simbach convent.

The sun was disappearing rapidly behind the mountainous shoulders of the Watzmann range, and the air's chill had a knifelike sharpness as night fell. Shivering despite her tweed jacket and skirt, Eva used both the cold and the time as her excuse.

"Thank you. The one photo I cannot take is the one that includes me," she smiled, then added quickly, "If the Führer requests my assistance, will you please tell him I will wait inside, where it's warmer?"

"Yes, of course, Fräulein Braun," he replied.

She could hear in his tone that he understood that their interaction was now concluded. She avoided looking at him. The more practiced of them always showed decorum and formal courtesy, but sometimes the younger ones had that glint of disappointment in their eyes or, more often, at the edges of their jaw, a barely perceptible throb, or a tightening of their lower lip.

This was what she found most difficult in the times with Adolf when others were also in company, especially others who hadn't met her before. Since she appeared as one of the many unmarried staff and secretaries around him, she also appeared fair game.

Until they knew better, understood what was never spoken or publicly acknowledged, yet was an understanding that any within the inner circle eventually acquired. The ambiguity of it all sometimes created these awkward situations, ones to which there was only one way to respond, whether or not the man felt rebuffed.

It was a shame, really, because it made her seem uncaring and cold, when, if she could truly be herself, she would visit in a congenial way, perhaps even flirt a little, all harmless. But there was this front that had to be continually reinforced, even though others might never understand why—might find her aloof.

Inside the chalet's cozy living room, Eva warmed herself on the bench that framed three sides of the tall Kachelofen stove with its green ceramic tiles. She glanced around the room furnished in the relaxed, rustic style of any Bavarian cottage and wondered: would Adi settle here, someday, after he achieved his ambitions and plans? Retire to the mountains to live the simple life of the man he protested he truly was?

For now, it was just a retreat he got away to whenever he could, and Eva's working for Hoffmann made a very convenient excuse to come along. Sometimes, she brought the round green overnight case that she kept ready at the shop and spent the night at the Hotel Post down in the village, as she would tonight, waiting for Adi to join her there, if only for an hour or two.

As darkness closed in, it became clear they wouldn't return to Munich that day. Soon, perhaps, that same adjutant would come to advise her that a car was ready to drive her down Obersalzberg mountain to the town's twinkling lights below. A room would be waiting at the hotel. Coffee and cake, Sekt, and perhaps other light refreshment would also be laid out there, more than enough for the two of them.

Eva would have plenty of time to freshen herself for his visit, which would be made via a staircase only hotel staff knew about. When he arrived, she would be wearing her apricot silk robe with its embroidered sash. He knew she loved to dress for him, and though he teased her about it gently, she knew how much he loved it when someone went to any fuss on his behalf.

It was just over a year since his niece, Geli, had been found dead in her room in his Munich apartment. Timing—and planning—were everything, Eva knew.

Each of her visits with Adi, while at the whim of his scheduling, was carefully choreographed to surround him with love, comfort, and the feeling of coming home. No matter what did or did not transpire when they were together, she considered each occasion the making of love. In the way she served him his coffee and cake, talked to him, like Scheherazade, telling him little stories to help him forget his worries, saved up nuggets and tidbits of gossip to delight him.

Perhaps she'd even tell him about the surprising encounter at Hoffmann's today with the kind February Fräulein. He liked the British, and Peggy had that connection in her background. For once, Hoffmann's irresponsibility had paid off, both in the chance to help a friendly acquaintance, and to be in Berchtesgaden tonight.

Eva couldn't have imagined either possibility when she retired to bed the previous night after a particularly unpleasant interaction with Vati at supper, about her being out too late and away from home too often.

Home was a place she no longer wanted to be, what with Vati's insistence and lectures, or waiting on tenterhooks to see whether a call from Adi would come, one she'd be able to take without anyone knowing. How miserable it was when no call came.

She found it easier to await the calls at Hoffmann's shop, under the pretext of working overtime to carry out the ever-increasing responsibilities created by the Party's growing influence—the Party, which unleashed such vitriol from Vati.

The only place to sleep at Hoffmann's was the hard wooden bench. There were many nights she considered it the lesser of two evils, and always, when Adi's calls or invitations reached her there, it was worth every second of discomfort.

When she was with the Führer, Eva felt that their future together was assured, but each time they parted, a roulette wheel of uncertainty began to spin. She would dance on a razor's-edge of doubt that made her feel she could never rest, nor take anything for granted.

As she huddled near the tile stove, the door from the terrace swung open, admitting a blast of cold air as the adjutant stepped in, here like clockwork to advise her of the plan she'd already surmised, yet, as with everything, had to wait to be told.

By now, a call would already have been placed to Hoffmann, who would then telephone Eva's family, as darkness settled over Munich, to advise them that her work would keep her away until tomorrow. Hopefully, it would be Ilse who answered.

There was much work to do, with the Führer's northern campaign beginning next week, and Fräulein Braun's contribution was very important.

CHAPTER 11

Anna puzzled again that while her mother had written these latest installments, the point of view was Eva Braun's. Peggy must have learned a great deal about her in order to enter her world this way, perhaps after Eva had died. Or, maybe from Eva herself. How well had she known her—and had she ever met Hitler?

The date of this Obersalzberg visit was the same day Eva and Peggy had met again at Hoffmann's shop, not long before Eva's first suicide attempt. Three years after she'd first met him, the 20-year-old was happily absorbed in her photography, and her lover, but less than a month later, she tried to take her life. Because of him.

After both that and a second attempt in 1935, it was her older sister, Ilse, who found her. Anna recalled that the sisters' relationship was prickly, at times, with Ilse disapproving of her younger sister's paramour. Yet at these two critical junctures, Ilse was the angel of life pulling Eva from the jaws of death. Maybe Eva knew instinctively that her sister would be her calm, centered best at such turning points—even relied on it.

Stirred to depths untouched for years, Anna's memory called forth the face of another responder, her father, who had so often felt unreachable, and unreliable. Yet in one emergency, he'd been quietly competent, too.

Eva hadn't really wanted to kill herself on either occasion, Anna suddenly recognized. Instead, her actions had been an assertion. Her way of finally saying, no, and no more. She'd wanted to end her pain, and to be acknowledged.

Which is what I wanted, too. The attempt Anna made when she was thirteen, that slicing of the tender skin on the underside of her wrist, the mess she made of it, wasn't ever really about suicide. It was an assertion, rising up from a place within her that she'd had no conscious knowledge of in those distressing days.

Some inner imperative finally found a voice to speak from that part of her stifled into silence the night her mother was away from home, and her father had climbed into Anna's bed naked and sobbed against her.

Two of those who saw her self-inflicted injury characterized it quite aptly. The first, a neighbor who rushed over after she received Anna's frantic call, and later, the emergency-room nurse, each blurted, "Why, it looks just like a mouth."

Each also fell instantly silent afterward, as though she had let escape what should have remained unspoken.

Neither Anna's father, who drove her to the hospital, nor the doctor who closed the wound with stitches said anything about what, like gaping red lips, had uttered its wordless pronouncement: *"Listen to me! I am unwilling to carry this pain, this injustice, one instant longer—one breath further."*

From that point, Rod treated her differently, the way someone did when they owed you something. Mostly, he avoided her. Yet that night at the emergency room, he was subdued, almost kind.

Perhaps something in Eva's psyche also attempted to speak on its own behalf in the two attempts she made, each of which elicited the response she sought, or something she decided was close enough.

On the first try, the eve of November 1, All Saints Day, Eva used her father's gun and aimed at her heart. Could there be a more direct reference from a lost daughter to the father figure she'd given everything to, who had abandoned her?

She had the presence of mind to call the doctor herself after she barely missed hitting her carotid artery. She also chose a physician she knew would relay the news to the person she most wanted to hear it. She was cunning, even daring, as she made her play toward her desired destiny.

By the second attempt, in spring of 1935, after her anguished diary entries, after being ignored and left waiting far too long, watching all the other women angling to insinuate themselves into Hitler's life, the fire of outrage in Eva's heart had dimmed.

Unlike the assertion of power she had made with her father's gun, she simply sought to "fall asleep" to block the pain, rather than take strong action to end it. *Insist* that it be brought to an end. Already, she'd become pain's victim, on someone else's terms. By the second attempt, Eva already recognized how demanding the road to her dream would be, what self-sacrifice—denial—it would entail.

Both attempts followed long months of waiting around for Hitler. Ironically, even once he formally made her his mistress, waiting comprised the greater part of her life with him. From the start, she was in training for what her life, that of so many women, became: the surrender of your self to something that never quite paid the dividends you told yourself it would, while it came at very high cost. You were still one man's possession until you were transferred to being another's, for the benefit of both.

Eva's desperate action forced Hitler to capitulate, but the "treaty" was negotiated entirely on his terms. She gathered the spoils he bestowed: a house of her own in which to live her life of perpetual waiting, quarters at the Berghof as close to the house's master as any personal servant's would be, and the right to be seen as female head of that household. Eventually, she also obtained her own rooms at the Reich Chancellery in Berlin, including one that former President Hindenburg had once occupied. But she had to use the servants' entrance to reach them.

The "triumph" of life with Hitler also brought an enforced invisibility that weighed on her as the years dragged by. From that point, Anna knew, it required a great deal of fantasy, and of medicating herself with alcohol and pills, for Eva to keep her illusions alive. She had to focus entirely on the prize, rather than the price it exacted.

Life with Hitler also required that she relinquish the opportunity to make any decisions about her own future. Even when he left doors open to her about her life, she, almost reflexively, stepped forward to close them, to close off any possibility of self-determination, and the possible loss of her dream.

She claimed and exerted control over only one thing—her body and physical appearance, obsessively clothing herself in an enormously expensive stylish wardrobe while exercising rigorously and rigidly restricting her diet, so as not to gain an ounce.

Some underlying fear never allowed Eva to feel truly safe, no matter what Hitler said or did or gave her. His face was on the stamps, the coins, his image was everywhere one looked, like that of a monarch. While he portrayed himself as a father figure to all, he traded on the certainty that, because he was unmarried, every German woman could imagine that she might garner the prize. He would never have achieved his power without their votes, and he knew it, as he knew it was vital to keep them captivated.

Eva had to know that such extensive, excessive power meant he could always dismiss her—destroy her. Even if she desired the freedom that he allegedly offered to her later in their relationship, how could she believe it was really hers to claim?

Her insistent and undying loyalty to him became the ultimate protection; a strategy, if an unconscious one. Her ticket to *not* dying, *not* being annihilated, one day at a time.

During her first appointment with Karen, Anna talked as much about Eva, and Peggy, as she did about herself. When the therapist asked about the flashbacks, Anna realized that she hadn't experienced any in more than a week.

"What was different during that time?"

"Well," Anna pondered the question, "Hannes is out most days, finishing up at the magazine. This will be his last issue, before he goes back to Germany in a few weeks. I'm here at home, reading about my mother's past. And about Eva Braun."

"What's that like?" Karen asked.

"Like stepping into that world—sometimes, I wish I could."

"Can you remember what life is like when you experience the flashbacks?"

"I'm often feeling bad." Anna realized aloud. "About Lowell."

"Do you mean sad?"

"No. It's not that."

Anna looked up as a suggestion of guilt billowed like an oversized wave in her chest. She was expecting to encounter a look of disapproval, or even confusion, but the therapist's expression was neutral, as if simply waiting to hear more.

"My life with him was already feeling over for me, and I wanted it to be." She looked away out the window. "Then, it was. Is."

"How do you feel about that?"

"I don't know," Anna said. "I survived. He didn't. When I think about that, the flashbacks seem to return."

The truth was, when she thought of Lowell, she felt either an ugly weight of guilt or a blast of outrage at how his run for his life had trodden her underfoot, as it had in everything.

"You had no control over what happened that day," Karen said.

Anna nodded. "I know." Then she added, "I've had dreams, lately. Feeling as though I'm supposed to look for him, and I don't want to. I wake up panicked. When I go back to sleep, or maybe the next night, I have flashbacks."

After a short silence, Karen asked, "How do you feel about Lowell now?"

Anna was quiet for a few moments as she considered the question. "Before the accident, there were suddenly all these new possibilities for me. But it felt like I would have to choose between them, and him. I'd started to see that life with him meant giving in to him, the way I'd always done."

"Why did you?" asked Karen.

"I told myself it was easiest, as long as things were what he wanted. But even the good parts of that weren't there anymore."

"What were those?'

"What I thought, believed, was the way to feel connected to him—to feel that he cared about me. Now, I think that was all just me trying to keep some sort of peace."

She paused, sat quietly for several moments. "I was tired of it, finally. It didn't make any difference. But I think I was afraid that if I didn't figure out the right thing—"

Her voice broke as tears filled her throat. "It's as if I have always felt, somehow, that I had to do the right thing, so he wouldn't stop loving me. Wouldn't leave."

Karen moved a box of tissues closer. "Had something indicated he might?"

Anna shook her head. "It's ridiculous that I didn't recognize he was … seeing someone. I kept telling myself he was buried in work, like he told me he was."

"Did you love him?"

The question caught her off-guard.

"A few months ago, I'd have said yes. I believed I did. I somehow felt responsible … for keeping some kind of balance. So everything would be all right."

"All by yourself?"

Anna didn't look at her, said nothing.

"And was it?" Karen asked.

"I don't think it ever was. It's so confusing. The more involved I got in the reading and research about Eva Braun, and in uncovering my mother's life, the happier I felt. It was a topic I wanted to share, but he cut off every attempt I made.

"When I saw him with someone else, I was so angry. And hurt. But already I realized that he didn't really know me. He wasn't willing to find out who I was. I don't think he wanted me to be who I really am."

"How could he stop it?" Karen asked reasonably.

"He had me to do it for him."

The other woman watched her quietly, saying nothing.

"I wanted him to love me, want me. I began to see that he didn't, really. Whatever was even possible with him, it wasn't something I wanted any more. That's what I was starting to realize. Maybe it never had been."

"Perhaps you now understand what you want to choose, for your life?"

Anna nodded.

"And you can." The therapist's tone was confident. "The flashbacks will be temporary, Anna, if you're willing to meet them. I can offer you some tools for coping. It'll help if you let yourself be really honest about your feelings. Not judge—"

"He stepped on me!" Anna blurted out suddenly.

Looking startled for a moment, Karen said, "Can you tell me more?"

"On the plane. To get away. He *stepped* on me."

Anna squeezed the words out, barely able to speak them, then sat shaking.

Karen came to sit beside her on the couch. "Have you talked about this?"

Anna shook her head without looking at her.

"Well, you can, when you want to. If you want. But for now, I think you've done a lot today, including this very important truth. Shall we talk again, perhaps tomorrow?"

"I'd like that."

"Anna, what you've done today is really good, and very brave." Karen reached and gave her shoulders a small hug. "I encourage you to write down any more feelings or thoughts about this, as they come.

"And I think there's wisdom in those dreams. Your heart knows there's only one thing worth searching for. And it has absolutely nothing to do with him."

Hannes put in long days at *The Fighting Chance* office during the steamy July weeks in which he wrapped up his final deadline.

Between twice-weekly appointments with Karen, Anna resumed reading Peggy's manuscript. She had noticed that its installments were occurring at intervals about four years apart, in even-numbered years that were also leap years.

The next, set in Berlin, entered a period of her mother's life Anna knew nothing about. It felt as much like reading about a stranger as the chapter about Eva Braun had.

FELLOW TRAVELLERS

Shouted into Silence

CHAPTER 12

Hotel Adlon, Berlin
16 August 1936

I sat kicking my heels as I watched the diminutive grandmother clock that always looks so out of place in the Adlon's cavernous lobby.

Checking my watch was no help. It never keeps time properly, but it made Mutti so happy to give me something as fine as this gold Longines. She had to acquire it used, I know, with the help of the local tailor, Herr Niemeyer—a supporting member of the SS, who's often wearing a pin with its insignia in his lapel. I think he aspires to marry her.

I call him Herr Nadelkissen—"Herr Pincushion"—though only to myself, and still haven't made up my mind about him. He's younger than Mutti, always soft-spoken. He seems to truly care for her. But what would prompt him to declare support for the SS?

Today was the Games' final day, yet there was still no sign of Erich, and no way to get to the Olympic stadium now.

We spent the afternoon there yesterday, our first time alone in a week, without his co-workers tagging along. The foreign news correspondents in Berlin eat together, drink as a group far into the night, and reassemble like a pack at every opportunity, as though putting off as long as possible the need for each to do his job, alone.

They rely on each other more than ever now that the Nazis seem to impose new rules almost every week. I've decided this is a strategy to keep obedient Germans too preoccupied to ask questions, and leaves those of us who might, increasingly unsure of where we stand *if* we do.

Erich seemed irritated and perturbed all afternoon, though his journalist's eyes followed everything with the kind of attention that always makes him appear interested.

"You see what's happening, don't you?" His voice was terse. "It's all by design, this pageantry we're supposed to feel honored to witness.

"And it's *working*. Because asking questions—living with your damned eyes open—is being driven out of fashion. All of them, the Americans and the British especially, think this is some Wunderkind savior at work.

"Und das Deutsche Volk," he'd sneered. "Well, *anything* to get their jobs and their bread back. Be 'purged' of that 'Bolshevik' threat."

Then his tone turned glum. "They worry that the wolf will come back to the door. So they welcome the most insatiable one right in." His voice climbed higher and louder, before it dropped to a low growl. "Hitler talks of peace so that they won't see this charade for the battlefield it already is. People don't *die* in truly 'free' elections."

His words wrenched out in fits and starts, alternating between English and German. I simply listened, knowing he needed to give vent to his frustration.

But when he got too loud, I shook my head in abrupt, discouraging "no's," gave the look mothers give children talking in church, even punched his arm when two SS men strode down the adjacent aisle, their conversation punctuated by bursts of tight laughter.

"You *must* be more careful, Erich!" I consciously chose English to deliver this command as I pressed close to him. "We cannot have this discussion *here*."

To my relief, he relented, fell quiet and watched the games without further comment. Eventually, he'd even joked a little and wondered where we might have dinner.

I feel a hard knot of dread, these days. It warns that egalitarian views like ours are becoming less acceptable, possibly dangerous. A kind of mass hypnosis is escalating all over the city, the entire nation, erupting every so often in outbreaks of mob rage.

I still can't believe its driving force is that man whose unnerving eyes glared back from those photos in Hoffmann's Munich shop. I hadn't even heard of him then, hadn't been interested enough to pay attention. Yet within months, he became Reich Chancellor, claiming he'll lead Germany to its "great destiny."

All I know is wherever I go now, I feel observed, unsafe. This isn't a new feeling, but a stronger version of one that's always traveled with me, like a low-level infection that's grown inflamed.

I'm terrified for Erich's safety, though it seems indecent to acknowledge or disclose this, as though doing so might actually make something terrible happen.

It isn't fear about the risks that come with his work as a reporter. In a way, the German censors protect him from being his own worst enemy as they dilute the texts of his broadcasts to America into something increasingly tepid.

I fear that danger's trailing him because of *who* he is, and what that might lead him to do. His loathing of injustice was obvious the night we met at a party at the American Embassy after the censors had done major surgery on his broadcast. When I walked past where he sat looking dejected, he reached for my hand. There was almost a note of desperation in his voice when he asked whether I couldn't offer more intelligent conversation than what he'd encountered that night.

I've since learned it was an uncharacteristically extroverted thing for him to do, but something in me saw through that veneer of banter to the hurt in his eyes. His background gives him the kind of looks many here consider exotically handsome. That family tree flies in the face of new laws the Führer imposed at Nuremberg, however.

Erich's paternal grandparents, an "Aryan" man and German-born Jewess, gave him his German surname, Geisler, his unaccented German, and the increasingly dangerous heritage his grandmother inherited from the tribes of Israel, though she hasn't gone to Temple since childhood.

His maternal grandparents are an unusual mix, even for freewheeling Americans: a marriage still forbidden in many parts of their country. His white grandfather has New England roots, while his black grandmother's beautiful skin, like Erich's mother's, is a slightly darker shade of Café au Lait than Erich's. His own is precisely the sort of tan the wealthy try to maintain.

Though his family acknowledges this mixed ancestry candidly at home, Erich and his sister have passed for white everywhere they've gone, whether

Ivy-League colleges, or in Germany, where their father's parents still live near Kassel. Maybe I feel kinship with him because he also comes from a mix of peoples with sharp divides between them.

As we watched the Games yesterday, I wondered just who I am. I cheer for the Germans and the British—in fact, a British classmate from my Salzburg school days won a medal in a women's swimming event. Now, with Erich, I cheer the Americans, too. The section where we sat was an international crowd, so multiple loyalties aren't unusual, at least in Berlin. It wasn't like I had to *choose* between them, as Father always insists I do.

On the Games' third day, American athlete Jessie Owens crossed the finish line first in the 100-meter sprint. This was a comeuppance for the National Socialists, who were counting on the games to showcase not only the resurgence of Germany's fortunes, but Aryan superiority. Those with roots in Africa are people they deem inferior.

Yet Owens went on to win three additional gold medals. As Erich watched with bird-of-prey attentiveness, his eyes weren't on the finish line where Owens was doused with water and cheers of triumph, but on the box where Hitler sat. He raised his binoculars to follow every move the Reich Chancellor made as he presented the gold medal to Owens—dark face shining in the flickering flashbulbs—but did not extend his hand to this victor.

"What does he propose to do *now*?" I wondered, just loud enough for Erich to hear. "Refrain from shaking *any* winner's hand?"

"We'll see," he said quietly.

That's precisely what Hitler has done—or not done—in the Games' ensuing days. Anyone who attempts to show this treatment of the Negro athlete for what it truly is, especially someone with a background like Erich's, is putting himself in the path of danger. This realization sowed the beginnings of a dull ache at the back of my head as we waited in the interminable lines to exit the stadium afterward.

We dined on the avenue of the Unter den Linden, lingering at our sidewalk table in the evening's soft air and golden light. Afterward—well, how can someone lie in your arms yet feel simultaneously all the way across the room? It's as though Erich can only have a conversation in the most public of places, and treats the private ones as if there are listeners behind every curtain. It leaves me so confused.

Something he said as he held me in those last moments before he left for the Rundfunk studio gave a glimpse of what's going on inside him. Maybe he hadn't been able to express it as directly in his angry frustration during the Games, and it took a sense of defeat to draw it out: "There's nothing possible now but to tell the story *they* want told. Do my part for the Fatherland."

That, I know, is something Erich can never do. His tone had been bitter, nearly choked. The developments with Jessie Owens no doubt felt like a soured victory.

I know he's furious about the increasing censorship. He protests it regularly in the councils he shares most nights with William Shirer and the other foreign journalists. "I'm lucky if 40 percent of my copy gets through now, unless it's what Herr Doktor Goebbels wants," he declared in the hotel's bar one night last week. When he described his strategies for avoiding this tight-fisted censorship, I again pleaded caution.

His tone turned resolute. "You know what this work *means*, for me. I have to do whatever it takes to get the job done. There may be even bigger demands coming, so I cannot back down from what's simply right and decent."

But danger is following you, more closely than ever, I wanted to cry out. This looming dread is a premonition, I realized, not my own thoughts, but the assertion of something larger that I can never ignore or escape.

It feels so unbearably awkward when I try to give it voice, as though it will be unwelcome, make me seem foolish. Superstitious. It's been this way, especially with men, from the time Father rejected such awareness when I tried to offer it. When I knew as a child that my brother Peter was in deadly danger if he went to France in the war, and tried to warn about what I'd seen as I lay in my small bed, I was shouted into silence.

Then, those awful things I saw happened, and it was as though Father held me accountable for having introduced such a morbid idea at all.

After Erich left for the studio last night, I had the taxi drop me at the Adlon. I was planning to have a nightcap when I overheard Campbell, one of the other newsmen, talking at a table in the corner of the bar with two Americans I'd met once or twice. Drink had obviously loosened his tongue, and increased the volume of his voice. He was tossing out phrases like, "The Nazis *this*," and "the Führer *that*."

Then I heard him mention the name of one of Erich's contacts, a friend who has begun to stir rhetoric against Hitler.

Something blinded me, an instant outrage—perhaps an eruption of all the fear I'd been clamping back on. I stormed over to where they sat, their table haloed with blue smoke. When they turned at my approach, I hissed, "Are you *mad*?"

The three immediately begun struggling to push back their chairs.

"Oh, do not trouble yourselves to get up on *my* account." As they stared at me, I remembered to switch to English.

I wanted to shake and slap them like badly behaved schoolboys. "Are you really so mindless of the risks? Are you all that *stupid*? Or simply arrogant?"

"Peggy, please, " Campbell began objecting.

I cut him off, my voice lowered so they had to crane forward to hear me. "No—it's time you listen to someone who's actually a part of this country and the mania it's disintegrating into. Every time you sit here comfortably with your drinks idly airing your opinions, you put people at risk."

I knew they still believed the Nazi promises; saw Hitler through the lens of their cultural bias, rather than as the threat he truly is.

"Whatever your beliefs or politics, let me remind you that even if they've taken that miserable hate-rag newspaper of Streicher's off the streets this week for the Olympics, taken down the 'No Jews' signs, and convinced thousands of happy tourists that Germany is a brave new world, people are still disappearing. And turning up *dead*."

"And your lack of discretion could land any of you—*any* of you—" my voice caught, finally overcome by tears that had lurked at the periphery all day.

Campbell leapt from his chair and moved toward me, his expression solicitous. "Now, Peggy—if it's Erich you're worried about—"

"I have *nothing* more to say to you." I put my hands up as if to ward him off. "Just don't say you were never warned." Then I spun on my heel and bolted away.

This morning, I was surprised by a call from Campbell. He apologized, then relayed a message asking that I wait for Erich in the Adlon's lobby: "He said to be sure to wait for him right there."

I certainly had waited. I couldn't possibly drink any more coffee; my hands were trembling. I'd stationed myself in one of the lobby's expansive maroon leather chairs so I could spot him immediately when he arrived. Half-hidden by the marble column beside me, I had an unobstructed view of the front entrance's revolving door.

Two women entered, heads bent close in conversation. I followed their movements as though watching a silent film. One was pale blond and buxom, the other slight, almost waiflike. Both wore brightly colored sundresses whose skirts tossed and fluttered with each gust borne in by the revolving door. Finally, they moved several steps away from it as they continued to converse. The taller one seemed to be trying to convince the other of something, bending close to catch her eyes, placing a gloved hand on her slender arm.

The smaller woman, whose hair showed several shades of gold from beneath her broad-brimmed straw hat, turned to gaze longingly toward the front desk and I saw her face. *It couldn't be.* My eyes must be playing tricks.

Then I saw her look of far-away sadness and felt sure of it. Her posture and demeanor were unmistakable, though also steeped in discouragement and dismay, rather than exuding their usual effervescence.

Eva was strikingly dressed, from her flawless make-up and lips that matched perfectly the soft strawberry color of her dress to the white peep-toe pumps that looked leather, Italian, and expensive. She appeared on the verge of tears, eyes wide, fixed, staring. Her companion was obviously attempting to console her.

Part of me wanted to race over, express my happy surprise to see her *here*, of all places, when we'd only ever crossed paths in Bavaria. But something held me back, suggested a need for privacy, as if she had recently received bad news, and I couldn't just rush up to say hello.

Eva's companion led the way to the lobby desk, closer to where I sat watching from behind the column.

Two young men in Leibstandarte SS uniforms approached them deferentially. One bowed slightly, then addressed the women in a strident voice loud enough for me to hear: "Gnädige Fräuleins, we are instructed to assist with transportation of your luggage."

"Very good," the companion said, then turned toward Eva, whose expression remained blankly forlorn. "Fräulein Braun and I will ride together. Come," she reached to tuck her arm through Eva's.

"Leave *now*?" Eva spoke at last. "We're not going to wait?"

The other woman shook her head. "It will be a long trip. The maid can finish your packing, and the men will bring the trunks down later. The cars are ready now."

Eva's eyes darted back and forth from the lobby desk to the hotel entrance, never once alighting on any of the three figures standing around her. Finally, with a look of dazed resignation, she turned to leave.

Throughout this exchange, I pressed back in my chair so the column hid me from view. It felt wrong to be visible, a witness to whatever was clearly such a source of difficulty for Eva. The adjutants' uniforms indicated they were part of the exclusive force responsible for Hitler's personal protection.

The women were leaving. I watched their backs as they disappeared through the revolving door, followed by the two men. If only Eva hadn't looked so crestfallen, and that other woman so in-charge, I'd have approached without hesitation. But it was as though some sort of protocol blocked the way, especially once those adjutants appeared.

I hurried over to the entrance. As I watched through a window, Eva and her companion were joined outside by two other women, both dark-haired. One had a stolid appearance and moved slowly, while the other had a curvaceous figure set off by a well-tailored suit. She tossed her hair back as she laughed.

As the uniformed men held the car doors open, the women climbed into a long, black Mercedes parked near the curb. Eva looked very small as the others pressed around her and she disappeared into the back of the car. Moments later, one of the soldiers closed the doors and waved the driver on.

Rain was dotting the ground in great plops, its ozone lifting from the pavement, wafting through the door. It had held off until the Games' final events. And still, no Erich. Was I supposed to wait all day? How lovely it would have been to pass the time with Eva, while she waited for whatever she'd seemed so loath to leave behind. Dressed like a film star, she looked almost imperious when she arrived, then seemed shadowed by disappointment, as though there was a party she wouldn't get to attend after all. Two of the women looked like Hitler's secretaries. Was *that* Eva's connection with the adjutants?

Why had I felt I couldn't approach her? It had seemed the only choice, for the sake of discretion and courtesy. But the truth of it was, when those two

Leibstandarte had appeared, I felt as barricaded as those who lined the streets when Hitler rode by in a great black Mercedes. Like the one in which Eva left. Wherever could she be going?

The watch was right where Anna remembered leaving it in the spare bedroom that day she'd been rushing to get to the airport. The gold Longines had a diminutive rectangular case, Roman numerals, and hands that, for as long as she could remember, stayed fixed at the same right angle: 3:30. When asked why she wore a watch that didn't work, Peggy always said its sentimental value was more important, its connection with the life she'd known in Germany.

The time it showed was just about right now. Without thinking, Anna turned the handspring's tiny knob and was surprised to hear soft ticking. The watch was still running when she showed it to Hannes the next day so she decided to wear it.

He had made sandwiches and urged that she eat before her appointment with Karen that afternoon. After the therapist's first visit at the house, Anna had been seeing her at her office twice a week. The alarming flashbacks were receding, though they hadn't disappeared entirely. Most nights now, Anna's sleep was undisturbed.

"My mother had a life in Berlin I never knew about," she told Hannes as they ate. "Even knew foreign correspondents there. Maybe that's how she met your aunt?"

He raised his blue gaze to meet hers. "I didn't read that far."

"Yes, at the Hotel Adlon, where Eva used to stay. In fact, in the section I've just read, she sees Eva there, with some people associated with Hitler." She shook her head. "I've been reading so much about that time, and it turns out that my mother had this whole life then that seems as much a mystery as Eva Braun's."

After a short silence, Hannes said, "Many of our parents probably did. It just doesn't occur to us to ask."

"Maybe they didn't want us to, didn't want to talk about it."

He nodded. "It's possible that we only think to ask once we've lived enough of our own life that we're less apt to judge theirs."

"I wonder when my mother finally recognized Eva's connection with Hitler? Maybe she didn't really know her all that well, beyond running into her a few times when they were young. Oh, and today I learned about a man she knew, someone named Erich."

Hannes was on his feet, beginning to clear away dishes from the coffee table.

"His *name*," Anna remembered. "That's what I wanted to ask. It was Geisler. Isn't that Nati's name?"

He paused in mid-step, nodding. "Yes, that's right."

"Is it a very common name?"

Hannes shrugged, "As common as my own, Ritter, I suppose. At least in Germany. Would you like some coffee before you go?"

"No, thanks. Karen asked me to avoid caffeine before my appointments." Anna reached for the manuscript in its box and paged through it. "Here it is: Erich Geisler," she said as she found it. "I don't ever remember hearing about anyone with that name."

"No?" he asked.

She shook her head. "She certainly sounds in love with him, but also clearly frustrated." She shrugged. "Well, the two go together often enough. Look at poor Eva."

After her appointment, Hannes dropped her back at home, then headed off for his final day at *The Fighting Chance*. The therapy session was uneventful, though Karen brought up the question Anna knew she must face soon: was she ready to make the trip to Germany? Each time she contemplated it, the flashbacks came roaring back. Curling up on Peggy's couch now, she sought escape in the next chapter of the manuscript.

FELLOW TRAVELLERS

Like Entering a Nest of Snakes

CHAPTER 13

Munich
22 August 1936

As my train glided into the station, I realized how much I'd missed Munich, and Aunt Paula. This little surprise for her birthday would be my last visit for a while, now that my Foreign Office job anchors me in Berlin.

The intercity express picked up many more carriages on its overnight trip south, so the procession from the platform into the station took forever. The swarms of passengers dispersed the morning quiet like a stadium cheer. Most are tourists visiting Bavaria on their way home from the Olympics.

Exiting onto the street, I heard a chorus of bells from three churches, then saw the blood-red banners with their dark Swastikas everywhere I turned. I'm accustomed to this in Berlin, but seeing them on these lovely old façades is like finding graffiti scrawled on my grandmother's house. The Nazis are relentless with this display, like dogs marking territory. Do they imagine it will make us forget a Germany untainted by them?

In a week-old American newspaper I found on the train, some stupid reporter claimed that the Olympics have made Germans "more human"— than what? Starving in degradation and humility after the "Great War" wasn't human enough?

Idiots like that always fall for the propaganda. They parade their opinions but do nothing as thugs ruin the country. In the end, they'll protect their own interests by sending boys off to slaughter, just like last time. Like they always do.

But I mustn't think of that, or the awful visions will return, though I fight so hard for them not to. What good is it to "know" things, see dangers, horrors, when no one listens? Believes?

Erich says he may leave Berlin soon. I don't know how I'll bear it. At least cognac's still cheap. And working in the Foreign Office will help me know where he is.

I can't believe how much has changed since he brought me to Erich Mühsam's grave last Sunday. Campbell finally came and found me that afternoon I sat waiting in the Adlon's lobby, his face flushed. I knew it wasn't drink—he never starts *that* early, though he looked like he needed one.

"They took Erich for questioning." His voice was so low I could barely hear him. He grabbed my arm when I nearly fainted. I didn't need to ask who "they" were.

"It's all right," he tried to reassure me. "He's safe. I've come to take you to him."

He didn't speak to me during the half-hour ride in the crowded train out of the city. Instead, he handed me a book to read and sat a short distance away.

Sitting with it open on my lap, I kept reading snippets of things that made no sense. Or the same paragraph over and over. I had to remember to turn the pages. I couldn't think, my mind like a deer with three weapons trained on her.

We got off the train separately at Dahlem, as he wanted to be sure we weren't being followed. He walked with me as far as the gatehouse entrance to the Waldfriedhof cemetery. "I'm truly sorry, Peggy." He looked contrite, as well as nervous. "You were right. I didn't know."

"Don't worry about that now. I appreciate your help."

"I hate to leave you here on your own. But it's what Erich instructed."

I shook uncontrollably after he'd gone as I fished in my handbag for a cigarette. It finally lit on the fourth match. Perspiration trickled down the backs of my legs under my skirt. I ducked under the canopy of a big chestnut, as much for a sense of shelter from lurking danger as for shade. Its leaves were like giant green hands with oversized fingers.

Within minutes, Erich approached from the opposite direction from which Campbell and I had come. He wrapped his arms around me as I threw myself into them, kissed my hair, and pressed his cheek against it. "I'm so sorry you had to wait all that time. Didn't know—"

"Campbell told me." I gripped him tightly. "Oh, thank God. Thank *God*." I didn't want to let go of him, ever. I searched his face and saw that its tan glow had been eclipsed by grey pallor. Shadows were like smudges under his dark eyes.

"Did they … " I couldn't bring myself to voice the rest.

"Let's talk in here." He led me through the arched gateway. We were out of sight of it when he stopped beside a narrow grave, reached into his pocket, and set a smooth oval stone down on the flat headstone.

He described how two Gestapo agents intercepted him near the entrance to the zoo park that morning, not far from the Adlon. They bundled him into a car and took him to a police station. He sounded surprised that their inquiry had been mostly wheedling and probing, with a hint of threatening when they mentioned his Jewish grandmother.

I realized I'd been holding my breath as I listened, and finally let it out.

"It was mostly a warning, to let me know that they're watching. I've known that my office phone is tapped. I imagine my room at the Adlon is, too." He pulled out his handkerchief and dabbed at his face. "That's why I've never wanted to bring you there."

I'd been so hurt about this, and that he never came to my tiny place, not far from the hotel. Instead, he insisted we go to the apartment of his diplomat friend, who was always out. It was closer to the Rundfunk studio for Erich's midnight broadcasts so we'd have more time, he had said, and he could send me home safely by taxi.

"I don't want anyone to know you have any connection with me."

My head was just starting to clear when these words struck like a lash.

"Peggy—Sweetheart." He reached and pulled me against him when he saw my expression. "You must know how much I want to be with you. More than anything. But I can't put you in danger. Things are likely to get much more dangerous, now."

So. There it was. What I'd been feeling. He'd known about the danger, too, but hadn't said anything. To protect me.

Tears were sliding down my face. I knew this meant that soon I might not see him at all. I swayed, feeling off-balance. The life I thought I could count on was being pulled out from under me. Again.

"If I can convince them that I want what they want—that's the key," Erich said. "Once they believe that, their own arrogance about it blinds them to anything else. Then I can do the real work, from behind the scenes."

As he described those with whom he'd be working now, I wondered, surprised, "Aren't they Communists?"

"Yes, some. I'm an ally of all who are my enemy's enemy and resist the Reich."

I asked about the cemetery plot beside us.

"Erich Mühsam was a good friend of my family," he said. "I'm named for him, though it upset my grandmother. Jews usually only name a child to honor someone who's already died, you see. Ever since we heard what happened to him, she's been inconsolable. Now, it all just keeps getting worse, for Jews." His face was pallid.

The date of death on the headstone was 10 July, 1934.

"How?" I asked.

"Oranienburg," he said quietly.

I felt a sickening lurch inside. I'd already done the mental calculations to determine that this man had been 56. No one was dying of natural causes in the camp known by this name that now represented something so sinister.

I wanted to ask what his grandparents would do, but I've learned to let him tell me about difficult things, rather than ask. We're all learning to do that, these days. I knew they had means and, everyone hoped, time to get out—if they could only bring themselves to leave the home they'd shared since their wedding day.

"Erich loved my parents," he said. He called their marriage living proof we're all 'citizens of the world.' That's how he wanted to be known." The warm reminiscence in his voice vanished. "I have to tell you why he died, so you'll understand why I need to do the things I must. Especially now this blight is so … inescapable."

I glanced around nervously, though the open space in which we stood offered no hiding place for eavesdroppers. He knows me well enough not to be explicit. He seems to understand how deeply images can imprint in me, stir that inexplicable knowing—and seeing—that can often feel too painful to live with. People sometimes call me "sensitive" with a tone that makes it sound like a defect. Erich calls it what Mutti does—my "Geschenk"—my gift.

It was enough to tell me that Erich Mühsam spent sixteen months and nine days in three concentration camps before he died in the one at Oranienburg. Erich didn't use the word "torture" although deaths ruled "suicide" in such places unquestionably included this.

"He was supposed to get out. He had a ticket to Prague the night they arrested him." Erich's eyes looked glossy, now. "Then, the way he always did with things, insisting he needed so little. … He gave it away." Erich broke off; first his voice, dissolving, then his expression, before it disappeared behind his strong, beautiful hands.

I reached and held him as he shook with soundless sobs.

I sensed sorrowful guilt, something more than grief about a tragedy that might have been averted. *What had this man tried to give Erich that he hadn't been able to receive?* I couldn't imagine where such a thought came from, though it resounded in me.

He fumbled for his handkerchief and wiped his eyes. "He was killed just days after the Putsch that killed Röhm and all those others. It was too dangerous for his widow to even come to the graveside. She had to leave Germany. But she knew the truth about how he died. She'd visited him just days before."

"Was it because he was Jewish?"

Erich shook his head. "They hated him for it, of course. Though it wasn't even that important to him. He was an artist, a poet. Published journals in which he spoke out. He knew how to be clever about it, for a long time."

Things had been alarmingly violent that week of what had come to be known as The Night of the Long Knives. So much brutality and murder had occurred overnight behind closed doors that many Berliners greeted each other cryptically, "Lebst du noch?—*You're still alive?*" for days afterward. If Hitler could eliminate his longtime friend, Ernst Röhm, and "purge" a hundred others who might get in the Reich's way, what chance had there been for an outspoken intellectual?

"Those in the camp with him, who were later released, say he was unbelievably brave, as if he'd already gone on ahead beyond it all," Erich said. "The bastards couldn't touch him, though they savaged him enough." He stopped then. "I'm sorry."

"No, it's all right," I said.

"I wish you'd known him." He smoothed back hair that the breeze was blowing around my eyes. "He was one of the kindest people I've known. You'd understand why I have to make the decisions I'm about to. No matter how small a voice justice has now, it's the only one worth working for." Unspoken, though heavy as the clouds massing overhead while thunder rumbled in the distance were the words: worth *dying* for.

Now, he'll toe the Party line in his broadcasts to the States by night, and by day, enter more deeply into the world of the Resistance. The mere sound of that word scares me. There'll be so much he can't tell me. When I asked how he'll do his work as a journalist, he said, "That's over. I'll simply read their scripts now, more or less."

I must have looked shocked.

"It's the only way to gain a cover. Avoid suspicion." He shook his head. "They're determined to mask the truth about what's happening here, and the U.S. isn't listening. If Ambassador Dodd, who's right here and sees it all, can't make his warnings heard, the time for journalists doing that has passed. Most correspondents are simply drinking at the Adlon bar, biding time until they go home.

"I won't be," he added before I could ask. "In order to stay, I'll eventually have to take another identity. Go somewhere outside Berlin."

I couldn't take in any more, and finally let my tears pour out.

He tried to reassure me, reminding that my Foreign Office job will help us stay connected. I wonder how, when so many of my new co-workers are Party members, though some, like Erich, are working against the Nazis. The work of the Resistance seems to require that you go into their midst, like entering a nest of snakes.

The sound of a soft cling interrupted my reverie, alerting me that I was in a little swarm of bicyclists going every which way, including straight toward me as I stepped to one side quickly. Beside me, a travel bureau's storefront showed a poster with an image of the Harz Mountains in deep blues and greens.

I had nearly reached Munich's Marienplatz square—my attention had wandered far, with my thoughts about Erich. I was so certain I knew this city that I never actually bothered to find out where Balin's is. I did have the address of this framing shop where Aunt Paula works, and knew it was somewhere near the Frauenkirche.

Turning left, I explored the little lanes that wind around that big church, and asked directions of a few people, but none of them knew. They seemed hesitant to even stop and speak with me. Surely, Munich used to be friendlier than this?

At the end of one street, the traffic lanes split on either side of a park that stretched like a long finger down the middle. Tram tracks framed its narrow span on either side. To the right, the Hotel Bayerischer Hof took up almost the entire block.

A tram clanged its bell before it trundled past on my left; then I saw the wrought-iron sign at the tram stop: "Promenade Platz." Across the park, the building on the corner showed the number 7 on a blue metal sign. I'd wandered right to it. I remembered coming here years ago with Mutti, when we'd both noticed the row of whimsical stone cherubs in little niches just below the building's roofline, each playing a different musical instrument, like an angelic orchestra.

I had barely stepped into the shop and asked about Aunt Paula when Herr Balin himself emerged from the back, wearing dark protectors over the sleeves of his shirt.

"I'm sorry—Frau Vogel isn't here," he said. "We encouraged her to take the day off. She wanted to visit a friend who is sick."

I had planned so badly. Herr Balin's words hit me like a dousing of cold water.

In a rush of memory, I heard Father accusing Mutti, "You do nothing but indulge her impulsiveness! What man's ever going to want her?"

A woman standing at one of the display cases spun to face me, her smile luminous in her tanned face. Blond curls peeked from the brim of her jaunty hat, and her white-linen suit accentuated her healthy glow.

"I *knew* I recognized your voice!" she said.

Now, I was truly speechless. *Ich bin sprachlos* was literally the only thing I could think of to say.

When Anna heard Hannes pull into the driveway in Peggy's noisy Jetta, she raced to station herself beside the kitchen table. She had set it for coffee around the centerpiece of a towering Black Forest cake, the first baking she'd done in months.

"Congratulations!" she called as he came through the back door. "No more deadlines."

He set his briefcase on the closest bench at the Bavarian-style table. "I think this next issue is going to look pretty good."

"I know it will," Anna said confidently as she planted a kiss on his cheek.

"Connie still had a laundry list of requests. I expect I'll hear from her, even once I'm back in Munich."

Anna placed a hand on his arm. "You've fulfilled every commitment that you made. Just fob her off on me, now. You've protected me long enough."

He gazed at her for a moment. Then his eyes widened when he noticed the table. "What's this?"

"A little celebration—of all you've done."

"You baked a *cake*?" He stood staring at it.

"And for a master baker. How brave was that?"

"It's a master*piece*," he exclaimed.

"Have a seat. I'll get the coffee." She moved to the stove "If I hadn't been so caught up in my mother's manuscript, I'd have paid better attention to the time."

She smiled to herself as he settled into the chair at the end of the table. She'd never seen him try to fold his tall frame into the confines of the breakfast nook. He probably knew better than to try.

"What have you discovered today?" he asked.

"Quite a lot, including what happened after she saw Eva at the Adlon. They met up again, just a week after the Olympics." She poured the water she'd kept on a low boil into the French press she'd filled with coffee.

"In Berlin?"

"No, Munich." She spun around to face him. "Oh, Hannes, the more I read, the more I long to see those places where they met."

"Well, that's an easy enough wish to satisfy."

"And, there's more about that man, Erich," Anna added quickly. "The Gestapo questioned him. She was terrified, especially when she didn't know where he'd gone. And there was another Erich, someone he knew. A poet, who was arrested and killed."

"Erich Mühsam?"

"You've heard of him?"

Hannes nodded. "It was the 60th anniversary of his death last year. I wrote an article about him—I can find it for you." The corners of his mouth worked into a lopsided grin as he eyed the cake. "But don't we have more important business at hand?"

She smiled at him with all the affection she felt well in her heart. She had something more to tell him, what she'd decided today while reading her mother's pages.

"Of course we do." She reached for Peggy's silver cake knife, cut into the cake, and served him a tall slice.

"The Erich my mother knew worked with the Resistance," she told him.

Hannes looked up. "Does she say much about that?"

"She didn't know much. Only that he might have to take another identity and go away somewhere. She was working in the Foreign Office."

"Doing what?"

"Translation—German and English. She had an ear for languages." She poured coffee for each of them. "I must have been a real disappointment to her, that way."

"Anna!" he chided. "You do very well. You just need more chance to practice."

"That's a generous assessment."

"What do you mean?" he protested. "I'm *German*!"

"Yeah, well, based on my experience, you're a pretty tame one. That American stepfather must have had quite an influence."

She looked up to see him watching her. "That's certainly true," he agreed.

"Most Germans I know say they don't speak a language, when what they mean is, they don't speak it *perfectly*."

His features dissolved into his irresistible smile. "We can be an exacting Volk."

Anna moved to the stove to refill her mother's Meissen coffeepot. "I'll have my chance to find out, soon."

He set his fork down and turned in his chair to face her.

"I'm coming to Germany," she announced. "I've finally made up my mind, though you might change yours, when all is said and done."

There were two or three seconds of silence before he sprang from his chair and moved to catch her up in his arms. Her feet lifted off the floor when he spun her around before her mind could even keep up with him. Her heart was pounding when he set her down gently, as if his response had literally taken her breath away.

"*This* is the real cause for celebration. Is it obvious enough, how happy I am?"

"That was certainly a very enthusiastic response, yes."

"Whatever you need, Anna. You know that. I want to help in any way I can. Shall I call Nati now, and Mutti? They can help with your plans."

Her head still felt like it was spinning on her neck. "Yes, let them know. But let's talk a little more, before arranging the flight, OK?"

Then she gestured toward the table with a smile. "And what about your cake?"

His face creased in a grin. "It just shows how excited I am."

Though she'd looked forward to sharing this news with him, Anna felt anxious because of what she wasn't going to tell him, at least not today. She needed to confirm for herself that the pull of following her mother's life, and Eva's, was the reason for her decision to go. And that was true.

What she couldn't tell him, didn't want to acknowledge herself, was that each time she imagined this house—and her days—without him, it felt like another death.

But this couldn't be her reason for going. She didn't even know how much she'd see of Hannes, once they were in Germany. She had to make her own way now, no matter where in the world she was, including the university classes he'd urged her to teach there.

For now, she wanted to bask in his happiness a little longer. She would wait to tell him about flying to Munich on her own. The time with Karen had convinced her that if she wanted to go forward with her life, she had to face getting back on a plane by herself.

She'd lived through the accident alone, after all. She had to get used to the idea that the closer she got to Germany, the more Hannes's own life was likely to reclaim him.

Aug. 22, 1995
Flight to Munich

Slanting rays of morning sun were infiltrating the plane's dark cabin as the smell of coffee roused the dozing passengers. With an hour left in the flight, Anna reached for the envelope of her mother's manuscript pages that was tucked into her bag along with Eva Braun's handkerchief and the photos that she had taken of Peggy that day at Hoffmann's. Anna kept all of these together, now, and always carried them with her.

She opened to the section of the manuscript that had solidified her decision to travel to Germany. As she reread it, she was immersed again in a visit between Peggy and Eva nearly sixty years earlier on this very date, in the city where Anna was about to arrive.

FELLOW TRAVELLERS

Nothing About You is Ordinary

CHAPTER 14

Promenade Platz 7, Munich
22 August 1936

Eva's eyes were alight as she grabbed my hand and tugged me toward the counter in Balin's shop. "I'm so happy *you* are here to see this!"

Resting on top was a portrait in a gilt-colored frame. The face gazing back over the subject's left shoulder was meant to be hers. That much I knew.

I could feel how eager she was for my response as I struggled for words. "Ah … from the photo. The one you gave to," I hesitated before adding, "the artist."

"You remember!" Her expression was like an adoring mother's as she gazed at it. "He kept his promise. He can only get to Munich for a day or so, sometimes not for weeks. I wanted it framed in time for his return."

Her tone sobered then. "He'll have no time for drawing now."

Hardly a sacrifice, I couldn't help thinking. This was clearly no artist; at least no portrait painter. While he'd captured Eva's sparkling eyes and satiny hair with technical precision, the overall image seemed to suppress her very vitality. The clumsy composition also made her face appear superimposed, as though on a mannequin or statue. *Or on someone else's body.* The illegible signature looked like a tattoo scrawled on her shoulder. Why would he place it there, so visibly?

Surely her photographer's eye saw how mediocre this was?

But Eva seemed enthralled, as though grateful simply for its existence. What could one possibly say about a job this unworthy of her? I couldn't help wondering whether the man was, too.

"Have you time for coffee? A little second breakfast?" She checked her watch. "We could go across to the Bayerischer Hof."

"That would be wonderful," I said eagerly, especially now I had more time than I'd expected, and hadn't eaten since last night's meal on the train.

Eva finalized plans for the portrait's delivery then linked her arm in mine as we left the shop and crossed the slender strip of park to the hotel. We were seated in the spacious comfort of the elegant salon, our petite table and overstuffed chairs directly beneath an enormous dome of stained glass. We ordered quickly—boiled egg and ham with rolls, butter, and marmalade for me, a fruit compote for Eva—and asked that the coffee be served first.

"Tell me your news," she urged. "You've come all the way from Berlin?"

"Yes, to surprise my aunt, for her birthday. But the surprise seems to be on me."

"Frau Vogel is the Aunt Paula you told me about?"

"Now you're the one with a good memory," I smiled. "I hope I can catch up with her this afternoon."

"Does she live on Widenmayer Strasse, near the river?"

"You *know* each other?"

"My sister and I lived in her building, until we moved into my house this year. Your aunt was our favorite neighbor, so warm and friendly. Just like you!"

"I can't believe you know each other!" I said. "I'm very fond of her. She's my godmother, and always feels more like my big sister than my aunt."

"She's been so kind," Eva said. "It was our first time living away from home, you see. I brought the portrait to Herr Balin's so that she could do the framing. I wanted her special touch to be a part of it."

I leaned in close to meet her eyes. "I've never had the chance to tell you how much I love the photos you took—the special touch that *you* brought to them."

Her gaze dropped demurely when she thanked me. Her features brightened as she remembered, "There was a man," then stopped, as though catching herself.

"That's right."

"I don't mean to pry."

"No, no," I assured.

Did etiquette now dictate we be more guarded in our sharing? I hoped not. Eva was always so easy to talk to. "Now, there's another man," I smiled. "He likes the photos very much, too."

"Ah!" she chuckled. "Then they've served you very well!"

"But more important to me is that I liked them. I'm forever grateful you gave me that gift, especially at that time."

"It was my pleasure. It's important to see ourselves as others do, as the men do, certainly. That's why the portrait means so much to me."

Can you even recognize yourself in it? I wondered.

"He says it will show me as I was when we met, an ordinary girl—before destiny brought us together. He wants me to remain that girl."

I'll bet he does. I felt rising impatience I had to find a way to vanquish.

"Nothing about you is ordinary," I declared.

Eva blinked back at me.

"You've always struck me as quite extraordinary. You certainly looked that way the last time I saw you. Like a film star."

She frowned, confused. "At Hoffmann's?"

"No, in Berlin." I instantly had doubts about bringing this up. "At the Adlon."

"The *Adlon*?" For a moment, her expression was guarded. Then her features showed recollection. "Ah, during the Games."

"Yes, the last day. You were with someone, in the lobby. I wanted so much to come over to greet you."

Eva's gentle eyes turned deep gray.

"It was *very* hard not to," I said. "I felt terrible. But you were both occupied with something—it seemed best not to interrupt."

She reached across the table for my hand. "You are always so thoughtful. Just like your aunt. You understand exactly." She opened the leather clutch purse on her lap, drew out a silver cigarette case and offered me a smoke. "There were plans. Ones I was really looking forward to. But then," she paused to light my cigarette, then her own, "well, things worked out differently. It was a difficult day."

"You looked so beautiful." *And so sad*, my thoughts added.

"Even when I was unhappy?"

"Absolutely. We should all look that good under duress."

She adjusted her diminutive cup in its saucer. "Well, thank you. It helps to know one can make a good appearance, whatever the circumstances."

"If it's a man who changed those plans, I think he has a lot to answer for." I clapped a hand over my mouth. "Oh, I am far too blunt."

Her grin was agreeable, "No, my dear Fräulein, you are quite right. He did disappoint me. But it was a very busy time for him."

She tucked the cigarette case and lighter back into her bag. "I'm glad that day's behind me." After a deep pull on her cigarette, she asked, "Do you sometimes find it challenging? Adjusting your life to theirs?" then added, "I hope that is not too personal."

"Oh, not at all," I assured her. Without the chance to see Mutti or Aunt Paula, there'd been no one to talk with this way, and I'd missed it. Most of Erich's cohorts are men, and the few women I've met in Berlin seem to function more like men.

"That's why I've come away, to think about things." I tapped the ash of my cigarette against the porcelain ashtray. "This other man ... well, some things are making life very confusing."

Her glance invited more before she turned to exhale smoke away to the side.

"A lot is going to change, soon. For him. For us."

"Is that difficult?" Her tone was sympathetic.

"It's—he feels he has a mission. As if he's called to it."

She nodded. "That sounds very familiar."

"Which means he may never have the kind of time for me I'd hoped for."

Eva was shaking her head vigorously from side to side. When she started to speak, her voice caught in her throat, like a sob. She looked away for several seconds, as though composing herself, then said, "What you say exactly describes my own situation." Her tone showed disbelief. "Do you love him very much?"

"Sometimes, I think there's no way I can love him enough to ever change this. To have a life with him."

"I understand. I do," she said. "And there's often so much they can't tell us."

"Or won't."

"*Cannot*," she emphasized.

I drained my coffee and Eva reached for the silver pot and refilled my cup.

"I'm so terrified about it all. Especially for him," I said. "I feel selfish. Because all I want is to go away together and have him to myself." I'd said more than I planned to. As though I'd finally found a place to let it out and couldn't stop.

There were tears in her eyes, though her voice was calm. "You must find the way that allows you to be in his life. It often means knowing less than we'd like. Focusing on the parts of life we *can* share with them. Their world can be so different from ours."

"Does that ever make you angry?"

She didn't answer right away. "It has," she said finally. "But if I must sometimes be alone, perhaps even more than I am with him, then that's the price."

She raised her chin, as though trying to reinforce the resolve in her words.

"Are there times when you're not sure you can bear it?" I asked.

Her features tightened. She cleared her throat with a small sound and gave a meaningful look, as though I ought to understand. "Yes, sometimes it can feel desperate. And desperate measures may even be called for. It wasn't long ago I thought I couldn't go on. Even … made that known.

"Now, such a short time later, things are better than I could ever have imagined. That's why the portrait means so much to me. He made time for it, when so much is demanded of him. It shows me that he cares, that I'm an important part of his life."

"You're willing to have it this way? Even though you can't see him very often?"

She nodded as the waiter approached with rapid steps and set our plates before us with a flourish. "It's what our mothers had to do, during the war," she said after he left.

My mother's wartime experience undoubtedly differed from hers. Mutti was in England, and my father's officer status and age kept him safely on British soil.

"We have to meet—rise to—the challenge," Eva said. The words sounded like a borrowed slogan. She craned forward and lowered her voice. "That's how we offer what we really have to give, nicht? They believe it is one thing, when we know it's another—something much more important. We give what they don't even know their heart wants. Let them think what they will, while we do what we must."

I recalled Erich's words about the convincing impression you had to create with the Nazis in order to do the work of the Resistance. Women do much the same: appear complicit, and execute our plans from behind that ruse. It all just takes us away from the truth, and ourselves; our feelings.

"You said something that day at Herr Hoffmann's about taking our opportunities wherever we find them," I remembered.

She nodded. "And keeping a positive view is important, too."

"I worry there'll be even fewer opportunities, soon. When there are already so few, for us."

"What do you mean? They're just beginning, for you!" she protested. "With your skills? In *Berlin*? Your work could even bring *intrigue*!" Her tone made the word sound like one of life's most sought-after goals.

It was true that many of the documents that crossed my desk were marked "STRENG GEHEIM—Top Secret." But that's inflated Nazi fuss about what's usually insignificant. You can assess people's support for the Reich by how seriously they take such things. Of course, even non-supporters are careful to at least appear concerned.

I wasn't sure Eva understood what I really meant. I wasn't sure I understood it myself. It was that unwelcome feeling I'd always had that there'd never be enough for us, because *we* weren't enough. Weren't allowed to be. That the most you could hope for was to find the better scraps of a portioning in which you had no say. To maximize those crumbs—and to be very careful never to let it show that that's what you were doing.

I've never yet known a man who believes that he is obliged to act this way. Surely, I can't be the only woman who feels a burning rage about it?

Exactly what had Eva settled for, that she was always insisting was so good? It wasn't happiness that I felt from her, but some sort of compromise. Of course, perhaps she saw it as the way to maximize her own limited opportunities.

"We have to know our priorities and make our decisions accordingly." Now that we'd finished eating, she reached for her cigarettes again and offered me one. "It may mean we must give up what's important to us for what we decide is most important, and forgo the things we'd hoped for," she continued. "But then opportunities come that are so very much better." Her eyes lit again. "That's why I have a little house of my own now. Perhaps you'd like to come see it?"

I glanced at my watch, suddenly nervous as I remembered Aunt Paula. "I'd love to. But I have to return to Berlin tonight, and still need to find my aunt."

I inhaled deeply from my cigarette, as if it might calm my rising anxiety. I'd been so spontaneous about this trip, never bothering to let Aunt Paula know—intent on fleeing a life where everything kept changing too fast. Coming back to Munich always felt like coming home, though not one where I ever seemed to be allowed to stay for very long.

"I was desperate to get away, just like that day we met on the train," I told her.

Eva grinned. "Two little escapees, we were! Must you really go back so soon?"

"I have to be at work tomorrow." In the Foreign Office's demanding atmosphere weekday absences were considered indulgent, thus inexcusable, unless you were literally too sick to make it in to work. I couldn't afford to lose the job. I'd barely survived on translation work before I'd been hired.

"Let me come with you, show you the way to your aunt's," Eva offered.

"Oh, you needn't go to such trouble."

"It's right on my way home. Then we can visit some more, and I can wish your aunt a happy birthday."

As we stood to leave, she seemed very small, despite her high heels.

"I'm glad my bad planning has brought this time with you."

She laughed. "Me, too. And please, whenever you see me again, no matter the circumstances, promise you'll always come say hello."

―――――――――

All those years, you knew, Anna realized as she studied the sheet of little photos that Eva had captured of Peggy in Hoffmann's studio. Her mother had sat under that portrait of Eva in the dining room knowing exactly who'd drawn it. But she hadn't known on that Munich morning when she ran into Eva.

When had she found out? Had Eva finally *told* her who her lover was?

Yet how could she? Everything Anna had read confirmed that she'd been expressly forbidden by Hitler to disclose her relationship with him to anyone outside his inner circle. Even there, inexplicably, the couple maintained an elaborate charade to appear as associates, rather than lovers.

In each leap-year encounter, Peggy and Eva were on the verge of transition, and in this 1936 visit, after all of the uncertainty that he'd put her through, Eva was soaring on the triumph of finally being the Führer's favorite. Peggy sensed the changes to come as Erich joined those working against Hitler.

The women didn't know that their men had opposing ambitions because their confiding only explored personal struggles, never more incriminating details. But why had Peggy never even mentioned her friendship with Eva?

Hannes, raised amidst post-war destruction, understood. "She had to distance herself from it after the war. Otherwise, she could have been seen as a Nazi sympathizer—even sent to prison. The fact she had worked in the Foreign Office could have implicated her even further, once the records of its activity were made public after the war. Later, she probably wanted to protect your family from the stigma that a friendship with Hitler's mistress would bring. Plus, you say your father hated him."

A lot had been changing for Eva and Peggy when their paths crossed in Munich that day, and a lot was changing for Anna as she embarked on following the trail of their friendship. When she finally told Hannes about her decision to fly alone, he first seemed confused, even alarmed.

"But the plans are made—it's all arranged! In first class, so you can be comfortable." He paused, as though stopping himself. "I know you said to wait."

As his voice trailed off, his expression shifted to uncertainty. Then hurt. Anna both saw and felt these as she watched him try to mask them. He stood in her mother's kitchen looking as though he didn't know what to do next; like an anxious boy who thinks he has done something wrong.

"I don't ... understand this."

Anna instantly recalled that day with Peggy near the seashore. Sipping lemonade in a circle of dark faces, she'd heard a man say these exact words to her mother, in much the same way.

"I'm not sure that I can help you understand."

His gaze seemed to be retreating from her.

"This is something I know I must somehow get through alone," she said.

His expression was guarded, his tone flat. "Does this mean that you prefer to be on your own, in Germany?"

"Oh! Not at all!" She hurried toward where he was standing so stiffly and put her hand on his arm. "Hannes, this has nothing to do with you, or anyone. I can't wait to be with you there, and meet your family. It's only for this first part, which sometimes, I still can't imagine getting through. But my heart tells me I need to do it this way."

His expression softened, along with his posture as he inclined toward her. "You can still fly first class," he suggested, leading her to explain why she felt she needed to revisit the same scene she kept seeing in her flashbacks. "I think it's my only bridge away from these demons."

At last, that aching vulnerability of hurt left his face. For anguished seconds it had very nearly made her change her mind.

"Of course, I want you to do what you need to." His eyes searched hers. "But please understand. After all that has happened, I need to know you are safe."

Anna did feel safe during the flight, and though he wasn't there with her, Hannes had played a big part in that.

She had time to reread one more chapter of Peggy's manuscript.

The next encounter also came four years after the previous one, yet the visits seemed worlds apart. While the two friends were still relatively carefree when they caught up with each other at the Bayerischer Hof, by the fall of 1940, they were immersed in the dangerous uncertainties of war.

FELLOW TRAVELLERS

The Whole Sky to Fly In

CHAPTER 15

Platterhof Hotel, near Berchtesgaden
18 October 1940

It was dreamlike riding up the Obersalzberg yesterday after all of Berlin's shattered mess.

Just outside Berchtesgaden, we began halting at a series of guard shacks on the ascent of what's now called "Hitler's mountain." This was pristine countryside when Aunt Paula brought me here ten years ago after my graduation. The locals treated us like neighbors. Most have lost their pastoral homes now as the "Führer Zone" spreads like a cancer on this hillside with acres of barbed wire and checkpoints to examine your papers and search your bags—and your person, on unlucky days.

My two co-workers had traveled down ahead of me so I rode alone in the long car that fetched me at the Berchtesgaden station. They're here, as I am, for a meeting Hitler will host. But they're really here to scout his Alpine environs without suspicion.

I rode up the mountain's gauntlet of hairpin turns and precipitous drop-offs with two SS men who barely spoke. That's their style, unless they're drunk, when they're talkative as magpies and sentimental as grandmothers—even prone to gossip. The Resistance relies on this.

I hate what's happened to this beautiful mountain. On my last visit, Aunt Paula and I stayed at the Türkenhof inn right beside Hitler's house. I don't even want to think about this upcoming meeting. Like everything these days, it will require acting some rehearsed role, because spontaneity is downright dangerous.

Still, I'm happy to come away, especially since the surprising telegram two nights ago, advising me that Eva could meet me for dinner where I'm staying up here at the Platterhof Hotel. I can't imagine how she knew my plans, or why she's even here, but I'm more thrilled about this than I am about the food.

Which is saying a lot because back in Berlin, it's all I think about: what there will be to eat, and how I'll find it. Since Italian restaurants still don't require ration coupons I load up on pasta when I can afford to. Meat's so hard to find—I was appalled to discover I'd recently feasted on donkey Schnitzel. In the cafeteria at work, they coin lofty names for positively revolting dishes. "Vegetable Mélange" is linear slabs of red and white cabbage and potatoes with a pitiful teaspoon of mustard sauce on top.

But at least it's available. Food shopping is like an unpaid second job—standing in line two hours for a clothespin-sized piece of cheese. Fortunately yogurt's not rationed and I can find it in Berlin. I now socialize with people I don't even like for the prospect of a meal with protein. Who knew hunger would be so humbling?

Then there's trying to keep warm. And, since the bombings started in August, trying to stay alive, to go on living—even sleep at night. Not just because the nightly poundings interrupt our sleep so often, but because of what you see in the streets afterward the next day, and then can't stop seeing in your mind.

There were times last week when I felt too exhausted to even get out of bed when the sirens sounded, and I'm on the ground floor, a much shorter trip to the cellar than my neighbors'. I'm tired of trying to "bathe" only twice a week in the paltry three inches of water that regulations allow. Weary of sleep that counts for nothing when it's interrupted so often, though there are advantages to fatigue. When truly numb with it, I almost don't feel hungry, the way you can only feel one kind of pain at a time.

More exhausting than the physical discomfort is how we have to constantly choose our words as if the whole world is listening. When the subject involves war, or the regime, it's vital to sound pleasantly curious, never critical or defeatist. Erich recommends adopting a mild, interested tone and letting others do the talking.

"Conversations" are mixtures of half-truths, talking at cross-purposes, and a cryptic code of creating one impression while masking something else. In the Resistance world, "Give your uncle my best, when he visits Tuesday," means an older Jewish man will be smuggled through your town that day and need your help.

Even family members spy on each other; neighbors step forward like loyal dogs to assume this odious role. During a seemingly innocuous exchange with a woman in my building, I realized she was trying to draw out information about another neighbor. "I don't know a thing about her," I told her with the satisfying glare of a false smile.

Always cordial, though often slightly reserved, Eva surprised me with vigorous kisses on both cheeks when she arrived at the Platterhof, like someone home from a long journey relieved to let down her guard.

I wasn't sure how to respond to her inquiries. Would she want to hear about Berlin, when here in Berchtesgaden it's as if that disintegrating world doesn't exist? Whatever would she think of the cycle of eating and sleeping I've fallen into since arriving here, interspersed with long spans of doing nothing, simply because I can?

I did talk about my Kindertransport experience, though not at first, and not in specific terms. I said nothing about how my mother's beau, Herr "Nadelkissen," shocked the daylights out of me when it turned out that he was helping the Resistance—and Jewish families. The perception others had of him as a supporter of the SS, for whom he sews handsome uniforms, was proving very useful indeed.

Mutti asked me to go with him as chaperone on a weekend hiking trip for teenagers. Minutes after we crossed into France's Alsace region and stopped to rest, he took me aside and informed me quietly that several youths would wander off soon to be met by others, who would help them continue their journey into safety outside of Germany. I should act as though I noticed nothing.

At first, I didn't understand. Then I didn't believe him, and thought it some bizarre test of my loyalty to the Reich.

"It's one way that we can help the parents." He gestured toward my wrist. "They're the ones who gave us your lovely watch, though I've never wanted anything for the little—far too little—we are able to do."

I stared at him until stinging tears seized hold of me as intensely as if ripped free.

"Take some time for yourself, child," he said softly. "I'm sorry I couldn't tell you, that we can't say good-bye to them. You've helped do something very important."

Then he moved off, perhaps as much to draw attention from me as from those who'd leave us soon. All day, those same tears continued to ambush me. So much was not as I thought; so much that others were risking bravely in a world gone mad.

I didn't hesitate to say yes when, during a visit that Erich and I made to my mother last spring, Herr Niemeyer asked whether I'd travel to England as one of the escorts for several hundred Jewish children.

During the conversation, Erich inadvertently called him Herr Nadelkissen. After a moment's lapse and a look at my steadily reddening face, Herr N. burst out in laughter and Mutti squeezed his arm and exclaimed, "That's a perfect name for a softy like you!" I was mortified, but he doesn't seem to mind, and we all—even Mutti—call him that, now.

My task as escort would be risky, he advised, even if the Reich had agreed to allow it, and Erich concurred. I wanted to feel a part of the dangerous work Erich does, even if I wish he'd stop doing it. For two sleepless days, I trained my attention on the children assigned to me, tried to follow those impossible instructions to be kind, but also distant, so they wouldn't become attached to us.

I felt their terror in my own heart when those brutes in leather coats boarded the train at the Dutch border barking orders. At *children*, for God's sake. This intrusion was cushioned by kind local women who passed bread and cocoa through the windows.

There are such idiots parading around with conferred authority, now. Most of the real *Untermensch* are walking around in SS uniforms, convinced that woman are just waiting for them to take them off. I caught one stealing looks at me as I had a smoke in the ferry's canteen once we were finally on the night crossing from Holland to Harwich.

Moments later, he made his way over and asked, as though it were the best line he could think of, "Why do you travel with this trash?"

My gaze bored into his. I flashed a tight smile. "Oh, there are many ways to keep what's worth keeping, and to get rid of what is not."

So often, these days, my words infer one thing when I intend its exact opposite. I knew he'd mistake my meaning.

"Where will you sleep tonight?" he asked then. "Surely, not with them?" His tone showed his horror at the very prospect. Was he about to offer himself as an alternative?

I glared back, shook my head as though I couldn't have heard him correctly. "Surely," I mimicked his words, "your mother never taught you it was acceptable to ask such questions, especially of a daughter of the Reich?"

I knew I'd hit precisely the mark I'd aimed for when a port-wine color overtook his face as quickly as if it had been splashed there.

Later, when I joined the children in our cramped sleeping quarters, I lay awake as the rough seas tossed the ship. Lotte, who at thirteen was older than the others, was also awake. Tears rolled down my face as we lay in the dark and she described the changes that had descended on her life in Vienna overnight. All public places were suddenly off-limits. She'd seen a boy she knew hurled through a shop window. One afternoon, she waited hours as none of the classmates she'd invited for her birthday came, then forced herself to choke down the cake her mother had baked, when all she wanted to do was cry.

She was among those we left at a camp in England where the children would wait to be "chosen" by British families, like pets, or orphans. The hardest part, for me, came once they finally reached safety, and I saw how it was really going to be for them; or would never be. What they'll endure far outweighs any good I might believe I've done.

I found the courage to ask Father to sponsor some of them. He'd kept going on about how England was the one country willing to take them; that America only talked about it endlessly before letting the proposal die in committee. He thought I was coming back to England to stay, of course. I never told him that the escorts were required to return to Germany, or the transports would be discontinued.

I'd do anything I could to help those children. Each time I remember their frightened faces, those numbers on cardboard signs around their necks, I can hardly breathe for the ache in my heart. The one small act of decency I may have managed in a world gone immoral, I did with duplicity. I don't know that I've ever felt such hate and anger and sadness all at once as I did during those days. I refused to feel fear.

Father provided enough money to sponsor three children, all from the same family. At the station, their parents were trying to summarize the kind of guidance they'd thought they had a lifetime to impart. "Learn English," nearly every parent was urging, adding, with a heartbreaking sort of emphasis, "And we'll follow soon."

I can't imagine what it must be like to send those children off, and never know. Yet it's just what my own parents did, sent me away. "So you can have a better life," Mutti always said. "But I like your life," I tried to tell her. At least the part she managed to save for herself.

"We'll outlive this," she keeps saying since the war started. In the same way she used to say, "We'll outlast him, child," after she and Father separated.

"Do you enjoy your work?" Eva asked as we sat in the evening air.

I longed to talk, tell her everything. "I also worked with children, for a while."

"How lovely!" She broke into her wide, sweet smile. "As a teacher?"

I paused before I said, "I helped with the Kindertransport."

I decided to set the words out boldly as my barometer. Either we'd be able to go forward from here together, or not. I needed to know.

"You mean—"

"To England. I was asked to help because I have a British passport."

I waited for her reaction.

Her eyes widened. "How brave you are! As brave as any soldier."

I was trying to gauge how much of a door this had opened. Then the memory came tumbling out, that scene from the Frankfurt Bahnhof burned into my heart like a brand. As we'd waited at the station, the juxtaposition of the city's Christmas decorations and all those children being sent away had seemed impossibly cruel.

"We were on a train, ready to depart, when I saw a father reach through the window of a carriage and pull his daughter back out through it," I told her. He had run onto the platform, where the parents weren't even supposed to be, to try to retrieve her.

"It was like a birth." I heard Eva's intake of breath as I described this. "She nearly slipped under the train. He was clutching her against him as it left the station."

I started to speak again and my words broke off when tears stung my eyes like sharp light. I didn't know exactly what I cried for—that child and her likely fate, trapped as she was in Germany now, or how abandoned my own heart had felt.

"To be loved—and wanted. *That* much," I said finally.

Tears glistened in Eva's eyes.

I thought of my own father, furious I hadn't stayed in England. I said nothing about how that man in the station had sealed his child's fate, as surely as if he'd let her fall under the train's wheels. Whatever faces her here, I know it isn't good.

"My father offered another ultimatum," I told Eva.

"You saw him?"

"Perhaps for the last time, now we're at war. My German will come in handy there, when they need to learn it." I'd said this reflexively, the way I often did now, to cover myself in this treacherous place our world had become.

I didn't mean it. I hated the thought. Living under the Nazis was like pretending you like someone simply to avoid suspicion. I was still here because this was my home. No one was going to take that away, though I had no doubts they might destroy it.

But my feelings toward the Allies were confusing, now, too. What did they imagine they were doing, dropping bombs on civilians—sleeping, helpless people?

And Erich ... I couldn't possibly leave Germany now. Though I hardly ever know where he is, at least I know he's here. Somewhere.

"I had to make a decision, about where my home is," I told Eva.

"It is never easy," she nodded her understanding. "When you must decide with your heart, and others don't understand. But it is the right thing."

When she smiled at me the way she did then, I saw all the generosity I'd first seen in her sixteen-year-old face.

"So much is not as we thought it would be." She seemed restless as she said this, and a little preoccupied, her eyes roving toward the doors at the entrance.

She apologized then, and reached for her camera to begin winding a roll of film into it. "I regret that it's always possible that my work may call me away. But I can't tell you how happy it makes me to see you sitting here." Smiling, she indicated the plate on which I hadn't left a crumb. "And getting something decent to eat. I'm so sorry about how it is up north. We hear it's awful."

Who, I wondered, was "we"?

For the first time, I detected there was something she hid away, like a dangerous secret. A life not her own that she tried not to think about, while distracting herself with other things. As we talked about clothes and films and she sipped another cognac, she said, "It's much more pleasant to focus on these things."

Sunset had turned the sky into an indigo field feathered with long wisps of coral clouds. It was warm for October, so she'd reserved us a table on the Platterhof's terrace.

"I love it up here, because you see so much of the sky," she said. "As long as I can see it, get out under it, I feel free. No matter what may happen."

"And how is your work?" I asked. "You seemed such a natural at Hoffmann's."

Her expression was thoughtful. "I'm lucky that the photography is my war service. It lets me be near my man—as near as any woman can be to … a soldier, now."

She glanced away at the sky again. "Sometimes, it keeps me here for weeks. Other times, I travel to Berlin, though I never stay long."

Her look seemed very direct as she asked, "Didn't it once seem that there would be the whole sky to fly in? Now, I feel like a bird that must always return to a cage."

I wasn't sure how to respond. My work sometimes kept me captured that way, especially since the war began last fall, but I sensed this wasn't what she meant.

"I used to travel … Italy, Norway, Iceland," she listed them off with a tone of longing. "It's freedom I didn't appreciate enough, before. Now, with the war, everything's changed. At least in Munich there's still some normalcy."

She accepted one of my cigarettes. After I lit it for her, she stared down into her glass. "There's so much I have to wait to know." Her words were tinged with something like melancholy. "Yet we must all make sacrifices now. As you have."

I felt as though she kept beginning to share something, then had second thoughts, perhaps deciding that it was territory she couldn't wander into any farther, and serving the topic back to me. This was something Erich often did, too, as though eager to talk, but unable to find a safe subject.

I let silence fall as we sat under the sky.

When she spoke again, her speech was faster, as though forced; her voice higher as she talked about my bravery and that of everyday citizens. Though I can't explain why, it seemed she was trying to distract herself.

Then, almost shyly, she wondered about the bombings.

My words had come easily so far, but I felt sick at the prospect of trying to describe the raw terror of air raids. How I lost all sense of time in the darkness, when it seemed the bombs would keep falling forever. Couldn't stop thinking about how trapped I was, how many had already narrowly missed me, like an oxygen supply being used up.

The air pressure was so awful I was sure my ear drums would rupture. Or feared I'd be buried alive, wishing for death, as I'd heard voices say when they called out from ruined buildings where no one could reach them. How could I describe what it felt like to walk past something like that and do nothing? Be able to do nothing. Walk on and try to work in the comparative safety of my office, which, because of the damage to streets and tram lines, I now walked more than an hour to reach.

I told her only a watered-down version of this, and agreed that many were being very brave, but denied being one of them.

"And your man?" Eva asked finally.

"Well, you know how it is now. He can't tell me much of anything."

"How *well* I know." She reared back, cigarette waving in the air. "Was there ever so much secrecy? It wasn't like this in the first war. But we were children then."

Her eyes misted over again. While she seemed self-possessed much of the time, her eyes instantly shone with emotion whenever it descended on her.

"Sometimes, I go to the country, where my grandparents lived, where I spent wonderful summers as a girl," she said. "Each time, I look forward to going because of what I remember from the past. But once I'm there, it's so different—like searching for what can never be found. Each time, I promise myself I won't do it again."

She shook her head. "No one's left, only the graves. And memories. Those things we think will always last are suddenly gone, and it almost feels as if they never were, or were simply a dream."

A chorus of voices was rising around us. Someone had started a record on a phonograph, a song from one of Zarah Leander's films: "Eine Frau wird erst schön durch die Liebe—*A woman only becomes beautiful through love.*"

We joined in. Eva's voice, whose Bavarian accent was thick in speech, almost like a lisp, was smooth and sweet when she sang, as though its natural inclination was to speak in song, like a bird.

As the music came to an end, my two co-workers from the Foreign Office were suddenly beside our table singing along. When I introduced them, each bowed low to Eva and kissed her hand, which seemed to please her. Neither is especially handsome, but they have excellent manners, something I know she appreciates.

They'd been called back to Berlin, having notified our boss that there'll be no meeting with the Führer after all, but I am permitted to stay on another day or so.

Eva looked amused, knowing what good news this was for me, though she may have wondered why I wasn't more disappointed about not meeting Hitler.

I've simply been a "beard" on this mission, I realized, to reinforce its credibility as Foreign-Office business. Hitler's whims will provide my co-workers' excuse. He's always canceling or changing plans, though in this case there never actually were any.

My not knowing that was an asset, as I'd talked about nothing else at work for days, making the ruse appear all the more genuine. The presence of several foreign dignitaries visiting here this week provided the foil for the resisters at the Foreign Office to construct this ploy. Perhaps those dignitaries were why Eva was here with her camera.

My co-workers had gotten a close look at Hitler's Berghof and its surroundings, intelligence they'd pass on through a convoluted network of people many of whom would never meet, or even know each other's names. This, it seems, is the best and safest way to be of help, these days.

I certainly wasn't going to complain about the chance to languish a little longer in my round of eating, reading, sleeping—and trying not to feel guilty about how awful it was back home. Now, I'd have time to walk alpine trails and breathe mountain air deep into my lungs after Berlin's shroud of smoke that never washes out of my hair or clothes.

Another day of the Platterhof's endless banquet. It's not like they didn't know there was a war, and rationing, yet the lavish spreads offered so many meats, succulent fruits and vegetables, caviar, champagne—even chocolate.

Here I was, obsessed with food, while Eva seemed thinner than ever in the midst of this plenty—anxiously so. She'd only picked at her meal, and the bones of her shoulder blades poked like wings against her woolen shirtdress when I hugged her.

As she held me for longer than usual, I wondered whether I would see her again, though I ponder this with every person I care about these days.

"When it's over—and God willing, it won't be long, now—try to come here, if you can," she said. "All you'd have to do is ask for me. Someone will find me, and let me know you've come."

I nodded, surprised. Did she spend as much time thinking about life beyond this war as I did? This, I knew, we could not talk about. Not safely. And not here.

"I *know* we'll see each other again." Her tone was uncompromising, as though any alternative was unthinkable. "Let's plan for it to be here. Afterward." Her dove grey eyes searched mine. "To celebrate," she said, raising her chin.

She reached into her purse and pulled out a powder-blue calling card with her initials embossed in a Kleeblatt above her name. Uncapping a fountain pen, she leaned on the table to write on the back of it, then handed the card to me.

"If you get to Munich, you can reach me at this address. Or write me there."

I thanked her as I took it. "How I wish I could extend the same to you, in Berlin. But I honestly don't know how much longer I may even have an address."

She took hold of my hands. "Come to me, especially if you lose your home. I'll always be happy to see you. And to help you, in any way I can."

Then, far too soon, she was gone.

I missed her for hours afterward, and slept very poorly. All night, I kept waking, as though I'd been overhearing a conversation—or more accurately, the sense of a group of people captured and held by one voice speaking that never seemed to stop.

CHAPTER 16

A s nearly 300 passengers disembarked with their minds on the next stage of their journey, Anna re-encountered the sense of urgency an arrival often brings after long hours of captivity in a plane. Munich had become a destination in her mind, an end in itself. Now that she'd arrived, it felt like a beginning filled with unknowns.

Her limbs seemed weighted with exhaustion as she squinted in the sunlight streaming through the terminal's broad expanses of glass. She needed to focus past the fog enveloping her mind as the overnight flight's sleepless hours caught up with her.

She moved through passport control, retrieved her suitcase, and emerged into the arrivals hall, where a throng of waiting faces pressed along the cordoned-off exit lane. Many held signs, or called out to those they were there to meet. Her aloneness felt acute.

It's what I have to get used to.

Glancing around for some indication of where to go next, she turned back from the sea of faces as someone stepped toward her from her side of the barrier. Directly in front of her at eye-level was a hand-lettered sign with her name on it.

When Hannes appeared from behind it, his beautiful smile made her stagger back with a cry of disbelief.

"You never said I couldn't be here to meet you!" His clear eyes shone with excitement, while her own felt glued to the inside of the back of her head.

She fell into the arms he closed around her as he kissed both her cheeks. "Oh, *Hannes!*" She hugged him tightly. "I'm so glad to see you!" She drew back to look at him. "But how can you possibly be here, when you were there to see me off?"

"Traveling light." He gestured toward his single carry-on. "I had my luggage sent on ahead a few days ago." His eyes twinkled. "Flying first class helped, too."

She shook her head as she stared at him.

"I kept one of the tickets and used it myself."

"On the same plane."

Nodding, he looked away toward the floor as a smile overtook his face.

"And never said a word—you trickster!"

"How could I surprise you, otherwise? You were so stubborn, I was afraid you wouldn't come at all, if I told you." He stepped nearer, touched her cheek, and breathed, "I *needed* to be nearby. I hope you can understand. Everything went all right?"

She nodded, smiling up at him. That flight attendant who'd come to check on her by name had surely been his doing. "Aside from my useless attempts to sleep."

"Ah, but you could have relaxed in such comfort!"

"I know. You're well-rested, I suppose?"

"Thoroughly refreshed, thank you, and at your service. My mother can't wait to see you—and Nati, too, of course. Her flight from Rome is delayed, but she says we can use the car that she left here.

"I've told them they'll need to be patient a little longer before they see you, though. Because—with your permission—I'm appointing myself your chauffeur for the 'Eva Braun Memorial Tour.'"

Anna felt more confused than ever.

"Only an abbreviated version, I'm afraid, what we can cover between Munich and Berchtesgaden in the next two days or so. I have meetings at the university after that. And only if you *want* to," he added. "Perhaps this is too much spontaneity."

"I'd love it! Will you be my interpreter, too? Oh, I've got a hotel reservation—"

"Nati will take care of that. Naturally, I'll help with translation, but I've been thinking, Anna. I'd like to speak German to you now, to help you warm up."

"Even with jet lag?"

He switched to German, as he replied, "Answer in English, if you prefer. But I think this will be good practice."

Anna felt something near her heart slip. It was so different, hearing him speak this way. It evoked an old, confusing mix of anticipation laced with anxiety, as though everything would suddenly start moving very fast, and she wouldn't be able to keep up.

"Yes," she said finally. "But please be patient with me. I'll try." Her voice sounded young, small.

"Anna, don't *worry*." He circled her shoulders in a reassuring hug, then changed back to English, as he reached for her suitcase. "There won't be any quizzes or grades!"

Outside the terminal, he led her to a bench. "Relax here in the sunshine. Mutti says it's been like early fall, very beautiful. I'll go get the car."

His sentences had already become a cobbling together of English and German that Anna had to strain to understand. She rested back on the bench, watching scores of bustling travelers in their impeccable business attire.

Hearing German brought those same feelings that it sometimes had with Peggy—as though she might suddenly do something wrong. She recalled being afraid to be caught speaking German with her mother, after her father had forbidden it. When she was 13, she'd waited with him at the airport as her mother left for Germany. Anna had already visited there twice with Peggy, but her mother had gone alone that time.

"You're not German," Rod had said angrily. "There's no reason for you to go."

She'd been afraid during those two weeks that her mother wouldn't come back, had left her alone with him forever. He'd probably been afraid of the same thing that night he'd climbed into her bed beside her.

The emotion that erupted in her now made it difficult to breathe, as gray haze began clouding her vision like a shroud. How had she forgotten all this?

Because she'd wanted to forget. Only the scar on her wrist carried its indelible reminder in a faint white line. She fumbled in her purse for a tissue as tears welled with choking force.

Seconds later, Hannes drove up to the curb in a white BMW station wagon.

"Anna," he said, when he saw her face. "What's wrong?"

She waved a hand at him and turned to pick up her carry-on from the bench. "I'm fine. Just glad to be here."

"Perhaps my plans aren't the best thing." He looked doubtful. "Would you rather wait? Rest a little?"

"Not a chance. I'm far too excited. But tell me about this car." She pointed toward it, eager to shift the subject. A sign on the passenger door read: "Sankt Antonius Bäckerei" beneath an image of a sweet-faced saint cradling a tiny sparrow in his hand.

"Our transportation comes free of charge, as long as we don't mind being a rolling advertisement."

"Now, I am truly in Deutschland! Does it smell like a bakery inside, too?"

He grinned, and opened her door for her. "It will. Soon enough."

He began with a drive through Munich's Schwabing district where Eva Braun first met Hitler at Hoffmann's photography shop. Her birthplace, a modest apartment building on Isabella Strasse, was just a few blocks from the family's second, larger apartment. Hannes's mother had a bakery on the same street so they stopped to buy rolls and pastries and some plums and creamy Camenbert from a neighboring market.

An hour's drive through rolling hills and picturesque villages brought them to Beilngries, where Eva's maternal grandparents had lived. After a stroll through its narrow streets to find the house where Eva had spent childhood summers, they were back in the car. Hannes urged Anna to rest during the ride to their next stop on the Austrian border.

Only a bridge across the River Inn separated the sleepy town of Simbach from Braunau, Austria. During her days at the convent school, Eva had lived literally within sight of her future lover's birthplace. No one at the Kloster remembered her now, though her notoriety brought many curious visitors to its door. Afterward, as Anna stood with Hannes on the train station's platform, she imagined her mother, so young, and lonely, recognizing that same loneliness in Eva as she reached out to her.

"This is where it all began," said Hannes. "Imagine if either had taken a different train—or your mother kept her original plans, back in Salzburg."

They found a café and stopped for coffee to fortify themselves for the last and longest leg of their trip, the ride south to Berchtesgaden. When Anna finally fell into bed that night, her dreamless sleep lasted only until 4, long before any sign of sunrise. She felt in a state of suspended animation, as though she hadn't fully arrived here yet.

Hannes had arranged for them to stay two nights at the Hotel Türkenhof. The balcony of Anna's room looked down toward where Hitler's Berghof had stood on the adjacent parcel of land, now an overgrown woodlot that showed few traces of its former identity beyond a remnant of the retaining wall and sections of crumbling foundation.

The views were the same ones Eva's camera had captured, what Peggy had looked out at fifty-five years before. Any evidence of the manmade "Thousand Year Reich" had now been erased by man and nature in mere decades while the surrounding mountains endured unchanged, a sovereignty Anna found comforting.

The previous evening, she and Hannes had sat in the Türkenhof's cozy lounge while the proprietor, accustomed to curious visitors, described the impression Eva Braun had made on her family in the 1930s. This woman had been about twelve when her mother had visited with Eva on the train from Berchtesgaden to Munich.

The mother had returned home, gathered her family together, and emphasized, especially to her children: "No matter what you may hear about Fräulein Braun, I found her to be bright and thoughtful. She also has excellent manners, something we see too little of these days. She was kind and friendly to me, when others barely spoke beyond the grunt of overfed pigs. Greet her warmly. Show courtesy when you see her."

The mother may have made this effort because on the "Berg," as Hitler's inner circle called this mountain, many in that circle treated Eva shabbily. Anna remembered her own mother's visit with her on the train, and Eva's assertion that the kindness that Peggy had shown would be returned to her. Perhaps it had inspired Eva's own kindness.

Anna took out her mother's manuscript now to revisit scenes that had taken place on this very mountain.

The next one occurred the day after Peggy's visit with Eva at the Platterhof. If Rod had despised Hitler—disliked all that was German—he would have been shocked to know how close to the Third Reich's epicenter his wife had come.

FELLOW TRAVELLERS

A Very Dedicated Person

CHAPTER 17

Platterhof Hotel, Obersalzberg
19 October 1940

I woke from such a horror of a dream.

I seldom go near the Reich Chancellery in Berlin. I take pains to avoid it. But in the dream, I approached that monolith of a building as if I visit every day. Strode into its courtyard as if on a mission, then stopped when I saw the legs—an elegant pair beneath a dark skirt, wearing stockings but no shoes. A woman's body lay there. I couldn't see her face. The scene was riddled with bomb craters, like many parts of the city now. Flames were engulfing the legs in little waves.

Who knows which of the hotel's guests I woke with my screaming? Eva's face gazed at the body from the fire and asked, "How can I look so young, when I felt so old?"

Perhaps I dreamt of that place because of where I am, or my indulgence in all that rich food. Or maybe it's guilt about having another day in paradise, away from Berlin.

For my extra day of freedom, I planned to linger over breakfast but slept so long, it was after 11 when I got to the dining room. I was hoping for a window table with a sunny view of the mountains but the room was a frenetic symphony of clinking and clattering, and the maitre d' stuck me in a dark corner.

I had just poured my coffee when a young male voice shrilled, "Fräulein Peggy Adler?" from the entrance.

I turned as he reached my table in a handful of long strides. He wore the stiff uniform of Hitler's Leibstandarte: dark tunic, breeches, tall boots, and rounded helmet. All that was missing was the rifle customarily slung over the shoulder.

"Come with me, please."

Terror struck so hard, I couldn't speak—not even to ask where. Especially not that. It seemed incriminating. At last, I stammered, "I-I—"

"You have been requested for an interview," he said.

What kind of interview? I still couldn't find words to ask. Should I get my stenographer's pad? Or was this about questioning *me?*

"We have a car waiting outside." His tone was threaded with impatience, as though I were already taking too long, being too slow to understand. I'm surprised he didn't check his watch, tap his foot. His face had a youthful softness. He was perhaps 19 or 20. I thought of my brother, Peter.

I noticed the waiter at a neighboring table and glanced at my unfinished cup of coffee, as though it might offer some possibility of reprieve—he would insist I stay, since I hadn't finished.

He also seemed uneasy around the guard as he told me, "No trouble, Madam. We will keep your table for you."

But would I return to it?

Then I remembered my co-workers—and Erich—and blanched with fear as cold as the sweat that rose instantly on my neck. Hadn't I been careful enough, yesterday? Had I said too much? Had someone besides Eva been listening, or had my cohorts from the Foreign Office somehow been found out?

My mind raced to the worst of all possibilities: they'd been apprehended. I refused to let that thought take root. I claimed my mind back from it the way I tried to rescue my breath from panic in the air-raid shelter.

Appear unfazed and cooperative. I'd heard this tactic from Erich and other resisters, many times. If stopped or called in for any reason, seem slightly surprised, untroubled, and entirely willing to comply.

I reached to gather my things. I had only my purse, and the book I'd brought along. "Will we be going far?" I found courage to ask.

"It is right nearby."

When we reached the car, his brisk movements included a snap of his heels as he opened the door for me. Clearly, he wasn't going to manhandle me like a suspected criminal. Not yet.

I clambered into the back, toward the middle, and closer, of the two bench-like seats. The mammoth Mercedes had as many huge tires as a delivery truck. Its convertible top was down, and bright sun blinded my eyes.

The young uniform joined the driver in front. The car exited the Platterhof parking lot, made a hard left, and rolled down a sharp incline, though only a short distance.

Göring's house was somewhere off to the right, hidden by trees. I'd learned recently that beneath us was a burgeoning network of tunnels and bunkers under construction, a subterranean complex that those who dwelt above ground might not even know was there. Perhaps it would open up suddenly and swallow us all.

The car blocked the narrow road when it stopped at a guardhouse barely big enough for one person to stand inside. Behind it was the Hotel Türkenhof where Aunt Paula and I had stayed. It looked to be in use as barracks of some kind. Is that where they were taking me?

The uniform turned toward me. "Your papers, please."

I had them ready in anticipation of this, though I'd already gone through all the rigmarole of admission to the Führer Zone two days ago.

He took them, got out, and strode to the guard shack.

I'd been taken in for questioning once before, after I'd helped with the Kindertransport, summoned by a petty Nazi bureaucrat because of my dual citizenship. I'd dressed conservatively in a simple cotton skirt that hinted at a dirndl's lines, and a borrowed white blouse tied loosely at the throat so the top half of my décolletage was visible, while the rest remained virtuously concealed.

During my inquisitor's first burst of questions, I'd offered simple answers with a demeanor of complicit meekness. Finally, I'd evoked tears by imagining the inevitable fate of that child I'd seen pulled back through the train window into her father's arms. "Can't you imagine how thankful I am that Germany is my birthplace? That my mother is so faithful?" I nearly shouted at him.

More advice from those in the Resistance: act indignant, even insulted, at the very dishonor of being suspected of disloyalty. "Doesn't her returning to Germany, and my own, tell you everything about where our true loyalty lies?"

"There are many spies," he said. "Dual citizenship makes an excellent cover."

It does, indeed, my thoughts concurred.

"How can you even suggest such disgrace?" I tried to sound hurt. "When my British blood is disgrace enough?"

Then I'd covered my face in the refuge—and strategy—of sobs. It had been over-dramatic, but I wanted to leave no doubt in his mind. I used my best high German for these impassioned declarations. Once I saw he was softening, I lapsed into the Schwäbisch dialect I'd detected in his own speech, thanking God for my ear for nuance and language.

The inquisitor turned almost paternal, even invited me for coffee. I'd had to pretend disappointment, say I was expected home to help Mutti.

"You are the kind of maid who will assure the Fatherland's triumph!" he'd avowed, like the final line of some Wagnerian drama.

"Whatever you do, use the language of the current view, and mold it to your needs," Erich had advised me before I had accompanied those Jewish children to safety. It was the only way to deal with these fools. These very dangerous fools.

Whatever was taking so long? If my escorts and I had simply walked from the Platterhof, the interview might be over by now. Our stumbling down this road as steep as stairs would have been an undignified spectacle, but no more ridiculous than the three of us piling into this oversized car to crawl forward a few dozen meters.

The driver sat staring straight ahead, as though we were both inanimate objects. Hysteria tickled at my insides, ready to burst forth. *Oh, God, not here.*

At last, the guard—I'd come to think of him as "my" guard, we'd been in this together so long—was returning. He halted, when the soldier in the shack shouted to him.

"There *is* no luggage," he called back. "She stays at the Platterhof."

They'd never asked to inspect my purse, I realized suddenly. Adrenaline shot through me at the thought, probably just the sobering influence I needed before whatever awaited me. I couldn't even remember what was in it. I tried to be so careful, to never have anything with me that might endanger anyone.

The guard climbed back in and handed me my paperwork, but kept the special pass he'd been given. "All is in order," he said.

I was preparing to climb out when the driver started the engine and the car rolled further downhill a short distance. As it wound left at a curve and slowed for a turn, I realized what our destination must be.

I watched in disbelief as the Mercedes labored up the narrow drive toward the gleaming white building at the top. My mind was mobbed with a confusion of questions and thoughts. Was there going to be a press conference after all? Were there other special forces here who would question me? Why were they taking me to the *Berghof*?

Anxiety raced around inside me like a small, panicked animal as I gazed at the unreal vista of the surrounding mountains. I remembered what Eva had said, about the sky—that if you could see it, feel yourself out under it, you could always find freedom.

The car had barely come to a stop when another uniformed man, an adjutant, appeared at the bottom of a set of marble steps. He held the car door open for me, took the pass from the guard, and said politely, "Good afternoon, Gnädiges Fräulein. Will you follow me, please?"

Though broad, the steps that I trailed up behind him were as steep as those in my mother's old timberwork house. The adjutant walked a few steps ahead of me as we crossed the flagstone patio at the top to reach the entrance to the house, where he executed a stiff bow and gestured me in ahead of him.

Then he led me through an arched doorway to the right, down a flight of shallow stairs into a room as spacious as the Platterhof's lobby. He seemed to disappear into thin air, as my eyes adjusted to the dim light.

Finally, I saw the figure standing before the fireplace when he turned to face me.

From the moment I realized what was happening, I tried to contain my shock, but I imagine he saw it. His posture was somewhat bowed as he approached me in small steps. When he took my hand and thanked me for coming, his voice was mild, almost shy, as though not quite sure how he'd be received.

I'd seen him once before—in person, that is, for we saw him everywhere we looked in Germany. The week after Eva took my photographs at Hoffmann's, I was walking down a street in Kassel where he'd stood on the roof of a car delivering a speech to a small crowd. His entire body had worked like a machine to push his voice out forcefully, as though that would make it penetrate more deeply.

I'd ducked down an alley to avoid it, but there was no escape route now. The contrast between what I'd seen that day and the almost deferential display before me held me in a kind of thrall.

"Do you like art, child?" He paused in front of a large canvas of Titian's "Cupid and Aphrodite" that hung to the right of the fireplace.

Had he invited me here to offer the same pedestrian tour any subordinate could have? I was determined not to call him "my" Führer. I recalled the protocol I'd heard used at the embassies and opted for the respectful, if awkward-sounding third-person. Let him think I was smitten with shyness. I knew I had to choose my words very carefully.

"The Führer must know what an unexpected opportunity this is for me. As for art, well, I wonder whether there can be any civilization without it."

His face grew as animated as a child's, almost naively so. "That's exactly right!"

I'd clearly scored some point with this.

He began to elaborate about the painting, almost as though following notes in his head, more aware of his words than of anything around me. This gave me the chance to study him without appearing too probing.

His body seemed ineffectual, almost rigid, as he moved, like an appendage that he was forced to drag behind him. It was an odd thing to watch, until I realized with some alarm that I wasn't seeing him now, but in some future, deteriorated state suddenly showing itself to me. Perhaps it's more accurate to say that, while he appeared to present himself as kindly host, fully in command, my inner impression of him was so opposite, and so strong, that this was what I actually saw as I watched him.

As I tried to push this from my mind's eye, he expounded on the painting's significance in a lilting Austrian German. When he turned back toward me, he used his eyes the way someone operates a searchlight, boring in with an unblinking ice-blue gaze.

I sensed that he wanted me to meet it and when I did, I encountered a strange, vacillating polarity. Like waves in the action of a tide, it surged forward, as if to engulf me, then receded rapidly.

When I followed its retreat, I met a blank void, like the eyes of an animal when life leaves its body. Having passed through his eyes' mesmerizing quality, almost like a layer to be penetrated, I spied something in a glimpse so quick, I couldn't be sure I'd seen it, or whether it had been visible to my outer or inner sight—or perhaps both.

Beyond that great power that radiated out at you, there was a hollow, like that of an unfilled vessel. And, for a fleeting second, it was as though a shadow had flitted through that emptiness and peered out.

He looked away, as though he knew what I'd glimpsed. But how could that ever be possible? His eyes were like torches as he turned them back to me. "I would like to ask you a question. What do you imagine that the British think of us, at this point?"

As I collected myself, I decided tepid transparency was safest. "Well, I must admit to the Führer I know little about this. Personally, I have rather lost my taste for England, since it is determined to ruin so many nights of our sleep—and so much else."

"Oh, but don't worry," he said, patting my arm. "We'll take care of them."

I was so stunned at this gesture that I barely felt it, as though the site had gone numb; as though I'd shrunken from it, retreating deeper into my own skin.

His tone was solicitous, his expression nearly apologetic, like a host confronted with an unwelcome discovery such as an infestation of rats or fleas that he assumes responsibility for rectifying, yet doesn't want to prolong discussion about.

A voice within me wondered, *Ah, but will you take care of us?*

Then he asked, "Do I understand correctly you are both German and English?"

Oh, dear, here it was. The question. And, surprisingly, he had asked in English, which I knew he understood, somewhat, but seldom used. I also knew he rather admired the British, saw them as a nation that would eventually "come to its senses" and understand it was essentially "Aryan."

"Well," I began, electing to stay with German, "the Führer no doubt understands how my situation is like the story of King Solomon and the two mothers who claim the same baby. Except that my mother would rather let me go than see me hurt in any way, which is why I choose to be with her, and in Germany." I felt as though a part of me were standing outside of myself talking to him.

He nodded vigorously. "Yes, yes. The decision that you would naturally make. Your mother knows the honorable road, and it is she who first sets our compass for us, like a true north."

I was already worrying about the "Heil Hitler" I must offer at the end of this bizarre exchange. I'd only ever used it mockingly, in ridicule. How could I ever have imagined where I would actually have to use it in earnest for the first time? God help me. Why was I even here?

He reached for my hand, raised it to his lips in an unhurried motion and kissed it with restrained delicacy. What came next was a shock even beyond that.

"I asked you to come because I want to thank you for being so kind to Fräulein Braun."

I couldn't possibly have heard him correctly. Did he mean Eva?

"Her war service is often a lonely post." He shook his head. "Few understand the sacrifices she makes. She is a very dedicated person."

I could only offer the slightest nod, as he talked; couldn't imagine what I'd say, when words were finally required of me.

"She is very grateful for your friendship."

This made my response easier than I'd expected, as well as sincere: "Fräulein Braun's friendship means a great deal to me, as well."

"Tell me," he said then. "Is there anything that you need?"

I'm amazed I managed to say anything, rather than faint dead away. A host of possibilities flashed to mind as my crazed humor pictured me carting home crates of food on the train, handing him an itemized list of the delicacies I'd been gorging on at the Platterhof before I had to return to Berlin's yawning hunger. My reply sprang out of my mouth before I could stop it. "The ending of the war will serve all of our needs."

He couldn't have seemed more delighted, nor I feel more disingenuous. He naturally assumed I meant Germany's presumed victory. He practically danced as he said, "That is *precisely* the thinking that keeps me going on the most difficult days."

Then he thanked me again for coming to meet with him and, before I could speak, the same adjutant who'd led me into the room appeared, posture erect, hands clasped behind him, as he stood a respectful distance from us. "It is time, my Führer."

With a hasty, "Be well, child," my host quit the room, and the adjutant said, "I can escort you to the car now."

Instantly, I remembered others describing how Hitler's presence cast a sort of spell that made it feel as though the air went out of the room with him when he left it.

That was exactly how it felt.

Anna had been left with a headache the first time that she'd read this back in Peggy's New Hampshire house—no doubt because she'd barely drawn breath. She certainly hadn't seen what was coming, any more than her mother had.

"Whatever did she think after she was summoned this way?" she asked Hannes. "She must have known Eva was behind it, begun to suspect her connection with Hitler?"

Hannes looked doubtful. "I think the Eva that she knew would seem nothing like the kind of woman she'd imagine would love Hitler. Though obviously, this showed that Eva was somehow a part of his world."

He paused a moment, then added, "Of course, Eva would have considered the opportunity of a visit like this to be the epitome of a gift. Even if she wasn't directly involved in organizing it, she may have told Hitler about her time with your mother at the Platterhof and *he* may have orchestrated it all."

Later, as Anna continued her rereading of Peggy's pages, the next installment came four years later, and it was Eva who was pondering the effects of Hitler's presence and sudden departures.

FELLOW TRAVELLERS

Up to the Light

CHAPTER 18

Obersalzberg
20 July 1944

With the Berghof's terrace to herself, Eva began the day the way she loved best: sipping strong coffee in the morning quiet, savoring the pleasure of the day's first cigarette. It had been weeks since she'd been able to do this.

The sky was finally visible again, now the cursed fog machines were shut off. Surrounding hillsides rolled like green waves under its morning-glory expanse, and red-tile roofs dotted the hollow of Berchtesgaden below. Even the shoulders of the majestic Watzmann were in view today, carved in silver and shadows on the western horizon.

The sunlight felt like a divine pronouncement after weeks in which the Berghof had been sealed off from the world in a shroud. The guards and their complicated machinery had worked around the clock to create the artificial mist that camouflaged it when the Führer and his entourage were in residence.

Of course, the protection this was designed to afford evaporated like a wake once he left and the machines were turned off. Everywhere in Germany, the people's safety was linked to his. His confidence that his destiny protected him seemed unshakable as ever. Eva vowed to renew her trust in it, despite the inner voice that woke her drenched in terror in the middle of so many nights, especially the ones she spent alone. Death could seize him anywhere, like a firestorm. *If he must die, let me die with him,* she pleaded silently when this anxiety struck. Any alternative seemed unthinkable.

In the dull silences in which he'd felt increasingly removed, Adi would startle suddenly and demand that the machines keep pouring out their screen of thick fog, even on murky days when nature provided its own. Whoever was there with him was his responsibility, he reminded. It was for *their* safety that the Berghof must remain hidden, when they were so often mindless as children of the dangers; unwilling, whenever the sirens sounded, to go down to the bunkers, especially if it interrupted their sleep.

He always couched his decisions here in terms of the needs of those around him, admitting none of his own. Even the hours of relaxation that lured him to this retreat were, he insisted, solely to boost his strength for leadership.

For himself, he expected nothing beyond a life as Spartan as his personal sleeping quarters always were. Although he came to the comfort of Eva's soft bed like an eager child, it was only the stoic, self-sacrificing soldier the world ever saw. This was the great confidence he entrusted to her, a trust she knew he gave nowhere else. It was her treasure.

Over the last week, the fog's shield had encased the house for days. It became increasingly difficult to find the will to get out of bed each dreary day, particularly when Adi's monologues around the fireplace had lasted so far into its earliest hours.

At last, one golden afternoon, he relented long enough for them all to enjoy the customary walk to the Mooslahnerkopf overlook and teahouse without the manufactured mist. They'd soaked up the sun's warmth as summer's bright hues reappeared around them. Eva had been reluctant to relinquish this when they reached the teahouse's cave-like interior, where the Führer spent every afternoon he was here, which meant his companions did, too.

Even before their climb back to the house, he'd phoned ahead to order the all-consuming veil to reappear. As they dallied in the sunlight watching the misty wall gradually swallow the Berghof, one of the secretaries spied a rainbow in the ersatz clouds but Eva, eyes trained on her two bounding terriers, was too distracted to notice.

She had to believe in Adi's assertions of confidence about his safety, that any apprehensions he had were for *them*, so dependent on his protection. She was the only one who saw the small, vulnerable signs of fear in the man who slept with a light on—or, she had been told, slept very little, when she wasn't there to sleep with him.

She'd had to stop herself from crying out when she'd first seen him on this last visit, had actually wondered: *Who is that old man, so hunched and bent?* And then realized, in unbelieving shock, who it was.

That was when she'd had the unbearable thought, like a stabbing wound, that this might be his last visit here. She refused to let herself believe it, even though she had seen him going slowly from room to room gazing at things, as if saying good-bye.

He'd been gone for nearly a week. There was a possibility that he'd stop in Bayreuth on his way back to Berlin. She only knew this because she'd overhead his adjutant Heinz Linge telling Martin Borman. Any stop in this near midpoint of his journey north would have been a last-minute decision.

But no matter what decisions were made, or when they were, she was never privy to them, and seldom informed about them. For *her* safety, as well as his own, Adi emphasized, time and again.

"I know that things are kept from me," she'd confided to the youngest of his secretaries, who always seemed friendly and sympathetic. Eva had come to believe that she would be the last to know about anything, or, perhaps, would never know at all.

Adi was gone, and, now that Gretl's wedding day had passed, her sister was gone, too. Thank heaven that Herta and her girls had come, so she wasn't left all alone. Herta, who understood her, and been such a good friend, for so long—more like a sister.

Her feelings about Gretl still confused her. Although her sister so often seemed at loose ends without Eva's guidance, she'd conducted herself with remarkable poise on her wedding day last month. She moved with the confidence of a film star, or a new young queen, during the civil ceremony at the Salzburg town hall alongside the handsome, restless Fegelein, and later, as the champagne flowed high above Berchtesgaden at the Führer's Kehlsteinhaus.

Of course, her clothes had been perfect. Eva made sure of that. For the ceremony, a suit of rich silk in a meticulous cut, pencil skirt accentuating the bride's willow slimness. Lace and tiny bows at the lapels drew the eye up to where her dark eyes gleamed from behind the tulle veil of her broad-brimmed hat. Then, for the reception that lasted until dawn, Eva's dressmaker fashioned a romantic ivory taffeta gown—with sleeves, thankfully, so Gretl didn't have to hide it under a wrap.

Though it had been early June, remnants of snow and ice still covered the cliff faces along the winding four-kilometer ascent to the Kehlstein. The passageway that led inside from the car park had been a virtual wind tunnel. The wedding party and guests struggled through it awkwardly in the cold, and then a long line of women had to queue in the narrow vestibule, waiting to repair their hair in the powder-room.

How short-sighted Borman had been, approving a design for a ladies' lounge as small as the one in this building that had cost such a fortune. And he thought himself such a connoisseur, of women *and* architecture. Eva wrinkled her nose at the thought of him.

It had been far too unfriendly a day for any outside photographs. The skies stayed gray all day as wind ripped around the stone building where it clung to the summit, and moaned through the adjoining colonnade. Gretl's complexion glowed in candlelight from wall sconces as she floated from room to room, greeting guests with sanguine ease, and taking quick but generous sips from any champagne glass she happened to find.

So often, she could seem shy, even a bit gangly. But when there was libation to be had, you could watch her shrug off that burdensome weight of wondering whether she was doing the right thing and grow nearly indifferent to anything but her own enjoyment. Yes, Gretl had been all smiling calm, even during the photographs with the Führer.

One would have thought that it was Eva's wedding day, nervous as she'd been, unable to eat very much, though eventually she had fruit and sorbet later that night, with more of the champagne she'd sipped all day long. She had taken on the task of ensuring that everything went perfectly that day with a desperate determination. And it had, from the dinner around the massive table to the pantomime in which, dressed as adorable Cupid, Herta's daughter, Ushi, bestowed good-luck wishes on the new couple.

Fegelein, in a self-absorbed state of inebriation by then, hardly seemed to notice—though he didn't miss an opportunity in one dark corner to cup the breast of a young kitchen helper as she trailed past with a tray.

And at last, there had been dancing. To revive her energy toward dusk, Eva began drinking strong black coffee once the dinner settings had been cleared. Her legs felt like India rubber, but she'd been determined not to miss this rarest of opportunities. She hadn't even asked Adi's permission, since he was leaving anyway, off to hold a briefing with some officers down at the Berghof. He had marshaled himself through the day's events like a man reviewing troops at some front, his thoughts just as far away.

After a few turns on the dance floor, Gretl pleaded fatigue in order to do what she enjoyed most—sit and sip, and talk and smoke. That's when the bridegroom found a ready partner in his new sister-in-law, who so seldom got to dance, and loved it so much. Especially the tango.

For those next hours, Eva could finally forget all the things she didn't want to think about and fall into the embrace of a life—a world—that, in such candlelit hours, still felt close to her skin, like Fegelein's arms. He was as good a dancer as he was a horseman. No doubt his mastery of one enhanced the other.

Once the day's success was assured, and Adi had left, she rested in Fegelein's arms, danced as though there were nothing she need do but drift there. No doors to watch, no details to police, no moods to gauge. She'd taken care that her gown didn't outshine Gretl's, that her presence kept a muted distance while she shepherded the day along.

Aware of Adi's penchant for matchmaking, she had pressed for this marriage for many reasons, Gretl's future uppermost. But her personal advantage in this union was that, as new sister-in-law, she'd contrived a role that legitimized her presence in public with the Führer, since, as chief liaison to Heinrich Himmler, Fegelein occupied a prestigious place in the SS hierarchy. At last, she could stand up in a respected role, beyond the ever-present shame of being "die Geliebte"—*the unmarried companion.*

The wedding day passed as suddenly as it came, then Gretl was gone. Eva had been so busy with the preparations she hadn't given thought to how sweeping this change would feel. The adjustment was easier while Adi was still here, and thank heaven he'd stayed another six weeks. But now he was gone, the empty house felt like a mausoleum.

Even if Gretl was often moping, less imaginative, at times, than Eva's two little terriers—or flirting and carrying on almost embarrassingly with any number of men—she was company. Someone to show things to, share news or have fun with, to pass the time. Gretl had *been* there. The void seemed so much bigger without her.

Adi's departures always brought mixed feelings, too. First, the weight of sadness, as Eva felt cut adrift. Then, undeniable relief, like a return to herself. When he was there, she must be ready. To be seen, to receive him, to be no more and no less than he required: the sure, soft touch of solace, scrubbed of any dire reminders or demands.

How delicious it would feel to dive into the jade-green waters of the nearby Königssee today, like a waiting oasis. Stretch out fully again in her own life. As soon as Herta and the girls woke, Cook could pack them a picnic of cold chicken and potato salad and they'd spend the day beside the lake in the mountain air.

She'd relax back and relive feeling important to Adi as she catalogued his glances and affectionate murmurings, especially those that others had witnessed—affirmations that were like transfusions to a bloodless heart, evidence that she existed, and mattered. Captured like snapshots inside her, they recalled his indulgent teasing, his little jokes, so very less frequent now. Sometimes, in the heavy, extended silences of the past weeks, she wondered whether she would ever hear them again. The moments she replayed most were those in which she felt his eyes on her, that look of pride, something that also had occurred less often, now that his head was downcast so much of the time.

This was how she must sustain herself. If she fell into the trap of dwelling on possible dangers and sorrows, she'd never get out again. Like the fog, it would envelop her, forever. It was vital to find where the good things were and call them to mind, as she so often did in her letters to him.

It was like those days when Vati had been at war and there'd been so much less to eat. Eva and her sisters had sat at Mutti's table with its freshly ironed cloth and shared an evening meal as slight as a child's. Mutti spread the butter on their bread, evenly dividing its pale-white smear between her three daughters, saving none for herself.

It had been hard to see, let alone taste, the butter. Eva had said—something now retold at family gatherings—that in order to know whether your bread was buttered, you had to hold it up to the light, where its shine would show you it was.

It was the same with life, especially in these times. She had to hold things up to the light, look for the blessings. Even the smallest specks of jewels can catch the light, after all.

And if not, there were cognac and pills, though these could no longer be the means for the kind of escape she'd once attempted. She had used them then to show him the pain his abandonment caused her. Now it was she who must not desert him.

Her turn had finally come, to prove herself, prove her love. The fact that the temptation of an almost irresistible man, like a reminder of something waiting, forgotten, had appeared in her life only reinforced the value of the sacrifice she knew she must make. Adi had given her a life she would otherwise never have known. She would not betray this generosity, or relinquish the honor of being one of the few who had his trust.

On a day as bright and glorious as this, she would turn toward the light, wherever she could find it. Time in the sun was what she needed. She'd immerse her body in the lake's icy water, drop her guard and relish those moments to be harvested from these last days before they, like the mist, evaporated, too.

She and Herta and her girls would enjoy a swim. Then they'd all share an early supper in the lingering light on the terrace, and after the girls had been put to bed, she and Herta would watch a film or two. She'd choose something romantic, imagine herself the heroine, and mingle the afterglow of Adi's recent attention with the role of the hero.

Later that day, July 20, 1944, every danger Eva ever imagined for Hitler seemed to come true at once when a message arrived while she was at Königssee, alerting her that someone had attempted to assassinate him using a bomb.

Hitler survived, though several of his companions were killed or gravely wounded. Hundreds of Germans were then executed as plotters in a savage reprisal. Peggy knew several of them, and would fear that Erich Geisler was among them.

The next three manuscript segments were her shortest, like jotted notes, as though she hadn't had the time to write them. Or could hardly bear to.

FELLOW TRAVELLERS

None Shall Know My Way

CHAPTER 19

Berlin
Midnight, 20 July 1944

O h, treacherous day. First we're told that the Beast is dead. Then—his voice on the radio just now! There can be no doubt that he survived. And no hope.

A wickedly teasing lifetime passed before us in a single day. We were going to be Germany again, *our* true Germany. Then, it all went wrong. Some of the plotters have been shot already. Better that than waiting to be found. Or, the aftermath.

They came for my co-workers this afternoon—Oh, *God*. I felt it, what's coming for them, as if it was being torn from inside me. My face was going to give me away, even while they were so careful not to look at any of us as they were detained.

I stepped forward to cry out and a hand gripped me from behind like a claw as a secretary who knows the same secrets I do hissed, "Nein!" in my ear. I bolted to the lavatory and retched up the little I'd been able to eat in my anxiety. I feigned illness all day as some of my co-workers expressed shock and outrage about the "conspirators" while others acted as though they felt those things. I was incapable of pretending anything other than illness, or even of speaking.

Then he was here at the apartment when I finally got home, after I hadn't seen him in weeks. I dare not even write his name, now.

I begged him to go, though they wouldn't look for him here, as he's never come before. I've tried to reassure myself that he's in less danger as he wasn't directly involved. But he knows so much, and so many of them know him, know the work he does. And they've already been arrested.

He's sleeping now. I cannot. I want to touch him and have it never end; and I feel as though I will never have the chance to touch him, be held by him, again. Never again be able to sleep, or eat, or believe.

Sunrise, 21 July

Last night was the first time my body hasn't responded to his touch. Before the day was out, I'd had to pretend after all. I was too tangled in fear, for him, and for what I see in the days ahead. Not only in my thoughts, but in my body, I feel it.

Afterward, I wanted to melt into holding him when he fell asleep in my arms but all I could do was lie awake listening. For the first night in many weeks, not a single Allied bomber flew over. But the real danger was out there in the night's dark silence.

I never heard him leave. It was light when I woke and found the two pages he'd left on the nightstand. The first had a stanza from a poem of Erich Mühsam's:

> I will go alone over the mountain,
> And none shall know my way;
> Because who would see my pathway to the heights
> Would tear me away from that path.

On the second sheet, he had written:

> My precious darling, my brave heart,
> I love you, always. How I wish our love had come in different times.
> I'll only endanger you, now. No matter what, find a way to go on. It
> is the only real way to win. Please, do this for me. Remember what
> your mother always says: Outlast them.

Anna opened the folder of papers Hannes had given her the night before, which included his article about Erich Mühsam.

"We grew up with his writing. My stepfather loved it," he explained when she asked why he'd chosen to write about the poet.

The article made a rather surprising comparison between Mühsam and Hitler. Both had been born in the same timeframe, with similarly domineering fathers and regular beatings, a popular approach to childrearing at the time that advised breaking the child's spirit, preferably before the age of six months.

One man became a genocidal tyrant, the other a lover of mankind. The difference, Hannes proposed, was their mothers. Hitler's, who was his father's niece, was uneducated and, though well-intentioned, reportedly obsessive in her relations with her son. Mühsam's had received a formal education that prepared her well for both life and motherhood and her son had credited her as the reason he reached maturity with an intact spirit despite the considerable abuse he received from others. He had also been a vocal champion of women's rights, in a time when they'd had none at all.

Anna picked up the pages of her mother's manuscript to continue reading.

Berlin
7 November 1944

Still nothing from him, or about him. He's always found a way to let me know. It can only mean one thing. Now that Herr N. has gone back to Westphalia, I feel so alone after all of today's news.

First that pig of a doctor, leering at me. "You probably gave up hope, at thirty-three. But you're proof it's never too late to have a child for the Fatherland." If he'd said "Führer," I'd have struck him. Instead, I left without saying a word.

Afterward, back at the office, Herr Niemeyer was waiting for me. God knows how he got here. The train service is so bad now that it had taken him almost two days. He asked if we could talk in private, at my place. Then he held me as I screamed, rocked and soothed me. Was there ever anyone so kind as dear Nadelkissen?

Mutti is dead. Three nights ago. RAF bombers attacked Bochum. She'd gone there to help a friend. I'd already read of the raids—their inferno—in an intercepted British communiqué at the Foreign Office. Felt grateful that she doesn't live in the Rheinland, near the industrial areas, but in a town planes fly over like disinterested birds.

Part of me keeps forgetting it has happened, until something reminds me. Then I want to wrench it out of me, run as fast and far as I can. But there is nowhere to run to.

Herr N. didn't want me to hear it any other way. I'm to take a train to Munich, stay with Aunt Paula. He brought me a pass, when it's nearly impossible to get out of the city now unless you've been bombed out of your home. He also arranged with my boss for me to leave, though not until the week before Christmas.

When I asked why I couldn't go back with him, he said, "I won't be staying there. I'm needed elsewhere, now. Your mother wanted you safe, out of the city." His voice was shaking. "I had promised her I'd find a way for you to go to Paula."

Then I told him about my visit to the doctor.

His eyes were the first thing to show response, like a parent's astonished joy. What I would never receive from my own father. For a moment, it made me feel close to Erich, that this first person I'd told had been so unhesitatingly happy.

"I believe your Mutti knew," he said. "You must leave Berlin. For the child, and all of us, your family. Your mother, Erich. And me. No matter where you are, we'll always be with you." He took hold of my hands. "Honor your Mutti by doing what she believed most: if we can go on, we will go on."

He took such a risk, coming to tell me, and to help me. Yet again, someone asks me to go on—if only for the sake of the others who cannot. When all I want to do is die.

Anna stared out at the morning's rosy clouds hanging low over the mountains. She had read these pages before, but their effect seemed even more penetrating now.

This must have been what Peggy wanted to talk about, that day before she died. On the night of the July 20 attempt on Hitler's life, when her mother and Erich Geisler made love for the last time, Anna's life was the result. If only she'd made time to talk that day last fall, this might not all seem as though she were reading about someone else's life. Had nothing about her mother's life been what she'd thought? Or her own?

Throughout the weeks she'd read Peggy's manuscript, Anna had shared its revelations with Hannes. But she hadn't shared this. She wasn't even sure why.

Perhaps because it stirred that same confusing pain whose cause she could never identify, the one she'd always felt about that music of Beethoven's that made Peggy cry, that door with its shape of a dark butterfly. A painful feeling that also brought shame.

She hadn't disclosed this discovery about who her father really was because of something that made her feel small and sad: the possibility that her mother's life, the one Anna had known, wasn't ever the one Peggy wanted at all

CHAPTER 20

Minutes later, Hannes knocked at her door to suggest they have breakfast quickly so as to reach Königssee before the tourist boats disturbed the lake's early-morning calm.

Soon they were following a trail that climbed alongside its mirror-smooth surface to the Malerwinkel, the "painter's corner," with its view of the red onion domes of St. Bartholomew's Church on the far shore. The setting looked just as it had in Eva's films, right down to a rowboat drawn up onto the shore, oars at rest against the sand.

A little later, they arrived back at the lakeside beach near the dock from which the boats departed. "You don't mind," Hannes asked, "that we're not taking a cruise?"

"Not at all. I'd probably fall asleep on a boat today."

He smiled. Then he bent to unlace his shoes, pried them off, and reached to pull his shirt off over his head. As she watched, Anna was startled to see him unbuckle his belt, tug it off, and drop it on top of his shirt on the sand.

His legs were a light tan under his shorts. She thought of how white her own were beneath her filmy cotton skirt, and how angry the scar still looked, sometimes.

It hadn't occurred to her that either of them might go into the water. The Königssee cut like a fjord through the steep rise of the surrounding mountains and even in summer, its waters were as icy cold as the Alpine snows that fed it.

"You're going in?" she asked as she kicked off her hiking sandals.

"What else does one do at a lake?" His tone was teasing. "Don't you want to recreate Eva's experience? This is where she swam, after all."

"Yes, well, she was younger—and athletic. And used to it," Anna said. "I am unconditioned, and cowardly. No, I don't think I can." She turned and burrowed in a tote bag for the blanket they'd brought, pulling it out and shaking it open in the air before draping it onto the ground. She dropped to her knees to smooth it out.

As she rose and reached for her sandals to anchor the corners, Hannes stood directly behind her. The smile overtaking his face nearly closed his eyes as he scooped her up in his arms. "Of course, you can!" His gaze probed her own with a glint of challenge. Then she was jouncing in his arms as he sprinted toward the water.

"Hannes!" she cried as air whirred past their heads and the surroundings became a blur. "What are you—?"

He had reached the water and was splashing in. Anna shivered as water sprayed against her legs, even her arms, which she tightened around his neck.

"See?" he said with a satisfied smile.

"It's too cold!" she protested as she wriggled against him.

"Now, now. Don't make such a fuss. It's not as if you have to go in all at once. You can try it a little at a time. First this way … "

She let out an involuntary shriek as he tilted her legs down until her toes dipped under the water's surface. Shifting his weight, he lowered her backward slowly until the crown of her head was close to the small waves reaching the shore.

"Hannes! Please stop!" She was trembling now.

He raised her back up gently and held her, gazing into her eyes, "Anna," he said, every trace of humor vanished from his face. "It is only play. I didn't mean to scare you."

The sun emerged from behind clouds and she felt its heat, along with the warmth of the skin on his chest and arms.

"Now, this is better." She looked up at him as a flush encircled her own limbs. "The sun, and you, keeping me warm."

"Is it?" He drew her closer, higher against him, until his face hovered inches from hers. Then his mouth descended and pressed softly against her lips.

Surprised, at first, Anna returned the kiss.

He broke away gently. "Very good then."

Stepping back from the water, he lowered her legs until she stood beside him.

"Now, if you'll excuse me," he said in German, "there's something of a code of honor to keep here." With a grin, he splashed off into the water, which drew a whoop from him before he dove beneath it and surfaced with a loud gasp.

"How'd it take me this long to figure out you're completely insane?" she called to him, wondering whether that code involved continuing with his chilly swim, or interrupting something before it could go any farther.

They returned to Berchtesgaden a few hours later for a tour of the Kehlsteinhaus, the "Eagle's Nest" Martin Borman built for Hitler high above the Berghof. Eva loved spending time there with family and friends, while Hitler had visited a mere five times.

Over Currywurst at one of its restaurant's outdoor tables, they discussed Hannes's upcoming schedule and when Anna might offer her lectures. Afterward they hiked down from the summit on a trail that ended near the former Platterhof hotel, where Eva and Peggy had visited. Bombed at the end of the war, it was later rebuilt by the U.S. Army as a resort for military personnel.

"I thought we could have dinner here tonight, but it's closed, now," Hannes said. "They're turning it over to the German government, so it will likely be torn down."

They continued down the steep road past their hotel to where the Berghof had stood. Though Anna knew the site literally from the inside-out, both from research and the strange journeys of her dreams, it looked like any random patch of forest, now. As she had several times over the last two days, she experienced a ghostly sense of not being quite present in her surroundings, in a place that could be anywhere.

"Hard to imagine there ever being a house here," she said.

"It's not a place the government wants to call attention to," said Hannes.

They found the ruins of the Mooslahnerkopf teahouse and its overlook farther down the mountain as late-day light cast an amber glow on the trees. In the valley below, the River Ache wove a silver-green ribbon through a landscape dotted with chalets.

"You must be ready to drop," Hannes said when they arrived back at the Türkenhof.

"Just a little hungry."

He suggested they eat a light supper there rather than drive down into town. Later, when he asked in German how she felt about the day, she told him, "Immer dankbar, dass du Alles möglich gemacht hast.—*Forever grateful you've made all this possible.*"

His smile was shy where he sat across the table. He studied her face, then asked, "There's something else. What is it?"

"Well, maybe I expected to find something, in these places where my mother and Eva were. And it's not just that it's gone, but long gone. Gone forever.

"I know that probably sounds silly," she added.

"Don't edit yourself, Anna. What did you hope to find?"

"I don't know. After feeling so much closer to both of them, I thought there'd be *something*. A sense of reunion."

"Don't give up." His smile was encouraging. "Tour's not over yet—there's Eva's house tomorrow, once we get back to Munich. But for now, sleepy eyes, it's upstairs to bed with you."

However tired she'd been feeling, as they climbed the stairs, she suddenly recalled the moments in Königssee that morning. She longed to feel his arms around her again after a day that had woven an affectionate aura between them.

On the landing outside her room, Anna turned and kissed him. It was a clumsy kiss, urgent-feeling, as though she were daring herself to do it.

Caught by surprise, he circled his arms around her and guided her toward the wall so gradually it was as though it rose to meet her. The feel of his mouth, the salty warmth of his breath, the Alpine smell of mountain air on his skin and clothes—she wanted to be swallowed in all of it. Everything she'd ever let herself imagine about him was suddenly real, immediate and close, and a new mystery to discover, all at the same time.

His eyes flashed like fragments of jewels from behind his lowered lids when his mouth travelled downward toward her neck and throat, then tenderly brushed her earlobe. She felt his hands slide to the small of her back then trail upward until his fingers cradled the nape of her neck and he kissed her lingeringly again.

"Anna!" he nearly gasped when he broke away and laid his cheek against hers.

His arms wrapped her tightly, held her fast so her hands could reach no higher then the middle of his back. Her fingertips tingled when they made contact with the smooth flesh there under his shirt. Heat was rising from them both; his body so close along the length of her that she responded with a reflexive arch.

"*Anna.*" His tone was more emphatic as he reached to grip her shoulders and drew back to create space between them that felt like an instant ache.

He didn't step away, only used his strength to hold her in place in a way that prevented her coming close again. He looked as though he were catching his breath, collecting his wits, steeling himself for a task.

He began in German that changed quickly to English: "Ich glaube das—I think that, perhaps, I have pushed us too hard, today. With our schedule tomorrow, it is best if we let this be a very lovely way to say good-night."

He spoke as though trying to make a case for reason, for something the exact opposite of what had been melding them moments before.

Anna remembered holding the phone in *The Fighting Chance* office, wishing she could disappear through the floor. "I'm sorry." She couldn't bring herself to look at him as she edged toward her door.

He stepped toward her. "Annchen," his gaze was steady when he used this affectionate form of her name for the first time. "Don't even think of apologizing for what we both so obviously enjoyed." His expression was kind, coaxing. He reached to stroke her cheek.

"Then—"

He laid a finger against her lips.

"But—"

"Please understand," he interrupted when she tried again. "For reasons, all of them important, none of which I can go into now, it's truly better if we get our rest tonight." His eyes looked tired, his expression a little distracted, or confused.

She nodded quickly, eager to get on the other side of the door before something inside her gave way. The instant she was behind it, it tore out of her so abruptly she reached for a pillow to stifle it and moved to the bathroom so as not to be heard.

A little later, she sat in the bathtub shaking and sobbing. When she lay down at last, exhausted, her mind kept circling back, like an animal on a scent, to the feel of him; the response she'd believed they both had felt. Until he had reached some—decision. Remembered something that had made it impossible to go on.

Her tears should be wrung dry, yet they poured out, still, with a keening she had to bury her face in the pillow to silence. Lonely sadness, like that day she'd realized there would be no answer from behind the door with her mother on the other side.

"*Anna.*"

Her heart erupted in flight like a startled bird.

Hannes's voice. Right at the door, as though he were already in the room.

She dabbed frantically at her face, then leapt up to the sink in her room to splash water on her eyes. She switched on the light above it and saw there was no way to hide what had left her looking so ravaged. She'd either have to ignore him, or face him.

"Anna," his voice was more plaintive this time. "Open the door. Please."

When she did, he stood before her dressed as he had been an hour or more before.

"May I come in?" he asked quietly.

She nodded, stepping aside.

His voice was soft, its tone grave. "Did my thoughtlessness cause this?"

She swallowed hard, not sure whether her voice would work when she tried to use it. "You weren't thoughtless. I was rash. Today was just," she paused, then said quietly, "very lovely."

"It was," he agreed. "Especially those last moments. I'm sorry if my interrupting them has hurt you."

She shook her head.

"Anna," he said after a few moments of silence, "I need for you to trust me."

"I do," she protested, almost defensively. "I mean, of course I do."

"Right now, you see, I am your host. I feel responsible for you. There are things that I want you to have time to adjust to. So many things will be new. And I have already watched you go through so much, in these last months."

After a pause he asked, "Can you understand?"

She nodded, her eyes clouding with tears again as she looked away.

"I felt that what could have continued for us tonight is one more new thing too many, right now."

She said nothing as he stood looking at her.

"Please, tell me why you've been crying."

Part of her wanted to snap, "What does it matter?" but the undeniable concern in his voice stopped her. "I must be tired. You're right about that."

"You sounded very sad."

She looked at him, unbelieving. "You heard me?"

"I stayed in the sitting area on the landing. Afterward." He was rubbing his forehead, above his left eye. "I was worried about you."

"All this time?"

He nodded. Then he surprised her again. "Would you like me to stay with you?"

She felt too uncertain to respond. Thank God he was using English or she'd be too paralyzed to speak. She wanted to say yes; felt she should say no.

He reached to fold back her bedclothes, then stepped away from the bed.

She didn't take her eyes off him as she moved toward it and climbed in slowly.

He pulled the duvet up over her. Then he reached into his shirt pocket. "Your schedule's been turned upside-down. I brought this for you. It's made from herbs, from hops. It can help you sleep. Not too strong. Nati uses it when she travels."

Her gaze travelled from his eyes to the single tablet in a tiny packet in his palm.

"Will you take it?"

She nodded and he went to the sink to fill a glass, and brought it to her.

Shall I stay?" he asked once she'd swallowed the tablet. "Until you fall asleep?"

Her eyelids were already heavy as she lay back, as if fatigue, together with her crying, had finally weighted them down. "You can stay forever," she heard herself mumble and he laughed softly where he had moved to switch off the light.

Anna wondered what he would do next as she waited in the dark. Seconds later, she felt him sit lightly on the bed, then stretch out along the edge of it beside her. He wrapped one arm gently across her waist, on top of the covers. It was the most comforting thing she could remember in a very long time.

"You're going to get cold," she told him.

"No," he said in German. "This will be just right. Gute Nacht, Anna. Sweet dreams."

The Autobahn's last 20 miles into Munich were one long traffic jam, as they often were in August.

"How did I *forget*?" Hannes seemed frustrated as he worked gearshift and clutch in the slow-moving sea of cars, trucks, and buses. Afternoon sun seared through the windshield. He repeatedly checked his watch and finally chose an exit to a smaller road.

Anna had wakened that morning with no idea where she was. Minutes later, his knock at her door had begun their day.

Once off the Autobahn, it took an hour to reach the Munich suburb of Bogenhausen where he parked across from a building on the corner of two busy streets. "Hitler's apartment was there, on the second floor," he told her.

The four-storey structure had broad balconies on its upper floors, which had displayed long, red Swastika banners in Eva's time. Hitler's niece, Geli Raubal, had died in this house from gunshot wounds alleged to have been self-inflicted, and British Prime Minister Neville Chamberlain met with Hitler here in his study during talks of the failed Munich Agreement. Eva later remarked to a friend that Chamberlain might have been shocked to learn the "history" of the red velvet sofa on which he'd sat, suggesting this was where she'd offered up herself to her first and possibly only lover.

Hannes drove on, navigating narrow residential streets where he repeatedly pulled over behind parked cars to yield to other drivers. Anna felt a surge of excitement when she realized they were getting close to where Eva had lived.

Often referred to as the house Hitler gave her, it had actually been paid for by her boss, Heinrich Hoffmann. Hitler suggested she be "reimbursed" this way for the hundreds of photographs of him she'd supplied that made Hoffmann so much money. Hitler always found creative ways to spend other people's money while his own amassed in great quantities, especially royalties from the sales of *Mein Kampf*.

"I like it best here in Munich, where her real life was. Her *own* life," Anna said. "Rather than what he commandeered."

"What she *let* him commandeer," Hannes said as he parked the car at the curb.

A red-tile roof was visible above the tall stone wall beside Anna. Hannes had parked in front of the house, where a shrub extended over the top of the wall toward the street. *Reaching for "Lebensraum"* was the thought that came to Anna—living space.

"Eva had so much time to herself here. More than she ever spent with him." Anna opened her door to get out. "I wonder what that part of her life was like?"

"Isn't that what your mother wrote about?" Hannes asked in German.

She shrugged. "Most of what she wrote about Eva makes it sound as though she was always waiting for what someone else dictated or decided."

"Maybe she felt she couldn't have a life of her own that didn't put someone else first," he said. "Girls still get that message, but not in ways they can easily challenge."

Though he had switched back to English, Anna still took in his words as though on some sort of time delay. He'd seemed silent, a bit remote, during the drive. What had sparked these thoughts? Perhaps he'd been thinking about his upcoming semester.

"I watch too many women postpone their lives." He climbed out and turned to lock the car with an edge of impatience in his voice. "Accommodate what's unworthy of their time, let themselves be convinced it is. Or that they're somehow obliged to."

Anna stared at him now. The words struck close to home. Maybe fatigue really was catching up with her. "Do you think I do that? Did that?"

His eyes softened as he joined her on the sidewalk. "I feel happy to see you taking up more space in your own life. It was very hard, watching you with Lowell. Perhaps it was also difficult for people who loved Eva to watch how she let her life be so confined. Society still tells women one thing while expecting—demanding—its opposite."

Anna's attention had snagged on the words "people who *loved*."

"And it was far worse in Eva's time, and your mother's," Hannes said.

"But in some ways, Eva stepped outside the bounds of her time. Asserted her own choices," Anna said.

"She did," he agreed. "But did she do it for herself?"

"I don't know. Perhaps she did the most she was able to." Was she actually defending Eva Braun? And to him? She was starting to fade, lose perspective, after the whirlwind of the last two days that sometimes felt more like dreams.

He looked apologetic. "I know I feel strongly about this, no doubt because my mother's so strong. She had to claim that strength, though. Women who think for themselves are usually more suspect than admired. It's as if they've stepped outside some dictate that says: 'You can act free. Just don't expect to be free.'"

Anna wondered again whether there was a woman here who was waiting for his return. She redirected her attention to what she'd waited so long to see.

Delp Strasse, known as Wasserburger Strasse when Eva Braun lived there, was a small, quiet street where trees provided an oasis of shade. But it wasn't as easy to see the sky here, what Eva found so vital to feeling free. Instead, it felt hemmed in; cloistered.

Like women's lives. Like what Hannes was describing. How often did women feel they had the whole sky to fly in? How often did she?

It was surreal, standing outside this little villa the same sand-colored stucco it had been in Eva's time. Again Anna felt as though she wasn't really here, but floating in a disembodied limbo. The air was heavy with the smell of soil and the lemony scent of the Clerodendrum beyond the gate whose blossoms were like crimson stars.

The house sat close to its neighbors. This and the fact that the wall in front masked everything below the second floor made it difficult to get a good look at it without feeling like a voyeur.

What she could see from the sidewalk—the small balcony off Eva's bedroom on the upper floor, the shutters, even the scarlet geraniums crowding the window boxes on the balcony railing—looked much as it had in Eva's photos, and in the films Anna had pored over trying to catch glimpses of detail before the action sped on, as it always did. Eva didn't seem to keep her attention on anything in her surroundings for very long, other than Hitler.

"It's a shame the wall hides so much," Anna sighed. "It's not as though we can stand at the gate peering in."

"What do you mean?" Hannes used German again as his hand slipped around her arm and he led her back toward it. "Right here." He pointed to a gap alongside the gate. "Have a look," he offered in English now. "It's no problem." His eyes had that curious glint that mischief never quite allowed him to mask.

"You're teasing!" she accused. "Damn you!"

"No, my suspicious one. In fact, would you like to see inside?"

Anna gaped at him now. "How's that even possible?"

"I have a key." He reached into his pocket and pulled out a small ring of them, singled one out, inserted and turned it in the lock, and the gate swung open.

Anna staggered backward as though something might leap out from behind it.

"Sesam, öffne dich!" he announced triumphantly.

"But—" Anna didn't know which question to ask, so many came to mind, in a mix of two languages. "You know the owner?" she asked finally in English.

"I do, as a matter of fact." His tone was still playful as he gestured her through ahead of him.

Though excited, she stepped inside hesitantly and paused to look around. Her stomach lurched with a swirling sensation and she was lightheaded in the humid air. Jet lag really was catching up with her. She felt on guard, too, as though Eva's Scotties might come growling out of a hidden corner at any moment.

"There are no watchdogs here," Hannes said from behind her as though reading her thoughts. "That warning sign came off the gate a long time ago."

The flagstones on the driveway, the plantings that crouched close to the house, the set of four stone stairs leading up to the simple entrance on the left side—everything looked just as it did in Eva's films. Only the small garage was a new addition.

"What do you think?" he asked.

"It's like standing inside one of her photos."

Hannes nodded. "There've been a few renovations. But it's much the same."

He strode toward the steps and took them two at a time. Pausing on the landing, he unlocked the door, then called with mock impatience, "Are you coming, or not?"

Anna climbed the stairs slowly, glancing from his smiling face to the open door as he stood waiting for her to go through it ahead of him.

The entry hall was as tiny as Eva's films had shown it to be in scenes of her packing a huge trunk for one of her many trips. When Hannes closed the door behind them there was barely room for the two of them to stand together in the entrance foyer.

"Not much when it comes to square meters." He reached past her to switch on an overhead light. "But economical to heat."

Dear, practical Hannes. What would a little extra expense for heat matter when you stood in the footsteps of *history*?

The air held cooking smells Anna couldn't quite identify, a little like baking bread. She tried to imagine the aromas that would greet them in Eva's time. Those of cooking, certainly, though Eva wouldn't have been likely to produce them. Perfume. Cognac, perhaps—and coffee. Plus the all-pervading cigarette smoke.

Hannes led her through what must have been the living room where she paused to study the fireplace tiles painted with rustic designs. In the light that shone through windows that faced the street, Anna saw that the room was nearly empty.

At the foot of a winding staircase, Hannes said, "Maybe we shouldn't go up. It's only bedrooms. You know. Might be a bit messy."

"I think we're invading enough privacy, as it is," she agreed.

He moved toward French doors that led out to the small yard at the back. They swung open when he unlatched them and Anna felt the warm afternoon air on her face.

"Why don't I make us some coffee?" he suggested from where he'd ducked into a miniscule galley kitchen. "We can sit on the terrace.

"Perhaps some cake, too." He unwrapped a bakery package on the diminutive kitchen counter. "Ah, Himbeer Torte," he said, sounding pleased, then reached into a drawer and found a knife. Gesturing toward the wrapper that wore the same logo as his mother's car, he added, "From the best bakery in town."

"What are you *doing*?" she asked from where she stood watching him.

He was pulling a canister of coffee down from a cabinet. "Anna, don't worry. We're completely welcome here."

"When will the owner be back?"

"The owner is already here."

She was leaning in for a closer look at the vibrant colors of a Kandinsky print hanging near the dining table and spun to face him. "*What*?"

"I said the owner is already here."

"For God's sake—where? Upstairs? We can't just sit here, making free with someone else's cake and coffee!"

"Actually, this is my coffee," he said quietly.

Then it hit her. "And, these are your things? Your furniture?"

There wasn't much of it in the curious mix. While this larger room with the French doors to the terrace looked fairly lived in, the other two ground floor rooms were mostly unfurnished.

"Some of it, yes," he replied over his shoulder before the coffee grinder droned into action.

Anna moved to stand in the kitchen's doorway.

Hannes finished his preparations and said nothing, only watched, as though waiting for her to speak.

"I don't understand," she said at last. "Do *you* live here?"

"I sometimes stay here, yes."

Her head was reeling again. She couldn't focus properly. "So you are the owner?"

He shook his head.

"Then why do you live here?" she demanded, adding, "If it's not rude to ask."

"You know you can ask me anything, Anna. I stay here because a house shouldn't sit empty. Nati's spent some time here, too, but she and Mutti have encouraged me to use it when I'm in Munich."

"Your family owns it?"

"You could say that." Then he added, "Actually, we've been keeping an eye on it. For the owner."

"Well, who owns it, then?" she asked impatiently.

His long pause was familiar. Anna knew it by now, knew how this always preceded whatever he was figuring out how to say.

But the pause seemed shorter this time, before he spoke again, in German, first, then appending in English. No doubt to make certain she understood.

While his gaze was steady on her face, his arms worked uncertainly at his sides when he finally spoke. "This house ... belongs to you, Anna."

She groped for words to respond, heard the sound of a phone ringing.

Hannes stood for a few seconds, looking torn. "We must talk more," he said near her ear before he bolted toward the sound.

"Ja. Ja, Mutti," she heard him say in German as he answered a phone in the front room. "We got in just a little while ago. The traffic was bad. It took much longer.

"I know. I was going to call and see if you could come join us. But I think it's better to wait just a little bit. We can come for dinner, yes?"

As Anna stood listening she heard another sound, a buzzer this time, followed a few moments later by a quick, impatient-sounding knock.

She met Hannes's eyes as she moved past him toward the front door. When she opened it tentatively, Nati burst in. Amidst the peals of her effusive greeting, Anna felt herself clasped in a firm hug as kisses were planted on her cheeks.

"Endlich! Endlich bist Du hier! Herzlich wilkommen in Deutschland—*At last! At last you are here! Welcome to Germany.*"

Hannes appeared in the doorway and hung back against the doorjamb, as there literally wasn't room for three of them to stand together in the entry. "I just talked with Mutti," he said in German. Looking confused, he asked, "How did you get in?"

"You left the gate open," Nati told him. "I rang before I noticed. I wouldn't even have stopped, but I saw the car on the street as I was coming by and wondered why it wasn't in the driveway. Did you find those things of Mutti's that I left?"

Before he could answer, she rushed on, her voice chiding and teasing, "Or are you too busy keeping Anna all to yourself when we're dying to see her?"

Hannes's face actually reddened, something Anna never recalled seeing before. "I—there are a few other things we need to tend to, first. The driving was slow, we didn't make good time." His eyes blinked rapidly, that uneasy wince. "I wanted Anna to see the house. We couldn't get to Mutti's in time, so I thought we could meet for dinner. Later."

Then, as if remembering his manners, he asked, "Will you stay for some coffee?"

"Ach, nein. I must run, before the shops close." Nati gave Anna's shoulder a small squeeze. "Can't wait to see you tonight, Anna. I only stopped to see if you both were here. Mutti was wondering."

She cast an admonishing look toward her brother. "Don't let him keep you here drinking coffee and talking, now." And, as quickly as she had come, she was gone.

CHAPTER 21

Anna sat across from Hannes at the dining table, where he'd urged they sit to talk. "I don't understand what you mean, about this house. And me."

The smell of coffee was evoking so many memories: mornings at Peggy's breakfast table; afternoons savoring the last moments she and her mother often shared together before Rod came home; hundreds of after-dinner scenes under Eva Braun's portrait. Anna felt transported through a span of decades in snapshot glimpses.

"Really, it's just as I said. There are legal matters to tend to, some papers to be signed. But this house is now yours," Hannes told her.

She shook her head, uncomprehending. "How can that possibly be true?"

"It was purchased by your father, because he wanted to give it to your mother, and you are her heir."

"But why—" She stopped abruptly, staring back at him. "You mean, the man who really was my father?"

He nodded.

Then it hit her: Erich Geisler. After a silence in which he said nothing, Anna asked, "He was your stepfather?"

"Yes."

"When I asked you about Nati's name," she remembered, "that it was the same—then later, you told me he liked Erich Mühsam's poetry."

"Yes," Hannes said. "I was sure you were finally going to guess."

"Why didn't you tell me?" Anna's voice grew louder as astonished disbelief rose inside her like a bird flushed from its roost.

Hannes didn't answer right away. "There is so much that I have to share with you, Anna," he said at last. "I never seem to know … what is the right time. What you can bear, with all that has happened."

He was using German again. The furrow between his brows was a deep chasm. "I kept hoping that your mother's words would do it. Because she wanted so much to tell you herself, you see."

"How do you know that?"

He swallowed hard. "Because she told me."

"*Told* you?" Anger was coming in flashes, now. Was everything in her life going to remain a blurry mystery; kept from her? Shrouded in a tissue of lies?

"When? For God's sake, aren't I entitled to know the truth about my own life?"

"Of course. Anna, please," he reached across the table but she pulled away, glared at him, unblinking. The anger felt hot behind her eyes now.

His gaze looked defeated, and sad, as it wavered between her face and the floor. He caught his lower lip between his teeth, his blinking rapid and pronounced.

"I-I-I." A series of other small, ineffectual sounds followed. He took a sharp breath, as though struggling to regain control, make his voice work at all. "I ha-have … fa-fa-failed you."

Anna could feel his struggle, viscerally, as she watched. It congested up toward her heart and throat, as though she were experiencing his distress in her own body.

She felt harsh, suddenly. Cruel for pressing him so insistently, like an adult bullying a child. When he was so obviously floundering.

He'd continued trying to force words out in English this time, she realized, when before he'd always slipped back into German to avoid stuttering when he grew anxious.

"Hannes," Anna worked to make her tone softer, neutral, as she searched his troubled eyes. "Just answer my question, please. Tell me how you met my mother." She added, "Tell me in German, if it's easier. Just help me have the truth. Please."

He rocked in his chair slightly, then faced her, as though he'd found focus again. "I visited your mother, not long before I first saw you," he began in German. "I had a plan, to tell her. Deliver the message that Erich had asked me to before he died. But once I'd met you, I never seemed to know what to do next. It was all so fast."

"*When* did you meet my mother? What did you have a plan for?"

"The week she died," he explained in English now. "I visited her, and she asked me to wait so that she could tell you the things you didn't yet know about." He was rubbing his forehead. "Then, she died, and so much else happened."

He had been Peggy's visitor that day she called. "You talked with her? I never even *knew*?"

"Please, try to understand—she asked me not to tell you, Anna." His expression was pained. "I wanted to honor what she'd asked. I was there to tell her that Erich had died, and left this house to her. He wanted me to go and tell her personally because he wanted his whole family reunited. My mother wants this, too.

"Your mother said she needed to talk with you, first. Und dann ... there was Lowell. Und dann kam das Magazin." He'd lapsed into German again and corrected himself. "And," he shook his head, wordlessly.

"And what?"

"It got so much more complicated than I ever imagined it would be."

"Complicated?" Anna continued to stare at him.

Before he could reply, she rushed on, "Maybe if you'd just talked with me, rather than keeping things from me, it wouldn't have *been* so complicated."

"Ja." He looked contrite. "It was complicated because you had just lost your mother. I understood this. For me, Erich was also a very big loss. This is part of why knowing you is such a gift.

"And, it was complicated because of Lowell. I felt that he might be difficult, if information were shared about your mother's past. And that it would be a shock for you, to find out what you hadn't known, especially so soon after she had died.

"I thought that if you could just come to Germany, meet our family, who want so much to welcome you, then, even if you didn't know the truth about your father, in time, it could all work out. It might be easier for you to learn it this way, once you had seen that you will always have family here, too."

"Why did you bring me here today? Tell me this way?"

"I hadn't planned to." He looked uneasy again. "Dragging my feet caught up with me. Nati and Mutti were expecting that you would already know. I thought I'd have time to talk with them, first. Tell them we still needed to wait a little longer. Then, we were so late getting back here."

Anna remembered the conversation she'd overheard in Peggy's kitchen. Nati had been asking him whether he'd told her, she realized now.

"Nati thought you'd already told me, back in the States?"

He nodded. Then he said with a sigh, "I think Erich gave this task to the wrong person. Nati would know exactly how to do it. I'd never imagined that I'd have to find the way to tell you, with all that it would involve."

"So," Anna said dryly after a pause, "you must be glad to have it over with."

His expression was alarmed. "Anna! Nein! That is not how it is, at all. The more I came to know you, the more important it was to me to get it right. I was watching you go through so many difficult things. And then," he looked grim as he added, "I was always afraid I would somehow make a mess of it. Turns out I was right."

Anna stared into her coffee, no doubt stone cold now.

"Am I your sister?" She could barely get the question out. Was *this* the explanation for his reserve last night?

"We are family, through your father. And Nati already loves you like the sister that you are to her."

When Anna said nothing, he continued, "My mother and Erich are her parents. Which makes her a sister to you and me, both. Well," he corrected, "Halbschwester—half-sister."

Anna's weary mind struggled to understand.

"Your real father, Erich, was also Nati's father," he elaborated. "But, while he acted as a wonderful father to me, you and I are not actually related."

In the midst of more than she thought she could take in, these words sounded like some sort of small pardon. What would she have done?

She couldn't think about it. Something inside her was retreating. She had to pull the words out of herself, as though she'd not only spent her energy but gone into a negative balance.

"It's all … so much."

"I know," he said gently.

"So much for you to carry, all this time. Knowing," she realized aloud.

He reached across the table for her hand. "Be honest, Anna. Would you rather not go for dinner at my mother's tonight?"

Her head was throbbing. She couldn't imagine eating. Felt weak. Faint.

In a few days, this man who had been like a vibrant lifeline, his role as messenger complete, would disappear back into his own life, while she tried to find hers.

Whatever it was. Who *was* she? Caught somewhere between her mother, who now seemed a stranger, Eva Braun, who felt like someone she *had* come to know, and this family, waiting here for her, though she barely knew them.

She heard herself say in German, "No, no. Naturally, it is important to go." She pushed back her chair. "I think I'm going to have to rest, though."

"Of course." He was on his feet.

It felt as though there was distance between them now that would only grow, until these last days together and all of the previous months faded like a dream. Everything would change from here, and never be the same.

"Would you like to lie down upstairs?" he asked.

She nodded.

"You're really sure, about tonight?"

"Yes. Perhaps we can talk more about the house and things another time?"

"Whenever it seems best. My mother is looking forward so much to talking with you. She also knew your mother, you see."

Anna hadn't thought one more thing could surprise her today, but she'd been wrong.

After a moment he said, "I'm sorry that I botched this all so badly."

She looked up to meet his gaze. "No. You did what you could. You have been so kind to me. For so long."

Now that he could deliver her to his family, he'd finally get a reprieve.

"Give me just a minute or two to make things ready for you," he said.

She wasn't looking at him, felt numb, as his arm went around her shoulders and drew her against him gently.

"Dear Annchen, I can't tell you how happy it makes me that you are finally here. I hope that you are going to want to stay," he said, with a light kiss on her temple.

Sunrise bathes the Berghof in a spectral glow, though its far side remains plunged in shadows, as if the house itself is a demarcation between dark and light. Surrounding hills show the deep green of firs, while all the other trees are now exposed skeletons.

A cloud of oak leaves whirls toward Anna on the rising breeze like a flock of paper sparrows in tight formation. Then, as though dispersed by a giant breath, they vanish and a single leaf cartwheels down in front of her, its edges curled like a scroll.

Her steps make tiny echoes off the vaulted ceiling as she enters the house. On her left, the dining room's double doors are open, revealing the table's long span, the walls' blond paneling speckled with dark knots like a Dalmatian. At the far end, tucked in a rounded breakfast nook, a smaller table is set with coffee, bread, marmalade, and butter. The odors that waft toward Anna have a cloying sweetness, like decay.

She turns toward a flight of broad stairs to the right. At a landing two-thirds of the way up, she imagines a servant pausing in this spot with luggage or a tray, to accommodate another person's descent. If it were the host coming down, he would insist that you have the right of way. So often, the one who chooses to yield is really the one assuming control. As Eva did. And Peggy. Though this must remain concealed.

When she reaches the hallway at the top, Anna feels transported from one dimension to another so removed from the first that the inhabitants there can have no awareness of what dwells here. The quiet is funereal, air as thick and still as if it never moves; as if all sound has been smothered out, the way a blanket subdues a fire. The atmosphere has weight, and simultaneously seems a vacuum.

Two small, shadowy figures crouch on the floor. She sees their pointed ears first, like cathedral spires in a miniature skyline—Eva's Scotties, posted sentry on either side of the entrance to her suite of rooms.

Anna senses that all is stillness behind that door, as though the occupant is asleep, or absent. A thread of pale morning light seeps onto the carpet from beneath it. Otherwise the hallway is dark as dusk.

Across the hall, there is the sudden sound of a man's muffled cough, then words uttered in a deep voice and the treble of a female laugh. A brusque shushing follows, as though some things ought not be audible, and certainly not from the same direction.

The dogs raise their heads like small Sphinxes; first the larger one on the right, then the smaller, as though following suit.

Anna hears a sound like that of a cup being set back in a saucer.

The larger dog rumbles a low growl, struggles to its feet to stand ramrod stiff. The hair on its neck and hackles bristles. Perhaps it has finally noticed her.

Then Anna sees the man, who wears the uniform of an officer of significant rank. His breeches are tucked into leather boots buffed to a shine that catches the light now pouring into the hallway from the room behind him.

He moves to the top of the stairs, greets whoever has just climbed them. "Gnädiges Fräulein." His tone is silky, if also ironic. "Wherever can you be coming from?" One of his brows arches, as if in surprise. He surveys the woman with a frank gaze from where he blocks her path.

"A walk, of course." Her tone is impatient. She looks him in the eye, her chin thrust out. "The air's finally clear, before those wretched machines fog it up again."

"Ah, but only for your *protection*. To hide you, safe from our enemies."

"I already know how to hide well enough," she snaps in reply.

He gestures toward the small guards outside her door. "Why go out alone, without your little friends?"

The larger terrier emits a low growl.

"Don't be a fool!" she hisses. "They'll wake the house." Then she adds firmly, "Excuse me."

He steps back and offers a deep bow, gesturing down the hall toward her door, as a servant might. "You know your wish is my command."

She moves past him and signals to the dogs, raising her right hand, and they settle back to the floor in silence.

The man catches hold of her other hand and steps around in front of her again, pausing, as though waiting to see what will happen.

This time the dogs make no response as she gazes back at him.

He frames her face in his hands. "You shouldn't be left on your own. You're always alone. It's too much."

She watches him, seemingly as on guard as the dogs.

Anna sees her neck soften, her head relax into the hand that cradles her cheek.

"You know how much I care for … your safety," he murmurs, this time using German's familiar "du" as he addresses her.

She seems suspended in time, in his hand, as she stands swaying slightly.

He moves closer, his breath stirring tendrils of her hair as his finger traces the curving outline of her lips.

She makes no move or response for more long seconds. Finally, she takes a decisive step backward. Her eyes look glazed.

"Thank you, Hermann." The words sound robotic, as though repeating something said before. "This is the concern that you must now have for my sister, Gretl. Your wife."

In a more personable tone, she adds, "Well, after a day as long as this— one that's never had its night—I really must go to bed."

She steps around and past him with a purposeful stride. Not hurried, yet decisive, perhaps even a little final in its feel. And, it seems, a little sad. Resigned.

She does not look back. She lets the dogs in ahead of her then closes the door slowly. The sound of its lock latching into place is loud in the hall.

He gazes after her, sighs, "But, can't you understand? You need not do so *alone*."

Anna wakened to a stripe of burnished sunlight on the wall across from the bed. At first she thought she was still on the Obersalzberg, wondered for several seconds whether she actually was, had been, inside the Berghof. Then she remembered Hannes, and Nati, and the revelations over the coffee and cake she hadn't been able to touch.

Whatever was this dream? About *Eva*? She felt lost in time, outside of it. Wasn't it just hours ago she'd been on what had once been Hitler's mountain?

Hannes had carried her bags up the red-carpeted stairs to where a queen-sized bed filled nearly half of what had been Eva Braun's bedroom. As Anna struggled to sit up, her dream felt like an amalgam of all that had transpired in this last 24 hours, distorted by her utter exhaustion. It also felt as real as any of the stops she and Hannes had made in the places where Eva lived her sequestered life.

At first, she couldn't tell whether the light shining low into the room was that of late day or early morning. Then she realized it was coming through the window at the front of the house, which faced west. Why hadn't Hannes woken her?

She pushed herself to the edge of the bed, mind scanning for what she could wear. A clock-radio at the bedside showed 20:26, nearly 8:30 in the evening. Beside it was a note, in English, this time:

> *Annchen – When I saw you sleeping, after all I've marched you through, I couldn't bear to wake you. We all agree you should rest before anyone asks one more thing of you. Nati stocked the kitchen a little. Please feel free to call the number below at* <u>*any time*</u>*. If we don't hear from you, Nati and Mutti will come tomorrow morning at 9. I'll see you tomorrow afternoon.*
>
> *Bis dann - until then,*
>
> *Your Hannes*

He really did understand her; understood she needed a chance to catch up. She longed for him. But she also needed to find some center from which she felt flung loose.

She had spent long years feeling alone, some of the most pronounced, when she was with Lowell. Yet time for herself had always carried a weight of guilt, as though she were stealing it from him. Whatever she had hoped to experience and share with him was actually what she resisted finding with herself, she saw now.

Was this what Eva had experienced in her restless life of never-ending waiting—waiting for her own life, while simultaneously allowing it to be pushed down or aside? Had Peggy done the same?

Being in this house, the very fact it was this house, felt nearly as disorienting as her dream had. Yet something about it was also unexpectedly comforting. She decided to explore its rooms, beginning in the empty bedroom across the hall that had been Gretl Braun's. It was barely big enough for a bed and dressing table, but after years of sharing a room in the family apartment with their older sister, the Braun girls must have felt palatial freedom here, out from under their father's watchdog vigilance.

This little villa in which Eva had lived her private life was surprisingly small, and ordinary. Perhaps that made it a refuge from the cavernous spaces of Hitler's demanding world. Situated on a postage-stamp lot on an unremarkable side street, it had been close to his Munich apartment, in a desirable neighborhood. During the war, this location on the city's outskirts was also safer than the densely populated areas that air raids targeted.

But just in case, the cramped cellar contained a curious reinforced space, almost like a bank safe, designed to function as a bomb shelter. Neighbors later described how Eva urged them to take cover there while she watched outside for incendiary bombs and tried to extinguish fires. Once the all-clear sirens sounded, she searched the surrounding streets to see whether anyone needed help.

Anna decided she would take a walk there tomorrow, find a tram to the city center and visit more of Eva's world. And, she would finally meet Hannes's mother, the woman Erich Geisler—her father—had married. Had Peggy been aware of this, before Hannes visited her? More than anything, Anna knew, her mother had wanted a life with Erich. What had led to such a different outcome, and what part had Hannes's mother played?

With the evening back to herself, Anna decided to have a bath. Aside from a handful of items Hannes kept there for shaving, the blue-tiled bathroom between the bedrooms upstairs looked as though little had changed since the Braun sisters lived here. Refreshed after a long soak, Anna put on a paisley cotton sundress, rather than a nightgown. Her internal clock seemed so confused, who knew when she'd sleep again?

As she waited for the electric kettle to boil in the tiny kitchen, she noticed the torte in its bakery wrapper and remembered she'd barely eaten since noon. She cut a slice and stood at the counter munching delectable flavors of creamy vanilla and tart raspberry that were like something long-remembered. Warm serenity settled on her like a blanket, an embracing sense of safety that suggested: *Everything is just right.*

Whatever would her mother, or Eva, think of her gobbling scrumptious cake like an eager child in this kitchen? She reached for another slice.

So pleased. So very pleased. At last.

The impression of these words, as palpable as the sweet tastes on her tongue, arrived like an unhesitating reply. Anna felt it flow through her body, as well as her thoughts.

For the first time since her arrival, she experienced the feeling of reunion she had longed for all these months she'd been reading Peggy's pages.

She had wondered many things about her mother's life, and Eva's, and this house. But she never imagined it becoming part of her own life. What had Hannes said about that music of Beethoven's? That it was like re-encountering something you hadn't realized you were missing, that had been there all along.

Anna checked the well-stocked refrigerator and chose a container of yogurt, plucked a spoon from the silverware drawer, replenished her tea, and carried it all to a table beside the living room's soft-cushioned loveseat. It faced the tile fireplace before which Eva had posed so many photographs of her guests, and herself.

She pulled Peggy's manuscript from her bag and settled on the sofa to revisit its final chapters. It was time to remember how the war brought it all to an end, why Eva Braun left this house in that winter of 1945 and never came back again.

FELLOW TRAVELLERS

Did the Women of Coventry Give Way to Despair?

CHAPTER 22

Overnight train, Berlin to Munich
16 December 1944

Eva hardly recognized her, at first.

Of course, so many were on the run now. Exhausted and terrorized by nightly bombings, they staggered like sleepwalkers through the kilometers of rubble that had been their city. But Peggy, face ashen as the sky, didn't quite look alive.

In a curious reversal of the day they'd met, she was standing on the station platform like an abandoned child and it was Eva who rushed to help when she spied her through the window of the train.

You could hardly board one now, if you were allowed to travel on them at all. Most civilians were forbidden to, especially from Berlin, unless you had a bombing-victim's pass like Peggy's. Rail carriages were so crowded you had to hand your suitcase through a window then squeeze your way on, sometimes literally crawling over others. Peggy boarded through a window, helped by the adjutant who'd driven Eva to the station.

The weather was frigid and by nightfall, the carriages of this overnight train scarcely seemed warmer. When Eva guided Peggy to a seat, a conductor appeared, insisting her companion's pass didn't permit her to sit there.

"It is issued by the *correct authorities*." Eva's voice grew louder on these last words. "Sie sind es, der im Irrtum ist.—*It is you who is in error*." She flashed her own Reichspass in his face. "Go do your duty elsewhere."

Um *Gottes* willen, the worse things got, the more people showed the rudest stupidity. She would not tolerate one more affront from anyone. Like that Berlin shop where she asked about the alligator luggage and the clerk sniveled, "Doch, nein, Fräulein. We keep that only for display. No one can afford it now," as if Eva were a simpleton.

She certainly wasn't "no one." She had nearly barked the orders that it be packed immediately and delivered within the hour to the Reich Chancellery. Shop girl and manager turned pale and instantly attentive, and all week, Gretl had called her "Miss Crocodile." They could call her what they liked. There were times you didn't back down. She had learned that much in these last years.

This encounter with Peggy was truly the timing of Providence. It had absolutely nothing to do with chance, this Eva knew in her heart. She had been ready to give up, succumb, as she nearly had twice before. Twice that anyone knew about.

In these last lonely months, aside from a handful of staff who tended the Berghof, Eva had been alone there, the rooms echoing a great silence. She had started to take her meals in the Wintergarten, where afternoon light filtered in and it didn't feel quite so cold and dark. Facing north, she'd gaze in the direction of Berlin, as if it could reduce the distance of being at the opposite end of the country from where her heart longed to be.

Few visitors came to the Berghof now, since its most important resident had departed in July for the eastern front and hadn't returned. Something in Eva's heart knew he wouldn't, yet she stayed there, rather than return to her own little Munich house, as if doing so might somehow draw him back.

His calls, which often came only every second night now, were all that retrieved her from an inner abyss that deepened with each passing week. The two of them talked of nothing, really; simply clung to the sound of each other's voice, the fleeting reminder that there had been, could still be, everyday moments to push back the roar of impending obliteration that swirled around them.

Some days she spent more than an hour, pen in hand, mulling over what she might say, noting down what could distract or comfort him, now that she could no longer touch his face or hand. Often, what she said to him now, like his own words, was about the past. The present offered so few topics that felt sure and safe, and the dreamy visions of the future that had sustained them both for so long were much harder to summon.

This week, she had finally realized that she'd spent her life rehearsing a role she was never going to play. The pain had nearly torn her in two, pain for her and Adi, both.

But the minute she'd put her arms around Peggy, she knew. God bless the February Fräulein for bringing this reminder! Here was the role life had prepared her for all along: acting strong, no matter how afraid or uncertain she felt. She knew how to project that assurance, surround others with it—insist upon it, if necessary. Leave no room for vacillation. She could do that for this dear fellow traveller. And, she would go that distance for him, wherever it led.

How had she not understood this before? No doubt because she'd kept waiting for the fairy-tale ending, when now, she could help write a whole other one, make the best of things that she possibly could. She'd always been good at that, too.

Even before she'd learned what others had heard on the BBC, or listened to the London broadcasts herself, in secret, she'd known it was all coming to an end.

When he'd told her days ago that she must leave Berlin, and stay away, it brought that old cataclysm of mixed feelings: near-paralyzing fear she'd never see him again, like watching a departing train carry someone away forever. And also, welcome relief from the exhausting vigilance of trying not to be seen, knowing you weren't supposed to be. And avoiding, within yourself, what you were trying not to see.

This was the ransom for an opportunity that is one woman's destiny above all others. Even what Providence bestowed on *him* exacted its price of unceasing sacrifice, as he so often reminded her, his generals, and the members of the inner circle that sat around the long span of the Berghof's dining table. Though there hadn't been any gatherings like that for many months.

She had dreaded his staying in the dank, moldering confines of his headquarters in the east, where the wings of death's angel had brushed him so closely in July. At least now that the Russians had pushed that front westward, his base was back in Berlin, where he was accessible to her again.

This week, however, he'd gone where she couldn't follow, and insisted, despite her protests, that she go back to Munich until he returned to Berlin. Yet look what the workings of Fate had brought as a result! Four bleak years after that lovely visit with Peggy at the Platterhof, their paths crossed again on a train, as they first had when she'd traveled home from Simbach. That day seemed a long lifetime ago.

Before Adolf left Berlin yesterday, and insisted she leave the city, too, news had come that the Allies were making gains on the western front. He had readied for travel to Adlerhorst, his field headquarters there in the Taunus mountains.

When Eva tried to talk him out of it because he'd been so ill for most of the autumn, he'd told her that he needed to be near his generals. Communication breakdown being what it was, they needed to know what his orders truly were, now.

Her reply was so fueled by her feelings that it came before she had time to think about it: "Your health is more important than any victory, on any battlefield."

He held his head higher than she'd seen him do for months as he gazed back. His eyes, so often clouded now, had actually glowed. It reminded her instantly of that day he'd looked up to see her on the ladder in Hoffmann's shop.

His voice was filled with tender affection as he said, "You are the only one who would say that. You are the only one who cares."

In that moment, those standing around them in the Reich Chancellery became, for Eva, both invisible and like witnesses for all eternity. All she had ever wanted was to be to him what no one else could. And finally, he recognized that she was. Whatever the state of the war, for her, there was victory.

Perhaps that was why mention of the evil day—the one that had nearly killed him—struck so hard when it came up as she and Peggy talked. Of course, it was always too painful to bear remembering. She had survived mostly by trying not to.

When Peggy said, "Since that terrible time, in July," suddenly neither of them had been able to speak, nor contain her feelings.

Eva extended a handkerchief toward her then dissolved in her own tears, a boiling-over of fear and grief, as though her body had waited for just this moment to set it free; as though the whole world were coming to an end. The two of them had simply gulped with tears as they cradled each other's hands until the storm passed.

"I don't know where he is," Peggy said finally. "Whether he'll ever come back."

Eva's heart knew what was needed then, like the reflex of a well-trained soldier. Banishing her tears with an abrupt sweep of her hands across her eyes, she declared, "We *must* believe they will return to us! It is our duty, *our* service!"

Her voice softened. "You love this man, have loved him for so long. This is one of the most important ways you can show it."

"I fear he has … fallen." Peggy's voice was barely audible.

"Then you must resolve to believe—more strongly than ever. After all, did the women of *Coventry* give way to despair?"

Peggy's face showed her surprise.

"Honor is honor, no matter who shows it," Eva insisted. "Those English women were very brave, after they lost nearly everything."

She captured Peggy's gaze, as if to underscore what she was about to say. "Doesn't this all show how infinitely precious your baby is? Why do we try to do good, if not in the hope that it will make things better for those who come after us?"

Eva had seized on this opportunity, knowing from their conversation that Peggy hadn't fully accepted the presence of this child. No doubt she was simply numb, with all that had happened these last weeks.

One could look at another's life and judge or envy what it seemed to show. But things were almost always more complex than they appeared.

So curious it was, that Peggy and Eva's sister, Gretl, shared the same name, Margarete. They also shared new motherhood, yet they couldn't be more different.

Gretl's pet name had been adopted shortly after she'd arrived as the third and final daughter, to their father's unmistakable disappointment. Yet by virtue of her birth order, she'd also claimed the advantageous role of youngest child, with all for which it is automatically, and generously, forgiven.

Eva, the middle child, was so expected to be a boy that the printed announcements of her birth had already been worded that way. The error had to be changed by hand afterward, crossed out and replaced with the feminine pronoun, like a question marked wrong on an examination.

Gretl had always been so compliant, seemingly unable to act in her own behalf. Hadn't Eva set a strong enough example that life's purpose was to take hold of one's destiny? Even now, married to Fegelein, a flamboyant specimen of manhood many thought such a prize—blessed to be married at all, in these perplexing times—Gretl struggled to get a firm hold on her life.

Hermann was a cunning piece of work, to be sure, always the hunter seeking the conquest of prey. Yet he could be utterly charming, and welcome company, at times. It was no troubling thing to have a man, and such a virile one, look at you because he couldn't look away.

What a fool he'd been, at first, calling Gretl a "silly goose." He had changed his tune fast, once he learned the lay of the land, and just how close to the Führer the Braun sisters' parcel was.

Peggy had nodded off to sleep, now, arms crossed at her thickening waist, head rocking gently with the rhythm of the train's progress. Her right hand's ringless fingers curled loosely over the handkerchief like a child's.

Eva circled an arm around her and gently drew her close until her head rested against Eva's shoulder.

What must it be like? Carrying a child, like a secret? And how did one bear so much loss, at the same time?

Her mother, *killed*. In an *air raid*! There would never be a grave to visit; only a site of horror no one would want to remember. These were growing like a malignant cancer throughout Germany now.

And, her man, missing for months, Eva's own greatest fear. It was just as she'd written him after the assassination attempt, mere days after he left the Berghof that last time:

> *You know I have always told you that I would die if anything happened to you. From our first meeting on, I have promised myself to follow you wherever you go, even to death. You know that I live only for your love.*

Deep in sleep, Peggy's face looked peaceful, now, as Eva stroked her hair. She just needed someone to listen, help her put her thoughts right about it all.

How could there be any question about keeping a child? Oh, there could be troubling circumstances, like that sweet girl who helped her at the house. Raped! By *SS*! Eva's sharp intake of breath produced the sound of horror in her throat, as it had when she'd first heard about this. If the criminal were ever found, she would see to it personally that the Führer had him executed.

Remarkably, despite the girl's terrible situation, she already loved the child she carried. Her happiness radiated through the house whenever she came, like a candle whose glow remained after she left. Of course, she had watched over the babies in a Lebensborn home, and dearly loved children.

For years, Eva hoped she might have children one day, too. Once Adi no longer needed to serve as Father of Deutschland, she could become his wife, and have a family. He would retire to Linz, as she knew he longed to do; raise a pup or two of Blondi's to eventually take the dog's place; and reward Eva's patience when he came home to stay.

Now, that was all impossible. The pain of it was like remembering that someone has died after you find a gift with which you can't wait to surprise them. Like that emptiness in her grandparents' town once there were only graves to visit.

What would it be like, Eva wondered again as she gazed down at her companion. Carrying that precious gift? Someone who would go on out of your love, even if you did not, or the love itself did not?

She couldn't give Adi a child now, and she wasn't ever likely to become his wife. The one thing she could give him was what she knew no one else would: a reprieve from having to die alone.

A little later, as daylight began to streak the sky, Peggy fluttered her eyes open and looked around uncertainly.

"You've been sleeping," Eva said. "A very good thing for you, now. Are you hungry? Have you adequate rations, so you can get enough to eat?"

"Oh, thank you. I'm fine, not hungry at all. Just tired. I'm always tired now." Peggy excused herself and covered a long yawn with her hand. "As for the rations, I hadn't thought that far ahead quite yet."

"You've had so much to think about. Where will you stay, in Munich?"

"I'm going to Aunt Paula's. Thankfully, her place is fine, despite how close some of the damage is."

"My home isn't far from there," Eva reminded. "Just across the river, close to the Böhmerwaldplatz. You and your aunt can come have lunch and choose some provisions from my cellar. I'll arrange for a driver to bring them over, afterward."

Peggy's face creased in a smile. "You are so very kind. I feel much better, just being with you. How can I ever thank you?" She indicated the crumpled ball of cloth in her hand. "And now I've spoiled another of your pretty handkerchiefs."

Eva patted her hand. "Behalte es. Es wird dir von der sehr wichtigen Entscheidung erinnern, die du heute Abend gemacht hast.—*Keep that. It will remind you of the very important decision you have made tonight.*"

Eva felt a warm rush of hope, the way she sometimes did after prayers. "Bless you, and your baby. You've helped me make an important decision, too."

What, Anna wondered, had Peggy done after that? How had she gotten to America, married Rod? The only chapter that remained didn't reveal the answers.

In this encounter that so thoroughly reversed their roles from the day they met, Peggy had lost her mother at a time when her world had been broken into confusing fragments that could never be put back together the same way again. *And so have I.*

Returning to this Munich house for one of the last times, Eva had already written a will, begun getting her affairs in order, like someone whose life is coming to an end. As she prepared to take her final leave of family and friends, say the good-byes that mustn't seem like good-byes, she shared her innermost feelings with no one—not until she wrote her very last letters to Gretl and Herta from the Berlin Bunker.

She was hoping for a miracle, knowing that it wouldn't come. Gripped with terror she was determined not to show, even if she couldn't stop feeling it, she was going to prove herself to the end, as she finally surrendered her belief that this man would be the means of her dreams coming true. This man who cared nothing for anyone's dreams except his own. Just like Eva's father. And Lowell.

Once Hitler wasn't going to be a victor, he became, by necessity, Eva's betrayed and wounded hero, much as her father had been. At the end, her identity was undoubtedly meshed with Hitler's, yet she may have also looked for ways to stand apart, and act to compensate for his weaknesses, which became increasingly evident in those final weeks.

Reading about what was likely her mother's last encounter with Eva had saddened Anna the first time, back in Peggy's house. Now, with all that had happened since her arrival in Germany, it left her feeling rootless.

I miss them, she realized. *Peggy, and Eva, both.*

And, she missed Hannes, in a way that felt like an ache of confusion. She didn't doubt that he cared for her. But did she love him too much, for the wrong kind of reasons? Did she even know how to love, at all? How had she ever imagined that what she'd had with Lowell was anything like love?

That bond that Eva had prized so much with Hitler, being the "only one" who cared, who understood—was that how Lowell had hooked *her*? As though understanding him had been some sacred privilege? Whatever was important for her had been predicated solely on that, by both of them. This was the incomplete "bargain" she had accepted in return for the love she offered, when Lowell hadn't been any more capable of real sharing than Rod had. Or Hitler. Hadn't ever truly been available to her at all.

And now, like Peggy, she was drawn to another man who seemed unavailable, though for whole other reasons. Was this all that love ever led to? Investing your care, only to have others wrenched away from you? Why did love, more than anything, seem to leave her in a void of hurt and sadness? Perhaps because she had learned, so early, to act as though she didn't feel either of these.

Outside, it was finally dark, the August night heavy with a stillness punctuated only by the distant sound of an occasional car horn.

It was time to read the very last of her mother's pages.

FELLOW TRAVELLERS

Shrouded Silence

CHAPTER 23

Munich, Bogenhausen
May 1945

The immense quiet of St. Georg's Church wrapped me in the sound of my own breath, an atmosphere of safety so unexpected, I collapsed in tears.

Did you draw me there? Urge me inside, when the clouds towered like dark Alps and wind drove me backwards on the sidewalk? Every rain's been a torrent today. Are the heavens weeping for you?

Aunt Paula says you came to Mass whenever you were in Munich. Even in the worst times, when an air raid killed your neighbors and destroyed this parish's newer church, just a few years old. Maybe a name like "Heilig Blut" doomed it after all this preoccupation with pure blood, an offense the Allies wanted to erase from their maps.

Burned to ashes, reports said, the same words they use to describe what happened to you. To your body, I keep reminding myself. *After* you died.

Why does setting fire to a corpse seem like a second, savage murder? And why is it that the more specifically I think about it all, the easier it somehow is? It's the rough sketches of possibility that are worst, the infinite ways my mind can conjure atrocity.

I want to know what you were doing, thinking, feeling, in those days. How did you spend that final one, especially those hours you knew were the last? Or perhaps you didn't know. Maybe you paid no attention to the day, the time. Living underground, without daylight, without that sky you love, you were already so removed from them.

Oh, Eva, will I ever get over feeling there was something I could have said or done? Noticed? Was there anything that could have kept you from returning to Berlin and never leaving it again?

He married you, of course, there in the bunker. What you'd waited for, nearly as long as I've known you. But surely this was never the wedding you hoped for.

Outside St. Georg's Gothic walls, birds were letting loose a crescendo in the graveyard. It's one of so many outbursts this spring. The green on all the leafed-out plants seems flagrant. So does the scent that the blossoms are diffusing over the mounds of rubble and bomb-twisted trees. On my walk to the church, I saw wisteria draping the façades of ruined buildings like lavender mourning crêpe, while empty windows framed the clouds in moving landscapes.

In such mingling of destruction and new life, I was surprised to find the old church undamaged. The altar Madonna, queenly in her gold-leaf opulence, gazed at me with the sympathy you might see in the face of a stranger who hears something terrible has happened to you. She seemed to look at me the way you sometimes had.

Mother of God, pray for us. Have I ever really prayed? Had I come to pray for you? If I did, I'd call on Father Delp, whose church this was. He helped some of the resisters. Erich could have been with them. Then the Gestapo arrested the priest last fall, after dear Nadelkissen told me to find him once I got here.

God knows what Father Delp suffered through afterward, before they finally killed him. He was right there in Berlin, in prison, all through those horrible months before Christmas. Hilde says his letters helped her keep the will to go on. I know she has helped me find mine. As you did.

How can you be gone? Ashes. That's the last time I was in a church, just before Lent, after I'd met you on the train that first time as I escaped Austria, and Father. Now ashes will always remind me of you.

I hate that my "gift" saw you. That hideous dream, with your sweet smile in the flames. Just like with Peter, it feels as though I make these things happen by seeing them, being there with them.

I want so much to see you. I keep deciding it must be a different Eva, in all this news of "him." What could you possibly have to do with that?

My mind chases endless arcs, scanning over all you said for pieces I should have put together. But I was never looking to solve any sort of puzzle, with you. Only bask in the sweet solace of your company. I may never understand your being with him. But I can well understand why someone would want you near.

That determination you always showed to be happy, to make the best of things—what did that demand of you? What energy and effort were required to create such a confident impression of a satisfied life, when the reality was surely so different?

What price did you pay, even before you paid that ultimate one? How much of your life died away while you had to be always available, yet so utterly invisible? That enrages me most, that you gave away what was so precious—*yours* to give—to *him*.

My heart tumbled inside me when the church bells shattered the silence with their massive, resonating tones, as if to mask the words I screamed: "How could you DO this?" When Erich … And all those others.

I was on my knees, the stone floor like hard ice beneath them. Despising everything that could make this true, about you.

I see you in glimpses that vacillate between the ends of a spectrum. Lonely girl on the Simbach station platform that day we met, almost—not quite—resigned to your fate.

Then all assurance and elegance in Hoffmann's photo studio. I felt you infuse life into me that day, the belief that it was possible to hope again.

How forlorn you looked in the Adlon's lobby that final day of the Olympics. Now I understand what you'd dressed up for, the excitement you anticipated sharing, instead of being ordered back to Berchtesgaden like a child.

Just a week later, you were in raptures at the framer's about that awful portrait, about being remembered at all by a monster who surely had no ability to appreciate you, any more than he could draw a human face. Yet demanded you all for himself.

What was different, that October evening on the Obersalzberg? The war, of course, but what was it you said, about the sky? That once, it had seemed as though we'd have all of it to fly in, but already, far sooner than you would have expected—or never expected at all—you became a bird that must return to a cage.

During my uncanny encounter at the Berghof, I learned you were part of that circle that orbited round him, as so many were. I knew you worked for the Reich's photographer. But never for a moment would I have imagined the real role you played.

Finally, in December, you plucked me from the edge of death, kept me alive that night on the train, like a transfusion of new blood. I'll never forget that peace I felt when I woke and you were holding me. You, who always remembered me. It was as though Mutti was there, too. I know that you knew that, know how thankful I am for you, always.

So curious you were, like velvet and silk, sometimes; champagne bubbly and effervescent at others. But when convinced of the rightness and importance of something, you were a little steel hand in that velvet glove. Just the tiniest bit scolding as you told me, "Now, you know a child's a precious gift. And at a time like this, when you don't—when we *can't*—know."

Then your voice filled with certainty when you told me, "Children help us to be brave, and this child will do that for you," and shocked me when you said, "Even I can be brave, now, knowing this blessing is here for you."

Ever the pragmatist, you also encouraged me to keep a small, packed suitcase, to be prepared for any possibility. I'd already learned the value of that kind of readiness, though once again, our reasons were likely entirely different ones.

It was nearly the Solstice, and the Ardennes was a harsh, violent battleground. In those Advent days of long, dark nights, when our ancestors would gather to light their fires not knowing whether they would live to see another spring, neither of us knew, either. And now, you have died in springtime; disappeared in fire.

How could I not know, about you, the truth of it? But then, you never said, and I was just the same, about Erich. Not so much as a first name did we share, either of us, each with her reasons. The men's reasons. How we wept, that night, in our fear for them, when July 20 came up. It was the only time I'd seen you let yourself cry, not try to stop or distract yourself. My God, when I think of the gulf between the reasons for our tears!

It's just as Agatha Christie has said. War, for most women, is about the destiny of one person. For me, it became three—the one I feared was dead, and the two of you who now are. Has my struggle to have faith about Erich brought these hateful endings for Mutti, and you? Did I not keep faith, as you urged? Could it have been different, if I had?

I know it's true, what Hilde and Aunt Paula say. I must never talk about it. But I want so much to know. I feel I'll go crazy if you simply remain like a movie whose film broke before reaching the end.

Our price, for surviving, is to act as if none of this nightmare ever happened. Go on from our own zero hour, put the horror behind us, and bury the feelings, like fires that have raged in the streets, as the rubble buries the city.

We must go on because we have survived, so many insist. That we owe this to those who did not.

How do you build a life based on a feeling of debt? I've never found a way to accept this, though others obviously believe in it. Is this what drove that role you chose?

Even for survivors, now, there is nothing but roles. Like a bizarre reversal of animals playing dead, we are expected to act alive when we are dead inside. There is nowhere for the truth of one's feelings.

Why must I always choose one thing and deny or lose another, when both are a part of me? It's no different than when the Nazis pressed so hard to control everything, and the only safety was in shuttering the voice of your own heart.

If I cannot speak of you, I'll carry you with me in shrouded silence, like the church bells in Lübeck they're going to leave where they fell to earth the night that city was bombed. So as to never forget. I'll set Nadelkissen's watch to the time you died—almost 3:30 on a beautiful spring day—and never wind it again.

I refuse to choose between two things this time. I'll bring them both with me.

I'll watch for the sparkle of your *joie de vivre* in every day. I loved it so much—it seemed, so often, the most hopeful thing I knew. How could it all end this way? How can anyone ever know, now, all of the good and bright and lovely things you were?

I'll take what you shared with me and keep finding it in the world so it will never die. I'll write down every moment with you I remember and keep it with me always.

And I will absolutely hate that you loved him, and nothing, ever, will change that.

Anna woke from thick sleep where she lay curled on the sofa, with time only to comb her hair and brush her teeth before the door's buzzer sounded. She raced to answer, squinting into morning sunlight.

Standing on the step was a woman in a blue seersucker shirtdress carrying a basket over her arm. Fresh-faced as a girl, she had white hair with angular waves that stopped abruptly at her chin and smile lines just like Hannes. Her eyes softened into crinkles. "Grüße Dich!" She enfolded Anna in a one-armed hug. "Ich grüße dich, so sehr. Ich bin Hilde."

Anna felt the woman's warm tears on her cheek as if they were her own.

"Entschuldige bitte." Hilde then switched to English. "Please forgive—it is only that it is so wonderful to see you a—at last."

"I'm very happy to meet you." Anna's tired mind was only able to retrieve English as she gestured for Hilde to come in, surprised to see she was alone. "I'm sorry that things got confused, yesterday. I hope it was not too much trouble, for your plans?"

Hilde waved the concerns away. "Hannes did what you were not expecting, yes?"

When Anna nodded slowly, she laid a hand on her shoulder, as if sharing a confidence. "So seldom impulsive. But when he is, it is just like Erich. Spins off your head." She frowned slightly. "No. That is not it. How do you say it?"

"'Makes your head spin'?" Anna offered, smiling. She was already feeling relaxed with Hilde. "Yes, he can have that effect!"

"I must apologize, for *both* of my children. Nati took work when she got a call last night, because there may be no flights next week. Big-shot pilots threatened to strike, *again*." The word was as laden with angry impatience as Hilde's scowl. "Think the world owes them, so everyone loses work. She is flying to New York," Hilde indicated the basket on her arm, "so I will fix some breakfast for us, ja?"

"But you're the guest!" Anna tried, unsuccessfully, to take the basket.

"For today, when you have only just arrived?" Hilde's tone was coaxing.

"It would be wonderful," Anna admitted. "I keep forgetting when I need to eat."

While Hilde bustled about, Anna set the table and drew back the drapes on the French doors to let in more light. The bright blue sky was dotted with cottony clouds.

"Were you able to rest?" Hilde asked.

"Oh, yes." Anna opened a drawer beside the sink in search of silverware. "I fell asleep on the sofa while I was reading."

The smell of fresh Brötchen was filling the kitchen as Hilde unwrapped a package from her basket. "Ach, gut!" she exclaimed when she saw that the butter was already out. "Die Butter macht es für das Messer leicht—*The butter makes it easy for the knife.*"

Bittersweet nostalgia enveloped Anna. These were the same words Peggy used.

She reached into the drawer again and Hilde turned to look at her when she held up a petite spoon with a gasp. "It's her monogram!" Anna said in disbelief. The little spoon, one of several, was the kind used with cups and saucers here.

"There are four of Eva Braun's coffee spoons in that drawer." Hilde smiled. "I had Nati put them there. There's a little story about them I'd like to share with you."

Anna suddenly felt like a very small child—excited, and also confused, and sad. None of it seemed to make any sense.

Hilde came over and patted her arm, then pointed toward the table. "Please. Go and sit. The coffee is almost ready."

Anna carried the butter dish and silverware to the table and sat, leaving the chair nearest the kitchen for Hilde.

She approached the table carrying the coffee pot and a basket of Brötchen, paused, as if composing herself, then she said in German, "Kind, ich habe keine Worte dafür. Es bringt mir so viel Freude dich zu sehen—*Child, I have no words for it. It brings me so much joy to see you.*"

She set the rolls and coffeepot down, adding in English, "Sometimes we have longed for something so long, we've had to make peace with the possibility that we may never have it. That is when life's surprises come like heaven." Her gaze roamed over Anna's face. "After all this time, just seeing you is like a miracle. And I see, in your face, the faces of two people I have loved very much."

Anna felt something like the start of tears in her eyes.

Hilde's heavily accented English had the same rounded Bavarian softness as Nati's, with its occasional lapses into German. "Do I understand you did not know you were coming here, or that now, this house is yours?"

"Yes, that's right," Anna said quietly.

Hilde hesitated, then asked, "And, you learned about Erich, your father?"

Anna nodded.

"The plan was for Hannes to bring you to our house after your flight, so that you could rest." She poured coffee for them both. "But we also thought that you would already know all of these things ... which must seem like a shock?"

"They do." Anna chose a roll from the basket Hilde offered and thanked her. "But I'm beginning to understand why Hannes found it hard to know how to tell me."

"I hope it was not too tiring, the tour he took you on?"

"No, no. I loved it," said Anna. "I never imagined feeling so close to everything I've been learning about. Did you know about my mother's friendship with Eva Braun?"

Hilde's eyes twinkled. "Your mother and I met because of Eva."

Anna's voice was nearly a whisper. "You *knew* her? Knew them both?" Then she realized: "*You're* the Hilde my mother wrote about!"

"Peggy came to visit while I was here at Eva's one day. A friend of mine cleaned for Eva and invited me along to earn extra money." Hilde spread a generous portion of butter on her roll then used one of Eva's tiny spoons to add apricot jam from a cut-glass dish. "We were always so hungry, with the rationing. The kind of hunger that makes it hard to think. Eva gave us food to bring home. I already knew your mother's Aunt Paula because I was her neighbor, across the hall."

"On Widenmayer Strasse? Where Eva and her sister first lived?"

"Ja, Where we live still," said Hilde. "Your mother and I became friends quickly. We were both expecting babies." She smiled. "We used to imagine that the two of you would be friends, too, even joked that maybe, you would marry."

Anna avoided her gaze, studying the rosy pattern on the china.

"Peggy's friendship meant so much to me, and your fathers'—both of them." Hilde stirred milk into her coffee "The man you knew as your father helped me, after the war. And the one who really was brought happiness I never expected to know."

Anna wondered how Hilde had met him, but didn't ask.

"That spring the war ended, Peggy and I came here to Eva's house. Lots of people did, once the news came out about her and Hitler. Your mother knew that might happen, and said she wanted friends to come here first."

"She told you about her friendship with Eva?"

"She did. There was nowhere else she could talk about it safely," said Hilde. "We were shocked to learn Eva was Hitler's mistress. It was the very last thing we would have imagined. I don't know how she kept it secret, all that time.

"I knew where Eva hid a key, so one night at dusk, your mother helped me climb over the wall so I could find it while she waited with you."

Anna stared at her in disbelief.

"Oh, yes, you've been in this house before. Barely a week old. Your mother's Aunt Paula and I were both with Peggy the day you were born, the day before Eva died. We heard about her within the week, and came here a few days afterward."

She paused to sip her coffee. "It was important to Peggy to bring you here. She wanted to call you 'Eva' but Rod would not have allowed that, whatever he did or did not know. So, you are named 'Anna Paula,' Eva's two middle names, which also honor your grandmother and great Aunt Paula. That little secret always delighted your mother."

How many other little—and not-so-little—secrets had she kept? Why had Peggy never shared any of this, or talked about when she had arrived in America?

"The streets here in Bogenhausen were clear," Hilde remembered, "unlike in the city, with all the rubble. Lilacs were blooming everywhere. Air like perfume. It seemed wrong that flowers could bloom, the world be so beautiful, after so much destruction." Her eyes were downcast. "We kept thinking about that dark place where Eva died."

Anna recalled Peggy's dream of her looking out from flames, wondering, "How can I look so young, when I felt so old?"

Hilde fished a tissue from her pocket and dabbed at her eyes. "Hitler was an *Untermensch*," she declared with a shudder. "Under the ground is exactly where *he* belonged. But she was so light. Joyful. That tomb of a bunker was never any kind of place for her. She must have truly loved him, to have stayed."

"You really think so?"

"Your mother and I both did." Hilde's expression seemed distant, as though she were looking into somewhere Anna couldn't see. "I believe that all of Eva's hopes died away at the end. That may be why she chose to die, too.

"But even then, she cared about honor, decided what she believed must be done. Then she tried her best to be brave as she died beside him. I think she felt she owed him that." Hilde's eyes met Anna's. "But I also think she felt very afraid, and very alone. She had already been alone, so often. She gave him everything. And he tossed her a bone of marriage at the bitter end. Some Führer," she snorted.

Anna had devoured her Brötchen hungrily as she listened. Hilde passed the basket in which the little rolls were still warm and Anna chose another, then helped herself to slices of cheese and ham.

"Your mother insisted that the Eva she knew would want us to celebrate her, not be morbid. So we drank a little of her cognac. Well, I did. Your mother was nursing you. And we listened to one of her records, something of Beethoven's."

"Oh!" Anna cried out, as if the sound had been torn from her. Before she could stop it, a ragged sob escaped as memories collided in her mind: Hannes's cello, that scratchy recording of Peggy's. Always the echoing mournfulness with this music that she could never explain; the loneliness of being shut out from Peggy on the other side of a door, calling and calling, with no answer.

She was shaking when Hilde came over, drew a chair alongside, and wrapped her arms around her, muttering soothing words in German as she held and rocked her.

Anna sank into her, as though there was nowhere else left to go.

"So much sadness. Of course you felt it, too." Hilde smoothed back Anna's hair and stroked her forehead. "It felt important to come here, remember Eva the way we wanted to, especially when so many would believe and say such awful things about her."

"When was the last time you saw her?" Anna's eyes and face felt like dry, bleached bones as her tears began to slow.

"Eva invited us to visit just before that last Christmas of the war." Hilde reached to pull her cup and saucer in front of her. "She had little gifts for us all, wanted to make the day special, but it was obvious her thoughts weren't with us. She must have already known those would be some of her last days in this house. Your mother was very upset afterward. Eva held her for a long time when they said good-bye.

"When we came back here again after Eva died, we took turns carrying you, or pushing your carriage, on our way home, because it was so heaped full of things. It is difficult to explain, now, when it sounds so wrong, like stealing."

Anna nodded her understanding. "Rod was always reminding my mother what kind of life she would have had, if she had stayed. She never talked about it."

"When he came to Munich at the end of the war, he knew where to find her aunt, so he and Peggy were reunited," Hilde said. "Of course, there were rules against fraternization, and a ban on German women marrying Americans. That is when her British birth and citizenship really helped. And her talent with languages made it easy to find work with the Americans."

Hilde's expression seemed sad. "It was very difficult for her to make the decision to go with him to America, for so many reasons. But after the attempt on Hitler's life the summer before, after she hadn't heard anything from Erich, or about him, she came to believe that he was gone. That maybe he had been executed with some of the others."

In the silence that fell, a black bird trilled a string of melodic bars in the garden beyond the terrace.

"Only that turned out not to be true." Hilde shook her head. "It was all so confusing for her. Wonderful news, that Erich had survived. And heartbreak. Because by the time she found out, she was in a whole new life, and was very afraid of what would happen if her friendship with Eva was discovered."

"It was that dangerous?"

"She could have been imprisoned—separated from *you*," Hilde's voice rose as she emphasized this last. "Especially if it had come out once she was working for the Allies. Even Heinrich Hoffmann's daughter spent time in a prison camp afterward, her children left to fend for themselves.

"Once Peggy was in America, she was determined to protect you both from anyone finding out that she had known Hitler's mistress. Even though she had never supported the Reich at all, that would not have protected her."

"That's why she left Germany?" Anna asked.

"She had been through so much, especially after her mother was killed. When she heard Eva had died, and about her relationship with Hitler, I think it influenced her decision. Rod also tried to convince her there was no reason to stay."

After a pause, Hilde continued, "When we came here to Eva's that last time, your mother took that record album to keep. We also took some silver, like these little spoons. And clothes. And a few other things we could trade or sell.

"Then your mother saw a portrait of Eva. I thought she wanted it for some sort of memento. She said her aunt had framed it."

Anna's gaze shot up from where she was spreading jam on her roll.

"Later, she had me show it to Rod. She told him it would be very valuable in the future. She knew he was looking for war trophies, as many soldiers were. She encouraged him to pay me for it, mostly in cigarettes, which were like currency, and some food and other goods—probably not so very much, to an American. But for me, it was like an inheritance, at that time. It kept us alive, in those first difficult years."

"The *portrait*," Anna breathed.

"You know it? Your family had it, still?"

Anna nodded. "My mother knew, by then, who had drawn it. Do you?"

"Aber natürlich!" Hilde's blue eyes sparkled. "Had Rod known, he'd have destroyed it on the spot. It must be worth quite a bit, today. I ought to regret having 'sold' it to him! Your mother knew how much it would help me. She had a kind of survivor's guilt, when she left, though I know she would much rather have stayed in Germany."

For a few moments, Hilde said nothing, as she watched Anna.

"She wanted only to be family, with you, and Erich," she said at last. "And to live here. In her heart, she was always a Munich girl, but she never had the chance."

She sighed. "People, and the choices they make, can seem good or bad, yet they are always more complex than what we can see. Your mother thought she was choosing the best possible future for you. And she also chose to help me. And, at the end, when Eva chose to divert an order of Hitler's, it saved Erich's life."

"I don't understand." Then Anna remembered: "You mean, in the bunker, in Berlin? The order to shoot the Allied prisoners of war?"

Hilde nodded. "Many thousands of them. When Erich covered some of the final war-crimes trials at Nuremberg, he heard a former SS officer, Gottlob Berger, testify that Eva had made sure those written orders were given to him because she knew he would never carry them out. He seemed to want her to have the credit for saving those lives."

"Mostly you hear that she didn't try to influence things," said Anna. "Do you think she did it because she and Berger were both Catholic?"

"That may be. I suppose we'll never know. Erich was with those men."

"The *prisoners*?" Anna's tone was astonished.

"He had been using a false identity and destroyed his papers, then was rounded up and taken to a camp with some British pilots whose planes were shot down. I used to tease him that he had pretended he was so many different people, he couldn't remember who he really was," Hilde chuckled.

"When did he come back?"

"Shortly after your mother left for America. Like Rod, he came to her aunt's, hoping to find her. Paula wrote to tell her, but Peggy said she mustn't have contact with him, must honor the choice she'd made."

"She loved him," Anna said.

"She did. And it may seem shocking to you, knowing all this, that I married him. I did so, in part, because she encouraged it," said Hilde.

There was the sound of the buzzer at the front door.

"But that is a story for another time."

PART III

The Path
Leads the Way Home

Der Pfad führt den Weg nach Hause

CHAPTER 24

Hannes's smile greeted Anna when she opened the door. Hilde's BMW was in the driveway behind him. "Guten Morgen! Is it all right to park the car in here?"

"Of course. Why didn't you just use your key and come on in?"

"This is *your* house now, Anna. You decide who comes and goes." His smile was mischievous. "Perhaps in future, I will need an appointment?"

"You are always welcome in ... my house." It felt odd to say the words. She had never lived anywhere that was entirely her own.

"Even after yesterday? Then I am truly honored." His kisses landed to each side of her mouth as she held the door wide for him. "I hope you rested well?"

"I did, and thank you for your note. If you're lucky, we've left you some breakfast after all the Brötchen I gobbled." She led the way to where Hilde was clearing the table.

His mother gave a sigh of mock exasperation. "And I suppose you'll want to eat?"

"Nothing for me, thank you, Mutti." He bent to kiss her. "How are you today?"

"Having a wonderful visit," she beamed at him happily. "Your plans changed?"

"Yes, it all took less time than I thought it would. I don't seem very good at gauging German time yet. Out of practice, I guess." He winked at Anna.

"Now that I've been to the university, there are things I'd like to talk over with Anna. I was thinking that we could see some of the city and meet up with you at home later." He turned toward Anna. "Would you like to do that?"

She nodded, glancing down at Peggy's watch. "I just need time to change."

"I've brought the car back from the airport," Hannes told his mother. "Do you need me to make the trip to Starnberg?"

"No, no—you and Anna enjoy your time while the weather's so fine. I'll be glad for your help with driving tonight."

A little later, they caught a ride with Hilde across the Isar River into the city and set out on foot. Not far from the university, they explored Munich's Schwabing district, where a handful of addresses had formed the map of young Eva Braun's world as she plotted to capture—and keep—Hitler.

Their first stop was the Hotel Carlton, around the corner from where she had taken Peggy's photographs at Heinrich Hoffmann's shop on Amalien Strasse. Once, when Hitler dined at the hotel with another woman, Eva stood outside in a crowd hoping for a glimpse of him after she hadn't seen him for weeks. There had probably been more anguished memories than happy ones for her in these streets, Anna decided.

A few blocks over, on Schelling Strasse, the building where Eva met Hitler at Hoffman's first studio had also housed early headquarters of the Nazi party. The bland façade, rebuilt after the war, showed remnants of the party's eagle insignia—now headless—above the door. A little farther down the street, Hitler's favorite restaurant, the Osteria Bavaria, renamed Osteria Italiana, still served Italian food.

To save time, they caught a tram to the adjacent neighborhood where Eva's family had lived. The shop on the ground floor of the Brauns' apartment building, a bakery in Eva's time, was now a pharmacy. Anna went inside and bought a round tin of Peggy's favorite chamomile hand cream as a keepsake.

When their tram back into the city rolled to a silent stop outside a large hotel, Hannes pointed to a building across the way. "That's where Balin's frame shop used to be." He offered his hand to Anna as she stepped down onto the sidewalk.

She turned to look up at the roofline, where a row of carved cherubs all held musical instruments, just as her mother had described. "They're still there!"

"So is the Bayerischer Hof. Shall we have some lunch?"

He asked that they be seated in the hotel's atrium lounge, under the stained-glass dome where the two friends had visited nearly sixty years before.

"What do you think?" he asked after the server took their order.

"I think I'm a Munich girl," Anna declared happily.

His enormous smile made her heart skip. "I certainly hope that's true."

"That's what your mother called mine. It's what Peggy and Eva were, at heart.

Being with him again, after Hilde's embracing welcome, made Anna feel almost giddy. Perhaps it was simply her inner clock trying to bridge the five-hour difference between here and home—as if the very speed of her life had intensified.

"But how do I live in two houses with an ocean between them?"

He squeezed lemon into his tea. "Do you *want* to live in both?"

She shrugged. "I'll have to figure it all out. For now, I would *like* to stay here."

His eyes were kind as they watched her. Did she want him to ask her to stay?

"I would—we would—love for you to live here," he said, as though reading her thoughts. "But only if you choose to."

The server stopped to inform them that the meal would arrive soon. After she left, Hannes asked, "What if someone would like to rent your mother's house? In America?"

Anna regarded him quizzically.

"Someone you know, who knows the house, and would take good care of it."

"Someone from Marsden? Or the university?"

"No," he said. "It's Nati."

"*Nati?*" Anna exclaimed, loudly enough that the couple at a nearby table turned to look. Nearly whispering, she added, "Why would Nati want to live *there?*"

He looked nervous. "Actually, this isn't what I planned to talk with you about."

"Isn't it time you gave up making those sorts of plans?" Her tone was teasing.

The furrow in his brow disappeared as his features relaxed.

"Now, *tell* me!" she demanded.

"Well, she's been offered a job with a tour company that is based in the U.S. It's work she has always wanted to do. She has also met a man, an American, who she's probably going to marry, especially now that she has Mutti's blessing." The corners of his mouth curved in a small smile. "And mine, which is a lot harder to obtain."

"I'll bet it is. That's a lot of exciting news."

"Yes," he agreed. "She's a bit worried about Mutti, though there's no reason to be, now I am back in Germany. I have ideas that can help the plans our mother has for her business, so I think everything is going to work out very well."

The server brought their sandwiches.

"How can I be so hungry again?" Anna wondered.

"We did a *lot* of walking," he reminded as he examined his baguette.

"Something wrong? Or just *not* the best bread in Munich?"

"Surprisingly, no," he laughed and took a bite. When he finished chewing, he said, "I think, perhaps, I will ask for an appointment with the chef."

"When does Nati plan to make this change?"

"She's thinking that she can take the job and see how things go in the first year."

"Am I ever going to see her again? Or will we always be on different continents?"

"Oh, she'll be back the day after tomorrow." He reached for the teapot to refill their cups. "And the new job will bring her to Europe almost every month—plus they plan to marry in Germany. I know she would like very much for you to be part of that."

"I'd be delighted to have her live in the house. I think my mother would be, too."

"And if you decide you want to sell it, she can help," Hannes said. "You wouldn't have to worry, if you weren't able to be there."

"I have to go back eventually. At least for a while, to take care of some things. And since I have no visa. But now," she said, as they finished their meal, "what *were* you planning to talk about?"

His eyes flashed up to meet hers and his expression turned apologetic, even a little sad. "Anna, there are *so* many things. And they always all seem to come at the same time." He looked at her helplessly. "Really, my life was never like this. Until now."

She smiled. "I won't hold you responsible, if you don't blame me."

"*Annchen!* Of course I don't blame you!"

"But your life might be a lot easier if you'd never met me."

His expression grew somber. "I would not want to imagine life without you in it."

She felt a flush of warmth in her face as she waited for him to continue.

"At the university today, my co-workers showed me a copy of Lowell's book." He paused as she nodded, as though awaiting her permission to continue. "A shipment of them had arrived—I have one for you, at Mutti's. In all the confusion, that order was never cancelled."

"Because Connie insisted on handling it," Anna said, irritated. "Though to be fair, I sure didn't want to think about it. And didn't want you burdened with anything more."

Knowing Anna's circumstances after Lowell's death, the university's press had filled the orders already placed for the book, mostly from libraries and colleges, and avoided bothering her. Still, Connie had managed to create complications.

Anna felt a pang of remorse. This was Lowell's life's work. For the first time since he'd died, she experienced an almost piercing sadness about him.

"The history department would still like for a guest lecturer to offer seminars using the book, as Lowell planned to," Hannes told her. "Though not until next term, so there is time to plan. They wonder whether you might be willing to do it."

Anna's attempt at response came out only as a muffled gulp.

"Naturally, you can still teach what you've planned for this fall. They're proposing that you also offer a future course that includes his book, in any way you like."

As she sat silent, he said, "Perhaps I should have considered that, with all that has … happened, you may not want to teach at all?"

Anna shook her head. "No—I want to. Very much. It's one of the very few things that feels familiar, right now."

Hannes looked relieved. "But you don't need to decide yet."

She relaxed back in her chair. "It's a little surprising, but I'm actually grateful that this helps me feel some connection with him. I've always respected that work he did. I'm glad it won't be lost. But why didn't they ask *you*?"

His face quickly colored red.

"They *did*!"

He looked contrite. "I recommended you, instead. I suspected that you know the book well, that your part in producing it was considerable. Was I right?"

She nodded as she met his knowing look. "During those final months of publication, there were days when I felt like Hitler lived with us. Not just Lowell's research and writing, but as though the man himself took up space in our house. In our lives. The way he does so much in the world now."

"He does consume a *lot* of psychic space," Hannes said.

"But what I've learned about Eva—especially through my mother's eyes— has changed the way I see him."

"How do you mean?"

"He's so omnipresent, in awareness, while Eva is deemed insignificant. But she's been defined that way in relation to *his* larger-than-life persona. And that wasn't even *real*, but was inflated by the propaganda that he and others manufactured and projected. Lowell understood that, and wrote about it. I think he'd recognize the strange hollowness my mother saw in Hitler when she had an audience with him."

"She *met* him?" Hannes looked shocked. "Oh, you did tell me. But not that part."

"I lose track of what you know," she said. "Maybe it's time you read it all."

"Maybe it's time you publish it," he countered with a smile. "I apologize for interrupting. You were describing something about Hitler, and Eva?"

"In reality, *he* was the nobody, the non-person," said Anna. "He was obsessed with—possessed by—certain strong impressions. But he was also severely stunted, developmentally. As though he never fully inhabited himself. It was only *her* presence that lent him any kind of humanity at all.

"The paradox is that the very things he degraded and sought to suppress and wipe out, all those softer, caring qualities for which he expressed such contempt, are the very things he valued in her. This gives her a true Schlüsselstellung—a key role in any understanding we might have about him. But not for the reasons people think."

"Anna!" Hannes's eyes were shining. "This is fascinating! You even have your title: 'Die Schlüsselstellung'!"

"Yeah, well, we'll see," she grinned. "I don't even know how I grabbed that mouthful. Maybe German's finally kicking in. How do you think Lowell's book looks?"

"It looks superb." His smile was admiring. "Like it received the very best kind of editing attention. As I know it did."

From the moment she saw the building where Hannes had grown up, Anna felt a nearly instinctual sense of something familiar calling from just out of reach.

She was noticing angels and cherubs everywhere. Munich seemed full of them. Above the front entrance to Hilde's building, two chubby angels held the oval frame of a transom window. Something stirred in Anna as she gazed up at them.

"Liesel und Friedel," Hannes told her. "Your mother's Aunt Paula named them, and that's what we've called them ever since."

Two memories sprang to mind: her family's little schnauzers with these names, and a photo on Peggy's desk of Aunt Paula and neighbors standing in this doorway. The neighbors, Anna realized now, were Hannes's family—including Erich.

Eva and Gretl and their gang of friends had crowded the rooms of the Braun sisters' apartment in this building between the autumn of 1935 and March of 1936. How often had Hitler climbed these stairs during those wintry months? It seemed unlikely he would visit Eva in a place that felt this public.

When they reached Hilde's apartment, Hannes unlocked the door and said, "I forgot to get something in the basement storage room. Do you mind waiting here?"

"Not at all. Is it all right to look around?"

"Make yourself at home," he invited as he started back down the stairs.

Hilde's apartment was two stories above the ground floor, in a corner of the building that gave it lots of light. Many of its windows faced busy Widenmayer Strasse, a one-way thoroughfare that ran south to north along the riverside.

Anna peered into the sunny kitchen from the central hallway, nearly the size of a small room itself. Then she explored the living room, whose balcony faced the river, though trees masked the view at this time of year. Three doors on the hallway were closed, presumably bedrooms. The bathroom was decorated in black-and-white Art-Deco tile, and the table at the center of the dining room was covered with a creamy linen cloth. Dishes were set out on it, possibly in anticipation of her visit.

The room was filled with photos, on almost every surface, and all four walls, many in frames of old silver that gleamed in the light from the tall windows.

In one color snapshot, teen-aged Hannes held Nati's small feet as she did a headstand, her upside-down smile beaming at the photographer.

A double frame beside it held photos of two couples. On the left, the blonde groom—Johannes Ritter—wore a Wehrmacht soldier's uniform. The girlish Hilde beside him had a crown of flowers over pale braids nearly as white as her hair was now.

In the other photo, the second groom's gaze was commanding, though he looked good-natured and kind. His dark hair and eyes were like Nati's, and Anna's. It was startling to see him looking back, recognize who he was. Peggy's pages had given Anna a vague image of Erich that this photo instantly eclipsed, evoking feelings she couldn't even name, they felt so jumbled together.

She remembered the photographs in *The Fighting Chance* article about Charlotte Wald, Erich's twin. The two were much alike. And she looked like them, too, quite a lot like them. No one had ever thought she looked like Peggy.

The top shelf of a bookcase was crowded with black-and-white snapshots in small frames. One showed Hilde with a baby—Hannes, no doubt, so bundled up that only his cheeks and nose were visible. Beside it, an infant Nati had a head full of hair and huge dark eyes. An indistinct photo showed Peggy holding a baby, an image Anna had never seen. In another snapshot, Hannes, probably about eight or nine, held a *Schultüte* full of supplies and treats for school, a cone-shaped parcel nearly as tall as he was.

An especially attractive portrait of him, likely a graduation photo, was one of three in a trio of connected frames. Like most of his college contemporaries in the late 1960s, he'd worn his hair long, its wavy gold strands grazing his shoulders. In the right-hand frame, Nati looked as elegant as a model in her Lufthansa uniform.

And in the middle frame between them was Anna, as valedictorian of her graduating class at Smith, one of the few photos Lowell had ever taken of her. She felt her heart plummet, as though it, and she, had been set spiraling down a tunnel.

The shock deepened when she saw that the wall to her right displayed a dozen or more photos of her at ages ranging from kindergarten to adult. Some were school photos, one was from her wedding day, with her parents standing on either side of her and Lowell. How long-ago that seemed, more, in some ways, than the childhood photos.

Whatever she may have expected, it was never to find herself among these family photographs. It was like looking at someone you'd never even known you were.

Then she noticed a postcard-sized photo of two small children standing in a street strewn with rubble. She recognized Hannes easily. Why—

She grasped the edge of the sideboard to steady herself, and in the mirror above it, saw him leaning on the doorjamb, hands in his pockets, watching her. As though he'd been transported out of that faint image into a living-color one inside the mirror with her.

Anna struggled to draw breath as a sea of gray swam before her eyes like shifting clouds. Finally, she met his gaze in the mirror's glass, but didn't turn around.

"You found the gallery." He smiled, ducking his head as he moved toward her.

The closer he came, the more she wanted to melt into the mirror, escape. But he was there, too.

"Is everything all right?"

She averted her eyes from meeting his now, even in the mirror.

"Anna." He stepped nearer, placed a hand on her back.

"Why are all these pictures here?" She heard the edge in her voice, as anger seemed to summon back her strength.

Hannes looked away at them then back at her. "We've always had lots of photos. Mutti got her interest in photography from Eva Braun, in fact. And Erich enjoyed it, too."

Her tone turned insistent. "Why are there these pictures—" She was shaking, so hard she could barely force out the words. "Of *me*?"

Now he looked confused. "Because you're part of our family, naturally."

"How do you even *have* them?"

She saw a shift in his features, as if he was finally beginning to understand. "We have them because your mother sent them, to her Aunt Paula, who shared them with us. Eventually, your mother sent them to us, as well."

He paused, then said, "Anna, I didn't realize. Has this upset you?"

"I don't know what—" She broke down in tears that were like hot shame, thought she might choke as they burst out, a storm nothing could stop.

Hannes was too quick for her when she tried to turn away, and too strong when she struggled to pull out of the embrace he wrapped around her. "Anna," he said against her hair. "There have always been photos of you in our home, for as long as I can remember. Because for us, this is your home, too."

She couldn't look at him, couldn't speak, nor seem to stop shaking. Only when she let the tears come did the trembling stop, as though it squeezed them from deep, buried recesses. The sobs sounded like a child's as Hannes held her against him.

"Annchen, Liebling. It's all right."

The house she'd grown up in had few photos of her. When Rod had taken photographs, he'd make such a fuss setting up a shot that she would feel responsible for how well it came out. She and Lowell had few photos because he had little interest in them, and Anna was unaccustomed to having them anyway. Yet this house had so many that any visitor would think she'd grown up here.

She pulled away, reached for the photo of the two children, and extended it toward Hannes. "This looks like me. With you."

After a few moments of silence he replied, "It is."

"How can that be?"

"We played together, lived together. As children." His expression was solemn as he added, "After you went to America, Mutti and I missed you very much."

"What do you mean? When did I come here?" Her mind cast around frantically, remembering the few visits to Germany she'd made with Peggy.

He was watching her as though trying to decide what he should say. "It is from the time that you were living here with us."

Anna pulled back and stared back at him. "*Living* here? *When?*"

Hannes looked pale, now. "Anna ... I have known that there is so much that you may not have known. About your mother's life. About ... our family. Even though we are not related, there are ties that have existed for a long time. So often, the ones that truly connect us the most have nothing to do with being related."

When she said nothing, he continued, "This was your home, your first home. From the time you were born. In fact, this is where you were born."

"But why, after my mother finally got out of Germany, would we come back so soon? When I was still so small?"

Now Hannes's expression actually looked pained. "Your mother didn't want Rod to know anything about Erich. I think she believed he wouldn't want to marry her if he did, and by that time, she desperately wanted to leave Germany."

He paused to glance at her. "She told him you were a friend's child, whose mother had been killed in an air raid. Said she had promised to care for you."

Anna experienced an instant sense of disorientation, as though the room had shifted to face a different direction, or she'd been dropped into the middle of another conversation.

"She *lied* to him?" she said finally.

"She ... was trying to ensure that she would get out." His voice was quieter as he added, "Rod probably seemed like the only chance she would have."

"I don't understand."

"There was so much confusion, so many people without identity papers, that your mother told him the record of your birth had been destroyed, or never recorded. He was only willing to have her go with him alone, at first, however."

Anna shook her head. "*Why?*"

"I am not sure, exactly. I do know that he felt very strongly against Germans."

Anger pushed her confusion away. "Why'd he bloody marry one?"

"I understand that he loved your mother—had known her in England, when they were young, and knew her father. His own father was also English. Perhaps he thought of your mother as more English than German."

"When did they go to the States—and abandon me here?"

The characteristic wince seized hold of his features, and Anna realized how thoughtless her words must sound. She reached for his hand. "Hannes—I didn't mean—"

He nodded quickly, said in German, "Ich weiss. Das ist klar.—*I know. I understand.*" It was obvious he was searching to find words for what he wanted to say. He cleared his throat several times, then told her, "They left in January of 1947."

"I was nearly two."

"Yes. Rod told her she would have to wait a year before you could join them. As it turned out, it was closer to two." Hannes set the photo down gently on the sideboard.

Anna's mind had gone blank "What were they waiting for? Was he hoping she'd somehow change her mind? Forget? *Leave* me here?"

His eyes were directed toward his feet now as he said, again in German, "Das ist ... das ist möglich, ja.—*That is possible, yes.*"

Anna pressed her palms to her face. Her eyes, like her thoughts, darted back and forth, as though seeking something to alight upon. When she finally looked at Hannes, his whole face seemed filled with sadness, an expression like a mirror of her own, which she felt in her own heart, as she looked at him.

"Is there *nothing* I've believed about my life that is true?"

He shrugged and said, "Maybe there is much that is true that you simply haven't yet had the chance to know." He took hold of her hands as his gaze tried to capture hers. "What is *true* is that you have always had family here that loves you."

When she said nothing, he said, "I keep fearing that I will be clumsy, about these things." He released her hands as his arms reached wide in a gesture of helplessness. "Maybe you can understand a little bit why I haven't known just what it is best to share with you, or how. Or when."

Anna nodded and sat heavily in a chair at the table. "Why should I be shocked? This is *exactly* what I have felt all along. Separate from her, from them. Always." She shook her head abruptly, as though it might clear some sort of fog there. "It may have felt lonely, but at least it was the truth, as it turns out. That feels like *some*thing."

"Anna, your mother loved you. You must believe that," he urged. "Part of what she did, she did from fear—and wanting to protect you. Mutti can tell you much more."

Anna didn't voice the thought that stabbed inside: *I'm not so sure I want to know.*

"I'm sorry ... if I've seemed ... ungrateful," she said finally.

"No, no. Not at all."

"You have such a wonderful family, to make a place for me. Do *you* remember? That time?"

He nodded. "A little bit. Mostly, it is feelings, very nice ones. The way that ones from birthdays and Christmases can be."

"Why don't I remember?"

He hesitated before he asked, "Perhaps it was too difficult? It is never easy, to have to go away from what you know. Where you know that you are loved."

"To leave what *I* loved, perhaps." Her gaze was nearly a challenge.

"Yes," he said softly.

And still do. She loved this man. And maybe this was some far older, long-time love she *did* somehow remember. How could she feel so many kinds of feelings at once? Baffling confusion. Anger. Hurt. Sorrow too big to ever approach safely. Had she been avoiding it all her life?

In the ruins of war, her mother sought refuge in the comfort and safety of America, and left her behind. And later, Peggy had taken her from what may have been the only truly loving home she had known.

"*That's* the door," Anna realized aloud.

At his puzzled look, she explained, "As long as I can remember, that music, that movement from Beethoven, has reminded me of a door. My mother is always on the other side, and I can't get in."

Hannes was looking at her now with an expression of recognition, and of sadness. "After she had gone," he told her, "you used to wait beside the front door. Watching for her."

Something yawned open in Anna like a chasm. In seconds, she was on her feet, racing toward the hallway. There, like an inkblot in the wood grain of the front door's inside surface, was the dark shape of a butterfly. Anna's eyes clouded with tears as she stared in disbelief, tracing it with her finger as her body quaked with little tremors.

In an instant, she tugged the door open and was enveloped by the smell of frying onions as she bolted down the stairs. Where could she go? Where could she ever go? Desperate to escape engulfing grief, she had finally flown past the door that, as long as she could remember, had been an unyielding, impenetrable wall in her heart.

As she scrambled down the stairs, they all flashed to mind, almost as if she'd find them waiting at the bottom: her mother, Rod. Aunt Paula. Hannes and his family. *Eva.*

They had all been here, climbed these stairs. But she felt more alone than ever.

Hannes was calling her name down the stairwell when she reached the next floor and rounded the landing between the flights, where sunlight streamed through a window.

She stopped short when she saw the man. Hunched over, he was hauling himself upward steadily, if slowly, his breathing labored when he paused to look up. If she'd been moving any faster, she'd have collided with him.

The bleary eyes in his wrinkled face lit with instant brilliance, his expression as if he'd been waiting all his life to see her. *All of yours*, something within her suggested.

She was starting to apologize when he asked in German, "*Anna?* Is it really you?"

Hilde appeared behind him carrying shopping bags as Hannes caught up to Anna and touched her arm briefly before he extended his own to assist the man.

The name with which Hannes greeted him, while Anna stood gaping, was the affectionate one Peggy had given him all those years ago: *Nadelkissen*.

CHAPTER 25

Anna barely felt in the room where she sat beside Hannes on Hilde's camelback sofa. Herr Niemeyer—"Nadelkissen"—had settled into an upholstered chair on her right.

She had snapped out of shock in the stairwell long enough to take one of the bags from Hilde, who had driven their guest here from his home in nearby Starnberg.

The bag's contents made a sumptuous array for their afternoon coffee: Sacher Torte with dark chocolate glaze, its cake moist with apricot jam; strudel so fresh the apples were still warm; and plum cake baked from the season's newest harvest.

As she helped set them out on the living room's coffee table, Anna moved through the task as though watching someone else. Her life felt like a dream from which she would never wake. Maybe this disembodied feeling was actually life, and the part she'd navigated without thinking about very much was the dream.

The others talked animatedly, mostly in German, as she listened, trying to ride out her tangle of emotions so that she could. When Nadelkissen asked about her life, and her work, she did her best to answer, relying on Hannes for added translation. With the intense concentration of following another language, she hung on their words, scanned for tone and facial expressions as if she dared not look away, like a lip-reader.

At first, this helped anchor her in the room, prevented her from drifting away with the sounds of the traffic passing beyond the balcony's open door. But in time, no matter how she tried to focus, blankness swallowed her in the same cottony cocoon she'd experienced after the accident, and recognitions began arriving like wasps building a nest.

She had always been afraid of being left behind, unchosen. It was the very deepest ache of her oldest pain, what had impelled her to do everything possible to align her life with Lowell's satisfaction, *his* choices—in order to remain wanted. It was the tightrope she'd balanced on with Rod, whether she'd realized it or not. So that she could stay—be there, at all. Whenever she was scared, or things were hard, she'd teeter on the edge of feeling abandoned, then look to appease whoever could make that go away.

Even the promotion to editor-in-chief the university press offered last fall hadn't seemed safe. Before Lowell could utter discouraging words, she'd decided that helping him wrap up his book was more important. She let those same demands keep her home that last night Peggy called, as though forced to choose between the two of them.

Was this the kind of "loyalty" her mother felt bound by once she'd married Rod, then learned Erich was still alive? In describing her visit to St. Georg's after Eva's death, Peggy claimed she couldn't understand why anyone made decisions out a sense of indebtedness to others. But wasn't that exactly what she had done?

Had she and Eva believed they owed a kind of uncompromising duty that demanded self-deprivation? As if, to gain what you desired most, you were required to lose something first, most often, parts of yourself?

The pressure of tears made Anna's throat ache as she tried to hold them back. Hannes was sitting close, deliberately so, it seemed, his knee against her leg. She felt his hand slip into hers, where it rested between the sofa cushions.

Their guest turned to her suddenly, asked in heavily-accented English, "It is all right, Anna? The German? You can understand?"

"Ja, ja. Danke." Her smile felt molded to her face. She had kept her responses minimal not because she didn't understand, but because, like a small child, she could *feel* what she wanted to say but seemed unable to find words she knew for it.

Nadelkissen was intriguing to observe, a mix of things that ought to seem like contradictions. Though age made him bent and frail, his presence shone out of his eyes with exhilarating power. Anna recalled Peggy's description of Hitler's eyes, but rather than being probing or invasive, this gaze made something in her melt. Perhaps it was because his own expression shone with affection each time he looked at her.

She'd done the mental arithmetic to estimate that, though he'd been younger than her grandmother, he had to be at least ninety-three or four. In stolen glances, she observed with some amazement how he quietly consumed slices of each of the three cakes while he visited, as if the servings were disappearing into some hidden place by sleight of hand.

He caught her watching him and smiled, showing even white teeth. It wasn't hard to imagine how handsome her grandmother must have found him.

"This is what happens to a man if he's ever been too hungry for too long," he said in German. "He will eat whole cakes by himself, when no one is looking!" He gestured to Hilde. "And there has always been the most wonderful food in this house."

"Ach, Paula was a fine cook."

"*Both* of you," he corrected her.

"This was Aunt Paula's apartment, first," Hilde explained to Anna. "Nadelkissen lived in this building for a time, after the war—Erich, too. They would spend the week in Nuremberg, during the later trials in 1948, and came back here most weekends."

"We had ourselves a game of musical flats, " Nadelkissen chuckled, with a nod at Hannes. "Not what you play in music, but swapping the apartments."

"At first, Paula invited me to move in here with her and Peggy, so that she could help us with our babies." Hilde glanced at Anna. "After you had gone to America, Hannes and I moved back across the hall. Later, Paula invited us to stay here in her place again while Nadelkissen and Erich lived in mine—and for a while, she paid the rent for both. That is what a very special person your Great Aunt Paula was.

"Finally, when Erich and I were going to marry, she suggested we swap, since we would need more space, and she moved across the hall."

"I came home from school to the wrong apartment all the time." Hannes shrugged. "I couldn't keep track. We never used keys."

"We joked about taking down the wall between them," Hilde said as she poured them all more coffee.

"Gott sei Dank, this building had so little damage. Just blocks away, almost everything was destroyed," said Nadelkissen.

"Remember the *messages*? On all the ruined buildings?" Hilde shivered. "People would take a brick and write, 'We've gone to such-and-such,' or even, 'Leben noch—We're still alive' on what was left of their homes."

"My friend came home after a raid and found refugees camped in his house," Nadelkissen recalled. "Even though the roof was gone, and most of it was rubble."

"When did the schools finally close?" Hannes asked.

"That was in '45, in January. "Snow all month, and no coal."

"I wore my coat inside, by then," said Hilde. "We spent most nights in the shelters. Many kept their possessions in the cellars and lived there, like cave-dwellers."

"Or stopped going out, so they wouldn't get caught in a raid," said Nadelkissen.

"No pleasure to be out, either." Hilde wrinkled her nose. "Laundry soap so scarce—the useless stuff that passed for it. And hardly ever time to bathe without the sirens going off. I carried lavender sachets in my pockets, to hold under my nose."

"People got so silly about the rationing," said Nadelkissen. "When we were limited to a jar of jam a month, my landlady began hoarding it rather than eating it. We came up from the cellar one night after a bombing and it was all over her kitchen floor."

"I'd be down there with my spoon," Hannes said as they laughed

"And her husband?" Nadelkissen shook his head. "Argued I hadn't charged *enough* for the officer's uniform I made him. I'd found a more affordable source for cloth, but he insisted that the uniform represented the Reich, and dishonored it if goods came too cheaply. I let his pride pay me twice as much, then 'honored the Reich' by sewing it into the coats of a family that we helped escape."

Nadelkissen, who had never married, lived with his niece's family. After the war, he'd helped with the resettlement of thousands of people who had been displaced through bombings, forced labor, or the death of their families.

"I reached the point where I could look at a face and tell whether that person would make it." His own face looked distressed as he recalled this.

"My worst days were when I knew they would not. Something in the eyes— even the ones who seemed to have enough will to get home might not make it, if they had too much fear. I think that was what had damaged people the most. Living in so much fear, for so many years."

Hilde nodded her agreement. "Ja. And the disillusionment. Many never got over it, afterward. That was the difference between those who had been able to see the truth for themselves and the ones who followed blindly, like children."

"Which the Nazis groomed them to do," said Hannes. "From childhood."

"I realized later how lucky we were that we never had our faith tested— never felt betrayed. Because we never placed it in the Reich," said Hilde. "It was hard to live so long under the deception, the treachery. But when it finally brought its own downfall, we knew *real* freedom. So many simply felt despair."

Anna imagined the Germany Peggy had left behind, society disintegrating all around, people trying to go on as if things were still normal. An entire nation exhausted, terrorized, and malnourished after living for years in fight-or-flight anxiety. What had that deprivation and fear transmitted to the next generations, and what did such unremitting trauma leave that never healed? Had Hilde and Nadelkissen found good lives beyond it all because they *had* talked about it?

"I used to say that we already know what hell looks like," Hilde said. "It parades proudly as life when all the goodness has been squeezed out. And the suffering it causes stretches to the horizon, like it will never end."

"We survived it," Nadelkissen said.

"We did," she nodded. "Though sometimes, I still wonder how."

"By remembering what had once been good, and believing it would return," he said. "Deciding that we *would* go on, no matter what."

"Like the Zarah Leander song."

Then the two of them were singing as Hannes joined in, and Anna listened. "Davon geht die Welt nicht unter—*It's not the end of the world.*"

"Your Oma sang this all the time," Nadelkissen told her. "Nazi fanatics thought it meant Germany would win. But we sang because we didn't want the war, or the Nazis, and were determined to outlive it all."

"Those days can seem far away, now," said Hilde.

"And they come close again for the best of reasons." Nadelkissen reached for Anna's hand, showed surprise when he noticed her watch as his eyes watered with tears.

"Ich weiss," she told him. "I know why Mutti had it. Why it mattered so much."

"Your Mutti was so good," he said. "So brave."

And she left me behind.

"She had to keep many secrets. That was also brave. For the resistance, those who could keep the secrets were as important as those who did the work.

"And her friend, Eva—she turned out to be the biggest one."

Anna was surprised to hear these words.

"What your Mutti did not know is that Eva always had to be a secret, even when she was alive. Maybe that is why she made so many films and photos, so that people would know. Your Mutti knew, but could not tell. Always, she had to keep secrets about the ones she loved." Nadelkissen's inescapable gaze seemed to broadcast a message.

"Even … about me." Anna's voice was tremulous.

"Ja, Liebchen," he nodded. "Ja. But when she thought she had no choice, she made certain that you were with those who would love you very much."

Anna felt tears on her face as Hannes reached and drew her close.

"Child, there are so many things you are just learning," said Hilde. "But always, we have loved you."

"Why haven't I known? Any of this?"

"It was for Rod that your mother made the decision. Later, after Paula died, he didn't want Peggy coming back here again. He was afraid she would want to stay. And perhaps she was afraid she would, too."

Nadelkissen began to recite: "'Jeden Abend werfe ich, eine Zukunft hinter mich, die sich niemals mehr erhebt—denn sie hat im Geist gelebt.'"

"It's Erich Mühsam," Hannes told Anna. "'Every evening away I toss, a future into yesterday's dross, a potential that shall never be—some spirit that had lived in me.'"

"For the days that are gone, there is nothing to do. And many are behind me," Nadelkissen said in English. "Now, each is ein neues Geschenk. A new gift."

He reached for Anna's hand again, then Hannes's, and brought them together.

"Like Zarah's song, yes? Like your Oma always said. Sometimes, we must outlast even what seems worse than we have imagined, because we believe in the things that are good. So that there can be good things again."

Anna sensed Hannes's anxiety as they waited in the hall. The others were in the kitchen, where Hilde was packing food for Nadelkissen before Hannes drove him home.

"I know that expression." Anna moved toward Hannes and kissed the corner of his mouth. "You don't need to worry."

He pulled her against him. "I ... don't want to lose you, Anna."

"I've come home. I can *feel* it." She pressed the words against the warm curve of his ear, then stepped back and touched the mysterious mark in the door's wood grain. "Always, I've wondered about my 'butterfly door'—in my mind, it's so much bigger."

"Your hands were much smaller," he said softly.

"We remember," she asserted. "Whether we believe we do or not. I've remembered my life here. People have remembered the war. And it all has its effect."

"In Germany, it was mostly women and children left to do it," said Hannes. "And many broken men. I've never believed we can just skip over those things and go on."

"The ones who face it, like your mother and Nadelkissen, do move on. Trying to escape the grief only keeps people trapped in terrible thoughts. My mother was like someone always looking over her shoulder, waiting for something to catch up with her. Although I think remembering Eva gave her comfort, and helped her."

His blue gaze was vivid as he listened.

"I'm realizing now that war leaves so many different kinds of legacies," Anna said. "Some stay buried. Many are part-truths that become legends or myths. And others are what we know are there but try to deny or ignore.

"What allows us to outlast it is the part of us that *feels*," she said. "The emotional one, which history always leaves out. Or writes out."

"Or never allows in," said Hannes.

"It can't bear cruelty, or injustice. So those in power always try to silence it."

"What you said today, about how the Nazis demeaned compassion, yet it was what Hitler valued, even craved, in Eva ... " His eyes narrowed in thought. "I think it's that same humanity that the resisters never allowed to be silenced. In themselves."

"Without it, we can never find what is best in us," Anna said. "What's so much greater than anything that leads to war. My question now is, how do we value this enough to place it above everything else, and bring its power forward?"

"And meet the opposition that will inevitably result," he added.

"Imagine if mothers—parents—refused to let their children go to war? Banks refused to finance it? Soldiers insisted commanders go into battle ahead of them? *This* is the focus I want to teach from, Hannes. They may throw me out the first day, but it's where all of this is leading, for me."

"They won't throw you out," he said. "They may need time to catch up with you."

"I think I'm finally coming into the inheritance that matters most. My feelings about my mother are still confusing. But I'm grateful for what she wrote, what she tried to do. There's so much she didn't talk about. She couldn't, in her time, I know."

"That may be why she gave Eva a voice," he said. "Besides the fact that she knew she wouldn't have one, and what was true about her might never be known."

"Maybe knowing Eva helped her find her own voice, even with the shock of learning about her and Hitler. Did she know that what Eva did had saved Erich?"

"Ja," Hannes nodded. "Erich made sure that she did. It's why he wanted to buy Eva's house for her, when the opportunity came. He saw it as a way to honor both of them, and help her have the life in Germany she always hoped for."

His eyes seemed to search hers. "Your parents each had to make peace with the fact they would not be together. But I don't believe they ever stopped loving each other. Fortunately, because war can reshape people in so many ways, there was always room in my family, and in my mother's heart, for that."

The others' voices sounded closer as Nadelkissen got ready to leave.

"I wish you were coming with us," Hannes said.

"I'm ready to talk with your mother some more. Then I'm going to accept her very sensible offer and collapse into that bed she's had ready for me here." Anna reached into her jeans pocket and pulled out the key to her new home. "Will you stay in my little Braun Haus tonight? Watch over it for me?"

"If you agree to come back in the morning and let me make breakfast for you."

"Deal," she said.

<hr />

Hilde had set two places at the kitchen's café table.

"Ach, that was too many sweets," she said from where she stood at the stove. "But Nadelkissen loves them so. We will have some soup, ja? Nothing too heavy. I think that maybe you will sleep very much, tonight."

When Hilde poured tea at the end of their meal, Anna finally noticed the diminutive spoon on her saucer. "It's one of Eva's."

"Yes. We took six from her house. Your mother insisted I keep them. You and Hannes used to eat with them."

As Anna studied the petite monogram, waves of sensation rose in her chest, a mix of curiosity and excitement, along with puzzling despair.

"You saw a butterfly in Eva's initials," Hilde told her. "Called the spoon 'Schmetterling Schlüssel'—'butterfly key.' Big words, for such a little one!"

"The shape ... must have seemed like the one I saw in the wood of the door."

Hilde's eyes glowed with kindness. "Your reasoning struck me as remarkable. You would go to the door and put the end of the handle into the keyhole."

She reached toward Anna's hand before she broke off with a quick breath and wiped away tears. "You kept trying—my heart *ached*. I knew you were so sad. There seemed nothing I could do to help. Now, I fear it hurts you all over again … "

"No," Anna shook her head firmly. "Please don't feel that way."

"I wish you could have known your father. He was so proud of you."

Anna wondered how, when she knew so little about him. "You make me feel so welcome, Hilde. How can I ever thank you, for all you've done, for so long? I feel close to my mother again, because of you."

Hilde's guarded expression relaxed into happiness. "We knew many things about her life. But not what she may already have told you. We understood that it was little, if anything, about your connection with us. This is what she felt she needed to do. She had gone through so much that she had nearly given up, by the end of the war."

Hilde smoothed the edges of her placemat, her expression pensive. "We have to allow those we care about to do what they need to, in the way they are able to. Even if we think we can see a better way. That makes no difference, when it is another's life."

"It's often hard to do," said Anna.

"It is," Hilde agreed. "There is something I would like to share with you, what Hannes probably will not talk about. I think it still makes certain things confusing for him. Since it is also my story, I want to tell what it may help you to know."

Anna felt an uneasy anxiety forming inside her like a knot.

"The way he first learned about it was especially difficult," Hilde sighed. "From boys who bullied him. He nearly lost an eye trying to fight them." Her mouth drew downward with the memory. "So very small. Against three stupid brutes, all older than he was. It was me he fought for, because of what they said.

"Sadly, there was truth in it. We *don't* know who his father is. We never will. Because I don't know which of three he was. That's exactly the way those boys told it to him, so you can imagine what it made me sound like. What the woman—who is the victim—is so often painted to be."

Watching Hilde's soft face with its wide cheekbones, Anna didn't know how to reply.

"I hope it does not trouble you, I am so … direct?" Hilde asked.

"No, no. It only surprises me, a little."

"Always, for me, this way seems better, simpler. But for many, that is not so."

"I prefer that things be straightforward, too," Anna said.

"The reason we do not know is because I did not see the men, not one of their faces, when they attacked me."

Anna drew a breath so sharp it nearly made her cough.

"I've always felt it was a sort of kindness, in one way, that I could not."

"I am so sorry," Anna said softly.

"There were very many terrible things at that time." Hilde lifted a hand and let it fall back into her lap. "Because the war left us in such a mess, I expected different things from people, afterward. More understanding. But most did what they always had. Drew conclusions about you, when they didn't even know you.

"It works against them, in the end. Because it's the same thing that keeps them from doing what they really want, or even admitting to themselves what that is. If you know what matters, you aren't afraid to live your own life, and let others live theirs."

"Did the war teach you that?"

Hilde shook her head. "My father did. He said it was 'die erste Gabel auf unserer Strasse,' the first fork on our road. If we didn't choose to be true to ourselves, then the two paths only stretch farther apart, as we go along. People often have to go back to that fork and start over, to change their lives. Maybe that's why so many never do it."

Is this the fork I've been brought back to? Anna wondered.

"Germany is still filled with people worrying about what others think, rather than living their own lives. I loved your mother because she wasn't like that. In a lifetime, you may find one, perhaps two, who are brave enough. God blessed me with so many: Peggy, and Erich. Paula. And Nadelkissen. If Peggy had not been in so much grief, and so afraid, she might have stayed here in Germany. She would have understood that Rod was not a man who would make her happy."

"You think she was unhappy?"

"I think, like Eva, that she found a way to manage, once she realized how things were going to be," said Hilde. "She accepted it as her fate. You brought her much happiness."

"But she *left* me here," Anna protested.

"Please don't imagine it was easy. She felt she had absolutely no other choice. She came back for you as soon as she realized that Rod had tried to trick her out of doing so. Told him she would not stay with him unless you were there. That in her heart, she was your mother, first."

"Did she even want to stay with him?"

"It's complicated, but she did. She felt a loyalty. And she did care for him. She was confused. And scared," said Hilde.

"But she encouraged you to marry … my father?"

"That's right. By the time she saw Erich again, he and I had known each other for a while. Our friendship had grown, but even though we enjoyed being together, things had not developed further. Part of that was because when a spouse had gone missing in the war, we were required to wait seven years before we remarried. It also took Erich a long time to recover from what he had experienced in the camp."

"What did she do? What did she tell you?" asked Anna.

"She said I should ask him to marry me. 'You are strong enough to be the right partner for him,' she told me. She did not believe that she ever had been."

"And did you?" Anna wondered.

"In the end, it happened through Hannes, of all things. Erich was so kind to him. To both of us. One day, Hannes just asked him if he'd like to be part of our family, and marry me." Hilde's smile was affectionate in memory.

"And while I have never cared what others think, for Hannes, it was … well, normally a boy his age wouldn't understand, what had happened to me," said Hilde. "But so many women had to trade on their body in those days that he already knew certain things. Knew those boys were calling him the bastard of a whore who couldn't make up her mind who his father was."

Anna blinked at the harshness of the words.

"It got worse after I married Erich, an 'Amie.' They attacked Hannes for using English, made fun of his German. Called him 'Mischling'—half-breed. That's why he stuttered."

A small sound escaped Anna as she remembered the vulnerability she'd sometimes seen in his face, its pained expression when he wasn't sure what to do.

"Thank God that all seems so far off, now." Hilde shook her head, as if to clear away shadows from the past. "Those savage days sometimes seemed as bad as the war. Or worse. In war, more people had some altruism. Afterward, that disappeared, because of how hard it was just to survive. Everything became a commodity. I think people clung so hard to the physical things because they had lost so much hope, all at once."

"Hannes has almost never talked about those times," Anna said.

"I thought not."

After a pause, Hilde said, "The men were SS. Drunk. They came after me as I was leaving the Lebensborn home where I worked."

Anna felt the muscles in her jaw grow tight. Hannes had called it a "children's home" and she'd imagined an orphanage. A Lebensborn was something much more disturbing. Eva had also known about this happening to Hilde, she remembered.

"I hated what was happening there," Hilde's face showed disgust. "Nothing but a breeding farm. We had sunk to a new low in Germany with such things, though, of course, horrible things were happening in the camps, but most of us had no idea yet.

"I stayed there because I cared about those babies. They received so little attention, or love. It was supposed to make them strong. I used to sneak in to hold them and talk to them. I knew they were going to have such confusion, later, because of how they'd come into the world, bred just like a rabbit or cow, then left in that place.

"The men saw me that night and I had no chance. In the dark, I could barely see. And I didn't know them." She reached into her pocket for a tissue and blew her nose, then sat silent for a several long moments.

"I don't know how you survived it," Anna said.

Hilde's bright blue gaze, nearly the same as Hannes's, met hers. "I told myself I'd already survived the war. There was so much to survive, you see. Then, God sent me two blessings. One was your mother. The other was letters from our priest, Alfred Delp."

"That's whose church my mother went to, after Eva died?"

Hilde nodded. "Of course, by then, he wasn't there. He helped many Jewish families, spoke out against the Nazis from the beginning, though he was careful about it. He never wanted to endanger anyone. They arrested him that fall, after the attempt on Hitler in July. He knew some of those involved, the way Erich did."

"Eva's street is named for him, now?"

"Yes. Many streets in Germany are. Hitler's name came down, and those of the true heroes replaced it. In Eva's time, it was Wasserburger Strasse."

"Sadly, they executed him." Hilde said. "But those letters of his, from prison! Like a miracle to those of us who saw them. He was so close to death, and he knew it. The words were like messages from heaven, when it all seemed so hopeless. Even with hands shackled, he wrote. These were what helped me focus on loving my baby, and going on, no matter what was happening."

She paused to sip her tea. "In time, I told Hannes why those boys were wrong, but in stages. It was still too much for an eight-year-old.

"Instead, I told him about the good man he is named for. Curiously, he is a lot like him." Her eyes crinkled with her smile. "I think Johannes must be his guardian angel.

"It was Erich who finally helped me tell Hannes what my own bad judgment had guaranteed he would find out. I talked with the commandant at the home afterward, you see, and he turned it all around on me. Said I'd invited it—should be glad to have any man in wartime, let alone three. To be *grateful*, if you can imagine, that they were our soldiers. The 'elite,' even, rather than the enemy's. After all, what was a woman for, especially when there was the Fatherland to serve?"

She choked back a sound like a stifled cough, then blew her nose again. "That is the last time I was foolish enough to seek justice where people don't even know what it is. That man talked, and then everyone knew what had happened—his version of it."

Anna felt tears on her face.

"Child, I did not mean to upset you."

"It's just … it's so awful. When things were already so difficult."

"But you see, I also had so *much*. Most of all, I didn't have to feel alone with what had happened. Today, I understand how very important that was.

Peggy was there, and Eva, and your mother's Aunt Paula, who helped us so much. They were all so kind to me. And once you and Hannes came, we were like a family."

"Why did she leave me here?" Anna asked quietly.

"Because she was very afraid. Within a week of the Allies occupying Germany, people began to seek advantage by currying favor, denouncing others. It was like a witch hunt all over again, same as with the Nazis. Maybe worse, in some ways.

"And Rod also pressured her to leave. The fact that he hated Germans must have had something to do with it."

"But he didn't hate you?"

"Well, he made his exceptions, the way people do with those who come from groups they don't like. They decide, 'Oh, you're not really like *them*. You're one of *us*.'"

Anna shook her head. "Now that's something *I've* always hated."

"It's something your father—Erich—lived with. He felt more black than any other part of his heritage, yet most people did not see him that way. So he had a great guilt, because at times, he relied on that in order to have opportunities he otherwise would not have, especially in America. This is also part of why he stayed in Germany."

After a pause, Hilde said, "You love Hannes, yes?"

Anna was so startled by the question that she simply sat silent for several moments before she finally nodded.

"He loves you, I have no doubt. So, you must tell him, I think. If you are willing."

"*Tell* him?" Anna cried. "But how?"

"Directly, as a child would—as he did, with Erich."

Hilde's sudden smile was one of agreeable surprise, as though the most obvious and practical of solutions had revealed itself; as if the idea had been whispered into her ear. "A lovely way for family history to repeat itself! It would delight your father."

Anna felt a warm glow surround her, even as she couldn't imagine what to say.

"So often, we do not ask, nicht? We do not say what it is that we really want. Not with the things that matter."

When Anna still said nothing, Hilde added with a shrug, "That is how it is," as though she wished she could do more about it. "He will love you forever, but you must tell him. He will not *ask*. It is … complicated, partly because of what happened to me. He has been careful. So often, much too careful."

Her eyes were gleaming when they met Anna's. "But you do not have to be."

CHAPTER 26

As Hilde predicted, Anna slept deeply.

But from the moment she reached for her clothes the next morning, she experienced something she hadn't for years. *Butterflies*. Aside from that confusing day she'd dropped off her story at the magazine, and realized how much she was beginning to care for him, she'd never felt this with Hannes. What had provoked it?

"How long will it take to walk to the house?" she asked as she sipped the coffee Hilde had waiting. She'd already twice evaded her hostess's efforts to feed her.

"It is about 3 kilometers. Maybe half an hour?"

"And St. Georg's church is on the way?"

"Ja. I will draw a map for you." When Hilde finished, she took a long look at Anna and said, "Child, I think there is no danger in this."

"Only the danger that I'll lose my nerve."

"But why do you need any?" Hilde's tone was reasonable. "Really, it is the female who should do the deciding and choosing, nicht? Is it not this way with every other creature?"

Her eyes held the same mischievous glint that Hannes's often did as she pressed a crimson apple into Anna's hand with a look that left no room for refusal. "It is a long enough walk."

Anna approached her in a quick movement where she stood by the door and wrapped her arms around her. "I love you. Hilde."

"Annchen," Hilde breathed. "My precious Schatz. What joy it is to love you. Now go," she patted her. "And have fun. I think he has a surprise for you."

Anna followed a route that led along Widenmayer Strasse and crossed the river over the Max-Joseph Bridge into her new neighborhood of Bogenhausen. Within minutes, a right turn just after the bridge brought her to St. Georg's and its parsonage.

She paused at the memorial to Father Delp, a sculpture in granite and bronze that showed an Old Testament scene from Daniel. A little farther along, the church's small, pretty graveyard was filled with birdsong, an oasis of peace.

Yet Anna felt anxious. Again.

Don't let me scare him off, her silent prayer urged as she stopped into the church for brief moments. She was simply going to tell Hannes the truth, finally. Her truth.

She moved toward the altar, where a dynamic St. George was mounted on horseback, alongside the Madonna whose face had made Peggy remember Eva.

Hilde had described how Father Delp often went out on his bicycle after an air raid to check on his neighbors. Eva usually did the same, on foot. Each knew these streets Anna traversed now. Did their paths ever cross on those blacked-out nights?

When she reached Delp Strasse, Anna took her first crisp bite of Hilde's apple.

And remembered.

She had *dreamt* of Eva—right before she'd woken. In fact, at the time, the experience felt as if she had woken up *into* it.

The setting had been the Berghof's terrace. Though she could only see the sky and the scenery across the valley, she'd known immediately where she was. After all of the photographs she'd pored over, the jagged profile of the mountains around Berchtesgaden had become as distinct and familiar as the ridges on a key.

She'd heard deep tones of male voices, laughter, the ringing sound of cake forks on china. Then a woman's voice, bright and lilting, wove through these like a melody.

Anna had focused her entire attention on it, like listening for a bird as it sings above the noise in a forest. She'd turned in the direction of the sound to find that she was sitting on one end of a bench at her mother's kitchen table. Peggy sat in the middle, beside her, and someone else was sitting on Peggy's right.

When Anna leaned forward to see, the other person simultaneously did the same. It was *Eva*, radiant smile lighting her face as if a sunbeam had shone onto it through the window. The glimmer in her eyes suggested that their exchange was like a shared secret.

Then, with almost childlike excitement, she pointed toward the surface of the table. There in front of Anna was a large, old-fashioned key.

Anna's heart leapt as the door opened abruptly before her—the door of Eva's house, now hers. Hannes had left the gate open and she'd wandered through it, barely noticing, as her thoughts revisited the dream.

A smell of baking wafted out as Hannes, shirt sleeves rolled up, and a bit breathless, welcomed her with a quick kiss.

Anna eyed him up and down where his clothes were covered by a white apron that reached to his knees. For the first time since she'd woken to find him at her hospital bedside, his face showed a shadow of evidence that he hadn't yet shaved. "Whatever are you up to?" she asked.

He escorted her ceremoniously to the table filled with baskets of baked goods. "I have an agenda. I hope you don't mind."

"Never, if it involves food," she smiled. "Thank *goodness* I didn't succumb to your mother's attempts to feed me!"

"This is actually meant to be a tasting menu. As little as a bite of each, if you like," he said. "I'd appreciate your opinion."

"Am I limited to just one bite?"

"Natürlich nicht!" he grinned. "Shall I introduce what we have?"

Anna nodded eagerly.

"First, that German staple, Spitz Brötchen." He pointed to a basket of crusty-looking rolls with lines down the center that made them easy to pull into halves.

"Next are Mohn Brötchen—poppy seed—and Laugenstange," he lifted up a basket of chestnut-colored breadsticks that resembled pretzels. And, finally, Mehrkorn."

"Corn ... ?"

"'Korn' is grain. These are whole-grain," he explained. The rolls, shaped like little pillows, were sprinkled with sunflower, flax, and pumpkin seeds.

"I'll cut up some of each so we can try, ja?"

"Ja, ja!" she exclaimed as she surveyed the variety of jams, cheeses, and other foods he'd set out. The coffee was fragrant as he poured it from a silver-colored carafe.

"These are from your mother's bakery?"

"No." His gaze dropped away briefly as he untied the apron and draped it over a chair. "These are mine."

"You baked ... *all* of these? Did you *sleep?*"

"A little. May I prepare the samples for you?"

"Please," she urged.

"Close your eyes."

"Really?"

"Really."

"You want this to be unbiased. No judging a Brötchen by its cover?"

"Something like that," he said from where he was assembling ingredients on a plate. "Ready for the first one?"

She nodded, eyelids fluttering.

"Eyes closed," he said firmly.

"What a bossy baker." She opened her mouth.

He placed the sample on her tongue.

Anna chewed thoughtfully, made a few delighted sounds. "That's heavenly. Is it the plain one? The crust is so delicate. What did you put on it?"

"A small amount of cream cheese with herbs. Personally, I think the best way to eat these is with lots of Alpine butter and red-currant jam."

"Mmm. May I try one with those?"

"Of course." Anna heard clinking sounds, then felt him standing beside her again. "Here you are."

As she accepted the sample, she caught the tip of his finger between her lips briefly, capturing stray drops of the tart jam.

She felt him coax strands of hair away from her mouth and tuck it behind her ear.

"You're right. They're delectable this way," she said.

"Now, how do feel about herring? A stronger taste—maybe with some onion and pickle?" he asked.

"Yes, please. To all of it."

He stood beside her again. "Two different types, now. Here is the first … "

"Poppy seed," she identified. "Flavors are great together."

"Now, a palate-cleanser." He offered the next. "With some apricot jam."

" Ah, the Nadelkissen," she smiled as she finished the mouthful.

"I'm sorry?"

"Nadelkissen—the ones with all the seeds, that look like pincushions."

"I guess they do, at that," he chuckled. "Which do you like best?"

"I like them both. I love them all."

She heard him sigh and cluck his tongue.

"You might as well be asking a Golden Retriever, Hannes. I am your food slave."

"Anna! I want your *opinion*. Go ahead and open your eyes," he said wryly.

"I'll be serious," she promised.

"I have my doubts."

Their eyes met for lingering seconds. He kissed the tip of her nose. "One more."

She watched as he cut a pretzel-like Laugenstange lengthwise, placed half on a small plate, and extended it toward her.

"What do you recommend on this?"

"Please taste it plain, first."

She took a bite. "Oh, very nice—just the right saltiness. I'd make a sandwich with this. Ham, Swiss. Some good mustard."

"Here you go." Hannes set the other half on her plate and passed a platter of meats and cheeses. "Taste test's over. Bon Appétit."

"What I *can* tell you," she said, "is that while your mother's are wonderful, I haven't tasted Brötchen this flavorful since the ones you made in Marsden."

"Now you're being diplomatic."

"No, Hannes. I *mean* it." She stared at him until he looked up at her. "I want to know that you believe me."

"I do, Annchen." His eyes were warm with appreciation. "I do."

When they finished eating, he cleared their plates from the table.

"Is it some tradition in this family, that the guests serve the host?"

His laugh was soft as he returned from the kitchen. "We seem determined to feed people, don't we? Another legacy from the war, I suppose."

He set a brown leather photo album in front of her. "Nati had left this— Mutti asked her to bring it for you to see."

"More ... family history?"

"Yes." He pulled up a chair to sit alongside her. "Shall we have a look?"

Anna lifted the cover and sucked in a breath when she saw the first photo. Three women, two of them her mother and Hilde, sat in what was unmistakably Eva Braun's living room, an Advent wreath on the table in front of them.

"It's the chair!" Anna cried.

At his puzzled look, she explained, "The one my mother's sitting in, it was in lots of the photos at the Archives. I think Eva used to pose her guests in it."

"She's the one who took the photo," Hannes told her.

"Is this Aunt Paula, with them?"

"It is."

Anna turned to face him. "Does this ever feel ... unreal to you, that we're sitting *here*? All this time later?"

"I'm just glad we are. There were times I wasn't sure what was going to happen."

He shifted in his chair and reached for the carafe to pour them more coffee.

Anna turned the page to see a group photo. The dark-haired man in the center was Erich, she realized, as she studied his features. His gaze at the camera seemed warier than the one in his wedding photo with Hilde. Peggy sat beside him, with Anna next to her. She recognized her dress, a pink gingham Peggy had sewn for her eighth birthday, even before she recognized her face. On her right was a tall, thin boy she knew instantly.

That day in Maine, somewhere near the ocean. "It was *you*, that boy I remember."

Hannes caught his lower lip between his teeth, said nothing as he watched her.

"Where was this?"

"A guesthouse called Rock Rest, in Maine," he said. "Charlotte found it when their uncle, who was a musician, played at a beach club that summer. Back then, black people could not easily find places where they could stay. You and your mother came for a day. That is when your father's sister and some of their family met you both."

Family whose skin was a lot darker than Erich's and Charlotte's, Anna saw, as she turned the page to another group photo. Here they were, the uncle and his family. Those faces she had remembered all these years.

She looked up at Hannes. "*Our* family. Yours, and mine."

"Yours, really. I have always felt … that so much of what has been good in my life should really have been your experience."

"You've kept it all safe, so that now you can share it with me." She touched his face, felt the soft bristle of his beard's new growth as he turned to kiss her palm.

"Remember what you said, that day I first saw you at the magazine? About how when we find something that belonged to someone we love, who has died, it's like they've saved it for us, for when the time is right?"

They gazed at each other for a long moment. "Yes," he said finally.

"I've always remembered this day in Maine, though I've never understood why."

"I think your mother agreed to meet there because she knew that no one she knew would see her there," Hannes said.

"Was their mother—my grandmother—there?"

"No. Both of their parents had died by then."

"Why didn't your mother come?"

"She couldn't then, very easily." He paused, then said, "It was shortly before she and Erich married. I think she wanted for Peggy to have the chance to see him, and for him to see you both, before she took that step."

"Was that the first time he saw me?"

Hannes nodded. "And the last. Your mother was firm that they could not meet again. She was afraid about what might happen if Rod found out."

He reached and drew a well-worn leather wallet from his pants pocket and fished out a small black-and-white photo. "This has always been my favorite," he said as he handed it to her. The image showed two small children on the shore of a lake.

"It's ..."

"The two of us."

"At ... Königssee?"

"That's right. You see, we have been there before, together. When your mother came back for you, she asked to go to Berchtesgaden. She told Mutti it was the closest she would get to visiting Eva's grave. Of course, there wasn't ever one to visit."

Anna recalled Eva's concern that Peggy's mother would never have a grave for her daughter to visit. As it had turned out, there hadn't been one for either of these two people she loved. During Peggy's evening with Eva above Berchtesgaden in the autumn of 1940, Eva had urged that they meet up there after the war. And so, in a way, they had.

Anna turned away when her eyes brimmed with tears.

"Rod wanted to see the ruins of the Berghof," Hannes said. "They were still there, then. It was the last time I saw you, until that time in Maine." He gestured to the album.

"Did Erich and my mother see each other, when she and Rod came back for me?"

"No. He was in Nuremberg that fall of 1948, at the Trials. He and my mother had barely met, at that point."

"When did he find out he was my father?"

"Mutti did not feel she should tell him. But once they were going to marry, she insisted that he know. Your mother asked her to do it."

"And Peggy wouldn't let him see me, after that one visit?"

"No." Hannes's eyes looked sad. "But we were always aware of you. That's why the photographs she sent meant so much."

Anna looked at the album pages again. "She's wearing one of the scarves ... "

"Aunt Paula was the one who sent them, but your mother knew they were from our family. Mutti chose them. That one you were wearing, the day I first saw you at the magazine's office, was one she had sent with me. I was surprised to see it—I hoped it meant that your mother had had the chance to talk with you."

"What was it like, that day you visited her?"

"She was very kind to me," he said. "She always had been. But I think my visit was a shock. She was so concerned about what she would tell you ... how she would."

"Why?"

"I don't know," he said. "Once Rod had died, once we heard about it, it was almost a year afterward. Erich and Mutti had already bought the house, Eva's house. They wanted to invite your mother to come to Munich. That was their plan.

"But then Erich got sick very fast. He asked me to go to America to tell your mother. He hoped he might see you both, one more time."

Hannes broke off, then. Anna felt sure his voice had, too.

Sure enough, his eyes were glossy when he raised them to meet hers. "My own inattention deprived him of that."

She watched him, not knowing what to say.

"I was busy with work. I kept putting it off."

Anna's heart seized, remembering the last time she'd spoken with Peggy. How similar his words were to exactly what she had anguished over, after her mother died.

"He might have had his wish, if I hadn't waited. And you might have been able to see him. I carry the responsibility for that."

"No," Anna insisted, "there's no way to know that. How can we know whether my mother would even have come? If she wanted you to wait until she talked with me, who knows what would have happened, even if you'd come sooner?"

Then she asked him, "Why didn't you simply tell me sooner?"

His gaze was directed toward the photo album, which she'd left open in front of them. "It seemed ... unthinkable. So soon after she had died. That awful time, for you. And you didn't even know me."

His hand went to his forehead, rubbing above his left eye. "Telling you then seemed the absolutely wrong thing. Even if I didn't know what the right one was."

He glanced at her, his expression confounded, as if explanation still eluded him, and said in German: "Alles ging so *schnell*, Anna. Ich wusste nie, was zu tun war.—*Everything happened so fast, Anna. I never knew what to do.*"

His eyes met hers again. "Und ich war verwirrt. Da ich dich auch geliebt habe.—*And I was confused. Because also, I loved you.*"

Then he said in English, "I thought I was simply the messenger. Then everything ... so many things." His hand massaged his forehead harder now.

"I saw what it was like for you. With Lowell. And losing your mother. Each time I thought I'd found a way, something would happen, something *terrible* for you. I wanted to help. To protect you. But I was also afraid, of doing the wrong thing."

His eyes seemed nearly pleading. "And then, the accident. God, Anna. Those *days*! If you had died, I thought I was going to die, too. And none of it would have happened, if I hadn't tried so hard to get you to come to Germany, for so many of my own reasons."

After a pause, Anna asked quietly, "Is it still true?"

He looked confused. "What I have told you? Of course. What do you mean?"

"That you loved me."

He stared back at her for several seconds.

"That I *love* you," he corrected. "I have often felt certain that you must know." He looked away toward the table as he chewed his lip again. "And very worried, that it would burden you."

"Love me ... as something different than a sister?"

He swallowed hard. "Ja," he said, as his eyes softened.

With her next breath, she dissolved in tears that seemed to strike like a downpour.

"Annchen ..."

"I ... I thought there must be someone else." Why had she even let these words out? Like the tears that left her gulping, she couldn't seem to stop them. "All along, I've thought you wanted to get back to Germany because there is someone waiting here."

She stopped, then, because she couldn't speak without gasping for breath as the tears streamed down her face. Not even close to what she'd planned, acting bravely, confidently. Instead, she was just a vulnerable fool.

"There is no one else, Anna." Hannes bent toward her and brushed tears from her cheek so softly, she barely felt his touch. As if she might be fragile, breakable.

"Only you. I have never, ever felt this way, about anyone else. And it scared me. But if I could help you, be near you ... that is what I focused on. And then, there was Lowell."

Anna looked up at him, startled. *"That* early?"

"I felt it from the first day I saw you again." His gaze was steady, now, as he looked at her. Even that eye the fight had injured when he was a child, the one that usually appeared more narrowed, was wide, flashing a brilliant electric blue.

"I recognized this later, because, well, that day, there were things we both needed to do. And you were married. And I didn't know how I was going to tell you what Erich and my family—*your* family—wanted you to know."

Anna felt dismayed, unbelieving. "If you love me ... " Her voice caught in her throat. "Why did you stop? In Berchtesgaden?"

He reached for her hand and held it in both of his own. "Whatever would have started then, I'd have been unable to stop. I couldn't allow that to happen, not when you hadn't had the chance to find out what was waiting for you here. Make your own decisions, about what you want for your life."

His expression grew stern. "It would be wrong for me to complicate that. I'd already made a bad enough job of complicating things. I sometimes fear that the more you learn, the less you may want to see me." He shrugged as he released her hand, adding, like an attempt at humor, "I don't want to lose my visiting privileges."

Anna pushed back her chair, knowing she needed to be on her feet for what came next. "I don't want you to have visiting privileges, Hannes."

His expression froze into what showed that her words had struck hard. She rushed to add, "I want you to live with me," as much to dispel what she saw on his face as to head off her own fear.

He seemed without words. Perhaps he was catching up with her, or maybe trying to determine how he could backtrack.

"I already invited you to live in my house once. We seemed to get along well."

"We did," he said softly.

"I'm sorry to spring it on you this way. But I need to act before I lose courage."

After a brief pause, he asked, "Does this invitation apply to any place you live?"

"Well, of course!" She reached for the napkin at her place and dabbed at her eyes.

"Then how do you feel about marrying a man who gets up at three in the morning?"

Anna looked back blankly. She hadn't said "marry," though she'd wanted to.

"Three in the *morning*?" she repeated, trying to take it in. "Well, I mean … as long as I don't have to."

He laughed quickly as she gave a weak smile.

"Do you really get up that early?"

"I will be, soon. At least three or four times a week," he nodded affirmatively. Then he told her his plan, about why he'd baked all that he had for her to sample.

"Mutti has been thinking about what will happen with her business when she has to stop working. She's interested in something I've proposed. She'd be happy about anything that involves me in the bakery, of course.

"I have an agenda with this, as well," he continued. "The more that corporations take over food production, the likelier it is that food loses quality, in terms of ingredients. I plan to take one of her three bakeries and begin producing goods with ingredients from farmers in the region, with as much of it grown organically as possible."

Listening closely, Anna wondered whether her face showed her astonishment.

"If things go according to schedule, within two or three years, the young couple I hope to mentor will be able to take over. If things are really successful, they'll be able to take on all of Mutti's shops."

"And then?" Anna asked.

"One thing I've thought about doing is to take a market truck to some of the smaller villages a few times a week, and maybe to buildings where pensioners live. To bring a good product to them, at a price they can afford, on their fixed income. And because there aren't shops near them."

"The bread angel," she smiled. "Might your Frau come along?"

His eyes were bright. "Whenever she likes. Of course, depending on how it all goes, I may have to work at the bakery longer." He shrugged. "But it's not as if I'll be doing it forever."

"Be careful," Anna said. "I told myself that, once, when Lowell informed me about my new job at the magazine. Now, here I am, in a whole new life."

"Well," he said, "I have more to thank Lowell for than I'd realized." He stood and reached for her hand. "I'd like to show you something."

As he led the way through the entry hall into the living room, Anna followed his gaze to the wall above the fireplace mantel.

"It's Eva!" she cried. "Oh, Hannes, she looks wonderful there. However did this happen?"

"Something told me to bring the portrait back with me. I decided that I'd risk having to apologize, if I'd overstepped."

"This is exactly where it should be," Anna sighed. "She's come home. Like I have." She turned to face him. "Three o'clock, huh?"

He nodded slowly. "A lot will be negotiable. But not that."

"Oh, well, even if I start getting up at 3 ... " she took a breath, then attempted a throaty parody of Zarah Leander as she sang, "Davon geht die Welt nicht unter—*It's Not the End of the World.*"

He stared at her for a few seconds until his delighted laughter burst free.

"I've found if I sing things, it's sometimes easier to get the words to come out the right way. Kind of like what they encourage stammerers to do."

Memory reined her in with regret at her careless words. "Oh, Hannes. Forgive me. I can be such an idiot."

"Ee-dee-OHT." His eyes twinkled as he corrected her pronunciation of this last with its German equivalent. "And it's true," he added, smile lines deepening on either side of his face. "The singing does help."

She continued to look at him uncertainly.

"It's fine, Annchen," he assured. "It's never a problem, with you."

He stepped toward her and slipped his arms around her waist.

"But tell me. Does it help that I speak German to you?"

"I think it may help even more if you were to murmur it in my ear," she suggested. "That seems to work well. No performance anxiety at all."

He grinned at her insinuation.

"Maybe a little sexy German, even."

"Ach so, ein bisschen erotisches deutsch?"

Anna nodded eagerly.

"Only in private, my dear student."

"Understood, Herr Professor."

"No, no. *You* are Frau Professor, now."

"No baker's Frau?"

"Certainly not. You've worked too hard, and been uncompensated for too long." His hands framed her face. "I love you, Annchen, the way I've always imagined I want to love a wife. Though I had decided I probably wouldn't marry."

"No?"

"Most women would want children." His jaw tightened, along with his voice. "And I didn't want to carry on the bloodline of someone ... who acted as my mother's attacker did."

His hands dropped away as his eyes began that fast-blinking wince. "You may not want to marry someone who feels such things."

Anna touched his cheek. "I love you, Hannes, and I'd love to be your wife."

She reached to trace his uncertain-looking brow, caress the outer edge of his retreating eye, then trailed down to touch his lips.

She heard his breath shift, intensify, as she felt her heart do, with sudden beating that felt as though her chest wouldn't be able to contain it.

"You're always telling me to ask for what I want?"

He nodded as he watched her.

"I see a lot of carbohydrates in my future. Our future."

He laughed quickly.

"It would also be nice to hear a cello playing, from time to time."

"That is easily arranged." His features relaxed in a smile.

"I want it all," said Anna. "All that we have to give each other, after so long."

"I'll treasure every bit of it," he murmured against her ear.

She drew a sudden breath as she looked at him. "I don't want to wait a moment longer. And I want to share it with you forever."

Acknowledgements

Patrizia Masciarelli-Müggler, your wisdom about language has its roots in the language of the heart. Thank you for your wholehearted accompaniment on this path.

Hildegard Diebel, ich danke dir für die Begeisterung in deinem Gesicht, als du das erste Mal von diesem Buch hörtest. Vielen Dank für deine spirituelle Freundschaft mit dem Buch und mit mir.—*I thank you for the excitement in your face the very first time you heard about this book. Thank you for your spiritual friendship to the book, and to me.*

Elizabeth Sims, you are a star, and a writer's extraordinarily good friend.

Diane Kirkup, the beauty and courage of your intuition are my heart's grace.

Tracey Edgerly Meloni, just thank you. For all of it. All my life long.

Ed Fusco, you share a perspective of Eva Braun that extends far, far beyond even the wonder and talents of your gifted photography.

David Campbell, you're a living invitation to a more complete view of history, and of world citizenship. That day we all found the Mooslahnerkopf Teehaus together in the rain and mud was a vital turning point. Thank you, too, for introducing me to Frau Ingrid Scharfenberg, a generous and unexpected primary source in my research.

Susan Gorman, your seeing eye and hearing ear helped me understand that this book really is about what my heart desires on its path. Please, please write your book(s).

Julie Burns Walker, your devotion to the Light of this Day brings eternal gifts of love and healing. Thank you for helping me heed my heart's call to oneness.

Carol Felker, Jane Harper, Lesley Hayes, Mary K. Makoski, Eric Mondschein, and Rhonda Palmer, you bestowed the blessed gifts of a reader's eye and listening heart.

Patti Rae Tomarelli, you're a true sister of a writing buddy, and Diane Richmond, I thank you for the refuge of retreat, loon songs, and utterly scrumptious nurturing.

Ginny Towler and Carmen Buford-Paige, your love and friendship when journey's end brought so many endings and beginnings is a gift I'll treasure forever.

Len Smith, my brother, you believed. And you were right.

Marina Dutzmann Kirsch, you've helped me understand more deeply that no one of us walks alone. Thank you for the gifts of beauty you have given this book, ones that flow so naturally from your innermost vision.

And Jon, who keeps my heart company in numberless ways. You introduced me to "my" corner at St. Anthony's Bakery (thank you, Anthony, für Brötchen), and Kaffee VonSolln (danke, Yalçın für Kuchen). In all of those café hours that I sat beside my dear husband, I discovered that writing need not be a solitary pursuit, after all.

About the Author

Phyllis Edgerly Ring lives in New Hampshire and returns as often as she can to her childhood home in Germany. Her years there left her with the deep desire to understand the experience of Germans during the Second World War. She has studied plant sciences and ecology, worked as a nurse, been a magazine writer and editor, taught English to kindergartners in China, and frequently serves as workshop facilitator and coach for others' writing projects. She is the author of the novel, *Snow Fence Road*, and the inspirational nonfiction, *Life at First Sight: Finding the Divine in the Details*. She is co-author, with Ron Tomanio and Diane Iverson, of *With Thine Own Eyes: Why Imitate the Past When We Can Investigate Reality?*, an exploration of how to achieve balance between the material and spiritual aspects of life.

The author is available for a variety of presentations based on *The Munich Girl*, Eva Braun, and the era of World War II Germany. She also loves to hear from readers.

E-mail the author at:
info@phyllisring.com

Find the author's blog at:
http://phyllisedgerlyring.wordpress.com

Connect on Facebook:
https://www.facebook.com/PhyllisEdgerlyRing?ref=hl

On Twitter:
http:// www.twitter.com/phyllisring

At Goodreads:
https://www.goodreads.com/author/show/2890301.Phyllis_Edgerly_Ring

For information about all books by Phyllis Edgerly Ring visit:
http://www.amazon.com/Phyllis-Edgerly-Ring/e/B001RXUFD6/ref=ntt_dp_epwbk_0

33143664R10219

Made in the USA
San Bernardino, CA
25 April 2016